PICADOR

First published 2003 by Picador

This edition published 2004 by Picador
an imprint of Pan Macmillan Ltd
Pan Macmillan, 20 New Wharf Road, London NI 9RR
Basingstoke and Oxford
Associated companies throughout the world
www.panmacmillan.com

ISBN 0 330 39608 0

1 3 5 7 9 8 6 4 2

A CIP catalogue record for this book is available from
the British Library.

Typeset by SetSystems Ltd, Saffron Walden, Essex
Printed and bound in Great Britain by
Mackays of Chatham plc, Chatham, Kent

To the next generation:
Alexa, Aoife, Brian, Clare, Eamonn, Féilim, Jane,
Julia, Michael, Niall, Niamh.
In memory of Eoin

Contents

PROLOGUE

Eleanor's Journal

I CAN STILL remember the dark curve of my sister's face on the evening Mama and Papa brought her home from boarding school. Her eyes had the startled look of someone dislocated, as one thrust violently from some familiar country into a sudden, other universe. The whole house had acquired that air of still, hushful expectancy which I had learned long ago to associate with Mama's white, tight-lipped smile, and Papa's silent fingering of his moustaches.

I was frightened, for myself and May as much as for our eldest sister. I watched from the drawing-room window as Hannah alighted from the brougham. After a brief hesitation, she accepted Papa's hand, outstretched to help her. I counted the seconds it would take them all to ascend the steps – Papa first, his back very straight; then Mama, without a backward glance; finally Hannah, her head bowed as she gathered up the folds of her grey silk day-dress and followed our parents up to the front door. It seemed a long time before there was any sound of the door being opened. That in itself was strange: there was no bell rung, no warning peal to bring Katie and Lily running from their various duties around the house. Papa must have brought a key. This, then, was some private, family shame which no servant was to witness. I was impatient to find out: ever since the delivery of yesterday morning's envelope, addressed in a slightly cramped but well-educated hand, my small world had begun to tilt uncertainly. For a wild moment, I considered hiding behind the heavy drapes, but I knew of old that Mama's sharp eye would find me out. I would stay, then, until they sent me away. I needed to look closely into Hannah's troubled eyes, to offer her my wordless affection.

I have never been able to see my sisters suffer.

CATHERINE DUNNE

PART ONE: 1886–1896

Sophia: Summer 1886

SOPHIA MET LILY on the second landing. Both women almost collided, but Sophia stopped abruptly, just in time, averting disaster. Lily's arms were full of what looked like puffed, frothy bundles laced with blue and white ribbons. Her round, open face was flushed with effort; perspiration pinpricked across her upper lip so that the coarseness of her pores was suddenly visible. Sophia had never before noticed this faint suspicion of a moustache.

'Oops – I'm sorry, ma'am; I was just bringin' you the girls' dresses.'

Sophia nodded. She waited until Lily got her breath. She felt a moment's sharp sympathy for her: the July heat was intense, debilitating; the humidity unusual. Ironing the girls' best dresses must have made the kitchen all but unbearable. No wonder she was panting.

'Thank you, Lily. I'll take them.'

Sophia held out her arms.

'Are you sure, ma'am? Don't you want me to help dress baby Eleanor?'

Sophia smiled and shook her head.

'Hannah has become quite the little madam. She's

just given Eleanor her bath and now insists on dressing her baby sister herself. I'll stay with them.'

'Yes, ma'am. The carriage will be here to collect you and Mr Edward at three. The girls and I are to leave a little earlier.'

'Thank you, Lily. They'll be ready. I'll call you if I need any help.'

Sophia walked down the corridor towards the bath-room. She found it difficult to suppress the surge of anticipation which had kept her awake and on edge since four o'clock. She had tried to lie still, not wanting to disturb Edward; but her mind insisted on speeding ahead of her, cramming future days, months, years into restless, unknowing confusion. Keeping busy with the girls all morning was the only way she had been able to maintain her accustomed aura of control. She was deliberately trying to keep the three of them calm, and in the process had had to steel herself not to expect too much from this afternoon, not to be too disappointed if the unthinkable happened. She pushed open the bath-room door, but the children had already left; small pools of water beaded here and there across the chequered linoleum.

Sophia made her way into the bedroom which Hannah and May shared. Hannah was taming Eleanor's wild curls into unwilling submission. As usual, the baby sat on the floor, still and contented, her thumb in her mouth. She never protested as long as Hannah was within sight. May was struggling to brush her own hair, although she had been told to wait.

Sophia laid the dresses carefully across the bed,

smoothing the lacy ruffles, untangling ribbons. She took the hairbrush from May, and the child hardly protested. Her small arms must have become tired.

'Hannah, I want you to begin dressing now. Eleanor's hair is perfect.'

Hannah beamed. She loved wearing her best dress, although fastening the buttons on her petticoat was always tiresome.

'Yes, Mama,' she said. Eleanor whimpered a little and then stopped. Hannah had only moved away as far as the bed.

May seemed content to lean against her mother's knees while Sophia brushed her thick hair vigorously. She was surprised at the little girl's stillness, but then May had always been sensitive to atmosphere. Sophia wondered if the child was catching some of her mother's suppressed excitement.

Looking at her three daughters, Sophia felt pride mixed with the now familiar tug of anxiety. They were all growing up so quickly. Hannah was six, already showing promise as a musician. She had a good ear, had learned to pick out some simple tunes on the piano. May was four, a dark, intense child who wanted always to be with her sisters, but even in their presence succeeded somehow in remaining separate from them. And then there was baby Eleanor. A delightful child of two: happy and sunny. 'Mouse,' Edward always called her. She was a quiet, undemanding little girl. She suited her father well.

Sophia knew that she was ambitious for her daughters. She wanted them to have every opportunity to move in the best circles, to become young women of accomplishment and grace. If for no other reason, then Edward's advancement was essential for that. This house would soon be too small for them. Sophia had recently learned that in all the best families, each child was now being given a room of their own. Sharing would soon become a thing of the past. And good schools were important, too, with music, drawing and dancing lessons. She knew that the years ahead would be expensive; she could not expect her father to continue helping for ever.

Besides, Edward was clever: he was a competent, professional man, respected by his peers. He deserved to succeed. If he had a fault, it was that he was too modest, too self-effacing. Sophia was growing stronger in her belief that her husband needed to push himself forward more. She knew it went against his nature. She also knew that if he couldn't, or wouldn't, do it, then she would be driven to do it for him.

She dressed the girls and took them down to Lily. Hannah and May looked so pretty in their best dresses, matching blue ribbons in their fresh curls. Hannah's hair was fair almost to whiteness, her skin pale and translucent. May's dark looks were a perfect contrast. Sophia smiled at the picture they made.

'Now, girls, you must sit quietly for Lily until she's ready. Hannah, I suggest we leave Eleanor's dress until the last possible moment.'

Sophia had been thrown into turmoil some four weeks earlier when Edward received his invitation to the Lord Lieutenant's garden party. This was the most important event in the Civil Service social calendar: an invitation like this could only mean that Edward had at least put his foot on the ladder. He must be deemed suitable, satisfactory: perhaps he was already under active consideration for promotion.

Now, as Sophia checked through everything she had planned to wear that afternoon, her hands began to shake a little, her stomach shifted uneasily. She was not ashamed to admit to herself how badly she wanted this for Edward, for their family. She would be scrutinized almost as much as he. She knew she had to behave as an intelligent, sophisticated woman, one who would do the Service justice no matter where her husband might be posted. She said a silent prayer. Promotions did not always go to deserving Catholics. She would need to play her part well.

Hannah: Summer 1886

HANNAH HELD MAY's hand tightly. Lily pushed Eleanor along in her bassinet. The children's summer party was to take place in a separate garden of the Vice-Regal lodge, away from the adults'. The wrought-iron gate to the garden whined as Lily opened it and shooed the two girls in before her. Hannah thought that Lily looked very smart today: she wore a navy dress with a white collar; her hat was white straw trimmed with white and navy flowers and matching ribbons. It was not usual to see Lily all dressed up, and today couldn't be her day off.

Some lady had arrived at the house earlier and helped Mama dress. When she'd finished, Mama had looked more than smart: she had looked beautiful. She wore a pale blue silk gown with cream embroidery, one that Hannah had never seen before. Her hat was much bigger than Lily's and she had flowers plaited through the complicated arrangement of her hair. She had seemed pleased when Hannah blurted out how beautiful she was. Sometimes she was not pleased when Hannah spoke out of turn, but today was different.

Hannah had never been to a real party in a garden

before. Especially one in a garden like this. A long table was set out in the shade under the trees, with great glass jugs of what looked like Lily's special lemonade. There were long salvers of cakes and pastries too, filled with summer fruits, and jellies of every colour. Some of the children were already queuing for the garden swing; others were waiting politely to play musical chairs. Hannah's eyes widened when she saw a young woman seated at a piano, ready to strike up for the game. She nudged May.

'Look!' she whispered. 'A piano in a *garden*!'

May laughed out loud. Hannah turned to Lily.

'Lily – please may we go and play musical chairs?'

'Off you go, Miss Hannah. Mind you take care of your sister, now. I'll be here with Eleanor when you want me.'

Hannah dragged May over to the waiting line of children. None of them spoke to her. She didn't care. She had her sister. And perhaps that smiling lady at the piano might allow her to play something later, when things were quieter.

At six o'clock, the carriage came to take them home. The piano-lady had been very kind, patting the stool beside her to show that there was enough room for Hannah. She taught her to play the opening bars of 'Für Elise' and praised her for the speed with which she'd learned.

'My word, Hannah, but you've picked that up quickly! Do you take lessons, dear?'

'Not yet,' said Hannah shyly. She felt suddenly breathless with excitement. She would ask Mama now – at once – tonight – if she might have piano lessons. The lady's question seemed to have made some hidden wish settle comfortably into a place already prepared in Hannah's mind, as though it had been wandering around looking for somewhere to sit. This was something that she wanted badly enough to fight for.

She wished they could stay longer, but May had had enough. Her long dark eyelashes seemed to sweep her cheek as she fought tidal waves of tiredness, struggling to keep standing. Eleanor was already asleep, her cheeks pink with contentment, her bonnet still in place.

Lily helped them all into the carriage, her face more flushed than ever, her eyes bright.

'Wasn't that a wonderful party, children?' she asked.

Hannah was surprised. Lily had never called them 'children' before. She had always been very careful to give each of them her proper name. Perhaps she was just tired.

Hannah nodded. May's head had finally slumped to one side, coming to rest on her sister's shoulder. Hannah stayed silent, not wanting to wake her.

She wondered if Mama and Papa's party had been as enjoyable as theirs. She hoped so. Something about Mama's earlier nervousness and Papa's intense, hurried busyness for the brief time she had seen him had made Hannah tread carefully around the grown-ups. She had the feeling that today was a very important day for all of them.

Mary and Cecilia: Spring 1888

FATHER JOHN MACVEIGH left the presbytery quickly, just as soon as he had disrobed after seven o'clock Mass. The streets of Millfield and Carrick Hill were quiet, filled with the distinctive silence of Sunday. Thin, greyish plumes of smoke were already ribboning from the clustered chimneys above him, speckling the morning mist with the ever-present smudges of soot.

He had half an hour before the next Mass, enough time to visit the McCurrys and bring some comfort to that distracted woman. Her husband's death was slow and agonizing. Not for the first time, the priest felt a surge of bitterness on behalf of his flock. Why any of them would want to cling to what this life had to offer them, once all hope had fled, was beyond him. The McCurrys were in for a particularly tough time, he thought – no sons there to protect the three women that would be left behind. He doubted that Mrs McCurry would ever recover from her husband's death. He had seen it before, too many times. Husbands and wives seemed to hold on together to the tenuous threads of endurance and survival. Once one spouse was gone, the other seemed to relinquish their grip, and the whole strained fabric of family life began to fray, unravelling piece by piece. He feared that Mrs McCurry would follow her husband sooner than she needed.

And where would that leave her daughters? Cecilia was just a wee girl, still at primary school. And Mary couldn't be expected to hold everything together on her own. Only thirteen, she was in her first year full-time at the mill. She should still be a child, he reflected, playing with rope and ball, if there was any justice. But the truth of it was, there was no justice, not in this corner of Belfast, anyway. All three McCurrys would need someone to look out for them, someone to offer shelter and comfort when things went wrong. And things seemed set to go very wrong indeed, sooner rather than later.

The uneasy peace of the city was already straining at the seams. Father MacVeigh could feel the changes, the steady hiss and crackle of tension, in the air all around him. The lull of the last few years, the absence of street-fighting, of vitriol and violence, did not mean that it was all over. Far from it. He had enough experience to smell trouble, long before others did.

Father MacVeigh reached the McCurrys' door and knocked gently, twice. Mary started into wakefulness, her neck stiff and jerky from sitting up in the lumpy armchair all night. Her eyelashes felt sore and spiky, her whole face almost too tender to touch. She got to the door first, just as Cecilia came running down the stairs.

'Good morning, Mary.'

The priest's face was open, freckled, kindly. His sandy hair was receding, and he had developed the habit of smoothing it back from his forehead with the heel of one hand. Mary found the gesture to be a peculiarly calming one: it seemed to tell her that everything was normal, under control. She welcomed the priest's presence, felt a curious sense of relief, a conviction that once he was here, all could still be well.

''Mornin', Father.'

'How is everything this morning?'

Mary shrugged. Cecilia cut in: 'Da's not awake yet, Father. Ma says he's slippin' away.'

Mary was horrified at her younger sister's matter-of-factness. She was only ten, but still, death left no one around here ignorant of its merciless grasp. Cecilia must have seen neighbours die before: surely she understood that Da was dying now, and once he was gone, they would never see him again? Mary felt her eyes fill with the hot, unmanageable tears which had woken her time after time throughout the previous night. It was the strangest crying she had ever experienced. It wasn't like when you got hurt, or when someone said cruel things to you. Instead, it got you by the throat, forced you to weep helplessly, chokingly, before disappearing again, leaving you feeling no better. There was no relief to be had anywhere. Da had already lasted longer than the doctor said; whether he lived or died, the strange weight inside her still felt the same.

'I'll go up and see him,' said Father MacVeigh, patting Mary's shoulder. His kindness brought on a fresh impulse to wail out loud; Mary bit down hard on the inside of her lip instead. Cecilia turned, ready to go upstairs before the priest.

'Come back, Cecilia. I want ye here.'

Grudgingly, Cecilia flattened herself against the wall to allow the priest's large, bulky frame to pass her by.

'Help me with the tea, there's a good girl.'

Reluctantly, Cecilia followed her elder sister into the kitchen.

'Da's not goin' to get better, is he, Mary?'

Cecilia's voice was explosive, over-loud in the small space. Mary placed the blackened kettle carefully on to the gas ring, and turned around to face her sister.

'No, love. He'll not.'

Her sister's body suddenly looked terrifyingly small and vulnerable to Mary. Cecilia stood just under the window, pale morning light seeping into the hollows of her white face.

'What are we goin' to do if he dies?'

Her chin began to tremble. Mary put both arms around her, drew her close. She held her so tightly that each of them was hardly able to breathe.

'I'll look after ye – always. Ye're not to be worryin', d'ye hear me?'

Cecilia nodded.

They stood silently in the dim kitchen, neither moving until the kettle boiled.

Father MacVeigh looked after all the arrangements for the funeral. For three days and nights, the house was full of neighbours, friends, family who had travelled to

Belfast from as far away as Tyrone and Donegal. Men took off their caps, drank whiskey and sang songs. Women talked incessantly, hugged Mary and Cecilia over and over, produced food from everywhere. Mary was surprised that sometimes the surrounding sadness would lift abruptly, to change into something lighter, happier. Da's brothers told stories about him as a child, people laughed at their jokes, some recited poems and rhymes, others spoke softly of harder, older times. There were moments when Mary caught herself forgetting why everyone was there, crowding into the hall and the tiny parlour until she and Cecilia had had to go outside to make room for others to breathe.

Everything was very flat and stale after Da's body was taken away from the house. While his brothers were still remembering him in talk, while they could all look on his taut, yellowing face, his gnarled hands crossed peacefully over his chest, it seemed that something of him still remained behind. Then he was gone, and life, it seemed, still went on.

Ma was determined that Cecilia stay on at school. It was the one subject that would shake her out of her torpor, the only topic that made the glaze go from her eyes. Mary nudged her with it every time she wanted to bring her mother's vacant look back to the kitchen table, her mind back again from wherever it had strayed. Mary agreed, over and over again: she didn't want to see her little sister at the mill, under the harsh eye of some bitter and withered doffing mistress, learning a trade that brought little but mill fever, consumption and toe-rot.

Any dream that Mary had that her brothers would come back was long gone. She couldn't blame them; she'd have done the same herself in their shoes, given half the chance. Belfast was no place for lads who refused to be happy being second best; who refused to lie down for their masters. They were all safer where they were.

She'd promised to look after Ma now, and Cecilia.

She'd spend the rest of her life trying, if that's what it took.

May: Autumn 1890

HANNAH HELD HER hand all the way. At first, May protested.

'I'm not a baby any more. I'm eight. I can walk on my own.'

She tried to wriggle her hand away from Hannah's, but her older sister held fast. She pulled May along behind her and increased her pace so that the younger girl had to run to keep up.

'Mama said we were to hold hands. I'm in charge and Mama says I'm to look after you.'

In charge. The words reminded May of Ellie, now almost six and longing to be in the same class as one of her sisters. She hated being on her own in Senior Infants. She had never settled into school, unlike Hannah and May. She chafed under its routine, the unaccustomed restriction of her movements. She still couldn't understand why she was not allowed simply to leave her desk and seek out her sisters whenever she needed. She had cried this morning when the time came to say goodbye to Hannah and May, cried so hard that Mama had had to take her away while Lily gave the older girls their breakfast.

'Be good, now, Eleanor,' Mama had scolded, but gently enough. 'Hannah and May are big girls and they have to go to their own classes.'

That had only made Eleanor's sobs worse.

'I'm a big girl, too, Mama! I go to school! I don't want to be all on my lonely!'

Mama had promised Ellie that if she was good, May could take her to second class with her for one whole day, soon. May had heard the sobs subsiding as Mama made her way down the long hallway of their new house, soothing Eleanor as she went, stroking the small, struggling body into quietness. Lily would bring her to school, immediately after the older girls had turned the corner, taking her firmly by the hand. She didn't cry too much when Lily said goodbye; but Mama would be upset for the whole day if she took her. She said it shattered her nerves.

May felt a sudden, unaccustomed pride that she would be the one looking after her baby sister, that *she* would be the one Mama trusted. Up until now, it had always been Hannah, Hannah, Hannah: May never got even one chance to be in charge of her younger sister. Sister Paul had already said that Ellie would be welcome to spend the day in her classroom, to know where her sister was in case she needed her.

May stopped resisting the pressure of Hannah's hand; she'd better be good. She didn't want Mama to change her mind, to decide that she, May, was badly behaved, unreliable, not to be trusted after all. And Hannah *would* tell on her, she was sure of that. The school gates were only a few minutes' walk away, anyway, so it was worth it. She loved Ellie, loved the little girl's bright smile and trusting eyes. She longed to show her off to Sister Paul.

The sun was bright, the air humid even at this early hour, and the stiff material of May's new uniform was already scratching at her neck and irritating the soft skin above her knees.

'This is your line, May. Don't forget to eat your lunch, or Mama will be cross.'

The other girls were already queuing up, each with a school bag on her back, feet shuffling and scraping into a reluctant silence.

'Be sure and wait for me at home-time,' Hannah said, kissed her sister hurriedly and ran off to join the bigger girls in fourth class. As soon as May had taken her place, and darted a quick glance over her shoulder to make sure that Brid Byrne was nowhere near her, Sister Paul appeared at the head of the iron staircase. Immediately, complete silence descended on the yard. She hadn't needed to ring the bell even once this morning.

May looked up at the old nun, wanting to catch her eye, to smile and be smiled at. But she was busy just now, papers in her hand, her little glasses perched on the end of her nose. This was a different start from the normal. The girls sensed it and a low murmur began, rippling up and down each line, like the uneasy scrunching of boots on gravel.

'Now, girls, quiet please.'

The murmur died away.

'We have some changes today. Please listen carefully.'

Sister Paul settled her glasses more firmly on her nose, and turned over the first sheet.

'Sister Mary Immaculate will be taking Junior Infants from today. Juniors, please follow Sister Mary to your classroom.'

There was absolute silence now. Everyone held their breath. One change meant everyone changed. May's eyes were drawn towards the group of nuns just below the stairs. Sister Raphael, Sister Annunciata and Sister Olivia were the only ones she recognized from last year. No one ever wanted Sister Raphael, the elderly, crabbed nun who used the strap far more than most, and certainly more than Sister Paul, who had never used it at all, not even once in the two years she had been May's teacher. Sister Raphael's face was creased into a permanent expression of discontent; her hands, too, frightened May and it was whispered among the girls that they were the hands of a witch.

She held her breath. Please, please, she thought. Let it be any of the others; don't let it be Sister Raphael.

Waiting for the other classes to be assigned their teacher was agony. When it came to second class, May's heart was beating so hard that she hardly heard what Sister Paul said.

'Second class, please go with Sister Raphael to your classroom; I'll visit you later on this morning.'

May's legs began to tremble. It wasn't fair. Now

they would all have to be silent and terrified. Sister Raphael would have nothing less.

She watched as the sunlight glinted off the old nun's glasses. Without a word, with only a sharp movement of her hooked hand, she led the snaking group of girls across the unwilling yard, and in through the main door of the school building. One by one, they filed into the bright classroom, standing around the wall until they were assigned their desks. May hoped that she would not have to sit beside Brid Byrne. She smelt bad, and Mama said she had nits.

'Kathleen Mulhall, Margaret O'Connor.'

The tone was sharp; the crooked arthritic fingers indicated their double desk at the top of the third row. For a moment, May hesitated, startled by the unfamiliarity of her given name. No one ever called her Margaret, not even Sister Paul, once she had learned that 'May' was her preference. 'It suits you,' she had said, smiling at May's red-faced admission that she never answered to 'Margaret'. 'That's Our Lady's month – a joyful month.' May had sat down gratefully, then, pleased that she hadn't got into trouble for her outspokenness.

Now, she and Kathleen looked at each other and ventured a small smile. They slid along the polished wooden seat of their desk, almost colliding in the middle, each wanting to giggle, but knowing that they'd better not. She didn't feel so bad any more. Having a new friend always helped.

*

It was just after midday when Sister Raphael announced it was time for mental arithmetic. May felt the familiar sensation of panic: something stirred deep in her chest, just behind the buttons of her uniform. It was like the flapping of a tiny, frightened bird. Her mind seemed to close over, becoming a shuttered window, no small chinks of light anywhere. Sister Paul had understood that feeling, had told her, kindly, to take her time. Accuracy before speed, she'd always said, folding her hands in front of her as she waited for May's halting reply. She could see the nun's gentle face now, her intelligent eyes as they regarded her pupil over the tops of her glasses. Her face had been calm, her steady gaze encouraging.

May knew there would be no such understanding at Sister Raphael's hands. She waited, in growing agony, as the questions went all the way up the first row of desks, down the second, ready to start again at the front of her row, the third. She stared at the bright blue pencil lying in its little groove at the top of her desk, its paint indented here and there with tiny teeth-marks. She tried to focus on it, tried to stop her mind from skittering away in all directions as it usually did whenever she was frightened. She wished that something, anything, would stop the questions before they got to her. The problems had been getting steadily more difficult too, she was sure of it.

'Multiply twelve by three, and add four,' Sister Raphael said, nodding at Kathleen.

May thought what a cold thing it was not even to try to know her girls by name; she seemed to have no interest. 'You there' or 'Girl with red hair' seemed to be enough for her. May missed Sister Paul sorely. If only . . .

'Thirty-six plus four are forty,' said Kathleen.

The nun nodded. She turned to May.

'Add twelve, then divide by four,' she said.

May couldn't reply. She could see the nun's lips move, understood that words had been spoken, that an answer was now required of her. But she was unable to make sense of anything that had been said. Even her limbs felt heavy, leaden. She wanted to sleep, or to wake from this bad dream. She said nothing.

'You, girl, you're not even paying attention!'

The whole class sat silent, expectant. May stared blankly at the old nun, who was now beginning to harness the anger which had hovered around her, use-lessly, restlessly, all morning: waiting for its moment to come.

May felt the back of her neck growing hot. What was she to do first? Add something? Subtract? Divide?

Still she didn't speak. Even to herself, her silence seemed like defiance, a refusal to bend her will, rather than the muteness born of sheer terror.

'You're an insolent girl!'

Sister Raphael rose from the desk, her hand already on the leather strap tied around her waist along with the rosary beads.

'Hold out your hand!' she commanded.

May could feel Kathleen stiffen in the desk beside her. She well knew that if any girl didn't do as Sister told her, the whole class would be punished. Playground lore terrified children into submission long before they met Sister Raphael. The unfairness of it all suddenly struck May. She would make sure that nobody else suffered because of her stupidity.

'I'm not insolent, Sister. I need more time. Sister Paul said . . .'

The old nun's eyes widened in disbelief. The class held its collective breath.

'How dare you answer me back!'

'I'm not, it's just . . .'

May watched as the nun walked quickly towards her desk. Already she could feel the sting of leather across her palm and prepared herself for the inevitable. She spread her hands out in front of her, a gesture of apology, submission. Instead, there was a sudden sharp pain in her right ear as the nun dragged her across the classroom, pulling hard on her ear lobe. May was startled, conscious of nothing now except the jagged point of pain that seared its way down the right side of her face. She cried out, tried to raise her hand to ease the burning sensation which now seemed to flush hotly across her eyes, down the other cheek.

And suddenly, all was darkness. For a moment, May couldn't understand what had happened to her. There was the sound of a door slamming, then a sudden creaking and rustling all around her, unfamiliar whispers which made her heart beat even faster. Cautiously, she raised her hands and began to feel around her in the darkness. Dry, choking sobs escaped her from time to time. In front of her was a door, wooden, rough in places, but warm to the touch. Beside her were what felt like cylinders of paper, stacked four or five deep. Voices still reached her, but they were muffled, droning, sounding like your ears did under water. May pressed her cheek to the door and listened hard: the girls were chanting their tables.

'Twelve *threes* are *thirty*-six, twelve *fours* are *forty*-eight, twelve *fives* are *six*ty . . .'

The blood pulsed loudly, warmly, all down both sides of her face.

She knew suddenly where she was. She was in the map cupboard. The cylinders of heavy paper were like those Sister Paul had hung across the blackboard every Wednesday, when she had pointed out continents, sub-continents, countries with strange shapes and stranger customs. May had loved those geography lessons; she loved repeating the names of rivers, exotic, unfamiliar, sometimes unpronounceable words: Nile, Ganges, Poto-mac, Amazon, Tigris, Euphrates.

She pushed with both hands hard against the door. It wouldn't give. Not even a thin shard of light insinu-ated its way into the cracks and joins of its sturdy surface. The darkness was complete, terrifying. What if they all forgot about her? What if they all went home and left her? Nobody would know where she was – not Mama, not Hannah, not even Sister Paul. What if she ran out of air? She could feel the panic rising again; a different panic from before. She no longer felt frozen. Now she felt open and vulnerable, watery and insubstan-tial. Tears threatened. The lump in her throat was already making it harder to breathe. She tapped on the door with the knuckles of her right hand and waited.

No response. Sister Raphael was obviously determined to ignore her. She was afraid to tap again. She did not want to face the full force of the nun's wrath, and, later, Mama's displeasure, her tight-lipped silence and disapproval.

She felt around her, desperately. There was no room for her to sit down, and her legs were getting cramped. It was hot; the material of her uniform felt even more scratchy than this morning. And she was so afraid of the dark. Mama always let her and Hannah have a night light burning in their bedroom, a fat tallow candle with a gas mantle for protection. She wished she were at home now, snug in bed with Hannah, watching the patterns made by the diffuse light on the bedroom walls and ceiling, making up songs and stories, giggling in the chiaroscuro of the chilly bedroom.

Suddenly, she had an idea. How to take her mind off the darkness, the tiredness of her legs, the hot and stuffy cupboard. She began to sing to herself, not too loudly at first, but enough to hear the comforting sound of her own voice. Singing was always a happy thing to do, just like in bed at night, or when Hannah would let her sit down on the piano stool while she practised, and both of them sang together.

May began to sing a few lines, tentatively at first, clapping to their rhythm, just as Hannah had taught her. It was a new song, one that Hannah had just learned. Remembering her older sister gave May a great surge of confidence. She sang five verses, making up words here and there, singing 'la, la, la, la,' when her imagination, or her memory, failed her.

She had even begun to forget about her fear of the dark, about the oppressive heat inside the cupboard, about the unjust punishment meted out to her when the door was suddenly wrenched open.

There, red-faced and furious, stood Sister Raphael. Her head was wobbling from side to side, as though her neck had difficulty in supporting its weight. Her right hand fingered the smooth surface of her strap. All of this May took in, but her attention, for a couple of seconds, was drawn irresistibly elsewhere. Just over Sister Raphael's left shoulder, she saw Kathleen Mulhall's mischievous brown eyes looking at her, face pink with the effort not to laugh. She lifted her hands off the inky surface of the desk and slowly brought her palms together in silent clapping. Then she bowed with difficulty from the waist, still seated, trapped in the double desk.

'. . . to Sister Paul, right this minute. And don't think I won't tell her just what you've been up to.'

May snapped her attention back to the lined, angry face in front of her. Suddenly, light-headedly, she didn't care. At least the door was open and she could breathe. Kathleen was her friend and Sister Paul would surely understand what had happened. She hadn't meant to be badly behaved; it had all just come about, somehow, without her willing it.

She stepped out of the cupboard with an air of bravado she didn't quite feel, encouraged by Kathleen's grin and the admiring glances of some of the other girls. Most of the faces, however, were terrified, and May felt a rush of pity for them all, a renewed fear for herself.

She marched out of the classroom, her head held high. She walked much more slowly across the yard and into the hallway outside Sister Paul's office. She knocked on the door and waited. Suddenly, starting with her legs, then her shoulders, she began to shake all over. Under her arms felt hot and cold at the same time. Her stomach began to cramp, as though she had eaten too much. Her palms were damp, clammy to the touch. She tried to draw a deep breath, but something dark and unforgiving in her chest seemed to obstruct the clean air, refusing to let it pass. Then the pictures on the wall began to shift, one after the other, in front of her eyes. Even the walls began to sway, to crowd in on her. She cried out to Sister Paul just as her legs crumpled under her and a thin, warm ache filled the space behind her forehead.

She tried to hold on to the light, to keep her eyes open. She was dimly aware of Sister Paul standing over her, sensed her hands being warmly held until, once more, all was darkness.

Mary and Cecilia: Winter 1890

MARY JOINED THE queue that was shuffling its way damply, anxiously towards the desk on the ground floor. Late December sleet still sparkled across the shoulders of the people in front of her. The air was filled with the heavy, fleecy smell of wet wool drying. She had never been inside the workhouse before. She decided she didn't like the echoing corridors, the remote, cold ceilings. She wanted to be home.

Cecilia pulled at her sleeve.

'What am I t'say?'

'Nothin'. Just leave the talkin' to me.'

The whole room was filled with girls who looked about Cecilia's age or younger, all of them accompanied by a sister or a mother, a grandma or a granda. Mary felt a sudden stab of pity for all of them. They looked awful young to be starting. But it was worse for others. Mary knew dozens of doffers at her place of work, no more than eight or nine years of age, their small faces pinched and yellow with exhaustion. At least Cecilia was older and bigger than that.

Ma had sworn she would not send Cecilia as a half-timer before she was twelve. It already broke her heart, so it did, to see her youngest child now snared by the linen mills. She had held out as long as she could, but Mary's shillings were not enough to feed and warm the three of them. It had been a particularly harsh, unforgiving winter. Jimmy's brothers had been good to her after he died, but they had mouths of their own to feed, empty bellies to fill. She couldn't expect them to keep sending her postal orders while their own went hungry. And she had had such high hopes for Cecilia, too: the clever one, the wee girl so much at home with her books.

The man at the desk had iron-grey hair, surprisingly black and springy eyebrows. His collar was shiny, Mary noticed, and his cuffs had been turned more than once. He barely looked up at her approach.

'Name?'

'Cecilia McCurry.'

'Date of birth?'

'Tenth of January, eighteen seventy-eight.'

Now he looked up sharply.

'Is the birth certificate for you?'

'For me sister.'

'Why doesn't she speak for herself, then?'

Mary felt her face grow hot. Wee shite, she thought. Here he is, warm and dry, burdened by nothing heavier than a pen. What gives him the right to be snotty with me?

She felt Cecilia begin to stir beside her, and squeezed her arm in warning.

'Because she's shy. Sir.'

Instantly, his frown began to clear. Mary congratulated herself silently on her stroke of genius. It was the 'sir' that had done it; she was sure of that. Be respectful to them, Ma had said. At all times, show respect, even if ye didn't feel it.

'Address?'

'Number seven, Carrick Hill.'

The clerk filled in the birth certificate slowly, dipping his pen into the brass well of ink on the desk in front of him. Mary noticed that their clerk was writing much more slowly than any of the others. She sighed. Trust her to get it wrong.

Suddenly, he signed his name with a black flourish and turned the certificate over on his blotter, pressing on it with his clenched fist.

'Pay over there,' he said, pointing to the far side of the room.

Mary nodded.

'Thank you, sir,' she said. But he had already lost interest in them, his face cross again as he turned to the next in line. Mary walked rapidly across the room towards the cashiers and pulled Cecilia into the shortest queue. She watched the new clerk's face closely, watched as he summoned one person after the other, learned to judge the moment when he would avert his sharp eyes. Just before their turn came, she ducked swiftly out of the line, grabbing Cecilia by the hand. Then she turned casually away and walked towards the exit, nodding and smiling at her sister. Anyone watching would have seen two young girls, one only slightly taller than the other, chatting happily, glad to be on their way home. Cecilia had been warned to ask nothing, no matter what Mary did. Now her eyes were full of questions.

Once they were outside in the rapidly darkening afternoon, Mary grinned broadly at her sister, fixing her shawl for her over Cecilia's long fair hair.

'We have yer lines, Cecilia, *and* I still have Ma's sixpence. Let's go home.'

Mary couldn't help feeling pleased with her little bit of thievery. It almost helped her forget the reason for getting Cecilia's lines in the first place. They were close, as close as sisters should be. Every bit as much as Ma, Mary would have done anything to keep her younger sister out of the mill. Instead, she had just spoken for her a week ago and the spinning master said that Cecilia could start straight after Christmas.

Almost in spite of herself, Cecilia could feel her excitement mounting. She felt grown-up this morning, full of heady anticipation. She sipped at her tea, hiding her excitement from Mary, who had recently begun to get on her nerves. 'Ye're not to do this, ye're not to do that', followed by all the stories about how tough life was in the spinning room, especially for a half-timer starting out. Cecilia didn't care. She wanted to go to work, to know that she was being a help to Ma. And it didn't mean giving up school, either. She'd still be there – Monday, Wednesday and Friday one week, Tuesday and Thursday the next. She felt pleased that she'd be getting the best of both worlds. She didn't need Mary's grim face telling her over and over again that life would be otherwise.

'Are ye right?' Mary asked her. 'Have ye yer piece?'

Cecilia nodded, picking up the piece of bread she had wrapped earlier in a bit of cloth. She stood up.

'Aye, I'm right.'

Mary folded herself into her long shawl.

'Time we was goin', then.'

Cecilia had a sudden pang when she thought of Ma, who had hugged her and kissed her last night, and asked God to look after her precious wee girl. Cecilia had felt embarrassed, felt her toes curl in her stiff new boots as Ma had come over all tearful. She hoped she was still sleeping. Mary had said they'd not be waking her at half-five unless they had to. Anyway, Ma had said as much of a goodbye as Cecilia could take last night; she couldn't bear to watch her red-rimmed eyes fill up all over again.

They hurried to Watson, Valentine and Company, Mary anxious, as ever, about being fined.

'Hurry, Cecilia, it's tuppence docked if we're not there by six.'

Cecilia *was* hurrying; she was easily keeping pace with her sister, although her boots were beginning to pinch. When they turned the corner into Amelia Street, Cecilia almost stopped dead with amazement. Girls and women were converging from everywhere, swarms of them, jostling and laughing, joking with each other despite the early hour. Some even appeared to be

35

singing. Cecilia felt her heart lift with sudden hope: these did not seem to be the hard, careless girls that Mary always talked about. These faces were smiling, friendly; many seemed to be in high good humour.

Cecilia kept close to Mary's side as they crushed in through the narrow doorway, surrounded by a great, heaving mass of bodies.

'Hold tight,' Mary muttered.

Cecilia obediently linked Mary's left arm and together they pushed their way up the giant staircase, Mary's right hand holding on tight to the narrow banister. The crowd parted abruptly at the top of the stairs, and seemed to disappear at once into the vastness of the wet spinning room. Almost immediately, the machinery started up, and Cecilia jerked in fright. Her ears filled with sound, her head buzzed as the terrifying racket seemed to suck up all the air around her. She realized her sister was speaking only when Mary tugged at her sleeve. She watched her lips move, but no sound could compete with the roar inside her head.

Finally, Mary dragged her away to where the air was a little less thunderous.

'Ye'll get used to it soon enough, don't fret.'

Cecilia nodded, the inside of her head already beginning to feel numb.

'I've to bring ye to the doffin' mistress, Miss Morris – d'ye mind I told ye?'

Cecilia nodded again, but everything Mary had told her earlier seemed now to have cracked wide open and floated away from her like thistledown. Impatiently,

Mary pulled her by the hand towards a young woman standing in between two spinning-frames.

'Miss Morris – this is me sister Cecilia. I spoke for her before Christmas.'

The small, neat young woman smiled and Cecilia was flooded with relief. If this woman could stand there and smile while the world seemed to be exploding all around her, then maybe she could get to bear it, too.

'Right, Cecilia – are you ready to start?'

'Aye, miss, I am.'

Her tone was friendly and at that moment Cecilia felt she would do anything for her, for the kindness of her voice, the sympathy of her glance. Mary left, having said something else that Cecilia didn't catch. She didn't care; she knew her older sister would come looking for her when the time was right.

There were five other girls, about Cecilia's age, looking nervously around them, their eyes never leaving Miss Morris's face. She gestured to all of them to move closer to her, to pay attention.

'Now, girls, I want ye all to listen to me very carefully. I'll not say anything more than once.'

She pointed out a tall, stern-looking man who was walking purposefully along the pass between the rows of machines, his hands behind his back. His eyes were bright, missing nothing.

'That's Mr Thompson, the spinning master. Ye'll have nothing to do with him until I've finished with ye. If somethin's not clear, or if yer in trouble, it's me ye come to.'

She lifted the whistle hanging around her neck.

'When ye hear this whistle, that's my signal for yous to run and do yer work. It means it's time to doff the full bobbins from each machine, like this—'

She moved a handle at the side of the spinning machine and the frames came to a graceful stop. Cecilia felt the immediate relief of even this small reduction in the noise all around her. Then Miss Morris reached up and shifted a metal weight to one side.

'This weight's called a drag – it regulates the tension on each yarn bobbin.'

She took off what looked like a giant reel of thread from its spindle, and laid it quickly into one of several boxes laid out on the floor nearby. Then she took hold of an empty bobbin and attached the now loose ends of yarn to what she called the 'flyer eyes'. Finally, she readjusted the drags and set the spinning-frame in motion again.

'That's it, girls – pull the handle, doff the full bobbin, and put it into the box beside ye. Then ye've got to put back what ye've taken off: put the empty one on the spindle, attach the ends, fix the drag and off yis go.'

She paused, looking keenly at each girl in turn. She tapped on her whistle several times for emphasis.

'When ye're called, ye've twenty bobbins each to change – ye must be quick, and ye must be accurate.'

Cecilia listened intently. It didn't seem too difficult, and at school, Miss Graham always said she was a quick learner – deft at her needlework, good at sums and reading. She wanted to be good here, too, wanted to please Miss Morris. She liked her strictness, felt that if she did as she was told, then she wouldn't have to feel as lost and terrified as she did now. She promised herself to stay alert, to do more than her share, to be the best of all her group of half-timers.

By dinner-hour, Cecilia could barely stand with exhaustion. Her head felt light, her brain was whirling in time with the clamour of belts, the rattle of spinning-frames. Her lungs had had to fight for air all morning: each breath brought with it a sticky combination of heat, steam and the pungent fumes of oil. The greasy stuff that sprayed constantly from the machinery spotted everyone's aprons – 'rubbers', they called them – with streaks of smudgy black. It left a heavy, sour aftertaste in the air, potent enough to be almost visible.

When the hooter went, she was bitterly disappointed that it was still only midday.

'I thought it was home-time,' she confessed to Mary, so close to tears she could barely eat her piece.

Mary stroked her sister's hair.

'It's just a wee touch o' mill fever, that's all – ye'll be better by tomorrow, I promise.'

Cecilia hoped so. If she did really well under Miss Morris, then maybe she could move on more quickly to caging, laying and spinning. If she could be with Mary, it wouldn't be so bad. She hated to admit it, but her sister had been right. It had taken Mary three years to learn her craft and be promoted to spinner: only now did Cecilia take in the bewildering range of skills that had to be learned before she could occupy a stand close to her sister.

Hours passed, dragging their feet, shuffling reluctantly towards home-time. Cecilia thought she could never endure another day as slow as this one. But she did learn quickly; she was first to respond to the whistle, first to doff her share of the full bobbins. Miss Morris even showed her, and none of the others, how to judge the exact moment when a bobbin was full. She showed her what she meant by tension, let Cecilia feel the weight and substance of the drag. More than once, she glanced in Cecilia's direction and nodded her approval. Without it, Cecilia felt she would have withered and died that very afternoon. The heat and humidity had made her feet swell, and she was terrified that she would not be able to take off her boots when she got home.

Only the thought of Ma made her keep her tears in check. She couldn't let her see how bad it had been, how despondent she felt. Mary had been so kind to her when the day ended, letting her rest her head on her shoulder all the way home on the rattling tram. She hadn't uttered one word, not one syllable of reproach or 'I told you so'.

Cecilia couldn't wait to crawl into bed, could hardly keep her eyes open to drink the tea Ma had just brewed. She had a moment of cold terror, just before she slept that first night, as she imagined her whole life spinning out in front of her, yards and yards of years like yarn, with no relief from the airless whirl and blunder of huge, malevolent machines.

May: Autumn 1891

IT WASN'T FAIR.

Just as May was feeling happy in school for most of almost every day, just when she had her own best friend beside her, everything had to change.

'You have your sisters,' Mama had said firmly. 'They're your best friends.'

That was true, too. But Kathleen Mulhall was her best friend in a different way. And now, maybe she'd never see her again.

'Where are you going?' Kathleen had asked her. Her eyes had been wide and scared at the prospect of anybody going far away. She could not conceive of there being another world beyond Dublin, a world which had its own roads and schools and houses and people. Everything outside the small boundaries of what she knew filled her with misgiving. When they drew their maps in geography lessons, Kathleen always put a big red dot carefully where she thought Dublin was; the rest of the outline was blank, except where little blue marks radiated from the coastline to indicate the sea. She drew carefully and well, but she had no curiosity beyond her own place, her own streets.

'Belfast,' May said, feeling a faint thrill of superiority despite herself. 'Papa has new and important work there, Mama says, so we are not to make a fuss about going.' She paused. 'I'll show you on the map if you like.' She said this shyly, not wanting Kathleen to feel bad. She was a much better geography student than Kathleen was; in fact, she was much better at everything, except, perhaps, mental arithmetic and making people laugh.

Kathleen nodded.

'I'd like to know where you're going.'

May wetted her finger and traced a rough map of Ireland in the chalky film of dust that always settled on their classroom desks overnight. Even though she hated leaving Kathleen, she would be glad never to see Sister Raphael again. Ever since that day last year when May had been locked in the cupboard, Sister Raphael had kept a tight-lipped distance from her. She rarely addressed her directly. May must sit still and work quietly: she instinctively discerned the shadow of Sister Paul which hovered around this unspoken arrangement. It was her, May's, duty never to speak out of turn, a duty she gladly accepted. She never, ever wanted to be locked in a cupboard again. A tiny white scar just above her right eyebrow was reminder enough of her fall outside Sister Paul's office, her fall from grace. It was the only outer sign of her crime and punishment. May used to touch it from time to time, running her fingers over its bumpy surface. It gave her a peculiar kind of comfort, a reassurance that, once she continued to be good, she need never feel such blind and breathless panic again.

She nudged Kathleen, who was keeping a sharp eye

on the classroom door. She jabbed her forefinger at the crude map she had just drawn in the dust.

'See the teddy bear's head?'

Kathleen nodded gravely.

'Well, just across from his eye is Belfast.'

She drew a line from Lough Neagh to the coast and placed Kathleen's finger on the exact spot where Belfast should be. She assumed a teacherly, properly solemn expression. Kathleen was a far better mimic than she, but May liked to try from time to time.

'Papa says it's a very busy town, and an important port.'

They laughed together at her pompous tone.

'Will you ever come back?'

Kathleen was twisting a tendril of thick black hair around her fingers. In and out, in and out. May used to watch her, fascinated, as she spent hours doing just this, as though weaving her lessons into her memory. Sometimes her fingers moved at great speed, almost desperately, and May would know then that she was finding something difficult.

She felt filled with a sudden kindness towards her friend. After all, she, May, was the one going away on a big adventure. To start with, there was the thrill of taking the train from Amiens Street Station, and snaking all the way around the coast to Drogheda, passing through Dundalk, listening to all the unfamiliar place names until they arrived at Belfast. And Hannah and Ellie would be with her too. May couldn't help feeling excited, although it wouldn't do to show it, either here or at home. Not yet, anyway.

But poor Kathleen was being left behind, and she had only brothers. May didn't want her to be sad over losing her friend, as well.

So she nodded.

'Yes. Mama says we will be back and forth, mostly to see Grandfather. I'll ask to see you, too.'

Kathleen grinned at her then.

'You'd better,' was all she had time to say before Sister Raphael swept into the classroom, the skirts of her habit swirling chalk-dust into the air around her, some of which floated gently, suspended in the streams of light that shivered through the classroom windows in the early hours. It was as though her long black habit was breathing sudden life into all the dead words that had fallen from the blackboard during yesterday's lessons.

At once, fifty voices fell silent; fifty small faces became still and waited for the day to begin.

Sophia: Winter 1891

SOPHIA GRIPPED EDWARD'S arm nervously as they alighted from the carriage at Mount Eden Park. She kept her eyes down, negotiating the three treacherous steps that led on to the safety of the glistening pavement below. Edward held the umbrella over her head. Sophia had not been impressed with her first view of Belfast. It had looked grim and sooty, dirty rain falling heavily all the way from the train station. Even the buildings along University Road and Malone Road had struck her as stout and practical: workmanlike rather than elegant.

This was not what Sophia had had in mind when she'd longed for Edward's advancement, for a better life for their daughters. Leaving Dublin, her father, her wonderful new home, had been a dreadful wrench. She had been assailed by grief, a deep, searing sense of loss whose intensity she could never have foreseen. Belfast seemed a grey and frantic place by contrast, no green spaces to be seen anywhere. And there was not even the comfort of familiar streets to ease the transition from one home to the other.

She was not so much concerned about the girls. They would adapt, she knew: children always did. Her fear now was that she would not settle, that she would somehow let her husband down.

Edward turned to her, his normally stern face transformed by a huge smile.

'Well, my dear?'

Only then did she look up.

'Welcome to our new home.'

Sophia gasped. 'Edward!'

'Which one, Papa, which one?'

Hannah waited impatiently at the bottom of a flight of imposing granite steps. Now eleven years of age, she had developed a slightly imperious manner, a too-high regard for her own academic and musical abilities. Sophia found herself frequently disliking her eldest daughter. It was time she was taken in hand, time she learned modesty and restraint. The last few months had been so busy that Sophia felt she had neglected her eldest daughter's social formation.

'Be still, Hannah!'

But Edward was in unaccustomed good humour.

'Number eight, Hannah. Take your sisters up with you. We'll be there directly.'

Hannah went first, stung by her mother's sharp reproof. She didn't wait for her sisters. May took Eleanor's hand and helped her up the steps to the front door.

Sophia clutched at her husband's arm so tightly he winced.

'Edward, is this truly ours?'

'Yes, indeed, my dear. A fitting abode for Belfast's new Postmaster, don't you think?'

'It looks wonderful! Can we really afford it?'

Sophia was almost afraid to ask the question. She had grown used to the increasing benefits of Edward's advancing career; she no longer wanted to contemplate the possibility of their living any other way. An elegant home, servants, the ease that accompanied rising social status: all had become necessary to her comfort, to the comfort of her daughters, over the past five years. She waited, needing Edward to still the faint, nervous fluttering inside her that made her hands automatically reach to finger her necklace.

Edward patted her hand.

'You are not to fret. It's all taken care of, I promise.'

Sophia glanced at her husband as he gazed at the facade of the large house in front of them. The change in him over the last five years had been remarkable. He had taken to his new career with enthusiasm, had built a reputation as a thorough, reliable, if uninspired, senior civil servant. She was proud of him, proud of his new-found self-confidence. This house would suit him, she knew, even better than their previous home on the Rathmines Road in Dublin. This was solid, respectable red-brick: rather like Edward himself.

'Shall we?'

He smiled at her, leading her up the steps to the front door. She could feel how pleased with himself he was. He had refused for weeks to give her any detail of their new home, had stayed uncharacteristically tight-lipped after his last visit to Belfast.

'Wait and see,' was all he would say.

Lily was standing at the open door, her plain face wide with welcome. She curtsied briefly.

'I'll be in the kitchen if you need me, ma'am,' she said.

She disappeared back to the kitchen at once. She knew her mistress liked to find her way around on her own.

The house exceeded all of Sophia's expectations. Five bedrooms, a vast bay-windowed drawing room, a dining room, kitchen, bathroom, scullery. She tried to estimate quickly what it would take to run this household. She would need to speak to Lily and Katie at once; perhaps even more staff would be necessary. She would decide after they had all settled in. The pleasing aspect of the rooms, the well-tended back garden, the heavy furniture all delighted her. Happily, she mentally arranged and rearranged, calculated and estimated, mediated in the girls' disagreements over bedrooms, and finally dispelled the gloom that had settled over her during the carriage ride from Great Victoria Street.

Above all else, she couldn't quell the delightful feeling that they – she and Edward – had arrived at last.

Hannah: Autumn 1892

THEY WERE FIGHTING again. Hannah could hear the start of the angry, insect-like murmur just minutes after the last guests had departed. She turned over in the bed, pressing one ear into the pillow, pushing down hard on the other with the palm of her hand. She did not want to hear another angry exchange, did not want to listen to the buzz and hum of voices that would eventually separate somehow, each becoming distinct from the other, solidifying into words and phrases she did not want to hear. She'd prefer not to know; she was tired of it. Every weekend recently had been the same. She'd begun to hate coming home. If it weren't for Eleanor, she would have preferred to stay in school on Friday and Saturday nights. Mama and Papa could come to visit her and May on Sunday afternoon, perhaps, like the parents of some of the long-distance boarders, and stay for tea. They wouldn't be able to fight there, not in so public a place.

Her father's raised voice now reached her distinctly.

'Have you any idea, any idea at all how much that *costs*?'

Money, it was always about money. Despite herself,

Hannah now strained to hear her mother's words. What was so costly this time? Was it school, perhaps, or piano lessons, or Christmas? Could she and May help by giving up something – anything – in order to take the frost out of the atmosphere, not to be compelled to listen to the same old argument weekend after weekend? She lifted her head off the pillow to try and catch her mother's elusive reply, but at that moment her bedroom door creaked open. Eleanor stood, framed by the light of the sputtering gas lamp on the landing. Hannah was startled. She looked like a small forlorn spirit standing there, her long curly hair frizzing out in shocked waves around her face.

'Can I come into your bed?' she whispered.

Hannah was already turning down the blankets on the other side.

'Of course, Ellie. Come on.'

Eleanor scrambled up the side of the high bed, pulling the folds of her long nightdress out from under her knees as she struggled into the warmth beside her sister. She'd hated having her own room ever since Hannah and May, one after the other, had become old enough to be boarders at St Dominic's. She hated being abandoned at night. And May was no use to go to for comfort, once evening was past. Once *she* climbed into bed, she slept instantly, heavily. From time to time, May would wander into Hannah's room, still asleep, and Hannah would take her gently back to her own bed. The first time Eleanor had seen this, she'd been upset. She hadn't liked the absence behind her sister's eyes, the useless search for recognition. Sleepwalking,

Hannah had explained to her. Eleanor thought that that was a good word; naming it had seemed somehow to make it less frightening.

'Why are Mama and Papa fighting?' she asked into the pillow, cuddling into the warm space made by Hannah's body.

Hannah kissed her lightly.

'Grown-ups do. They can't enjoy themselves properly without it.'

Eleanor giggled.

'Will we fight when we're grown-up?'

'No – we're different. We're the Bright Brilliant Sisters of Belfast – don't tell me you've forgotten already? Anyway, it's men and women who fight, mostly.'

'Why?'

Hannah shrugged into the darkness.

'I suppose because they're different. Don't worry. They'll be friends again tomorrow.'

But the voices continued, a steady angry stream, suddenly lower in volume. Hannah knew what they must look like by now, could see both their faces, read the tiniest flicker of each expression. She had been an unwilling audience to last weekend's fight when they'd forgotten about her, left her seated at the piano in the adjoining room. One of the folding doors had been partly closed over, so she was hidden from sight. She hadn't intended to eavesdrop, didn't even want to be there. By the time she realized that she shouldn't be overhearing this, it was too late to move. She had sat listening to words she only half understood, most of them drowned out by the buzzing in her head. She hadn't realized until later that she'd been holding her breath.

Papa's face had been red and creased, his moustaches bristling. He was tapping agitatedly on his cigar, blowing out great plumes of blue-tinged smoke. He threw his head back from time to time, staring upwards, as though looking for answers on the ceiling above him. Hannah had seen him do it, watched him avoid Mama's steady gaze.

She had been standing by the fireplace, her hands clasped in front of her, like someone about to sing her favourite operatic aria. But there was none of the smiling and nodding that always preceded her drawing-room performances: instead, her face was pale, her lips almost translucent. She would not take her eyes off her husband's face.

'It seems that we must go without, while others in a lesser position . . .'

Her father had exploded then, rocking angrily back and forth on his heels.

'There's no question of anyone going without, for God's sake, Sophia!'

At that moment, Hannah had heard low voices outside the door leading into the hallway. Katie and Lily, on their way to draw the curtains, turn down the beds. She heard her mother murmur: 'Edward, please, the servants . . .'

'Damn the servants!'

Hannah chose that moment to make her escape. If they heard anything, they would assume it was Katie and Lily making their way upstairs. She would be safe.

She moved quickly then, leaving the lid of the piano open, taking no chances. She waited at the bottom of the staircase until Katie and Lily had disappeared to the left, along the landing. She prayed that her mother would have no reason to open the drawing-room door. She took the stairs two at a time, holding her breath again until she reached the safety of her own bedroom.

Lily was already there, smoothing the top of the broderie anglaise sheet over the counterpane. She'd just lit the lamp, and the light was still guttering, not yet settled into its pale, steady glow.

'Everything all right, Miss Hannah?' she had asked, with her usual warm smile.

Hannah had nodded, tried to calm her breathing, hoped Lily couldn't hear the hammering of her heart against her ribs. Luckily, she hadn't seemed to notice anything. The voices downstairs had been quieter after that, but the air was still tense and expectant the following morning.

It would probably be the same again tomorrow. Hannah sighed, looking down at Eleanor's now calm face. She was only eight: her little sister shouldn't have to be afraid like this. At least she'd fallen asleep almost instantly, her thumb just resting at her half-open lips. Mama had tried to cure her of this habit by putting oil of cloves on both her thumbs. But Eleanor had persisted in sucking, even growing to like the pungent, foreign taste. She had made her sisters promise not to tell.

Hannah lay awake for some time, trying to listen for voices below, but all had suddenly fallen silent.

Eleanor's Journal

I THINK I MUST have been aware for some time of the tensions in the household, but I was much too young to articulate any unease that I might then have felt. My life was full at that time – I loved school, loved the many kindnesses of the nuns and the pursuit of excellence expected of all of us girls at St Dominic's. Hannah and May had been boarders for ever, it seemed to me, but at nine years of age I had to wait for some time before I could join them. How I envied them! I, too, wanted to have that special status denied to the day-girl, to join my sisters in the recreation room each evening, to share whispered secrets in the quiet of a darkened dormitory. I hated being 'too young' for all the interesting things in life: I suppose I was in a hurry to grow up. However, I had to content myself with their company at weekends, and occasional glimpses during the school day. I have to confess that I missed them both sorely – Hannah and her lively talk and songs, May and her grave gentleness. It is from that time that I can date my passion for reading. How else was I to find solace during the dull hours of long winter evenings? Reading, study, anything to do with books became more than a pleasure to me. I visited Mama's bookshelves in secret and discovered for the first time the joys of the novel: Oliver Twist, David Copperfield and Emma Woodhouse became my constant daily companions.

Mama was very preoccupied all that spring, and I gradually grew resigned to the fact that she had little time for me, little interest in my ordinary daily activities. She was frequently absent in the afternoons when I returned from school, or else there would be a gathering of ladies in our drawing room, sipping tea and talking in high, tinkling voices. I was learning from *her*, too, that I had to be self-reliant, to amuse myself as best I could.

On one such afternoon, towards the end of April 1893 – I have no difficulty remembering the dates of that momentous week – Lily had just poured me a glass of milk and handed me a plateful of soda bread and home-made preserves. We were, as usual, in her and Katie's domain, the kitchen, where I had become accustomed to seek out Lily's company daily, needing her warmth. She was usually so cheerful and interested in all my daily doings that I chittered away about school and about Sister Monica, our bespectacled and highly eccentric schoolteacher.

It took a while for me to notice that Lily was quiet, that she was not interjecting and questioning in her usual teasing manner. She was seated at the long table, with her pile of mending in front of her. While her square, capable fingers worked busily, her face showed that her thoughts were not on the cuffs and collars that covered much of the table.

'Lily? Are you not well?'

I remember I spoke shyly, tentatively – this was a side of Lily I had never seen before, and it both puzzled and frightened me. I was even more alarmed when her chin began to tremble, and tears hovered dangerously on the brink of her eyelashes.

'I'm fine, Miss Eleanor. Drink up your milk there, like a good girl.'

Two large tears splashed on to the shirtsleeve she was holding. I don't know which emotion I felt more keenly: astonishment or fear.

'Shall I get Mama for you?'

I was already standing up, poised for flight. Mama would know what to do to make the tears go away.

Lily reached out then and held on to my arm.

'No, please, miss – it's nothing for you to worry your head about. My sister is sick, that's all, and I'm awful worried about her.'

I was shocked. A sister? Lily? I think I became a little indignant, perhaps even jealous. We were Lily's family, were we not? She and Katie had been looking after us, and Mama and Papa, ever since I could remember. It came as a novel idea to me that we were not the centre of everybody else's universe.

'Will she get better?'

Lily wiped her eyes again.

'She will, please God. But she's all alone in hospital, miss, and I'm afraid it might take a long time.'

I was afraid to ask what was wrong. Mama's stern face in my imagination made it very clear that this was a question one did not ask, that such matters were delicate and private ones. But I was becoming more and more curious. I needed to find out how it was possible to have a sister ill, in hospital, and have no one to go and visit her.

'Where does she live?'

'She's in service, miss, like me. Except she's in Dublin, in one of them big houses in Merrion Square.'

I only half remembered Dublin in those days. I knew that that was where we were from, that we would most likely return there some day. But there was nothing about it that I missed: everybody I loved was with me in Belfast; there was nobody left behind whose company I hankered after.

'Will you tell me her name?'

It was inconceivable to me that sisters would not always be together, that they would not at least live in the same city as one another. I felt suddenly anxious about some far distant day when Hannah and May and I might too be scattered.

'Her name is Jenny, miss, and she's my twin.'

'Do you miss her?'

I knew the answer already, of course I did. I knew how much I missed Hannah and May during the week. I think I just wanted to hear Lily say that she missed her sister terribly: I wanted to be sure that for a servant-girl like Lily, having a sister meant the same thing as it did to me.

Her face suddenly crumpled and she cried without restraint. I felt guilty and sorry then: I had been cruel. I had got my answer, my curiosity had been satisfied, and now Lily was suffering.

I stood and put my arms across her shoulders, just as Mama had done many times to one or other of us. I felt awkward standing there, awkward and compassionate at the same time.

'Don't worry,' I whispered. 'She'll get better, you'll see.'

That afternoon was the first time in my young life that I had ever experienced true empathy. I am grateful to Lily; it is a quality which I have been fortunate enough to possess, and nurture, all through my adult life.

Up to that moment, the concept of suffering for me meant only sore feet, or cold hands, or having to eat the vegetables I detested. Lily's tears spoke of another kind of suffering – one that was altogether foreign to me. It spoke of a wider world than the one I knew, of separations and loneliness which I had never even begun to imagine.

I think, too, that I was shocked: I regard that occasion as the first time when I became aware of personal conscience – the ability to discern justice and injustice, the rights and wrongs of an unequal world which, up until that afternoon, seemed to have functioned perfectly well around me. It was the first time I can remember ever having questioned the arrangement of my own life, and the lives of others.

Mary and Cecilia: Spring 1893

ST MARY'S HAD filled up more rapidly than any other Sunday Mary could remember. Those men who rarely attended Mass now crowded into the porch, crushing their caps between their large hands as they waited, shuffling occasionally from foot to foot as the waiting became uncomfortable. It was a strangely ill-at-ease group: the men looked out of place, unfamiliar with their surroundings. They had stood in a tight knot, and parted almost unwillingly to allow Mary and Cecilia through. The two young women blessed themselves quickly at the holy water font and walked up the centre aisle of the church. As soon as they had moved away, the group closed over again. It was as though they each needed the comfort and safety of numbers, even before any trouble began.

Inside, Mary and Cecilia had pushed their way into a packed bench midway down the church, and now sat stiffly together. Mary was squeezed tight against the wooden arm of the pew, almost unable to breathe. The other women had moved up without a word, crowding more closely together, taking children on to their knees in order to make room for the two sisters. It was understood among them: you didn't even try to separate the McCurrys. Even the way people greeted them spoke of the sisters' public indivisibility. Friends and neighbours would call out to them on the streets, waving cheerfully, nodding and smiling to *Maryancelia*, making no individual distinctions. Although Mary was three years older than her sister, most people referred to them as, simply, 'the twins'.

The men's benches had filled up, too, packed tightly with the usual scrubbed faces in their Sunday clothes. Mary caught a brief glimpse of Myles McNiff, along with his brother, Peter. She glanced away quickly, hoping that no one had seen her looking. But there were no covert glances being exchanged among the young people this Sunday: none of the whispering, or sly grinning and nudging that went on before Mass began every other week.

Where the women sat the air was almost unnaturally still: the small children seemed to know somehow to be silent, and sat quietly on their mothers' knees, no longer needing to be shushed.

Father MacVeigh walked out on to the altar and everybody stood. Tension hovered over the men like the threat of an electric storm. Faces grim with expectation, they knelt, waited: their eyes were fixed on the figure at the altar. It seemed as though they were looking for answers in the priest's broad back.

Finally, the time came. There was a brief scuffling of boots, a ripple of coughing as everyone sat once more, watching as Father MacVeigh ascended the pulpit. This was why they had been summoned; this was the part they had come for.

Father MacVeigh rested both hands on the pulpit and looked down at his congregation. His hands seemed larger than usual, strangely white against the bright red velvet surround. All shuffling ceased at once, coughing died away. Hundreds of faces were raised, tense, attentive, waiting for him to speak.

'My dear people,' he began. 'It is a great comfort to see so many of you here today. As your priest, and friend, and member of this parish for over twenty years, I have asked you all to be with me this morning, to pray with me to God to give us strength to face one of the most difficult weeks we are ever likely to know as a community.'

He paused. All eyes continued to be fixed on his face. He hardly needed to raise his voice.

'I know that some of you have felt the rumblings already, some of you have known disturbances in your place of work, and violence on the streets. All of that is nothing to what I fear is going to happen next Friday and Saturday, when the results of Mr Gladstone's Home Rule Bill become known in this divided city.'

The congregation shifted; a murmur arose, grew to an angry buzz, and stopped suddenly when Father MacVeigh raised his hand. When he spoke again, his voice was louder, more powerful; his whole demeanour was suddenly commanding.

'You have the right to feel angry, but more than that, you have the *duty* to protect your children, your families, your neighbours from the certain thugs of this city who will come looking for trouble no matter what happens next Friday night.'

Nobody moved. His words were measured, emphatic. Cecilia looked at Mary, her eyes troubled. Mary took her hand and squeezed it.

'Mr Gladstone is presenting his Home Rule Bill to the Government on Friday evening. The results will be known in the early hours of Saturday morning. I don't have to tell you that there are elements in this city that will want to punish our communities if that bill is passed. If it is not passed, those same elements will no doubt rampage in triumph through Catholic areas as they have done on other occasions in the past. You already know what their behaviour will be like. And although it grieves me deeply to say so, we can expect no proper level of protection from the police.'

His voice grew warmer.

'I do not wish to see one act of provocation, one act of retaliation, or one act in response to villainy, from any one of you sitting here in front of me, nor from any of your friends and family not present here today. I cannot emphasize this strongly enough: we are not responsible for what happens among government men in London. We have no control over anything: the bill's success or its failure; the behaviour of loyalist gangs; the attitude of the police on the ground.'

Older heads were nodding sagely now. Younger ones were held high, necks and backs speaking silently of defiance. Some of the men were seeking out other faces in the congregation. Their expressions were satisfied, urgent in their attention to the priest's words. It was as though they had not expected to hear this today; they looked vindicated, almost triumphant as the rightness of their own thoughts was now echoed by this good priest, revered by all as a man of God.

'The one thing we do have control over is our own *response* to the behaviour of others, our own sense of responsibility towards ourselves and our community. *We must be blameless.* The priests of the Catholic parishes in Belfast have consulted with the Bishop of Down and Connor. Our committee will monitor the situation over the next few days very carefully, and we will be making our report to the Home Secretary, Mr Morley. But we can have no control over ruffians.

'I appeal to you, to your dignity, to your pride in your community, to your love for your families: do *not* make the doing of evil any easier for those who have hatred in their hearts, for those who are bent on destruction. Stay home, I beg of you. Keep to your own firesides next Friday and Saturday nights. I will visit as many of you as I can during the next few days, I will help in any way I can. But you must keep your doors and windows closed, keep them shut fast.'

His hands were now gripping the top of the pulpit, fingers bloodless with strain. Those close to him could see the beads of perspiration across his forehead.

'Wives and mothers, I appeal to you to use your best influence with your families. Husbands and fathers, fulfil your God-given duty to protect your wives and children. I want no coffins leaving this parish church because one man was unable to keep a check on his anger. Hold fast.

Put your trust in Jesus Christ Our Lord. Let each one of us make sure that we do not let down ourselves or any member of our community. Now let us pray together.'

The parishioners filed out of the church afterwards, unusually subdued. Groups of neighbours gathered all along Chapel Lane, despite the driving rain, and lingered, talking. The women had anxious faces, men for the most part looked restless, edgy, on the verge of anger. Some of them stood apart from the larger groups, smoking, waving their cigarettes intently, stabbing the air now and again for emphasis. Others seemed disappointed, almost resentful, as though they had expected something different from this morning. It had been the most powerful sermon anybody could remember from their normally affable, kindly parish priest. Because he so rarely spoke strongly, his words had had a profound effect.

Mary and Cecilia hurried home together, keeping as close as possible to the shelter offered by the terraced houses, avoiding the worst of the rain. They didn't speak until they were inside.

'Will we be all right, Mary?'

Mary looked up from where she was poking the fire, and smiled at her sister, who was unwinding herself from her wet shawl.

'We will, surely. We'll not come to any harm. Just you don't worry, now.'

Briefly, Mary wondered what possible difference any Home Rule Bill could make to them, or any report to Mr Morley for that matter, whoever he might be.

Would it keep them safe and put bread on the table? Would it dampen the smouldering hatreds bred in the ranks of miserable two-up, two-downs all over the city? Or would it save the mill girls from dying in their hundreds every year from consumption? She thought not. She was suddenly, bitterly glad that Ma was no longer alive. She would have hated her to see this again, to live in fear of what might become of her girls. Aloud, Mary said to Cecilia: 'We'll sit tight, just as Father has bid us. Trouble won't come to us if we don't go looking for it. You heard what he said.'

Wanting to be reassured, Cecilia said: 'Aye, I'm sure you're right. Will I make the tea?'

Mary nodded.

'Aye. Do that.'

She bent towards the fire again, hiding her face from her sister. She had indeed felt the rumblings, as Father MacVeigh had called them. Myles had said the atmosphere in the shipyards was getting uglier. He and others from the engineering room had been taunted, marked out as taigs and fenians. Stones had been thrown by unseen hands. The outside wall of the workshop had, mysteriously, been daubed with paint overnight: no one had seen anyone, heard anyone, knew anything. 'No Pope Here' stood out in garish orange letters, at least two feet high. Paint dribbled downwards, extending the two 'p's of 'Pope' almost to the ground below. He had tried to keep his head down, Myles said, they all had. But it wasn't easy. The usual tacit acceptance by both sides of an uneasy peace, an unhappy truce in which nobody truly believed, had suddenly been suspended.

Instead, it felt like open season. Demarcation lines had been drawn; to be Catholic was to be the enemy.

The mill, too, was a powder keg waiting to explode. Mary had felt the tension rise there as well over the last couple of weeks. The usual heat and humidity seemed to have intensified; the girls had all felt the damp atmosphere to be more suffocating than usual. Mary had been glad to welcome the return of the normal April downpour, the chilly winds which put paid to any notion of the early arrival of summer. She hoped Cecilia hadn't felt the stirrings of bitterness: she had encouraged her sister's complaints about the heat, about how cranky it made everyone. Keep her safe, and out of trouble. Keep her innocent for as long as possible. Mary could only hope that all those girls with their rough hands and even rougher tongues would have enough sense to keep their powder dry.

Eleanor's Journal

THAT WEEK IN April continued to be, in so many ways, a rite of passage in my young life. It became one of those defining times after which nothing could ever be quite the same again. All memories subsequent to that week became coloured by my experience; I came to view all events prior to it in a different light, with the hard-won wisdom that is known as hindsight. I still think of that week as an ever-changing and shifting pattern, a kaleidoscope of events which I have rearranged in my imagination many times, to see if I could effect a better outcome. Lily had already shattered the comfort of my domestic view of the world, and now even greater changes awaited me. It was to be the first time that the real world intruded rudely into mine; the first time I would ever have cause to doubt Mama's ability to make everything better; the first time that I, or anyone else, knew anything of Papa's trouble and its enormous consequences for all our lives.

I know that we have spoken at length of this, you and I; you have indulged my painful reminiscences more than once. But this is the first occasion on which I find myself capable of real reflection: reflection without anger, without the soul-corroding rancour which, for so many years, was my father's living legacy to me. Indulge me a little more, now – I already know that love is patient.

A couple of afternoons after Lily's revelation about her ailing sister, I made my way home from school again in the freezing rain – showers which seemed to run one into the other so that they became a constant downpour of needle-fine sleet, and not the April showers which we like to think of as heralding the arrival of summer.

The wind felt like a knife-edge, peeling away at the delicate skin on my face. The chilblains on my feet were getting worse: stinging, weeping, sticking to my woollen stockings and causing me a great deal of pain. I could hardly wait to get my boots off. I wanted Mama that day, wanted her to make the pain go away.

Lily opened the front door to me before I had reached the end of the path. I saw, without really noticing, a carriage with two patient horses at the kerb outside our house. I probably thought it was for our neighbours. In any event, its significance only became apparent later on that afternoon. Lily's face was white, and she looked intently at me. Her brown eyes were startled, more prominent than usual. I wondered for a moment whether she had been crying over her sister again. She took my hand, and her palm was clammy.

'You come with me, Miss Eleanor,' she said, almost in a whisper.

I noticed that the door to the drawing room was closed. Not an unusual occurrence in itself, but this time there was no sound of ladies' laughter, no chinking of silver spoons on china cups. I thought I heard Papa's voice, but it seemed deeper, less familiar to me than usual.

'Where's Mama?' I asked.

'She's busy at the moment, Miss Eleanor. You just come along with me, now.'

'But I need Mama to look at my feet; they hurt.'

I began to cry, more, I suspect, because I could sense something in the house that terrified me, an air of catastrophe which cast its long shadow on to everything around me, including Lily's frightened face.

'I'll look after your feet. Come along, now, there's a good girl. The fire's lit in the kitchen, and I've just made some scones. Would you like that?'

I was won over. I wanted somebody to love me, somebody to make a fuss of me. Above all, I didn't want to be on my own that afternoon, not when whatever was going to happen happened. I sat with my feet in a basin of warm water, sipping milk and eating scones smothered in gooseberry jam. Lily had already peeled my sore stockings from my legs, had already begun the ritual of comfort and healing which was familiar to me from all the winters of my life. Mama preferred to use wintergreen ointment, but Lily's remedy for the agony of chilblains came from her mother's people in County Tipperary. She would put a turnip in the oven just long enough for it to soften. Then she'd cut it in half, and place thinly pared slices of its fibrous stuff over each of the broken chilblains. Next, she would carefully place a strip of cotton on top of each slice, the pieces of cloth already smeared with clarified lard.

Mama used to smile at her country ways, but I can still vividly recall the sense of warm comfort once the greasy dressing was in place, can still savour the oily, vaguely animal smells of it all. I have always found it strange how the memory of such small details remains the most potent, once the large events in our lives are over.

Poor Lily and Katie must have been frightened out of their wits that afternoon. The arrival of the police at any door was cause for anxiety, but their arrival immediately after my father, Mr Edward's, unusually early return from his business day was especially troubling. He was an important man, they knew that. Someone very high up in the Post Office, one who was not given to returning unexpectedly from work to the bosom of his family, especially not with two detectives in tow. I know now how fearful those two good women must have been for their livelihood, how disaster for their employer signalled even more immediate and complete disaster for themselves. Nevertheless, they minded me, Katie continued her preparations for the evening meal, and Lily continued to tend to my feet, even warmed a clean pair of stockings for me on the top of the range.

Suddenly, one of the little brass bells above us sounded. I looked up. Drawing room. Lily glanced swiftly at Katie and left the kitchen. Neither Katie nor I spoke a word. I knew that we were both waiting for something, but I didn't know what. I did not know until long afterwards, of course, that the two gentlemen in the drawing room, who had arrived some two hours before my return from school, had been sent to arrest my father. I opened the kitchen door just a little, and Katie didn't try to stop me. Instead, she watched with me as the two sombre-looking men, dressed in black, ushered my father outside to the waiting carriage.

'Jesus, Mary and Joseph help us,' Katie whispered, making the sign of the cross. Then I heard Mama wail, in a voice I knew immediately to be hers, yet not hers. I wrenched the door open fully and ran down the hallway to the drawing room. Mama was lying on the floor, her face ashen, her arms clutching at Lily.

'Quick, Miss Eleanor, ask Katie for the salts.' Lily waved me out of the room. 'Hurry now.'

I did as I was told. I felt strangely calm, a state I now know to have been shock. I remember watching, in a curiously detached way, as Lily was becoming more and more frantic. The salts had done nothing to revive Mama. She seemed to come to from time to time, only to lapse into fresh weeping again and again, and languish somewhere between consciousness and unconsciousness. She kept calling for Papa, or rather saying his name to herself over and over, as though trying to make it reveal something to her. His name was the only word I could distinguish; I could make no sense of anything else she said.

I ran to the window once I heard the front door close and I watched Papa leave. I understood even then that he was being taken away from us, and I wanted to cry out, to tell those men to leave him alone, but no sound would come. I can still see myself, all these years later, standing mute, frozen, by the drawing-room window. I was aware of what was going on around me, but powerless to respond.

Katie had come running from the kitchen once the detectives had left with Papa, and now I could hear her exclamations as she tried to help Lily with Mama. Together they tried to get her to stand, so they could at least carry her over to the sofa. But her body was limp and heavy; all her strength had abandoned her. I remember that the room and its occupants all came into focus once I heard Katie's tone, really frightened now.

'Surely we should call Dr Collins,' she said, and I could see her glancing in my direction. I must have looked lost and terrified, because Lily called me over to her at once, shaking her head at Katie, trying to smile at me at the same time.

'I'll go get some water and lavender oil,' she said. 'I think she's a little bit calmer than she was. If we bathe her forehead and her wrists, she should come round.'

She gripped my shoulders now, making me look up into her kind face. The touch of her large, solid hands made me feel real again.

'Don't worry, pet. Your mama has just had a shock. Come with me and help carry the water.'

I remember that I went with her obediently, glad to have something to do other than watch Mama's shaking body, and listen to her great, gulping sobs. When we returned from the kitchen, Katie was kneeling on the floor, supporting Mama's head on her knees. I was relieved that the sobbing had eased. I began to hope that everything would be all right again, that we would all get back to normal. The room seemed to be that little bit more familiar, the strangeness of catastrophe receding somewhat. Perhaps what had happened was the result of a misunderstanding. Everyone would soon be sensible again, the house would return to normal and Papa would come back, smiling and relieved.

'Just a mistake, Mouse,' he would say cheerfully. 'Nothing to worry about. Just a mistake.'

Carefully, I carried the bowl of lavender water over to where Mama was lying. I touched her hand.

'Mama? Are you feeling better?'

She smiled at me then, very weakly, but at least her face seemed to have lost some of its earlier formlessness.

'Thank you, dear, yes.'

I watched Lily wring out the excess water, and apply the cool cloth to Mama's forehead. A subtle scent of lavender drifted upwards. I liked the smell, liked the whole ritual of putting drops of oil into the water, wringing out the cloth, placing the compress on Mama's forehead; all these smooth, deliberate movements seemed to calm everyone, not just Mama. Katie handed her a glass of water, and she sipped from it until it was almost empty.

Eventually, she was recovered enough to stand up.

'Let me loosen your stays, ma'am.' I heard Lily whisper to Mama, but I pretended not to. Mama nodded, and allowed herself to be led from the room. She turned to face me, just before she reached the bottom of the staircase.

'I'm going to lie down for a while, dear,' she said. 'Lily and Katie will look after you. I'll see you first thing in the morning.'

I remember that I ran forward, then, and gave Mama a kiss. I felt suddenly sad for the sagging body, the ghost-like face.

The last remains of my innocent existence were shattered for ever that April afternoon. I gave up waiting for things to return to what they had so recently been. Mama lay down on her bed and stayed there until the following morning. I knew that she did not want company. Katie and Lily whispered together all that evening; I was no longer welcome in their kitchen. And there was no sign of Papa's return. I felt that jagged pieces of our former lives seemed to be all around us; nothing was whole any more.

As for me, I spent what I think still remains the loneliest night of my life. I crept into Hannah's bed, in between her freezing sheets. I left her door open so that I could see the low light from the gas lamp on the landing. I knew not to ask Lily or Katie for the warming pan that evening, or for the flickering company of a candle for myself. But even in her absence, Hannah's bed was far more comforting than mine. I know that I cried, but more than that, I wondered and wondered what my Papa could have done for those men to take him away. He still looked the same, had still said, 'Goodnight, Mouse,' the previous evening to me. His pet-name for me came from my babyhood, Mama had once told me. I was a very quiet baby, she said. Much more placid and contented than either of my sisters.

If someone didn't sound any different, or look any different, then how was one ever to know whether they had done something bad? My Papa had just been arrested for embezzlement. Although as yet I didn't know, all I could do that night was puzzle over his disappearance: wasn't it true that only bad people were taken away by policemen? People who broke the law? Perhaps it was still some dreadful mistake, perhaps they really wanted some other man.

But still, I could not ignore a strong sense that Papa had indeed done something very wrong. Mama's tears had been tears of desperation, of grief for something lost that had once been hers. They were certainly not the tears of a loyal, distraught wife protesting her husband's innocence. There was no fight in her, no righteousness. Instead, she had the air of someone enduring what was both inevitable and unthinkable at the same time.

I remember agonizing over this well into the night. I think I expected some outward sign, some mark of Cain to indicate wrongdoing, to symbolize a state of sin for all to see. I was beginning to learn, even then, that life is not always that simple.

My head began to ache with the effort to understand. I needed to escape to somewhere different, somewhere bright and happy. I began to tell myself stories, about elves and shoemakers, princes and princesses, all the myriad wonders of fairyland.

Finally, I slept.

Sophia: Spring 1893

SOPHIA GOT UP at half past six the following morning.
The whole house was quiet and dark. Lily and Katie
had not yet risen to light the range or to prepare
breakfast. She could hardly blame them. As far as they
knew, they might no longer have any livelihood to speak
of within this household. They would have a genuine
fear of being left, literally, at the side of the road by
their employers.

Sophia had lain awake most of the night, trying to
work out how to extract all of them from the awfulness
which Edward had brought on everyone's heads. Now,
this morning, she had practical things to organize. First,
she would need to visit Edward's solicitor personally, to
try and ascertain what was to become of him, of all of
them. She couldn't bear to think about it: for Edward,
the prison cell, the trial, the personal indignity. For all
of them, the unbearable humiliation which would
accompany such a very public fall from grace.

She could not stay in Belfast, that much was clear.
Apart from the shame of Edward's arrest, they had no
money. She couldn't possibly afford to keep the family
here.

At some stage during last night's sleepless hours, Sophia had held on to a faint hope that this might all be a mistake, that Edward was innocent. That hope had disappeared as soon as she had arisen this morning. In the dim light of her bedroom candle, she had seen his face clearly, as clearly as when he had stepped out into the hallway yesterday, flanked by the two detectives. He had turned to her in what she now realized was mute appeal – *save me from this*. She remembered that look now – and it made her angry. He was not a stupid man; he had to have known the implications of what he was doing. One simply didn't 'borrow' government funds, no matter how firm one's intention to pay them back quickly, no harm done. But she couldn't think about that, not now. There were too many urgent decisions to be made before she could afford the luxury of bitterness and recrimination.

She had to get her girls back to Dublin. And Katie and Lily. She owed the two women that much. They had been with her for almost fourteen years now; she didn't want to lose them, didn't know how she would ever manage without them. But that was a problem for later, for Dublin. She finished dressing, her impatient fingers fumbling with the tight row of covered buttons on the front of her dress. She sighed in exasperation when she finally reached the last button, only to find no matching fabric loop to close it. She must try to be patient; bad temper at half past six in the morning did not augur well for the rest of the day. And she had Eleanor to think of.

Methodically, she undid the buttons one by one,

and hooked them closed again carefully, making sure she got it right this time. She swept her long hair up into a simple knot that would do until later and made her way downstairs. Sophia felt her way around the carved rope-edge of the table in the hallway until her fingers made out the shape of the drawer in the centre. She opened it and took out a flat box of matches. Placed directly above the drawer was the tall, heavy gas lamp, its mantle clouded and sulphurous. Once lit, the flame guttered, throwing shadows on the wall in front of her. It settled, quickly, into a warm yellow glow.

She carried it with her into the dining room, its light sending strange, elongated shadows up the walls and on to the stretch of ceiling beyond her writing-desk. She pulled down the leaf of her desk and balanced the lamp carefully beside her, to her right. She took out headed notepaper and envelopes from the small compartments above. She needed to do this quickly. Her father must know, as soon as possible, what had befallen them. He was the only one who could help her in Dublin, once she got home. He would get his letter by this evening. That would give him time to reply, if he needed to, before they took the train tomorrow night.

Sophia addressed the envelope swiftly, pulled more paper down on to the blotter. She would write to Constance MacBride. She was the only person she felt she could turn to in Belfast. The imperious, elderly lady was a curious mix: discreet when discretion was necessary, yet straight, honest to the point of bluntness. She was a legend in Belfast society: her connections spread throughout the city, an intricate, overlapping tapestry of business, politics and philanthropy. She would have her letter by mid-morning.

Sophia would be back home again by early afternoon, and all she could do then was wait. She knew that Constance MacBride would not let her down. She would come, bringing sympathy and the smallest possibility of something, anything, to be salvaged. Sophia allowed herself that one last hope. Other than that, there was nothing else she could do.

She was going to have to rely on the charity of others.

There was a tap on the drawing-room door.

'Come in.' Calmly, Sophia put down the papers in her hand and waited.

Lily curtsied.

'It's Mrs MacBride, ma'am.'

'Show her in, Lily, and bring tea.'

'Yes, ma'am.'

Sophia felt grateful to Lily. No matter what she thought or felt, she was keeping up the pretence of normality.

Constance MacBride swept into the room, bringing a waft of cold air and energy with her.

'My dear,' she said, her round, plain face full of concern. 'I'm so sorry.'

Sophia returned the sympathetic pressure of her hand, unable to reply for a moment.

'I'm very grateful to you for coming.'

'Nonsense, my dear, I'm only too glad to help.'

Sophia waited until the older woman had settled herself on the sofa, her voluminous skirts spread out all around her. She stood up, then, agitated, and walked towards the window. She waited for a moment, making sure that she was composed enough to speak, that her voice would have no telltale tremor. Constance Mac-Bride's large, kindly presence had made her feel her humiliation all the more keenly. For the moment, she kept her eyes fixed on the window, seeing nothing.

'I need to get my girls back to Dublin, as soon as possible. Everyone is going to know about Edward by tomorrow, and even if I could afford to keep them here, Belfast is no place for them to grow up, not with that kind of shame.'

She paused. She had said it. No question of Edward's being innocent. That much had to be understood between them.

'Your father will help you.'

There was only the slightest change in intonation at the end of the sentence, as if Constance MacBride feared giving offence by asking the question too openly. Sophia turned away from the window now, her face composed.

'I wrote to him first thing this morning. I've asked him to meet us off the evening train tomorrow. I've just written to him again this afternoon, asking if he could help to place Lily and Katie.'

Sophia pressed on her temples with the tips of her fingers. The beginnings of another awful headache, right behind her eyes.

'I don't know if we'll be able to keep them with us,

but I have a duty towards them. On the other hand, I don't want us to be too big a burden for my father.'

Sophia paused. Of all the ignominious things to happen to her, she felt that nothing could be worse than this. Had Edward set out to punish her, to avenge himself for some unknown crime against him, he could not have chosen better. What could he possibly have been thinking of?

As though reading her mind, Constance MacBride said softly: 'You can tell an old woman to mind her own business if you wish, but have you any idea, my dear, any idea at all what drove Edward to do as he did?'

Sophia turned and looked at her sharply. The shrewd blue eyes were fixed on Sophia's, their gaze unwavering.

'How do you mean?'

Sophia felt herself react at once, stiffly, to the older woman's choice of words, to their implicit criticism. Nobody 'drove' Edward to be dishonest, he chose to be so himself. She felt the beginnings of indignation that Constance MacBride might assume that she, Sophia, could be complicit in her husband's wrongdoing. Nevertheless, there was a small germ of truth nudging at her from underneath the other woman's words, from the calm, almost benign expression on her placid face.

They had fought about money a good deal, that was true. But Edward had an important position, a civil service appointment of great seniority. Such a position implied a certain lifestyle, the maintenance of a certain standard of social intercourse. They had to attend the theatre, the opera; they had to entertain on a reasonable scale. She had never been lavish or wasteful, she was sure of that. But appearances were important. And the girls had to be educated at a good school. If there was a different way to do such things, then she didn't know what that way might be.

'Perhaps he felt under pressure, my dear. Living well is not cheap.'

Sophia did not reply.

There was a moment's awkwardness before Constance MacBride spoke again. This time, her tone was almost hesitant.

'May I ask – are you sure . . . let me be direct, my dear: is your lawyer to your satisfaction?'

Sophia nodded. How could she know, never having needed one before? Pride stopped her from asking the older woman's opinion of Morgan, Bradshaw and Company. The sting in the tail of Constance MacBride's sympathy smothered Sophia's reluctant impulse to ask for any other help. It was all too painful: she would soon owe even her daily bread to others. She would not crawl. Enough was enough.

Constance MacBride watched as the struggle played itself out on the younger woman's face. She watched as Sophia's mouth tightened, as pride battled with humiliation, as maternal duty fought with the natural resentment of the impotent. She decided to say nothing more. For a moment, she regretted her earlier outspokenness. Perhaps she could have helped more by saying less. But the moment had passed: it was too late now. Instead, she moved effortlessly into the next phase of the conversation.

'You must leave the arranging of this house to me. I will see to it that your belongings are packed and sent on to you. You need not worry about anything here.'

She let her crisp, no-nonsense words hang in the air between them. She knew that at least she had left Sophia thinking, and that was no bad thing. She was a good woman, a good mother, there was no doubt about that. Her girls were a credit to her. But she had a blind spot; there was no doubt about that either. She was more than impressed by money, by the trappings of solid, respectable, not necessarily glamorous, wealth. Constance MacBride suspected that she had pushed her husband too far, that she demanded a manner of living way beyond Edward's modest resources. He was a government man, after all; up until now, respectable to his fingertips; but no civil service posting, no matter how senior, was going to make him a fortune. Constance MacBride liked him, liked both of them, had warmed to their family. They were people for whom she felt a genuine, kindly impulse. She should like to help.

'Let's have a wee look at what we can do for you here before you go. What do the girls need?'

Sophia was grateful to her again. It was so much easier to accept help for one's children than it was for oneself. It made her present humiliation a little easier to bear.

She was glad to turn the conversation to more practical issues, too. Constance MacBride had made her feel uncomfortable. And she had far too many other things to deal with at the moment.

Hannah: Spring 1893

WHY HAD MAMA summoned them from school so urgently? Her letter had left no room for delay. Sister Canice's round face had been grave as she hurried Hannah and May into the carriage. 'Now, girls, at once, please – no dawdling.' She closed the door safely behind them.

'God bless you both. Joseph will see you to the train. Remember, now, no talking to strangers. Stay close to Joseph until your mother comes for you.'

'What's happening?'

May spoke only after Sister Canice had waved them away, her cheerful gesture looking oddly normal, strangely out of place. May had been puzzled by the nun's air of intense anxiety.

'I don't know – Mama seems to be in a hurry to get back to Dublin. Perhaps Grandfather is unwell, or something.'

Hannah's voice seemed unconcerned, almost as if it had shrugged its shoulders. May was somewhat reassured, but still a small germ of suspicion itched away at her, like hives. She didn't reply, looking out the carriage window instead as they made steady progress down the

Falls Road. As soon as they turned right on to Gros-
venor Road, she sat suddenly bolt upright, her hands
clutching at Hannah.

'What is it?' Hannah was startled by her sister's
terrified expression.

'Can't you hear it? The shouting? Really angry
shouting?'

Hannah shook her head once, then stopped and
strained to listen. Their leisurely pace had not been
interrupted, there had been no shout of warning from
Joseph to indicate that anything was wrong, and Hannah could hear nothing above the rolling rumble of the
carriage wheels. She was about to dismiss May's imaginings when, suddenly, she heard it. The whole world
seemed to burst open into riotous, human thunder. The
road before them heaved into sudden life; swell after
roaring swell of men's bodies erupted blackly from
behind every gateway, around every corner.

May clutched at Hannah's upper arm, digging her
nails painfully into the soft flesh.

'What?' she cried. 'What is it?' Her eyes were wide
and blank in a chalk-white face.

'Ssshh – I don't know,' said Hannah, trying desperately to see out over May's shoulder.

She tried to keep her voice level, but some intuition
was making the back of her neck prickle hotly. Instinctively, she crouched down low in the carriage, jerking
May with her. Her sister's body was limp with terror.

'Don't worry, Joseph will take care of us,' Hannah
whispered, wishing she felt as sure as she sounded. What
could this be? Was it, finally, the trouble that Papa's

newspapers had been warning about? She knew that something political was afoot – Papa had recently taken to reading his papers more and more intently at weekends. She had heard him grumble more than once about something called Home Rulers. Don't know when they're well off, he'd growled. Independence indeed. Stuff and nonsense. Biting the hand that feeds, more like. She had paid little attention; it couldn't possibly have anything to do with her. Nobody spoke about such things in school, and besides, she had always thought that they were much too young to have anything like politics touch their small lives.

But now, whatever it was that had been simmering away below the newspaper headlines, filling the streets of this city unknown to her, had suddenly erupted into daylight and now surrounded her on all sides. She tried to cover her ears and May's – the solid crunch of pounding boots was a sound she felt she would never forget.

'Keep low, May – don't listen! Keep your hands pressed to your ears – you don't need to listen!'

What had started as a strange murmur, like the distant buzzing of giant flies, soon became distinguishable as voices, hoarse with rage, harsh with hatred. Hannah tried to block it all out, to extinguish the angry words that hurtled through the greying evening, spreading menace in their wake. At the same time, she pressed her sister's body closer to her, crooning softly, trying to drown the ugliness that fractured the air all around them.

The masses of running bodies seemed to press closer.

From all sides, they surged towards some invisible centre, as though drawn by the irresistible power of a giant magnet. She and May were caught in some innocent place, the unknowing eye of the storm. Outside the carriage on all sides she heard the ugly shouts of the mob. Men were howling for papist blood, for the guts of fenian bastards. Hannah kept her head down and prayed. She knew that that was what she and her sisters were – papists, fenians. The nuns had said that they were ugly, ignorant terms, and to pay no heed to anyone that might use them. Turn the other cheek, they said, never acknowledge such disrespect. They were Catholics, Roman Catholics, members of the one true Church, and that was the beginning and the end of it.

Hannah begged God silently that Old Joseph would not lose courage, that he could steel himself in the face of whistling, studded cudgels and the crack and bite of hate-flung paving-stones. Make us invisible, she prayed.

'It won't be long now, we're nearly there,' she whispered into May's terrified ear. She had no idea where they were, how much of the journey to the station remained. The child was still trembling. Hannah put one arm around the thin shoulders and held her sister's body as tightly as she could, trying to still her whimpering. She felt every bit as frightened as May, but her two years' seniority made her feel responsible – Mama and Papa always trusted her.

Leaning forward, she caught a glimpse through the carriage window of the street-fighting which they now seemed to be leaving behind. Perhaps that was just an illusion; perhaps the worst was still to come. A solid line of RIC men, batons drawn, now charged the crowd on Boyne Bridge, their silence and the grim set of their faces a stark contrast to the howling mouths and angry faces of the mob which opened up and swallowed them. Just then, the carriage swung sharply to the right down Great Victoria Street, and into its tremendous silence. Hannah imagined she could hear the crack of skulls on stone, the sickening thump of flesh and fist. Her stomach heaved as the carriage pulled up abruptly outside the station.

Instantly, Old Joseph was at the carriage window. He wrenched open the door, muttering 'Poor wee wains' to himself, over and over.

'What's happening?'

Hannah felt almost faint with relief. Her legs trembled as she scrambled up from her position on the floor. Only then did May start to cry, the quietness of Old Joseph's kindness unleashing all her pent-up terror.

Joseph flipped up the step underneath the carriage and gave Hannah his hand. She was even more frightened to feel that his old, hard palm was sweaty and trembling visibly. His face was grim.

'It's the loyalists batin' up on the Home Rulers, miss. The bill goes to a vote soon, and they're not havin' none of it.'

'None of what?'

'Don't you worry about it, now, miss. It won't concern you – there's folk here as wants nothin' to change. There's others believes that Queen Victoria's men have nowt to do wi' us in this country.'

He lifted May on to the pavement beside Hannah. His face was red and angry.

'But why were they fighting and shouting like that?'

'Sometimes ye have to fight t'be heard. Man needs to feel he has a say in the runnin' of his own country. Then there's them as don't like it when you do.'

He looked at her closely.

'Stay away from the streets, miss. Things are goin' to be ugly again in this unforkunate city.'

May had started to cry again, loudly.

'Where's Mama? I want Mama.'

Hannah shushed her as best she could, and half lifted, half pulled the frail, small body while Old Joseph struggled with their trunk.

'She's here, just inside, waiting for us.'

Hannah hoped she was right. She glanced at the big clock outside the station entrance. Twenty to eight. The Dublin train, Mama's letter had said. At eight o'clock.

'Quickly, May. We mustn't miss the train.'

Her eyes scanned the platform as she dragged her now wailing sister along behind her. The station was eerily empty. It took Hannah only a moment to locate her mother. Her feeling of relief was matched by a great wave of anger as her eyes locked on to the distinctive russet travelling coat, the plumed hat. She wanted to shriek at her mother, to beat her fists against her, to make her suffer for the terror they had just been through. But there was something in her mother's stance that made Hannah pause as May ran down the platform, arms outstretched, her sobs now uncontrollable.

89

The eyes which met Hannah's above her younger sister's head were dark, haunted, the face paler and much more haggard than she remembered. Her mother's expression was one of mute appeal and Hannah knew, at once, that something bad had happened. Papa. Something must have happened to Papa. She said nothing. Old Joseph tipped his cap to Sophia. His breathing was laboured, his face beaded with sweat.

'Them's dangerous streets, tonight, ma'am. Your wee girls were very brave.'

'What is it, Joseph? What's going on?'

Sophia's question was bewildered, almost distracted.

Hannah was surprised that her mother didn't know. She must have observed something. She hadn't been locked up all day, surely – she had had to cross the city to get to the station. Had something even more momentous closed her senses to what was going on around her, right in front of her eyes? Joseph manhandled the trunk on to the train, grunting and sweating with the unaccustomed effort.

Now he turned to face Sophia, his old, creased face full of surprise.

'It's the loyalists, ma'am. They've took to the streets.'

'Oh,' was all she said. 'I didn't know.'

She bent down again to comfort May, who still clung to her mother. Her sobs had finally begun to ease. Hannah couldn't shake the feeling that her mother had stooped in order to hide her face. She began to feel really alarmed. What other awfulness had happened to make her mother unaware of the violence and mayhem that now claimed the streets around them?

'Thank you, Joseph.'

Hannah's mother pressed a coin into Old Joseph's hand and he tipped his cap to her again.

'The blessin' o' God on ye, ma'am,' he said, nodding towards May and Hannah, to say that he included them, too.

She smiled at him. Then she turned again to May, who was still clutching at her mother's skirts as though she were drowning. She held her daughter close, whispering to her.

'I've got you now, I've got you.'

Then she turned to Hannah, her voice urgent.

'Quickly, now, Hannah. We must board the train. Eleanor's waiting for us.'

Her face was set again, back to the severe contours that were familiar.

Hannah knew that, for the moment, there was nothing more to be said. She welcomed her mother's silence, the postponement of pain that it brought with it. She already knew that speech would make solid and real all the vague terrors of the angry, whispered nights that had filled her recent dreams. This way, she could pretend that nothing had changed.

At least there was some comfort in that.

The first hour of the train journey back to Dublin was a silent one. Hannah was very glad to be out of Belfast. She was still shaken by the carriage ride through the heaving streets. To be safely on the train was a relief, but this was no ordinary visit home. Mama's face on the platform had told one part of the story; Papa's absence seemed to confirm another. Hannah was now anxious to know the rest.

She waited until Eleanor and May had fallen asleep. The youngest girl was already half-asleep when the train pulled out of the station, seemingly oblivious to the atmosphere in the compartment. May had taken longer to settle, her memories of the riots still palpable. Shadows of the fear she had felt still flitted across her face, and her dark eyes looked huge, haunted. Hannah had comforted her as best she could, and now she was lying, sleeping at last, with her head cradled in Hannah's lap. When she was sure that neither of her sisters could be listening, Hannah turned to her mother.

Sophia had put her head back; her eyes were closed. Somehow, Hannah knew she was still awake. The eyes behind her eyelids were restless, jerky. Her face was white, bordering on an unhealthy yellowish colour, that dull, waxy sheen that reminded Hannah of the smell of church candles. The sharp cheekbones seemed more prominent than ever.

'Mama?' She kept her voice low.

Sophia's eyes snapped open at once.

'What is it?'

Her response was quick, anxious, her words full of jagged edges. It was as though she were arming herself to face disaster. Her eyes darted around the compartment, checking on each of her daughters in turn.

'What's happened, Mama? Where's Papa and why are we running away to Dublin?'

Sophia glanced anxiously at the two younger girls.

'It's all right, Mama. They're asleep. Please tell me.'

She saw her mother hesitate, as though trying to decide among many options. Hannah wanted the truth.

'I'm old enough, Mama. I'm nearly thirteen. I know that something bad has happened to Papa.'

Her tone was firm, almost like a grown-up. Despite the seriousness of the situation, Hannah was pleased with herself. She wanted Mama to treat her as an adult. Sophia stood and pulled down the blinds on each of the rainy windows. Hannah wondered why she was doing that. No one could see them here, hurtling through the darkened countryside at high speed. The drawn blinds did not make the atmosphere any cosier. Instead, the pale light cast pools of cold shadow on the sleeping faces. Hannah was startled to see that her mother looked like a dark, unhappy ghost.

'Your father has been arrested, Hannah. The police came and took him away two days ago.'

Hannah stared at her blankly. Of all the things she half thought, half suspected, half knew, this was not one of them. She found it peculiar to hear Mama talk of Papa as 'your father'. It made him sound like a stranger, someone distant from them all. It had none of the friendliness, none of the warm cigar-smells of 'Papa'.

'What did he do?'

Hannah was afraid of what her mother's answer would be. What could Papa possibly have done that was so bad the police had arrested him?

'He embezzled Post Office funds.'

Sophia almost threw the words at Hannah, leaving them where they fell, shattering into pieces all around them. She made no effort to pick them up for her, to arrange them into a pattern which made sense, into some sort of order which would give her daughter comfort.

'I don't understand. What does that mean?'

'It means he took money – borrowed it, without permission.'

'But if he borrowed it, then he means to pay it back. Why don't they just let him pay it back?'

'Because he hasn't got it, Hannah. And if you haven't got it, then borrowing like that is the same as stealing. That's the law.'

Awful thoughts were crowding into Hannah's mind as she tried to grasp the enormous implications of what her mother was saying to her.

'Will he go to prison?'

Her voice was unsteady, tears were threatening.

'We don't know yet. We must wait and see.'

'Why are we going to Dublin? Why don't we stay and help him?'

Hannah was beginning to grow indignant. Her mother's abruptness unnerved her. She didn't seem sorry for Papa at all, only angry. Hannah did not want to think of her Papa being locked into a prison cell, with no one to bring him comfort.

'Because—' Sophia's eyes glittered, whether with tears or rage, Hannah could not decide. 'Because we have nothing, and we cannot live on nothing.'

Her voice was hard and bitter, her features becoming more and more exaggerated as she spoke. Hannah watched her mother's face, watched as the mouth became a thin, tight line, shadowed mauve by grief. She remembered all the weekends when she had listened to her parents fight, wanting to spirit herself away somewhere else. Now she was frightened. She suddenly understood what her mother was saying – she meant no house, no school, no food. Hannah had heard about people like that already, too many of them, living on the side of the streets in Belfast. Was it really possible for a family like hers to become one of them, to slip through the cracks of what was normal, and fall headlong into a different sort of life?

'What are we going to do, Mama?'

'The only thing I can do – beg.'

She stopped for a moment, and her voice became gentler. She had seen some of the fear in her eldest daughter's eyes. Some of the anger seemed to dissipate, and her face became softer again. Hannah felt a wave of relief start somewhere at the top of her head, warming its way downwards, releasing the tightness in her chest. She sounded like Mama again, calmer, in control, with things thought out thoroughly for the sake of her children.

'I'm going to ask Grandpa Delaney for help. He'll look after us, I promise.'

Hannah nodded miserably. Her Grandpa was a crusty old man, often gruff in his manner to children. 'Old curmudgeon', Papa had called him, and she remembered laughing at the unfamiliar word.

May stirred, her head moving restlessly from side to side, as though shaking away a bad dream. Hannah looked down at her pale face, anxious even in sleep.

Eleanor's thumb had crept up towards her lips, but it looked as though she had fallen asleep again before she'd even had a chance to suck it. Hannah was filled with an enormous tenderness for both of them, even for her mother, whose sad, pinched face made her suddenly want to cry.

At the same time, she was filled with rage against her father. How could he do this to them? The shame of it – stealing money when he must already have enough, leaving his family with nothing, and then – going to jail. She would be ashamed of him for the rest of her life. She would never forgive him. Never, never.

Grandpa Delaney was waiting for them at Amiens Street Station. He looked severe, standing there on the concourse, dressed from head to toe in black. He stood out from the crowd. Nobody was standing anywhere near him – it was as though people sensed something forbidding about him, and gave him a wide berth. He looked like someone important, looked as though he might even own the station. His hands rested, one on top of the other, on the ornate handle of his walking stick. His back, as usual, was ramrod straight. Hannah had a brief memory of the only day he had seemed to unbend. Christmas. Sitting in Papa's armchair by the fire, warmed by good brandy. He had taken her on his knee and told her about his own Christmases, when he was just a lad. He had shown her a shooting stick that had once belonged to his father. His eyes bright with merriment, he had revealed its secret to her: the little com-

ANOTHER KIND OF LIFE

partment, concealed just beneath the handle, big enough
for one generous measure of brandy. He had twinkled
at her then, tapping the side of his nose and nodding
conspiratorially. Their secret. It was the only time Hannah had ever seen him really smile. His face now wore
its all-too-familiar expression – a mixture of impatience
and disapproval, and Hannah could feel something
inside her sinking.

They walked towards him. Hannah thought they
must appear to be a rather sad and bedraggled little
group by now. Mama went over and kissed Grandfather's cheek. She heard her say: 'You got my letters
then.'

Hannah did not hear his reply. She was too busy
trying to recover from her astonishment at Grandfather's
behaviour. He put both arms around his daughter's
shoulders and enfolded her in a mighty hug. Sophia
clung to him. All Hannah could hear was her mother's
voice, choking with sobs, saying over and over again:
'Oh, Father, what are we to do? What are we to do?'

He held her for a long time. Eleanor and May stood
beside Hannah, looking bewildered. Eleanor's thumb
was resting at her lower lip again, a thin thread of saliva
drooling from her open mouth. Hannah wiped her face
with a handkerchief, glancing over at her mother, trying
to smile reassuringly at her sisters.

'It's all right,' she whispered to them. 'Mama's upset
because Papa couldn't come with us. Don't worry.'

Sophia composed herself quickly. She turned to her
daughters. Hannah thought her smile was watery.

'Come along, girls, say hello to Grandfather.'

He hugged each of them in turn. Hannah felt his moustaches tickle her face, liked the strong smell of tobacco from his skin. May and Eleanor were timid with him at first – they were a little confused by this affectionate behaviour on his part. All they could remember was that he slept in his chair when they went to visit, and growled from time to time that children should be seen and not heard.

Sophia linked her father's arm and they made their way together out to the waiting carriage. Hannah followed, with May and Eleanor in tow.

It seemed to her that her first lifetime had passed away from her since early that morning. She no longer felt like the schoolgirl whose embroidery class had been interrupted by a visit from Sister Canice. That could have happened to someone else, for all the resonance it had for her now. It was like shedding a skin that had become too small for her. She felt that she had expanded since morning, that life had become deeper, wider, far fuller of shades of grey than she could ever have imagined.

She had never thought about the precariousness of things before. Now her life seemed like a fine thread woven along with others into the tapestry called family. It seemed that when one of those other threads snapped, the whole picture unravelled and life emerged from the wreckage, in all its messiness and confusion.

Hannah had the feeling that things would never be simple again.

Mary and Cecilia: Spring 1893

MARY WASN'T SURE what had woken her. Some unaccustomed sound had startled her into wakefulness, and now she was alert, watchful. The whole house was silent, but something was wrong. She could feel it. The street had been strangely quiet this evening; there had been none of the usual Friday night drinking, no rowdy return from the pubs on Peter's Hill. The men had gone home early, quietly, stayed close to their own firesides. The emptiness of the streets had had an eerie quality to it: no groups of youths hanging around the corners, dragging on a shared cigarette, shouting across to groups of disdainful girls. No children fighting over whose turn it was to hold the skipping rope, or play ball; not even the North Street dogs had barked.

There it was again: shouting, running feet, the sound of glass breaking. Cecilia stirred in the bed.

'What's goin' on?' she asked, struggling out of sleep.

Mary was kneeling at the window, pulling the corner of the curtain back a little.

'I don't know, but it's somethin' bad – I heard glass breakin' a minute ago.'

She peered out into the dimly lit street. At first she

could see nothing out of the ordinary. No doors opened, no lights blazed from the waiting eyes of the houses that lined each side. It was all much too quiet. Suddenly, there was a roar from the top of Peter's Hill, from where it adjoined the Shankill Road. Cecilia scrambled over to her sister's side, putting one arm around her shoulder, as much for her own comfort as Mary's. She started to tremble.

'Oh my Jesus – look at yon crowd!'

Mary felt the hair rise on the back of her neck. Gooseflesh roughened her arms; her throat went dry. She thought she had never seen so many men massed together before. The roar of their voices increased as they marched as one body down the narrow street, their boots sinister on cobblestones, their arms swinging. They had a swagger made of rage and drink.

'Yis 'uns will get bate! No fuckin' Home Rule here!'

'And no Pope, neither!'

Their bodies seemed to swell, to fill the whole street from side to side, crowding and crushing from pavement to pavement, their shadows looming upwards from gutter to street lamp. It was impossible to distinguish the men from the distorted shadows they threw, from the sticks and clubs they waved in the air, hurling them upwards from time to time and catching them again to the incessant drumbeat of stamping feet.

Their voices were ugly and discordant. Old insults were hurled at the same time as sticks and stones laid waste to almost every window on the opposite side of the street. Mary pulled Cecilia's head down below the level of the window sill.

'Keep low, for God's sake!'

Just as she spoke, there was the crash of glass as the McNiffs' front window shattered into tiny pieces and fell, in graceful, starry slow motion, to the ground below. The mob cheered and whooped, now kicking doorways and launching lumps of paving-stones through the doors and windows on both sides of the street.

The noise became intolerable.

'What are they saying?' Cecilia was clutching at her sister's arm, her eyes wide with terror.

'Sssh!' Mary warned her, keeping her eye on the street, trying to comfort Cecilia as best she could, patting her hand distractedly at the same time.

'Long live the Queen!'

Mary could see the shadowed faces of the mob uplifted into the greenish pools of gaslight. They were all shouting, all of them, each vying with the other for the worst insult, the most savage bite of triumph.

'We'll win, so we will! A British parliament for a British people!'

Their caps were pushed back from their foreheads: no need for subterfuge here. They don't care, Mary realized; they don't care who sees them, who recognizes them. They can do their worst and there's no one to stop them.

'We'll teach yis, fenian bastards! Ye'll not win!'

The shouts grew louder, the men working up their own anger, faces chiselled by drink and hatred. And yet the crowd never missed the beat of its own march. It made steady, menacing progress, like some sort of terrifying heartbeat, until the entire street was filled.

'Taigs out – we'll have no fuckin' Pope here!'

Still the houses sat tight. Not one broke ranks: no door, no window showed any sign of life.

Suddenly, as abruptly as it had begun, the noise of the mob ceased. As though at some secret signal, the marching stopped. The men stood still and silent, their sticks now by their sides, smacking from time to time off an impatient trouser-leg. All that could be heard was the shuffling of feet, the chink of nails on stone.

'Jesus, Mary and Joseph, but we're for it,' whispered Mary.

The silence was immense.

Suddenly, Cecilia nudged her sister.

'Look yonder,' she said, nodding her head to the right.

Some of the street lights had been broken in the fray, but those close to Peter's Hill were still lit. In the misty, greeny-yellowish light cast by a cluster of three or four lamps at the corner, Mary could make out a large group of RIC men.

'Them bastards is just standin' there!' Cecilia hissed, crouching down again.

'Aye – not a baton drawn between them.'

Cecilia craned her neck again, moving the hem of the curtain very gently. She began to count silently.

'There's at least forty of them – what are they doin'?'

'Nothin',' replied Mary, grimly. 'And I'll wager that's what they've been doin' all night – nothin'.'

The noisy shuffling of feet had begun again outside. Mary felt a strange sense of relief. Anything was better than the terrifying silence of the last few moments. A great roar came from the back of the crowd of bodies.

'Come on out, ye fenian bastards, and take what's comin' to ye! Take it like the men ye're not!'

Still the houses sat tight and silent. A moment's uncertainty hovered about the men's heads. Mary kept her head below the level of the window sill and prayed. Suddenly, they were off on the march again, as abruptly as they'd arrived. This time, they surged back in the direction from which they'd come, back towards the groups of policemen standing on both sides of Peter's Hill.

Mary and Cecilia watched as, with what seemed like breathtaking defiance, the men swung their sticks and clubs again, crashing into those windows they had missed in the excitement of their earlier rhythmic march down the cobbled street.

Their taunts continued; Mary and Cecilia could catch the same old insults, repeated over and over, accompanied by the crashing of paving-stones on doors and windows. The breaking of street lights went on and on, pools of darkness spilling out over the rough pavement as though released from the exploding stones. Still no baton was drawn. The two women waited, holding their breath, until the mob reached the policemen.

The men stopped there, congregating all along Peter's Hill. Each group kept its distance; neither moved towards the invisible boundary which kept them separate, each carefully apart from the other. The silence was palpable. Cecilia and Mary sat where they were, watching, terrified, waiting for the inevitable. It never came. They remained watchful, gritty-eyed, until five o'clock when the men finally dispersed, straggling off into the dirty dawn light.

May: Spring 1893

AFTER JOSEPH LEFT, May clung to her mother on the platform, too terrified to let her go. She held on tight to her coat, whimpering, convinced that the noise and black rages of the streets would erupt all around her again if she let go of the familiar. She had just escaped the path of the terrifying energy that had wanted to snatch and suck at Hannah, at her, and drag them screaming into its very centre. She had had a powerful vision of their carriage being swallowed and spat out again with its passengers already devoured, missing for ever. She wanted to feel familiar arms around her now, inhale the safe, comforting fragrance of lavender.

'You're safe, my love, you're safe now.'

Sophia rocked her daughter back and forwards, back and forwards as best she could, standing in the middle of the rapidly crowding platform. But the memory of the lurching carriage ride from school to train station filled May's senses: her head still reeled with the hoarseness of angry voices, her mind's eye kept replaying vivid flashes of running bodies, arms flailing in fury, stone crashing against stone. She had been able to see herself and Hannah as though from above, as they'd huddled together, low on the carriage floor. Now that it was over, she felt the invisible fist tighten its grip again inside her chest. It squeezed and squeezed so that her breath came wheezing, gasping, and her head grew light and dizzy.

'I've got you, I've got you now, you're safe. Breathe slowly, like Dr Collins showed you.'

Even Mama's whispered words, over and over, did little to still the rising sea of panic. May tried to slow down, to breathe deeply through her nose, but it wasn't working. It was always like this: once the crisis had passed, the waves of suffocation began, washing over and over her until some hand, usually Mama's, soothed her hot head and made the tide recede. But there was no comfort to be had here, not now. The hairs on May's arms and neck still seemed to stand to attention, prickling with the electricity of impending disaster.

'It's all right, loves, it's over, it's all over.'

May felt her mother's right arm reach out and draw Hannah closer to her. Hannah put her arm around May, too, and the three of them stood there, trembling. May wiped her eyes over and over.

'I thought those men were going to hurt us, Mama.'

Sophia hugged both girls to her.

'Hush, love, don't upset yourself any more. You're here now, you're safe. We – I had no idea that there was rioting. Let's just thank God you're both unharmed.'

People were now crowding and jostling on the platform. The noise and bustle of the station seemed to have increased tenfold. A red-faced little man in a GNR uniform was now pushing his way through the crowds in an absurdly cheerful manner, shouting above the excited buzzing that was suddenly everywhere. May wondered if he had any idea what they had just been through. How could anyone be cheerful if they knew what was happening out on the streets?

'All aboard! Dublin train in five minutes!'

Mama seemed to jerk suddenly into life.

'Quickly, now, Hannah. We must board the train. Eleanor's waiting for us.'

For the first time, May wondered where Papa was. Although they often went to Dublin without him, this time felt different. This time, they were surrounded by danger, the unexpected, the unknown. He should be with them, to keep them safe. She allowed herself to be bundled on to the train, still sobbing occasionally. Hannah held fast to her hand, but she treated her gently. There was no tugging or pulling at her to keep up. Ellie was already curled up on one of the seats, already half-asleep.

May felt the silence envelop all of them as they closed the door of their compartment. Mama stroked her head once in a distracted kind of way, and then gazed out the window. She kept patting her daughter's hand, murmuring, 'Good girl, good girl,' as May's breathing stilled, but she still kept her eyes fixed on something beyond the window. It was strange: there was nothing to look at, it seemed to May. Everything was blank and featureless once the bright platform had slid away, backwards, into the dusk.

'Why were those men fighting, Mama?'

'Sshhh – we'll talk about it later. It's nothing for you to worry about. No one can touch you now. You must rest, May, you need to breathe quietly.'

May wanted answers; she wasn't interested in breathing quietly. But it seemed that neither Mama nor Hannah felt inclined to speak. Underneath all the recent terror, her senses sharpened by fear, May was able to detect an undercurrent of something else in her mother's silence. She was different, somehow, more distant. Her presence with them in the carriage was somehow unemphatic. She had withdrawn that part of herself that made her Mama. It was as though May could have been anyone's daughter, sitting in any carriage, going anywhere on a normal, everyday journey. She felt suddenly afraid that in the midst of her terror, she had, somehow, done something to make her mother stop loving her.

Hannah whispered to her to lie down, pointing towards Eleanor and pressing her finger to her lips. There was nothing else for it. Her breathing felt more normal now, the hammering of her heart against her ribcage had eased, and Hannah's gestures were becoming insistent. She'd have to do as she was told. Reluctantly, she tucked her feet under her on the seat and lay down, nestling her head into Hannah's lap. Exhausted, she waited for sleep.

But sleep would not come. The wheels of the train failed to comfort her, the motion made her begin to feel sick. Rather than the familiar *taketa-tack* of its wheels, the usual, soothing rocking sensation, the train instead seemed to become sinister. The noises it made were an uncanny echo of the ugly shouts May had heard on the city streets, imitating their rhythm and ferocity. She felt the base of her throat start to constrict again. She was about to sit up when Hannah began to speak, quietly, to their mother. May decided to stay where she was. A strong instinct told her that this conversation would cease if she were suddenly to appear awake. She kept her eyes closed instead, and listened, straining to hear her mother's reply above the noise of the train.

'Your father has been arrested, Hannah. The police came and took him away two days ago.'

May felt her stomach lurch and fill rapidly with butterflies. At the same time, she was conscious of a wave of relief: it was always so much easier once the darkness was *named*: she had been deeply disturbed by the great silent cloud of distress which, up until now, had surrounded all of them in the dimly lit carriage.

'What did he do?'

May held her breath.

'He embezzled Post Office funds.'

May was puzzled. She had no idea what her mother meant. She waited, and Hannah spoke again, voicing her thoughts, speaking for her, as she often did.

'I don't understand. What does that mean?'

'It means he took money – borrowed it, without permission.'

'But if he borrowed it, then he means to pay it back. Why don't they just let him pay it back?'

'Because he hasn't got it, Hannah. And if you haven't got it, then borrowing like that is the same as stealing. That's the law.'

'Will he go to prison?'

Hannah's voice was unsteady. May could hear the tears behind her words, the tension suddenly stiffening the knees on which she rested.

'We don't know yet. We must wait and see.'

May heard nothing else. She wanted to cover her ears, to blank out her mother's words. She wanted to turn back time, to move the big hands on the station clock back to when they'd arrived, to make Mama greet her with a smile and a hug, a proper hug this time. This was not real: this was some other family's unhappiness which they had all stumbled into by accident. May wanted to sing out loud, to blot out the fear, to keep terror at bay as she had done when Sister Raphael locked her into the map cupboard.

But try as she did, she could not make anything change. Mama's tone continued to be angry and bitter. Hannah filled the air around them with her bewilderment. May wanted to be back in school, safe in the warmth of her dormitory, surrounded by all the girls who had become her friends. And she wanted Papa. Nothing could be as bad as Mama said; nothing.

Mary and Cecilia: Spring 1893

MARY CUT THE bread into large hunks. She put sugar and milk into Cecilia's mug, and filled it with a stream of strong, dark tea. She pushed it across the table to her sister.

'Here,' she said. 'Get that into ye.'

Cecilia drank it quickly. She stuffed the pieces of bread into her pocket. Mary was hurrying into her shawl.

'We'd best be goin', Cecilia – I don't want to get fined again.'

The younger girl nodded. 'Aye, I'm ready, but I don't know how I'm goin' to keep me eyes open the day.'

'Saturday's a short day – at least that's a wee bit o' comfort.'

'It's muck-up day – I hate it.'

Mary said nothing more. She could see that Cecilia was in no mood to be comforted. Both girls stepped outside; Mary pulled the front door behind them. There was now an unnatural silence on the morning streets. Debris was scattered everywhere. Tension hung suspended over the city like a lowering cloud. The air seemed to crackle with the memory of the previous night's violence; paving-stones and stout sticks were strewn everywhere, as far as the eye could see.

Since dawn, there had been the sounds of hammering and banging all over Carrick Hill. Mary and Cecilia had made tea and joined their neighbours in the wasteland of the street below, sweeping glass and stones off the pavement into the gutter. Men in their working clothes nailed planks of wood across the gaping holes where windows had once been. Women picked up shards of ornaments, precious things which varied little from family to family: little china dolls, toby jugs, a china vase or two. There were exclamations of delight when, miraculously, a sad brown and white china dog and a miniature Virgin Mary emerged whole from the wreckage.

Myles had come over just after the dawn silence had descended on the streets. He was anxious to make sure that Mary and Cecilia were safe. Mary had never seen him angry before. Frightened, yes – they had all grown to know fear, to acknowledge it to the others without shame. They had become a tight community, pulled even more tightly together by terror. It was what kept them close, wiped out any differences of opinion, old hurts, family enmities. These were all forgotten in their need to share the fear equally: just so much for everyone, so that no one felt overwhelmed. Just so much, so that people knew where their safety lay, and looked out for others, knowing that others were looking out for them. But Myles was angry now. His broad hands clenched the air, his large frame seemed even larger. Mary realized that he was standing up to his full height; he had suddenly forgotten to stoop.

'Bastards,' he muttered, his face set and pale with rage.

'Please be careful the day, Myles. Don't draw them on yerself.'

Mary was anxious for him. Father MacVeigh's words were enough to make her sharp-eyed, cautious about trouble, but she wasn't sure they were a strong enough antidote to Myles's anger.

He nodded and squeezed her shoulder, looking down at her tenderly.

'Aye, and you too.'

Numbed with exhaustion, Mary had gone back into the house with Cecilia to get ready for work. She had made breakfast for both of them to eat on the run. Hurrying now, they made their way through the streets towards their tram.

Handbills fluttered everywhere, uselessly, in the breeze. Bottles rolled and chinked against the sides of the gutters, as though marking time. The whole atmosphere was one of electric expectation; even these inanimate objects seemed content to wait for a new occasion of havoc, secure in the knowledge that it wasn't far off.

Mary and Cecilia joined the long stream of women headed for the mills of Bedford Street, York Street and the Crumlin Road. Nobody spoke of the night before. It was a silent march, a nervous procession that made its way towards the city trams. The girls' usual morning banter was silenced. Many of the younger faces were pale, pinched with anxiety. Girls and women linked arms with each other, taking some comfort from the presence of neighbours, the company of friends. The disturbances of the night before, and all the old tales, vivid with tribal memory, meant that these women moved carefully, watching their backs, all senses on the alert. Trouble had its own distinctive smell.

'Take care the day, Cecilia, keep your head down,' said Mary quietly as they walked the last hundred yards to Amelia Street. 'After last night, them girls'll be only lookin' for an excuse.'

The younger woman's face was even whiter than earlier, the fine blue veins along her temples almost garish by contrast.

'Aye, don't worry. I'll not say nothin', just do me work.'

The sisters approached Watson, Valentine and Company, its dark exterior forbidding even at six o'clock on a bright, crisp April morning. The mill girls were streaming into their place of work, converging from the right and the left of Amelia Street. In the ground-floor spinning room, they immediately took up their stands between the giant frames, ready for the day.

The coughing began almost at once. The filmy covering of pouce, disturbed by the influx of so many people at once, insinuated itself into nostrils and throats, snaked its way deep into lungs, setting off the harsh symphony which signalled the start of every morning.

Cecilia and Mary joined the throng heading for the stairs, long used to the morning jostling and pushing. Today, the crowd seemed to be denser than usual. There was an air of suppressed excitement among the girls and Cecilia felt herself being almost washed along by the press of urgent, hurrying bodies. Mary squeezed her sister's hand and had to let go suddenly as a group of three or four girls pushed against them, forcing their way between them. Cecilia said nothing as Mary was carried up the stairs before her on a wave of ascending bodies. They never spoke to each other once they'd entered the factory, meeting up again only when the day's work was over.

Cecilia struggled now to stay upright, knowing that any sign of weakness would bring her grief. It was important to stand your ground, to keep both feet firmly under you. She kept a sharp eye out for the known troublemakers, the Sandy Row girls with hard faces and tough, unforgiving bodies. She was careful to make no eye contact as she searched the sea of heads for Alice McLaughlin and Marian Ward, two of her few allies in the upper spinning room. Not for the first time, she wished that she could be with Mary. She consoled herself that the three years would be over at the end of the year; she'd join the experienced spinners before her next birthday. It couldn't come soon enough.

Her search for Alice and Marian distracted her for a moment and suddenly she stumbled on the stairway. She began to fight to stay standing and found herself being lifted by the elbows so that her feet no longer touched the ground. Instantly, she was terrified. Her heart began to beat faster, her palms to sweat. These were no helping hands. Almost immediately, the pinching began.

'What do ye say we pitch this filthy wee taig down the staircase, sister?'

The words were whispered, low and vicious, just at her right ear.

Cecilia looked around her wildly. Still neither of the girls she needed was anywhere near her, not even in sight. Her tormentors had chosen their moment well. She fought back the tears that sprang to her eyes as the tender flesh just above her elbows burned and flared with an almost unbearable pain. Nails were dug deep into her shoulders until she felt her skin must surely burst. She could not cry out. Any disturbance, any shouting or troublemaking, meant a fine, and she had already had enough of those.

'Aye, good enough for her, fenian bitch. Away over the banisters.'

They had just reached the entrance to the upper weaving hall, where Miss McCutcheon, the most senior doffing mistress, stood at her table, watching over the arrival of the girls. Even if the woman had glanced in her direction, Cecilia knew that she would see only an anonymous face flanked by two seemingly affectionate friends, one with her arm around Cecilia's waist now, the other resting her hand on her shoulder.

'We'll get ye,' was the final whisper as the two parted from her, one to the right, one to the left. Cecilia trembled with relief, her whole body now soaked with sweat. She took up her station and looked around her, trying to project a careless attitude which she was very far from feeling. She wanted to cry, to rub her arms and shoulders, to do anything to take the pain away. But she never moved. She wasn't going to give them the satisfaction. She wouldn't even recognize the two girls again if she saw them. They had come from behind, and disappeared before she could turn around. But their voices, she would never forget their voices.

Miss Morris was waiting for her. She looked at Cecilia closely. The girl looked unwell, flushed and bright-eyed, not at all like her usual self.

'Are ye all right, Cecilia?'

Her voice was full of concern, her eyes kind. For a wild moment, Cecilia almost blurted out what had happened on the way up the stairs. Just in time, she stemmed the impulse, forced back the tide of words already forming behind her lips. Telling tales brought its own punishment, and today was going to be bad enough.

'Aye,' she said abruptly. She gestured towards four children hovering uncertainly near Miss Morris's stand.

'Are these 'uns for the wipin' down?'

Cecilia looked at the unhappy faces of the four doffers who stood in front of her. What age were they? Ten, eleven, or younger? She tried not to feel too sorry for them: if she had been able to bear it, then so must they.

Miss Morris nodded.

'Go with Cecilia, now, girls: she'll tell ye what to do.'

For the next five hours, Cecilia supervised her charges as they emptied the water troughs under the spinning-frames and scrubbed them vigorously with wide brushes. Within an hour, their petticoats were soaked with brackish water and mucky residue. Their faces grew red, their small hands became raw and speckled with blood. Cecilia herself remembered how, within a very short time on muck-up day, her own body used to quiver with exertion, muscles strained and knotted by the demands of the unfamiliar. The young doffers did what they were told without question. Cecilia got down on her knees and showed them how to use their hands to drag out the black, silty mass of thread and dust that had accumulated in the bottom of each trough, her stomach revolting at the foul smell, eyes watering in her effort not to be sick. The children used their scrapers energetically, hacking away at the stubborn, dried dirt, freeing the shores of the gluey residue which had settled there since their last cleaning. Cecilia had to push them hard to stop them flagging: the longer the mucking-up took, the more work was lost as the machines lay idle.

'Hurry up! There's another frame off. How many for wipe-down?'

Voices were heard calling all over the spinning room as the half-timers were urged on to greater efforts. Finally, they carried buckets of water to each machine, which they dashed over the frames, washing them down and scrubbing the stone-clad passes beneath.

And then it was over, until the next time. No matter how well the half-timers adapted to the noise, the heat and the smell, Cecilia remembered all too clearly that the hatred for muck-up day was universal and abiding.

*

At twelve o'clock, the hooter sounded. Cecilia was grateful for the sudden silence, for the absence of the shouting and running and hurrying which had made her head split since early morning.

She deliberately played for time, wanting to leave only when Alice and Marian were well in sight. She'd have to be careful after this morning, watch her back. Such whispered threats as this morning's were rarely idle ones.

She caught a glimpse of Alice's fair hair and quickly pushed her way into the crowd, intent on their going down the stairs together, side by side. She couldn't reach her in time, so she held on to the banisters instead, scanning the crowd below anxiously for Mary's face. She saw her at once, and was overwhelmed with gratitude. Now she would be safe.

'Keep walkin', Cecilia. Don't even look round. Them 'uns are spoilin' for a fight. Hurry.'

Mary kept her eyes on the ground and walked rapidly down Amelia Street in the direction of home. Cecilia followed without a word. Just ahead, she spotted Alice and Marian, and then her heart seemed to stop. Blocking the exit from the street was a crowd of at least a hundred girls and women. She tugged wordlessly at Mary's sleeve. She could hear her sister's sharp intake of breath.

'Don't stop. They've t'other end closed off as well. Just keep goin'. Don't get involved.'

Cecilia couldn't help it. Her eyes were inexorably drawn to the crowd in front, following the progress of Alice's bright head. She just knew something bad was going to happen to her. As she made to pass through the narrow passageway between the two sections of the crowd, someone reached out and pushed Alice, hard. She lost her footing on the uneven street and her arms flew out in front to break her fall. But there was no fall. From the other side of the massed bodies, two girls pushed Alice back and she stumbled again, this time back into the first group. Back and forwards they pushed her, back and forwards, laughter and taunts ringing out into the now crowded street.

'Dirty wee taig! She's gone and pissed herself!'

Then the beating started in earnest. Four women set upon Alice, pulling her hair out in clumps, beating her around the head and shoulders with their fists.

Cries of 'We'll have no Pope here!', 'Fenian whores!' and 'No Home Rule!' filled the air as Mary and Cecilia looked on helplessly.

'Jesus help us, Cecilia, we're for it.'

For the first time, Cecilia saw fear glaze her sister's eyes. That, more than the waiting crowd, made her afraid as never before. Mary had always minded her, looked out for her, knew all the short cuts away from trouble. Her very presence last night had made Cecilia feel safe, that nothing really bad could happen once she had Mary by her side. But not today.

Alice was screaming, her eyes and her voice beyond terror. Suddenly, Cecilia couldn't stand it any longer. If they were trapped, then they were trapped, and she'd had enough. She was going to go down fighting.

She wrenched her arm away from her sister's and ran all the way down the street towards the waiting mob. Outside herself she knew there was confusion, the ugliness of hurled insults, Mary's terrified screams. Inside, a complete silence had descended; her mind was clear and unafraid. She couldn't just stand there and watch Alice, her friend, being beaten senseless. Her anger grew white, focused. Alice was such a gentle girl, she didn't deserve this. Nobody deserved this.

But Cecilia never reached her. Somebody's foot shot out and tripped her just as she reached the outer ranks of the crowd. She fell heavily, gashing her forehead on the cobbles. Suddenly, she felt as though her scalp were being torn from her head, piece by piece, as her body seemed to move of its own accord through the forest of kicking feet. She was being dragged by the hair right into the centre of the crowd of women, which now closed round her on all sides. Rough hands turned her over on to her stomach, wrenching her arms behind her back.

'Back to get more o' what we gav' ye this mornin', taig?'

That voice. She'd remember it for ever.

'C'mon, Agnes! Give her a hidin'!'

The crowd's blood was up. Agnes Neill was encouraged from all sides. A fist crashed into the back of Cecilia's neck and there was the sound of bone splintering. Her mouth filled with something liquid, warm and tasting of metal. There was nothing else in the whole world but pain. She closed her eyes, then, and welcomed the darkness.

*

Dr Torrens closed the door quietly behind him. Mary's anxious eyes seemed to fill the narrow hallway, her face a greenish colour from the weak light of the single gas lamp.

'Will she be all right?'

'She's badly shocked and bruised, and she's lost some teeth.'

The doctor paused. He suspected erysipelas, but couldn't be sure yet. He badly wanted to give this girl hope.

'She has a slight shadow before her eyes, and that's the one thing that worries me. The next forty-eight hours are crucial.'

Mary looked away from him.

'You must report this, you know,' he said gently. 'The people who did this must be punished.'

She turned to him then, her face alight with anger.

'There were two policemen *there*! They looked *on* while it was happening!'

Tears threatened to spill over as she remembered the complete, paralysing terror of her own helplessness.

'They *laughed* when that mob tore the dresses off two girls from Dover Street!'

Mary tried to stop her voice from shaking. She could still see the two RIC men standing at the edge of the crowd, impassive. They mostly looked away, off into the distance, above the heads of the people.

'Folded their arms, they did, and enjoyed the sport! Just like last night – just stood there, so they did. Don't tell me nothin' about reportin'!'

Dr Torrens put his hand on her shoulder.

'Nevertheless, you must report it. I'll write up Cecilia's injuries. Let me help you.'

Mary's anger disappeared as quickly as it had ignited; all that was left behind was a profound weariness.

'You are helpin', Doctor. I just want to see Cecilia well. I don't care about much else.'

He nodded.

'We'll talk about it again in the morning. In the meantime, keep her quiet, and lying down. If anything changes tonight, send someone for me.'

'Aye, I will. Thank you.'

'I'll see you in the morning. Try and rest yourself.'

Mary closed the front door and made her way quietly into the kitchen. She knew she was going to cry. Neighbours had been calling all evening, bringing food, blankets, anything they could lay their hands on. She was grateful for their support, for their companionable anger. But Myles hadn't come yet, and she was terrified something had happened to him, too.

She didn't want to live like this any more. She felt old at eighteen, as though she had lived several lifetimes in the last twenty-four hours. Cecilia might never be the same again; she could read between the doctor's words. At fifteen, she was finished; she'd probably never work again. They had nothing to stay for in this seething cauldron of a city. What she didn't know yet was how she was going to get both of them out.

May: Summer 1893

MAY HAD ALWAYS been afraid of Grandfather Delaney. On stiff family visits over the years, he had always appeared to her as forbidding, supremely impatient of children. Hannah was his favourite, if he could be said to have a favourite, and Eleanor sometimes raised an indulgent smile. But May seemed to be invisible. He simply paid no attention to her; it was as though she did not exist for him.

She felt obliged to sustain this illusion during the weeks they all stayed in his home, just after their hurried return to Dublin. She rarely spoke in his presence, and padded softly around his house, taking care not to disturb him, or anything belonging to him. Eleanor and Hannah, however, seemed to become more boisterous in his company: it was as though they challenged him to notice them. Mama simply worried: that was all she did these days. She worried. Her face was white and pinched, and May noticed more and more grey filaments invading the smooth cap of her dark hair. She felt vaguely guilty, sad and sorry all at once that her mother was suffering, and that she, May, could do nothing to make it better.

And so she had been surprised to find, in the unfamiliar surroundings of Grandfather Delaney's house, an unexpected refuge. Its very strangeness made it easier to forget Belfast, forget what they'd left behind, and the reason for their being here. It was like starting over. The three months spent with him before the move to Leinster Road were some of the happiest May could remember. His solid, gruff presence was somehow comforting. Once his long-established routine remained uninterrupted, he expected nothing from his granddaughters except impeccable behaviour.

And Grandfather Delaney's routine was nothing if not sacred. Breakfast was followed by some hours closeted in his study, where he wrote letters and attended to business. He preferred to lunch early, and alone. The afternoon was spent with his pipe and his newspaper in front of the drawing-room fire: very quickly the girls learned to place wagers on how long it would take him to fall asleep. Whoever timed the first snore correctly was the winner. He ate dinner with them in the late evening, and his testy manner softened, May noticed, after the first two glasses of red wine. Hannah, in particular, was often silent at dinner: May had learned that the dull, oppressive afternoons in town with Mama set her teeth on edge, sometimes made her want to scream.

May could still remember her mother's face when she impressed upon the girls the hours when activity around the house was permitted, the extent of that activity and the periods of time when silence had to be observed, no matter what their personal inclination might be. Behind all her words, May could hear her grandfather's language, even his inflexion. Sophia's face had been strained, anxious, and she spoke in a half-whisper, although before lunch was not supposed to be one of the quiet times.

May had no difficulty keeping the silences: she liked the afternoon hours of quietness which Grandfather had imposed upon her, hours in which she could slip away to his study and surround herself with the books which lined the entire room, floor to ceiling. She liked the old-fashioned, almost fusty smell of the room – a not unpleasant mixture of old damp, woodsmoke and pipe tobacco. She usually spent the time there on her own. Hannah was always needed by Mama for some errand or other, and Ellie preferred to play in the room she and May shared. She didn't like the study – found it too dark and dreary.

They were all allowed access to the books on the lowest shelves: a lot of Tennyson, lives of the saints, unbearably dull books on history and religion. There was not much to feed a twelve-year-old's growing appetite for novelty. Grandfather had said they were to read as much improving matter as they could, given that they probably would not start school again until September. May was particularly glad about this. To her own surprise, she had loved her time at St Dominic's in Belfast, but school in Dublin still held memories of gasping for breath in the darkness. She was glad to put off her return for as long as possible.

May was content to do as she'd been told for the first few weeks in Grandfather's study: she enjoyed simply handling the books, feeling the fineness of the binding, admiring the marbled insides of the covers. Some of the gold lettering of the titles was flaking away, and she made sure to treat the books carefully, as she had been bid.

Then she started to feel a little braver. There were shelves and shelves of books she couldn't reach; they grew more tantalizing by the day, their inaccessibility a challenge, and at the same time, an invitation. One cool, rainy afternoon, May planned her raid carefully to coincide with the hour of Grandfather's deepest sleep. With a confidence grown from almost a month of familiarity with an unchanging routine, May took herself to the study once Mama and Hannah were gone and Grandfather was already snoring, his newspaper sliding gently across his knees until it would eventually end up on the floor beside his feet.

She closed the study door firmly behind her. She marched straight over to the library steps, pulled the lever to free the wheels, and rolled them over to where she thought she had spied something interesting. The steps had fascinated her since the first day: she had never seen ones with wheels before. Once you pressed the lever, the wheels were locked and you were kept safe and stable. You could stretch out, she supposed, and choose your book without fear of falling.

Grandfather Delaney had travelled extensively in his earlier life, and Grandmother, for the most part, had gone with him. May remembered this from her mother's stories of her own childhood. Mama would tell her of the places her parents had been together, looking amused and still a little surprised at her own mother's daring. If all that were true, May had decided there had to be something better in this room than Tennyson.

On the very top shelf of Grandfather's study, May could see an enormous volume entitled *Atlas of the World*. On no account was she to climb the ladder to reach the top shelves: Grandfather had been very strict about this one rule. But her curiosity had now developed to such a pitch of impatience that such a petty rule seemed no longer of any importance.

Feeling suddenly nervous, May rolled the steps to just under where she had spotted the large atlas, and locked the wheels in place. She didn't like heights much, so she kept her eyes fixed on the tallest books on the top shelf, making sure not to look down. She reached out carefully, and pulled the atlas with difficulty from its position, wedged as it was between other volumes of equal size. It was as though their covers were stuck together. One last pull and it became free, but she almost toppled over with its sudden release. Staggering a little on the small platform, she regained her balance. She began to descend the ladder, clutching the atlas close to her chest, her hands and bodice already smeared with dust. Some instinct made her turn before she took the next step and a dry voice said: 'I'll take that for you, my dear.'

May felt the blood rush to her cheeks. Grandfather was standing at the foot of the ladder, his face grave. May began to look around her wildly, her head filled with ridiculous notions of escape. She couldn't speak: what could she say or do to excuse her disobedience? He had been fast asleep, she was sure of it: and the door was closed fast behind her. He shouldn't be here – she had heard no warning rattle of the door handle. How had he got in so silently? Her head buzzing, she handed the atlas over meekly, without a word. The truth was, she was far more terrified of Mama's probable reaction than Grandfather's serious expression.

He walked over to the table, which was as neat and precise as everything else about him. Papers lay in tidy bundles, bound with strong, dark ribbon. His blotter was fresh, his pens wiped clean and stored upright in their holders. He opened the atlas, at random it seemed, and smoothed the pages along the spine. He turned then to May, who had been holding her breath.

'I didn't know you were interested in maps?'

May exhaled suddenly with relief. His voice was kind, his eyes bright. It seemed to May that he was really seeing her for the first time as *May*, not just as one of his three granddaughters. She nodded eagerly, glad of the reprieve.

'Mama said you used to travel a lot. I want to go to different countries when I'm older.'

'Do you, now?'

His voice was amused. May felt herself bristle.

'Just because I'm a girl doesn't mean I can't.'

He nodded vigorously.

'You're absolutely right. You can do anything you want if you set your mind to it. Did you know your grandmother was a great traveller?'

May nodded, suddenly shy. She didn't know whether to admit that she knew, wondered if perhaps this was one of those private things which Mama would say should never be discussed. But his face was open, interested, and May decided to plunge in and hope for the best.

'Yes – Mama told me.'

He smiled at her.

'Come with me.'

He took May's hand in his and brought her over to the right-hand side of his bookcase. Just above head height, arranged in strict alphabetical order, were all the books that now began to transform May's solitary afternoons in her grandfather's study: a series of imaginative journeys that left her wide-eyed, greedy for more. She could hardly believe what had been opened up to her; she could feel her pulse race as she discovered that travel, adventure, the experience of the exotic were all possible – and here were books to prove it.

She started with ones Grandfather recommended, the ones written by the woman with the funny name: Isabella Bird. *A Lady's Life in the Rocky Mountains*, followed rapidly by *The Golden Chersonese* and *Journeys in Persia and Kurdistan*. She didn't care that she didn't know what 'Chersonese' was, or where it was – her ignorance was no barrier to feeling the magic pull of this woman's words. She read almost too quickly – her eyes raced across the page, terrified that something would happen to prevent her reaching the end of these enthralling stories. She wanted to live in a tent after Lady Anne Blunt's *Bedouin Tribes of the Euphrates*, but best of all so far was Constance Gordon Cumming's *A Lady's Cruise in a French Man-of-War*. A woman at sea!

May had no idea that such a thing was permissible. She had no idea, either, whether Mama would allow her to read such works: she suspected that she would not, so great was May's delight in their contents. Each afternoon she read avidly, one eye on the door, one on her book, always ready to cover it hastily with something wholesome should Mama enter suddenly, which she never did.

May was careful to replace all of Grandfather's books in the correct order. She showed him every day how she was gradually reading her way along the shelf, and once she noticed with dismay that his old eyes had misted over. He took out his handkerchief and blew his nose loudly.

'They were your grandmother's books, my dear, and you're very welcome to read every one of them. She'd have been proud of you.'

May felt herself glow. Nobody had ever said they were proud of her before.

'I promise I'll be careful, and I'll put them back in the right order.'

He patted her shoulder awkwardly, but gently.

'I know you will, my dear. I know you will. I think you might even be ready for Marco Polo.'

That afternoon of the atlas also began a series of meetings with her grandfather in the delightful seclusion of his study. They pored over the maps together, and he pointed out the towns and cities he had visited, the art galleries he had frequented, the buildings he had studied. The cities he described for her thrilled her imagination: Paris, Rome, Lisbon, Florence, Madrid, Venice. They made her long for the day when she could pack her bags and go.

But more than that, she loved the fact that this was their secret: neither Hannah nor Eleanor was invited. May began to feel less invisible, less like the middle sister of three, whom nobody really noticed. She now had something they didn't: and she had no intention of sharing it with anybody.

Mary and Cecilia: Spring 1893

MARY ROSE LATER than normal the following morning. The peal of church bells for seven o'clock Mass sounded louder than usual, their call harsh and jangling in the brittle morning air. She left Cecilia sleeping, and went downstairs to make her breakfast. She was glad it was Sunday, that she didn't have to face Watson and Valentine's today. Her whole body hurt, every muscle stretched taut and aching. She felt that everything about her was suddenly fragile; her spirit was all but broken, her optimism exhausted. She hated the thought of tomorrow, of facing yet again the tense tram ride, another taunting mob, the almost-certainty of more trouble on the streets. And yet she couldn't afford not to go to work. The walls of her small life seemed to be closing in on her; she felt that it was becoming difficult to breathe. She was the older one, it was up to her to make the best of what had happened to them, what was likely to happen in the long, uncertain days ahead. She had slept badly, wondering how they were going to manage if Cecilia could not go back spinning. They couldn't stay here; not that she wanted to stay here, but for now she had nowhere else to go, no other means of earning a living.

She thought about Myles. He would marry her, she knew that. And he would help look after Cecilia, have her to live with them, along with his ailing mother. She didn't even need to discuss it with him. That was how they would do things, she and he. That was how it was. She could see her whole married life stretch out in front of her, its sameness as assured as the streets she lived in. They would not go far: Carrick Hill, children, middle age. Daughters to the mill as half-timers, if they were unlucky; the same old vicious circle all over again. Or if they were lucky, to school until fourteen, followed by some gentler employment. Sons to the ropeworks, to the water plants, to the angers and resentments of Harland and Wolff, always second class, always poor. She would never get out, never breathe fresh air and see her children play in open fields, by the sea, somewhere healthy and happy.

And Cecilia. What chance did her health have here? She'd probably be dead before she was forty – ironically, having escaped the certainty of consumption to be cut down by the constant assault of ill health on a body already weakened by brutality and infection.

Mary cut a large hunk of bread while waiting for the water to boil. She made the tea as strong as she could, and carried the two mugs back upstairs to the bedroom. Cecilia was awake. Her eyes followed her sister, hugely, around the bedroom.

Mary put the mugs down on the floor. She stroked her sister's forehead, taking care not to touch any of the cuts and scratches that were now darker than yesterday, congealed blood thickening at the edges. Her whole face seemed to be one massive bruise, the skin a deep angry vermilion. Her lips were split, her cheeks swollen, puffy. Even her neck was discoloured, the skin from chin to collarbone red and inflamed. Mary was frightened at the heat from her sister's forehead. She was burning up. She prayed silently that the doctor would hurry.

Cecilia smiled up at her as best she could. Some of her teeth were missing, others broken, blackened with dried blood.

'How're ye feelin', love?'

The younger girl barely nodded in reply. Mary knelt on the floor beside the bed, as close to Cecilia as she could.

'I've brought ye tea; mebbe if I soak the bread in it, ye might be able to eat a wee bit?'

Cecilia shook her head.

'Dr Torrens is goin' to look in on ye this mornin'.'

Mary tried to keep her voice light, but her sister's face, the blankness of her eyes, the sweaty, angry skin, terrified her. She had a strong sense that Cecilia's injuries were even worse than they looked. What if she lost the sight of her poor eyes?

Cecilia squeezed her sister's hand. She tried to speak, and winced.

'Don't try to say nothin'. You have another wee sleep, there. I'm goin' downstairs to wait for the doctor.'

Cecilia's eyes closed. Mary wondered how it could be possible to sleep when you were in so much pain. Her eyes filled as she thought of her mother. She needed

Ma now; she couldn't look after Cecilia without her. She was afraid of what might happen, being on her own.

She went downstairs again to the kitchen, balancing her mug of tea carefully. She couldn't eat the bread she had cut. Its taste was stale, almost powdery, like pouce. She put it aside, and went to all her hiding-places around the kitchen. Ma had taught her to put away whatever money could be spared, no matter how little, 'for a rainy day'. Mary used to watch her, as a child, making a game out of hiding pennies, thruppenny bits, the odd sixpence. She and Mary would be the only ones to share the secret. As Mary moved about the kitchen now, opening canisters, prising the old lids off metal boxes, she felt an unfamiliar surge of bitterness. She remembered how she'd promised herself that she would have another kind of life.

Mary knew that her mother's death had been hastened, not just by her own years at the mill, and the wasting disease which seemed to come to all, sooner or later: more than that, she had become consumed by despair, watching with enormous, pool-black eyes as her two daughters became trapped, just as she had been. Mary had heard her mother's anguish during the long nights of her illness. Often, she'd crept into Ma's bedroom and into the cold bed beside her. From those nights, Mary knew that her mother's tears were not for herself, but for the daughters she had had such hopes for. Cecilia was the bookish one, so quick and clever at her sums, at reading. Ma had been angry at God, had shaken her fist at him in the darkness. Of all of them,

Cecilia should have been able to stay at school, to better herself, to pull herself out of the pit of Carrick Hill. Ma had always believed that a better life awaited her daughters, better than she had had, somewhere way beyond the mills of Watson, Valentine and Company. She used to have hot, heady dreams about the mill being like a giant spider's web, winding its flaxen threads around her daughters' waists, holding on tight, pulling them close, closer, into its remorseless centre.

And she never stopped missing her three boys. Life was good in America, it seemed, and the work plentiful. Father MacVeigh had tried to get in touch with them for her after their father died, but there had been no response. *Not known here. No forwarding address.* They'd moved on by then, maybe; or maybe they just didn't want to know. It happened. People here shrugged it off, as though such abandonment was natural, only to be expected. Sometimes, parcels kept coming from America for years, dressing and entertaining the younger ones in the large families left behind. More often they stopped after a year or two, to be replaced by the few dollars at Christmastime inserted between sheets of writing paper, folded carefully into blue envelopes with exotic stamps. Eventually, inevitably, these stopped, too. People made new families, created new memories, a whole new way of life. 'That's the way of the world, child.' One of Ma's favourite sayings. Nevertheless, Mary could always tell that it had scalded her heart.

She kept rummaging around the kitchen for almost an hour, looking twice or three times in the same places, dismayed at the paltry yield. A handful of copper pennies, a sixpence, a couple of ha'pennies. That would pay no doctor. He was a kind man, Mary knew, and that made it all the more important to be able to give him something. She hated relying on charity.

She spread her arms out on the tiny table and rested her forehead on them. Her whole head felt heavy. It was an effort to hold it up. At least this escape cost her nothing. She would sleep until he arrived.

Dr Torrens arrived punctually at ten o'clock. His knock startled Mary. She had been dreaming about being surrounded by a hostile crowd, her body powerless, her chest suffocated by fear and inertia. In the dream, she had no voice, no will. She tried to cry out, to move her legs and arms; instead, she woke whimpering, paralysed between sleep and wakefulness, saliva all over her hands where her mouth had rested. Hurriedly, she wiped her hands on her skirt and ran to open the front door.

Dr Torrens looked too clean, too cheerful, too well tended to be standing outside her front door first thing on a rainy Sunday morning.

'Good morning, Mary. How's our patient?'

'Still the same, I think. I don't even know if she slept.'

'Let's go take a look. And you?' he asked. 'Any ill effects?'

She shook her head.

No, she wanted to say, not unless you include fear for yourself and your sister, terror at watching the next forty unchanging years of your life unfold before you in dust, consumption and bitterness, or watching your unborn children's lives unfold in dust, consumption, bitterness. That's if you live that long. No other ill effects.

Cecilia was very still, lying just as Mary had left her. Dr Torrens leaned over her and very gently lifted one eyelid. He turned to Mary.

'Can you bring me some warm water and a cloth and we'll clean up her cuts? I've got antiseptic with me.'

She had the feeling he was getting rid of her, kindly. She'd go then, but she wanted the truth, all of it, when he was finished.

When she came back upstairs to the bedroom, Cecilia was weeping silently, the doctor peering into her right eye with a small light.

Mary was frightened. There was a strange atmosphere in the room.

'What is it?' she asked, almost dropping the cracked bowl full of warm water.

'Cecilia's afraid that the shadow in front of her eyes is worse than yesterday.'

He lifted her left eyelid.

'It's not even twenty-four hours, yet, Cecilia. Give things time to settle. Please try not to worry.'

He put his light away, and snapped the top of his black bag shut. He handed Mary a bottle.

'Put ten drops of this into warm water and wash the cuts three times a day. Keep the room dark and quiet. I'll be back again tomorrow morning.'

He laid his hand on Cecilia's forehead.

'I've given you something for the fever, my dear, and you're made of strong stuff. Don't lose heart.'

There was no reply. He didn't look as though he expected one.

Mary followed him downstairs.

'Her sight has got worse, I'm afraid. I'm hoping it's only temporary, but it's very distressing for her. You must try and keep her spirits up.' He hesitated. 'And your own. I'll do whatever I can to help.'

'Thank you.'

'You must send for me at once if the fever gets any worse. If you're in any doubt, please don't delay.'

He paused, and Mary knew that he was breaking things to her gently.

'It's very important that the fever doesn't get a grip. Watch her closely tonight.'

All feeling suddenly seemed to have left Mary's body. She clung to the door after he had left. Cecilia. Blind. She'd known by looking at her this morning that she wasn't going to get better. Now what? She sank to the floor, leaning her back against the door, resting her forehead in her hands. She stayed, unmoving, until pins and needles began to creep up her legs towards her knees. She wasn't going to be able to cope with this; all her familiar strength seemed to have deserted her. She had no idea what she was going to do next.

Look after Cecilia, that's what. Up off yer arse, girl, and stop feelin' sorry for yerself. This is no time for guernin'. She heard her mother's voice, startlingly clear inside her head. She felt, suddenly, some of the old energy begin to seep back into her blood again. Something under the

absorb so
... them; other people's
... ...eep into their very bones,
leaching out in later years, transformed into something
very different. I think that the first seeds of my desire
for independence were sown that year of our return to
Dublin. Whether I knew it at the time is not really
important: I came to know it later on. I wanted to hand
my destiny over to no man.

It is ironic, of course, that another man should
have been our saviour that awful summer. Grandfather
Delaney, with his stern face and kind eyes – I'll always

surface of her skin began to feel alive. Even her hands
had begun to tingle. She had a strange, warm sensation
that Ma was looking after her, willing her to do what
was right. She couldn't just sit down under this. She'd
promised to look after Cecilia, always.

She had today to get herself organized. Mrs McNiff
would surely come and sit with Cecilia in the mornings.
The old lady was a great talker: she had a wealth of
stories. She'd be good company for Cecilia. Then there
was Mrs Devlin. She'd help out, too, once her sons went
off on their afternoon shift to the ropeworks. Saturday
afternoons and Sundays she'd mind Cecilia herself.

And if she did go blind, maybe there was still
something she, Mary, could do without leaving Cecilia
alone. She might become a homeworker. She'd ask
Father MacVeigh. There was great call for fine needlework these days – embroidered sheets and table-linen
for all the big houses on the Malone Road.

She rubbed the backs of her legs vigorously and
made her way into the kitchen. She filled the bowl again
with water, this time cold water, straight from the tap.
She would bathe Cecilia's forehead all day, if that's what
it took. She would break this fever, for both of them.
That was today's work. She'd worry about tomorrow
when it came.

Cecilia slept fitfully all day. Mary stayed at her side,
filling bowl after bowl full of cold water, talking to
her all the time as she bathed her forehead. There
were times when she was sure that Cecilia heard and

understood her, other times when her sister seemed to have gone so far away from her that Mary was terrified. She couldn't leave her side for more than an instant. She had called out the window to neighbours who knocked anxiously, looking for news. She threw down a key to Myles for Mrs McNiff, just in case she, Mary, had to rush away for Dr Torrens. She willed the fever to break, willed her sister to come back to her.

Shortly after midnight, something in the room changed. Mary jolted awake, sensing the presence of something different. She had fallen asleep for an instant, still on her knees at the side of the bed, the cloth wrung out and clenched in her right hand. Cecilia seemed to lie more quietly. The childlike moaning had ceased. Mary stretched out her hand to touch her sister's forehead. Cooler; it was definitely cooler. Even by the light of a single candle, her skin seemed less livid, its rawness abating. Too exhausted even to undress, Mary climbed into bed beside Cecilia, pulling the blanket around her own shivering body. She slept.

Sunlight filtered through the thin curtain, filling the room with a warm, yellowish haze. When Mary opened her eyes, she knew she was already late for work. She'd overslept – it was much too bright. Nevertheless, the brightness made her cheerful until she remembered. All the unhappiness of the past two days came flooding back. She turned at once to Cecilia. Her sister was already awake, her face much cooler than yesterday.

'Cecilia?' she said.

'Don't gi
to worry.'

But the cracking of her own voice g
Two huge tears trembled on Cecilia's lower lids. She squeezed her sister's hand. Mary broke then.

'Oh, Cecilia. I'm so sorry. So sorry.'

She wept, her head on her sister's thin shoulder. Then, with a huge physical effort, she hugged the younger girl closer to her.

'I'll look after ye, Cecilia. I will. As God's my judge, I'll always look after ye.'

surface of her skin began to feel alive. Even her hands had begun to tingle. She had a strange, warm sensation that Ma was looking after her, willing her to do what was right. She couldn't just sit down under this. She'd promised to look after Cecilia, always.

She had today to get herself organized. Mrs McNiff would surely come and sit with Cecilia in the mornings. The old lady was a great talker: she had a wealth of stories. She'd be good company for Cecilia. Then there was Mrs Devlin. She'd help out, too, once her sons went off on their afternoon shift to the ropeworks. Saturday afternoons and Sundays she'd mind Cecilia herself.

And if she did go blind, maybe there was still something she, Mary, could do without leaving Cecilia alone. She might become a homeworker. She'd ask Father MacVeigh. There was great call for fine needlework these days – embroidered sheets and table-linen for all the big houses on the Malone Road.

She rubbed the backs of her legs vigorously and made her way into the kitchen. She filled the bowl again with water, this time cold water, straight from the tap. She would bathe Cecilia's forehead all day, if that's what it took. She would break this fever, for both of them. That was today's work. She'd worry about tomorrow when it came.

Cecilia slept fitfully all day. Mary stayed at her side, filling bowl after bowl full of cold water, talking to her all the time as she bathed her forehead. There were times when she was sure that Cecilia heard and understood her, other times when her sister seemed to have gone so far away from her that Mary was terrified. She couldn't leave her side for more than an instant. She had called out the window to neighbours who knocked anxiously, looking for news. She threw down a key to Myles for Mrs McNiff, just in case she, Mary, had to rush away for Dr Torrens. She willed the fever to break, willed her sister to come back to her.

Shortly after midnight, something in the room changed. Mary jolted awake, sensing the presence of something different. She had fallen asleep for an instant, still on her knees at the side of the bed, the cloth wrung out and clenched in her right hand. Cecilia seemed to lie more quietly. The childlike moaning had ceased. Mary stretched out her hand to touch her sister's forehead. Cooler; it was definitely cooler. Even by the light of a single candle, her skin seemed less livid, its rawness abating. Too exhausted even to undress, Mary climbed into bed beside Cecilia, pulling the blanket around her own shivering body. She slept.

Sunlight filtered through the thin curtain, filling the room with a warm, yellowish haze. When Mary opened her eyes, she knew she was already late for work. She'd overslept – it was much too bright. Nevertheless, the brightness made her cheerful until she remembered. All the unhappiness of the past two days came flooding back. She turned at once to Cecilia. Her sister was already awake, her face much cooler than yesterday.

'Cecilia?' she said.

remember the way he greeted us at the station, off the Belfast train. I know that he made me feel safe, made me feel that I had, at last, come home.

We all stayed with Grandfather until about a week or so before we went back to school in Dublin the following September. The four months leading up to then had seen our lives grow more and more difficult – Grandfather was not accustomed to three noisy young ladies disturbing his afternoon sleep, giving him indigestion with their antics after dinner. Mama had grown white and tense again – she shushed us angrily so often that we went around the house like ghosts, our very shoes made of whispers.

We were glad to move out – at least, Hannah and I were. Grandfather's house was full of male smells, and stiff, no-nonsense furniture. All traces of Grandmother's hand had long since disappeared: there was no sense of the feminine in any of the rooms to which we were permitted access. To this day, the smell of brandy, cigars, and the warm, heady aroma of cinnamon-smothered bread-and-butter pudding remind me of my Grandfather Delaney. His tastes were solid, respectable, upper middle class. Roast beef and Yorkshire pudding on Sundays, a good claret, a blazing fire beside which to open one's waistcoat in the late afternoon. Such were the joys of the masculine household. However, he and May seemed to form an unlikely alliance. They disappeared together to the study most afternoons, although May never spoke about it. I didn't mind – I had no wish to be singled out for Grandfather's attention. I was very happy to be left alone, or to play tennis with Hannah in the park opposite Grandfather's house.

As with many things, I learned later that the house we moved to – a pretty red-brick house on Leinster Road in Rathmines – was one of Grandfather's several properties. I have wondered often about the unhappy family who had to move out so that we could move in. I have often felt guilty that our misfortune was the cause of some other poor family's displacement. Bits and pieces of the previous tenants' lives were everywhere, and I know that my small self was distressed at finding some child's teddy bear hiding in the dust under the bed in May's and my room. I wanted Mama to find out where that child had gone, so that we could give her back her toy. But Mama got angry with me then, and I learned never to speak of it again. I still have the bear, as you know, somewhat the worse for wear, but none the less well loved for all that.

Lily and Katie set to cleaning the new house with a vengeance. It was smaller than we were used to, but I liked that. I liked sharing with May. On the nights when she snored, or went sleepwalking, I took my pillow to Hannah's room. I thought my heart would break when both of my sisters were sent away to boarding school early in the New Year. That they had been at day school since September had been the source of all my happiness. I cried and cried until Lily and Katie took pity on me, and brought me warm milk and comfort in the evenings. Mama was far too distracted to worry about my childish tears.

She disappeared several times that autumn, usually

for a day or two at a time. I think I knew that she had gone to see Papa, but I was too afraid to ask, and she never spoke of it. She would return to Leinster Road with red-rimmed eyes and creased travelling-clothes. Lily would always look after her, bustling her upstairs, disappearing for an hour or two, then reappearing with an armful of Mama's dresses. She would shake her head over the clothes in the kitchen, clucking at the mistress's unhappiness.

Perhaps it was because neither Lily nor Katie had children of their own, but they seemed totally oblivious to my presence by the range, where I sat sipping my warm milk, nibbling on Katie's cherry buns. I was always loath to go to my bed, and I made this supper last as long as I could. If I kept still and quiet, they would talk about Mama, about Papa, about us children and our misfortunes as though I didn't exist, as though none of us really existed. Perhaps that is why I now have a healthy respect for other people's children: what they do not understand of speech, they more than supply with intuition.

I sometimes feel sorry now for the little girl I once was, sitting in her lonely corner of the kitchen. In all senses, that range was the only warmth I received; by its side, I learned to decipher adult language, to understand the words that were spoken and, more importantly, to understand the significance of the silences in between.

I got books that first Christmas back in Dublin, and a new pair of boots. Grandfather Delaney came for dinner and slept in the big winged armchair by the fire all afternoon. We girls had to be silent. It wasn't hard.

There was no cheer for us that festive season. Hannah was disinclined to play the piano; May sat quietly, poring over the atlas Grandfather had given her from his library. There was little that was new. Grandfather didn't believe in making a fuss over Christmas.

I remember thinking, even as a precocious nine-year-old, how ridiculous it was that everybody had to pretend to be happy on the same day of every year. As if happiness were something we could experience to order.

We all went to bed early that night. I couldn't bear any longer to see Mama's eyes fill every time any of us looked at her. May slept instantly, but thrashed and tossed so much during the night that she kept me awake.

I took my pillow and made my way to Hannah's room. She was not asleep. Wordlessly, she turned down the bedclothes on one side and waited until I had climbed in beside her.

She kissed me on the forehead.

'Good night, Mouse,' she said.

I was glad. She didn't need to say anything else. I understood that this was now part of our private language. We were both thinking of him. In our own way, this was our gift to Papa, our way of wishing him a happy Christmas.

Mary and Cecilia: Summer 1893

'ARE *YOU* REALLY sure about this, Cecilia?'

Mary was braiding her sister's hair carefully. She tried to cover up the bald patches, brushing wisps of fine, tired hair from one side to the other, trying to hide as much as possible. Of all the injuries which Cecilia had suffered, Mary found these open, hairless patches of scalp the most difficult to look at. It seemed as if all her sister's vulnerability lay just below the surface of the tender pink weals that littered her scalp. They had been raised and angry before, in the days immediately following the attack; now they looked flat and defeated, like the discarded cocoons of some predatory insects. If she pinned up the plaits, then perhaps the scars wouldn't be so visible. Not that Cecilia would notice anyway, not any more.

'Aye. You heard what Father MacVeigh said. And Dr Torrens. Why should them girls get away with it?'

Mary didn't answer. Instead she said: 'All right, pet. Just so long as ye're sure.'

Mary didn't tell her what Myles and the others had said, how they'd been pressing her all week not to let Cecilia make her deposition. She had listened to them, growing more and more fearful for her sister, for herself. They had insisted that in this city there were great big yawning gaps between what was lawful and what was right. That too many times, the law hurried to meet you, and justice was left trailing somewhere behind, so confused by complexity and contradiction that it lost its way, disappearing like smoke. The law is not for people like us, Myles had said, and in her heart Mary believed him. But Cecilia wanted to do this. Something in her determination had made Mary realize that in some strange way, this was part of Cecilia's groping towards being well again. She couldn't stop her, not now.

'You'll be with me, won't ye?' Cecilia's voice was childlike again, all the certainty of a moment earlier suddenly evaporated.

'Aye, I will, o' course. Don't you worry yerself, now.'

Mary hugged her, resting her chin on Cecilia's shoulder, seeing both their faces reflected in the cracked mirror which Mary had propped up on the kitchen table. Something inside her lurched with pity as the paleness of Cecilia's skin was made even more apparent by the silvery shadows of mildew ghosting everywhere behind the old glass.

They made their way to Clifton Street for three o'clock. The policeman who had visited them at home the day before yesterday had been kind enough; a big, imposing man with a dark uniform and a deep voice. Mary had let him in, her face tight in the effort to conceal her hostility. She didn't trust him; didn't trust any of them.

The deposition was nothing to be frightened of, he had told them. All Cecilia had to do was to tell the 'whole truth'. He stressed this several times during the interview, until Mary wanted to ask him sharply what did he think Cecilia was doing now. She was glad she hadn't. Cecilia simply turned her blank eyes to him then and said with quiet conviction: 'I haven't ever told anythin' else, sir.'

Now they sat, Mary holding her sister's hand tightly, waiting for the Justice, Mr Dobbin, to arrive. A small, thin man emerged from somewhere among the shadows of the huge room and glided over to where they sat. His hair was a yellowing white, like old parchment, his bushy eyebrows startling in their blackness. Mary thought his face was as colourless as his hair, as though he spent too much time indoors, hiding from sunlight.

He whispered that Mr Dobbin's clerk, Mr Fleming, would be the one writing down everything Cecilia said, and that she must direct her answers to him. Mary nodded, and watched as this slight, somehow dusty man of indeterminable age effaced himself from the room. The door closed behind him with a sigh.

Cecilia tugged at her sleeve. 'Is he thick? Does he think I'm hard o' hearin' as well?'

Her tone was half irritated, half amused.

Mary felt instantly guilty. She had developed the habit of responding for Cecilia on so many occasions in the weeks since the attack. Sometimes it was to stave off situations which Cecilia couldn't see coming; other times she was as bad as everyone else: treating her sister as incapable of speaking for herself. Mostly, though, she felt on guard in her sister's presence, like a soldier charged with protecting the innocent. She couldn't help it; old habits die hard. Now she felt her nervousness increase on Cecilia's behalf.

She was afraid of what might happen to her sister's words, once they became indelible marks on paper. What if someone twisted them? What if someone ridiculed her, or made her change her story, or reduced her to tears? They couldn't just get up and leave – the policeman at the door would surely stop them, make them stay no matter what. Even the room seemed disapproving of them – its high, elegant ceiling, the rich, nutty wood-panelling everywhere, the vast desk: all were like a reproach to her and Cecilia, casting light on their shabbiness, their unimportance, their sad, ordinary lives.

Suddenly, a door in the panelled wall opened, and two men emerged, dressed in black, their expressions grave. One of them, the taller one, sat in the high-backed chair behind the desk. Mary was so terrified that her mind went blank, her ears filled with a frantic whistling. She was hardly aware of Cecilia's being led away from her to another table, much too far away for her to comfort. It was as though she became suddenly paralysed, rooted to the floor, unable to stop Cecilia before it was too late.

And then everything went still as Cecilia's voice, clear and steady, began to describe the events which now became eerily unfamiliar to Mary's ears. It was as though her sister were telling someone else's story, the tale of someone not related to her, someone she had never even met. Hearing Cecilia speak made everything become detached, separated from the reality they had both known and felt together. Drained of the emotion that had accompanied them in real life, the events lost their potency, their urgency. Mary wanted to interrupt, to cry out 'But it was much *worse* than that!'

'. . . A girl named Ward saw what happened. A mob gathered of about a hundred. They were all workers in the same factory as myself. A girl named Agnes Neill caught me by the hair and dragged me to the ground, and hit me on the back of the neck with her fist.'

At this point, Cecilia's voice began to waver. But she didn't stop. Mary wanted her to; she wanted them both to go home. She had the strongest feeling that every word Cecilia uttered was like the cutting edge of a spade slicing remorselessly into soil. It was digging deeper and deeper into a pit of trouble for herself, for both of them. A shaft of sunlight pierced the high window and Mary felt her face grow suddenly warm. At the same time, as though realization had come with the yellowy, dust-trembling brightness, she knew that she could never go back to Watson, Valentine and Company. She knew it as clearly as she knew her own name. She would never be safe in the mill, not after today. What before had always been a threat, breathed in as naturally as air, was now a certainty, a palpable reality. She would be singled out, marked even more than before. *Taig; fenian; traitor.* Her life there – their life there – was over.

As she listened to her sister, Mary was suddenly filled with an intense joy. This might not be how Ma would have wanted it: it might not be how any of them would have planned for it to come about, but the end result was the same. They were free, free of the mill's sickness and corruption. She would find something else for Cecilia and herself to do, she would make sure they didn't starve. The only important thing now was to look after her sister.

She felt filled with pride as she watched these men in their important clothes listen to Cecilia's story. They didn't bully her, didn't interrupt, didn't mock or threaten her. Maybe all of this would make no difference to anybody, ever. Maybe these pages would be filed away into obscurity somewhere, forgotten quietly, their dark ink left to fade into oblivion. It hardly mattered; whatever was done with them would make no difference to their lives. But the fact of the attack had miraculously brought something good in its wake: she and Cecilia had been given – no, had *earned* a second chance. Mary was determined that the rest of their lives would be lived out somewhere, anywhere, far away from the fears and cruelties they had learned to believe were an inevitable part of daily existence.

Something had been transformed in the telling of Cecilia's tale: its horrors had somehow been lessened; their grip around Mary's throat began to loosen. She felt suddenly light and giddy, and full of heady compassion for her sister. She had stood up to those girls with the hard faces and tough, brutal bodies; they no longer diminished her. Mary swore that she would never again have to be their victim.

Eleanor's Journal

LATE IN JUNE, some three years after we had returned to Dublin, Mama told us she had a surprise for us. Her voice was light, intimate – but I sensed effort beneath its brightness. We girls were all going on a little holiday, she said, to our cousins in County Cork. I remember Hannah looking at her sharply, as though she didn't believe her, as though her words contained more than their surface meaning.

I had noticed that about Hannah since our return from Belfast: she treated Mama almost as an equal, and was frequently bold and outspoken in situations where May and I kept our heads down. Whatever we might have thought privately, or indeed discussed later between the two of us in our bedroom, in Mama's presence, May and I were the very souls of meekness and discretion.

'Why?' Hannah asked now.

Mama had some letters in her hand, as Lily had just brought the morning post. We were sitting having breakfast together, with the French windows wide open into the garden. For once, there was warmth in the bright morning light.

Now Mama's smile faded and she placed the letters

and the silver letter-opener back down on the table again. She looked at Hannah coolly, and something in her tone warned Hannah to take her questioning no further.

'Because that is what I have arranged for you, Hannah.'

'Aren't you coming, Mama?' I asked, more to break the dangerous silence I could sense building across the table between the two of them than for any other reason.

'No. I have things I must do. I may have to go away.'

Her tone was flat, precluding all further discussion. It was the tone she always used when anybody mentioned Belfast – although nobody had dared to mention it here. That name was always left simply hanging: nothing was done with it once it had been spoken. It seemed to float in the air, trailing long threads of silence in its wake. May and I had learned long ago to let it hang, reluctant to get snared in the knotty complexities it brought with it. Once Mama said 'away', the three of us understood at once. May and I kept quiet, but in those days, Hannah was different.

'I'd prefer to come with you, Mama.'

Her tone was firm, adult, as though she were the mother, and Mama the child.

'That's not possible, Hannah, and I really don't wish to discuss it with you here. The subject is closed.'

Even Hannah wouldn't dare reopen it after that. I ate my egg and soldiers and watched my plate intently.

Somehow, I knew. Papa was coming home. By now, he had spent over three years in prison. We weren't supposed to know that, of course, at least May and I weren't. But Hannah had let it slip once, late at night, about a year after our return to Dublin. We were all in her bedroom, putting curling papers in each other's hair. She had clapped her hand to her mouth as soon as the words were out, and looked, stricken, first at May, and then at me. We two were actually standing behind her, with curling papers and a hairbrush in our hands. We stared at her reflection in the mirror, which stared back at us.

'I didn't mean to say that,' she whispered, the tears threatening. 'Please don't tell Mama.'

'I knew it,' said May softly. 'I heard you and Mama on the train that night we came back to Dublin. But you said I was wrong: you told me I hadn't understood what I'd heard.'

'Mama made me promise,' said Hannah, openly sobbing now. Her hands were clasped tight together, the knuckles showing white. 'Please don't say I told you.'

She turned to me.

'Mouse, you must promise, too.'

She only ever called me Mouse on very special occasions. I nodded, wordlessly, feeling suddenly important, like one of the heroines in Mrs Gaskell's novels. I wondered if I was going to faint. But nothing that dramatic ever happened to me. Papa was 'away', we had always been told, working in New York, learning new and important things about banking. Mama had a brother there, too, and she told us a lot about that young and thriving city; she had made it sound vibrant and exciting. She even read Papa's letters to us which arrived from America on a monthly basis. May always asked for the stamps, which were much more exotic than our own.

New York was so far away, Mama told us, and the sea journey too long and too arduous, and Papa had far too much to do. That was why he could not come home, not even at Christmas. One day soon, she had promised us, Papa would come home, and it would be for good.

I, for one, had pretended to accept her explanations; I voiced no word of doubt. I had grown over the years to believe her a little – because, as a child, I desperately wanted to. I knew that nothing could take away the shadow of the two tall men at my father's side; nothing could change the fear on Katie and Lily's faces; nothing could truly convince me that Mama's distress that April afternoon in Belfast had been anything other than despair laced with humiliation. Once I had recovered from the initial surprise of Hannah's slip of the tongue, it all made perfect sense to me. I was relieved by her revelation: now I could admit openly to myself that I knew, that I had always known.

That night, locked into Hannah's bedroom, the three of us solemnly swore to each other a sisterly pact: that we would pretend this had never happened, that we would allow the fiction of Papa's travels to take root and to grow with all of us as the truth.

When I think about it now, I am amazed at how expertly we all kept these things, each from the other. If Mama suspected, she never said. And so we lived, each concealing what we knew, child protecting parent just as parent protected child. And now it seemed the day had arrived for Papa to come home. I didn't know how I felt about seeing him again. Would he still call me 'Mouse'? Would he still be the same, or would everything about him have changed dramatically in three years? I couldn't ask these questions, of course. I had to believe what I had just been told: that Mama was sending us all away on a nice holiday to County Cork, where we could get to know our cousins.

I heard her and Hannah's voices, late that night, rising and falling in the empty air of the drawing room. I made myself stay awake, listening for Hannah's footsteps on the landing. I waited until I heard them, and the sound of Mama's door closing.

As silently as I could, I crept out of my room and made my way across to Hannah's bedroom door. I tried the handle noiselessly. It wouldn't give. I was afraid to call her name, afraid that Mama would discover me and that all our secrets would be out. I tried the handle again. Still nothing. Then I remembered the unaccustomed noise I'd heard soon after Mama and Hannah had parted on the landing.

For the first time ever, my sister had locked her door against me.

Hannah: Summer 1896

HANNAH REFUSED TO allow herself be drawn into the company of her girl cousins. At sixteen, she was a year older than Theresa, a full six years older than Frances. She had decided not to be impressed with Bantry; with her aunt and uncle; with their home way out in the countryside, miles away from anything civilized. She maintained an aloof silence, impenetrable in its iciness. Several times, she caught May and Eleanor about to melt, to respond warmly to the shy smiles and tentative invitations of their cousins. She would call them away at once then, ostensibly to braid their hair properly, to write a letter to Mama, to spend time together in their room. Her indignation followed her around like a cloud for four full days, until Uncle Paul brought home the bicycles.

The three girls were in their room after breakfast. The last button had been fastened on May's boot, the last bow tied on Eleanor's unruly braids when they heard a commotion just underneath their window. May and Eleanor fled from their seats by the mirror, not caring about Hannah's disapproval. They had had enough of her, she had already begun to sense their impatience – it was high time for diversion. Hannah had been no fun this week. She had even avoided all occasions for playing the piano. Aunt Elizabeth had not asked her directly, but Hannah could feel the invitation hovering in the air at night after dinner. Theresa's playing was stiff, her fingers wooden; Frances didn't play at all. Hannah felt the chill of her aunt's disapproval on the three occasions when she had kept her head in her book, rather than follow her cousin to the piano. The unspoken rebuke had hung in the air like a question mark.

Now Hannah stood behind her two younger sisters at the big, open sash window that looked out on to the driveway. There, on the gravel sweep in front of the house, were two brand-new, shiny bicycles. Theresa and Frances were jumping up and down in delight, Frances clapping her little plump hands together, her one fat plait leaping up and down her back in contrapuntal rhythm.

'Oh, Papa, are they really for us?'

'Yes,' said Uncle Paul. 'They're for you *and* your cousins. You already know how to cycle, Theresa, so you're to help the others.'

Hannah had the impression that his words were meant to be overheard. He was standing directly beneath their open window. She wasn't quick enough. Just as she had decided to stand back, to move out of his line of sight, he looked up. His broad face was smiling at them, knowingly.

'Come on down, Eleanor, May. Get a turn in before your big sister!'

There was no time to reply. May and Eleanor simply ran from the bedroom, pushing each other to get through the door first, no longer heeding Hannah's call. Reluctantly, she followed them down the wide staircase and out the front door to the driveway.

'It's too difficult here,' Theresa was saying. 'All the little stones make it too hard to pedal. Help me push them down to the gates – the laneway outside is much easier for bicycling.'

There was nothing else for it. Hannah followed the four younger ones as they hurried towards the gates, the high, childish voices of Frances and Eleanor bright in the summer air. Hannah kept her shoulders stiff, her back erect. She couldn't help the feeling that someone was watching them, smiling, from the drawing-room window.

May got the first turn.

Theresa sat on the saddle of one bicycle and instructed May to do exactly as she did.

'Mind you keep your skirts out of the way, otherwise they'll get caught up in the spokes, and you'll fall off. Look.'

Quickly, expertly, Theresa drew her skirts up and sat firmly on the saddle, a great swathe of fabric bunching out from under her. She kept one foot on the ground, the other turning the pedals which made a pleasant, whirring sound. Hannah had a moment's envy: she was older, after all, she should really go first. She had heard about this craze all last year in school: some of the more daring girls already belonged to the women's cycling clubs in Rathmines and Churchtown. Hannah had heard them discuss their outings at weekends accompanied by their older sisters. Some of them wore divided skirts to make the sport less dangerous, and there were whispers of more senior spinster ladies wearing trousers. Despite herself, Hannah had been intrigued. And now, here was her opportunity to try out 'the latest' for herself. She decided the time had come to be kind.

'I'll hold the saddle for you, May, until you get your balance.'

None of the others even noticed her magnanimous gesture. She could take part or not, as far as they were concerned. Theresa continued, enthusiastically addressing herself to May.

'Stand up while you pedal, at first. When you get up a little speed, sit back on the saddle. Hannah, you must run to keep up with her – but don't let her go until she's ready.'

Hannah nodded. Theresa's tone wasn't even bossy: she was far too excited at initiating her cousins into the secret art of bicycling. For once, she was way ahead of them at something.

May took off quickly, Hannah holding on to the saddle as her sister wobbled her way towards finding her balance. Theresa caught up immediately, shouting encouragement, her face already reddening in the sun, her bright hair escaping everywhere.

'That's it! That's it! Now sit! Hannah has you! You're safe!'

The two girls cycled side by side at a good, steady

pace. Hannah began to lose her breath, her boots were hurting her. Suddenly, astonishingly, May seemed to take flight – there was no longer any pressure against Hannah's wrists. She let go of the saddle abruptly, saying nothing. She could hear Theresa's excited shouts, watched as May went speeding away from her. Then just as suddenly as she'd taken off, May began to wobble again. She tried to glance over her shoulder, and the next moment she came crashing to the ground, ending up in a hopeless tangle on the grass verge, half on top of the bicycle, half underneath, the wheels still spinning. Hannah hurried towards her, suddenly anxious.

'May! May! Are you all right?'

May's face was pink and contorted. Hannah was frightened for a moment – was she crying? Had she broken something?

By the time Hannah helped her up, May was helpless with laughter.

'That was *so* wonderful! Hannah, you must try it!'

Theresa's smile seemed to reach all the way to her ears.

'I've never seen anyone do it the first time! Don't look back in future. You only fell off because you knew that Hannah wasn't holding you!'

Eleanor and Frances arrived, breathless, excited, wanting their turn, but too gleefully terrified to try.

'I think Hannah should go next,' said Theresa gravely. 'She can have my bicycle.'

Hannah felt instantly grateful. She understood the gesture of friendship, the need to accept it. It was time to melt, time to be gracious.

'Why, thank you, Theresa.'

She turned at once to little Frances, and smiled at her.

'Then I'll help you, Frances, shall I?'

The small face smiled up at her, bravely trying to conceal her disappointment at being the youngest, the smallest and always the last to try everything.

Hannah stooped and whispered in her cousin's ear.

'I'll give you three turns for every one I get – shall it be our secret?'

The child nodded, her eyes brightening at once.

It took Hannah a lot longer than May, just about the same time as Frances. Seven false starts, three tumbles, one of them painful – although the sense of her status as the eldest was the most badly bruised – and at last she was away.

Aunt Elizabeth finally had to send Nuala from the kitchen to come and fetch them for lunch. The girl arrived at the end of the laneway hot and gasping, her apron flapping, her face creased and cross with effort.

'Did ye not hear me callin'?'

Theresa and Hannah exchanged a conspiratorial glance and followed her meekly back to the house, each of them pushing a bicycle. They were all warm, dusty, and in the highest spirits Hannah could remember for at least three years.

She began to feel the first stirrings of regret about going home.

Eleanor's Journal

I DIDN'T ENJOY the first few days of our holiday in County Cork; nor did Hannah or May. Hannah was furious, and sulked the whole time. May missed Mama terribly, and grieved for her, for home, and for Grandfather Delaney. I wanted to put all thoughts of Papa out of my head, but the more I tried, the more impossible it became. I saw him everywhere, heard him call me 'Mouse', felt his moustaches tickle my cheek as they used to when he said goodnight.

Our girl cousins, Theresa and Frances, were very nice to us, particularly as we showed no appreciation of their kindness at first. I think we made them feel out of their depth: they were at an absolute loss to understand our unfriendliness. Each of the three of us was preoccupied in her own way. Each of us wanted to be home, and, with the cruelty of children, we made sure that our country cousins received the brunt of our discontent. I can still see the way their tentative smiles faded when yet one more overture on their part was rejected by one or all of us.

I think it was on the Thursday that Uncle Paul brought home the two bicycles. That was the turning point. Without their timely arrival, I suspect that our Aunt Elizabeth would have been very glad indeed to see the back of us.

Years later, I was able to tell Theresa, the elder girl, something of what had been happening in our lives at that time. She looked at me blankly – she didn't remember it like that at all. In fact, they had quite enjoyed having three girl cousins to show off to friends and neighbours. They lived out in the countryside, beyond Bantry, and we found their dresses and their accents strange, almost quaint. For their part, they admired our city ways, our different way of speaking. They saw us as somewhat exciting and liked to boast about us, to bask in the innocence of our reflected glory. Once we all learned to bicycle together, the hostility of the first few days disappeared, forgotten by them instantly. They were truly good-natured girls, much too used to being overshadowed by their older brothers, James and Arthur, whom we saw only fleetingly during that week. Theresa's reaction to my confession made me smile at the time, and makes me smile again now: it makes me recall a similar discussion between you and me after our first quarrel. Do you remember how we, too, had cause to ponder the wildly varying memories shared by two different people of the same event?

Lily and Katie came to Cork city to collect us when the week was over. They met us at the station and looked after us on the train journey home. They settled us into our compartment, with strict instructions not to move, and then they left us, reappearing from time to time with food and a thermos of hot chocolate. We became giddier and giddier as the train approached Amiens Street Station. We hadn't spoken of Papa at all during our holiday, but I think each of us knew that he occupied all our thoughts, particularly now, to the exclusion of everything else.

It was May who first brought up the subject.

'I wonder will Papa be there when we get home?'

'I don't know if I care,' said Hannah.

I was shocked. Her expression was cold again, disdainful, and she turned away from us and stared out the window.

Neither May nor I said anything. I think I understood instinctively even then that Hannah felt displaced, that Papa's return would somehow rob her of a privileged place in our household. She had been Mama's confidante for three years, sharing her joys and sorrows. Once Papa was home, she would return to being, simply, a daughter.

He was waiting for us in the drawing room when we reached Leinster Road. He seemed smaller to me, almost sunken, his head withdrawn a little into himself like a tortoise. I know I felt suddenly shy. I looked to Mama, standing with her back to the window. The air in the room was strange, almost brittle, but she was doing her best to smile.

'Hello, Mouse,' he said softly. 'My, but you've grown.'

'Hello, Papa,' I said, accepting his kiss, feeling a little wary. He smelt different, somehow, almost fusty.

He turned to May and kissed her, too. She went bright red and stammered, 'Papa – welcome to our home.'

There was a silence, and his smile faded. May burst into tears and fled from the room. Once her sobs had calmed later, she turned to Hannah and me in bewilderment. She had really meant to say 'Welcome home', but it had all come out wrong. Poor May, she was inconsolable.

I think he kissed Hannah, too, but I can't remember. My memory seems to fall apart at the moment when May ran from the room. I really don't know what happened next.

The following days were subdued. I don't think that anyone even attempted to keep up the subterfuge of New York – we simply never mentioned his absence again.

Papa moved about the house quietly, keeping out of everyone's way, as though he realized he didn't belong. And Mama? I don't know how she struggled through those days. She was the same with us, the same with Grandfather Delaney, and ladies started to come to tea again in the afternoons.

I suppose our lives settled back into some form of normality late that summer. We learned to live around Papa, not quite with him. At twelve years of age, I decided I was no longer comfortable with his calling me 'Mouse'. I was finally growing up. Still, I was reluctant to leave Mama when the time came to go back to school. I felt she needed someone to watch over her and, to be truthful, I felt, too, that Hannah had usurped far too much of her during the previous three years.

Mama was easy to persuade: I think she liked the idea of having me at home. And so the decision was taken that I should go as a day-pupil to Loreto on St Stephen's Green, rather than as a boarder like my sisters. They had each other, so they didn't seem to mind.

I settled into the luxury of my own room, my own books, and Mama. Papa and I circled each other warily for a time, and then he seemed to decide that I wasn't worth the effort.

Hannah: Summer 1896

PAPA'S FACE HAD gone quite white. He seemed not to know what to do with his body. He looked around vaguely, after May had left the drawing room, as though searching for her, or forgiveness, or an escape – it was hard to tell.

Welcome to our home.

The air in the room seemed to grow suddenly still, then fill up with tension. Hannah stood very quietly after May's outburst; Mama stood, unmoving, between the window and the heavy drapes. Her face was turned away from everybody. Nobody seemed inclined to speak. Hannah stepped forward.

'Welcome back, Papa,' she said, and allowed her cheek to receive a trembling kiss. 'I hope you're well.'

'Well, yes, well,' he agreed, nodding his head. There was an eagerness to his tone which saddened Hannah, made her suddenly want to cry. She wasn't sure why she had stepped forward – she supposed it was a mixture of duty, embarrassment at May's faux pas, and a sudden sympathy for the figure standing by the window. It seemed to come to life abruptly, to become Mama again, once the spell of silence had been broken by her father's kiss.

'Papa's tired, dear, he's had a long journey. Perhaps you could ask Lily to bring some tea.'

'Yes, Mama.'

Hannah turned to Eleanor.

'Come, Ellie. Come with me. Mama and Papa need some peace and quiet.'

She had not intended to behave like this at all, but the warm glow of her recent visit to Cork made her disposed to be kind. She had glimpsed a life where it might be possible to feel happy again, carefree, invulnerable: a life where the worst thing that happened was a fall from your bicycle, a dusty dress, some hurt dignity. Besides, she could take little satisfaction now from raging against the shell of a man whose eyes seemed grateful when his eldest daughter condescended to let him kiss her cheek.

Hannah went down the steps to the kitchen, still holding Eleanor's hand. A nervous Lily promised to bring tea at once.

'Let's go and play with May,' whispered Eleanor, once they were out in the hallway again. 'She looked so terribly sad.'

Hannah sighed. She did a rapid mental calculation. It was nearly July. Preparations for boarding school would begin again in late August. Seven full weeks, and then she could count herself as on her way, out of home again.

She wished she could will the time away, or spend the long days in Cork, or be anywhere other than under her parents' roof.

*

September came, and with it the promise of company, of ordered convent days which flowed one into the other without effort, and Miss de Vere.

Hannah felt a small thrill of delight when she thought about the lessons which awaited her. She had been singled out from the other girls after her music examination last term. Miss de Vere took only the brightest and most promising students for extra lessons. Hannah could barely contain her impatience. She wanted to throw herself into something that demanded discipline and focus. And Miss de Vere was known as a demanding teacher. Something of an eccentric, she taught her girls in a way that shouldn't have been successful, but nearly always was. Those she chose became the school's candidates for scholarships with the Royal Irish Academy of Music.

For the last few weeks before returning to school, Hannah thought about nothing else. She had daydreams about being the successful candidate when her final year came, modestly receiving applause, the admiration of others.

The dream brought with it a new determination to succeed. Something so wonderful and undreamt of would go a long way towards drawing a line under the last few unhappy years of everyone's life.

Mary and Cecilia: 1893–1896

ONCE THE DEPOSITION was over, Mary wanted to know nothing more about it. She no longer cared what happened to the likes of Agnes Neill, felt no thirst for revenge. It was over, done, finished with. Now she needed to pay the rent, feed and clothe Cecilia and herself: keep body and soul together, as Ma would say. The only way she could do that was by using all the skills she had garnered over the last six years with Watson, Valentine and Company. She set about doing so, filled with the most extraordinary energy she had ever known.

Mary knew that none of the mills could keep up with the demand for linen handkerchiefs, heard that hemmers were in demand everywhere, all over Belfast. Handkerchiefs, embroidered tablecloths, shirt-finishing: she would do it all, whatever it took, no matter how hard she had to work. She presented herself at York Street mill the Monday after Cecilia's deposition, unwilling to return, ever, to Watson, Valentine and Company. A taciturn foreman pointed her grudgingly towards the warehouse.

She felt almost eager when she saw the giant bundles

of unfinished handkerchiefs, tray cloths and tablecloths. They lay there, rows and rows of them, waiting for her practised fingers.

'What's the piece-rate?' she asked, pointing towards the handkerchiefs. The despatcher was tall, gangly, no more than a lad.

'One and ninepence for twelve dozen, miss.'

Mary was startled, thought she couldn't have heard him correctly.

'How many dozen?'

'Twelve, miss.'

One hundred and forty-four handkerchiefs hemmed and finished for one and ninepence? She felt suddenly shaky, the creeping numbness of disappointment filling all the spaces where hope had so recently been.

'How many stitches to the inch?'

'Sixteen, miss.'

Grimly, Mary carried the bundles home with her on the tram. Cecilia would have to come with her in future: she'd need to carry far more than this if they were to have a hope of surviving. She forced herself to be optimistic, to appear cheerful when she got home. Mary knew that she was good with her needle, that she'd grow quick and accurate before long. She'd find some way for her sister to help, anything to smooth away the lines of worry that were settling into permanent creases on Cecilia's face, making her look old before her time.

She and Cecilia quickly became familiar morning visitors to the York Street warehouse, often arriving long before six o'clock. Mary wanted to be first in line, wanted not to have to see the long queue of bedraggled women, of tattered children, their faces always snotty, their bare feet hard and blackened.

On the first morning she returned with the finished handkerchiefs, Cecilia came with her, holding tight to Mary's arm. She grew nervous long before they drew close to York Street; Mary knew she could smell the mill in the air. She wanted to get her sister in and out of there as quickly as possible. Once her work had been checked, the foreman handed her a chit for her pay. Quickly, Mary scanned the numbers. The sum was not what she had expected, not what she had carefully calculated with Cecilia the previous evening.

''Tis short,' she said. ''Tis more nor a shillin' short, sir.'

She stood her ground, refusing to budge, to lose her place in the queue, until he paid attention to her.

He snatched the piece of paper from her hand.

'Deduction for thread,' he snapped.

Mary looked at him.

'For thread?' she repeated, stupidly.

'Aye, for thread. A shillin' for thread. Take it or leave it, but move away on outa here.'

Mary felt her anger rise in a way she hadn't done for a long time. She used to take it quietly when they fined her for talking or sneaking a drink of water. She had not reared up once, doing all the muckiest, filthiest jobs they gave her. She'd never answered back the spinning master, not once in six years. But this made her blood sing in her ears. She felt angry not just for herself but for all the raggle-taggle line of humanity waiting patiently, hungrily, behind her.

Cecilia tugged at her sleeve. 'Come on, Mary,' she whispered, 'there's no point.'

She moved out of the queue, clutching her new bundles of handkerchiefs and tablecloths, and shed tears of bitterness and frustration. She wanted to dash the bundles on to the cobbles, dance them into the muck with her boots. But Cecilia was right, there was no point. She forced herself to be calm; her rage was making her sister's helpless face whiter by the minute.

'Aye, you're right. I know there's no bloody point. That's what makes me boil, so it does.'

Mary's anger continued to burn over the next several weeks. It was new to her, new and unwelcome, this raging sense of impotence and injustice. She and Cecilia began to hear stories of a Miss Galway, a lady who'd formed a union for women workers. She didn't just help those in the mill, they said, but the homeworkers, too. Mary watched as Cecilia's face grew worried. She had no difficulty reading her sister's expression. She feared Mary's new anger, feared that she might lose her to Mary Galway and the battles that none of them would ever win.

Silently, Mary wished the woman well, but she'd bitten off more than she could chew. Trade unions meant trouble; Mary had seen enough of it in Watson, Valentine and Company. The men in the weaving shed, mostly, fighting against unjust fines, demanding covers for their dangerous shuttles, things like that. Mary's memory of most disputes was the men silently filing back to their looms, sullen, angry, defeated; sometimes worse off than before. Whoever owned the mills in this city had no mercy. Power, yes; but no mercy.

In the early days of Mary's homeworking, the sisters loved being together, sitting over the tiny table in the parlour, piles of fabric covering every surface in the room. It was the closest they had come in years to being happy. Mary would describe each piece to Cecilia as she sewed – the scalloped edges of fine linen tablecloths, the embroidered flowers on matching napkins, the inter-twined initials of a bridal couple on sheets and pillow-cases. Most pieces were heavily ornamented, hard on the fingers and eyes. Mary grew used to the headaches brought on by sprigging, as her eyes strained over complicated patterns, often requiring hundreds of tiny stitches to complete each stem or petal.

Cecilia would make up stories to amuse Mary as she worked, stories about the big houses where all these pieces were to be used. She tried to imagine the luxury of the rooms, the duties of the servants, the quality of an existence which meant sleeping on smooth, fine sheets, rather than ripped-up flour-sacks. But, just as suddenly as she had begun to make up these stories, she stopped. Mary said nothing. She knew that her sister's sightless eyes had made her inner life all the more vivid. Eventually, the imagined pictures became a cruel reminder, day after day, of what she would never be, never have, never see again.

During the first year, Cecilia learned all the finishing

touches Mary could teach her. She used the tips of her fingers to check for knots and stray threads on the reverse side of each piece: she was delicate and accurate, learning by touch how to snip away the loose ends and make each side of the embroidered fabric virtually indistinguishable from the other. She became adept at spotting gaps or unevenness in the stitching, passing the pieces back to Mary, who worked quickly, neatly, confident that any mistakes would be detected by her finisher. Cecilia had even learned to iron and fold the smaller pieces, watched carefully by Mary. At first, she had been terrified that Cecilia would burn herself. She would heat the flat iron on the fire to the right temperature, and watch as Cecilia measured the distance from cloth to iron, using her hands to see. Mary had admired her sister's deftness: whatever else had been forgotten from Cecilia's other life, the skills of needlework were remembered by her hands, which were still strong and beautiful. The only part of her, Mary reflected bitterly, that hadn't been damaged beyond repair. It took Cecilia some time to grow accustomed to using the iron without her eyes to guide her. There had been scalds and burns in the early days, but not enough to quench her determination, her enthusiasm to be useful.

They survived. Mary divided everything they earned into individual piles of coin. Three shillings for rent, a shilling for food, sixpence towards material for a new skirt, or fixing their boots, or perhaps just a tram ride to the Botanic Gardens on a Sunday. She tried to save, as well, not telling Cecilia what she was saving for. Every week, she calculated how much she would need to put by for Cecilia, for the doctor, for medicines. She knew that the day was coming.

Mary had been aware of its approach for months, watched its stealthy, shadowy progress. First the loss of appetite, then the weariness when it seemed that Cecilia no longer had the strength to use her arms. Her head seemed to have grown more fragile, yet heavier too: for long stretches of each day, she could not summon the strength to lift it. Her face had grown paler, skin stretched tight across the cheekbones. Mary could trace the fine network of tiny blue veins underneath the opalescent surface. A death sentence, written in blue ink on the parchment of her face. The blank, empty eyes became bigger and bigger.

Neither of them spoke of it. Mary stayed bright, cheerful, allowing herself to worry only when she was alone. Cecilia slept more and more during the day now, and Mary worked downstairs, ears constantly on the alert for any restless murmurings from the bedroom above. The younger girl had taken to talking in her sleep, becoming more and more agitated until she would finally struggle into wakefulness, clawing at something invisible, fighting for breath. Mary would open the window then, and they would sit together on the edge of the bed, Cecilia gulping lungfuls of the dirty night air until, gradually, the panic subsided. These assaults had become more and more frequent over the past few months, and Mary felt frightened.

And now, almost three years after Cecilia's attack, Mary watched as her sister seemed to grow smaller with each passing day. She seemed to become separate from everything around her; it was as though her very presence was gradually diminishing. Finally, she no longer wanted to eat. Her face was ghastly against the white pillowcase which Mary had embroidered for her, the swirling, silky letters of 'Cecilia' stretching all across its cool surface.

'C'mon, love,' Mary said tenderly, trying to spoon some clear soup into Cecilia's reluctant mouth. She turned away, her face to the wall.

'Leave me alone,' was all she'd say.

Then the fever came back. Mary sat with her for three nights, bathing her forehead, reminded cruelly of the first forty-eight hours after the attack. Then, it had been the loss of Cecilia's sight which had terrified her; now, she knew that the slow disappearance of her sister's spirit, her will to fight, was a far more serious loss. Mary sent Myles to ask Dr Torrens to come, as soon as he could. Exhausted, she sat with her sister until the chill, grim hours of dawn, falling herself into an uneasy, dream-filled doze which brought her no rest.

On the third morning, Cecilia's eyes would not open. By the time Dr Torrens arrived, she had slipped away, her body already cold to the touch, unresponsive to the warmth of her sister's weeping.

Myles comforted her as best he could. Everybody came to the wake, bringing food and drink, overwhelming Mary with their generosity. Kindness was everywhere. But there was no relief for her. She had become obsessed by the vision of her whole family leaving this place: first her brothers, then three coffins: lives all blighted and blunted, each in its own way, by this unforgiving city. Myles watched over the storms of Mary's grief and waited for what he thought was a decent interval.

'Marry me, Mary,' he said, a week after Cecilia's funeral. 'Let me take care of you, like I wanted to before. There's nothin' stoppin' us.'

He was sitting in Mary's house, watching the speed of her needle, admiring the ease with which she embroidered a crisp linen tray cloth. Her stitches filled in the outline of a large basket containing dozens of what looked like sprigs of lavender. It had hurt him that she had had to go back to working so soon after her sister's death. Mary looked at him, his hands callused and blackened by years of oil and soot, his face streaked with grime. She had refused to discuss marriage with him, for as long as Cecilia survived. Now she knew she could put him off no longer. Underneath, she could see his anxiety, and one part of her wanted to say 'yes', wanted to be relieved of responsibility, to be taken care of. But the days after Cecilia's death had brought with them the harshness of realization. If she stayed here, and married solid, decent Myles, her life would never change. This house, this street, held too many memories for her. Da, Ma and now Cecilia. It was a nonsense to feel she would be looked after, even for a while. Her life, and the lives of those around her, were not built for ease or rest.

Mrs McNiff was still ailing, in need of care. 'The creakin' door', Ma used to call people like her. Always ill, but always surviving; she'd see all of them six feet under, while she went on to complain and creak and groan well into her nineties, just like her own mother had. There were years and years left in her, Mary knew, when she would need looking after.

She had been ashamed of her selfishness the first time she had had the thought: but it wouldn't leave her alone. It fought for space inside her head along with grief for Cecilia, anger at the hand life had dealt her, and the lonely certainty that she did not want to live like this for ever. She couldn't tell all of this to Myles: he wouldn't understand. He would probably despise her for her callousness, her betrayal of all she had known, and he might be right.

Cecilia's stories of big houses and servants and crystal and china had awoken something in Mary, some instinct which had returned to poke and prod at her over the last week to give her no peace. She wanted to be surrounded by something other than the grim streets around Carrick Hill, their ugliness and struggle. She wanted warmth and security, even if it had to be under some stranger's roof. She wanted to hide herself away where things were different, to work and sleep, sleep and work until each day ran numbly into the next and she could begin to bear her life again without Cecilia.

'I can't, Myles; I'm sorry.'

She almost crumbled then, as his eyes clouded over with hurt and bewilderment.

'I'll be good to ye, I'll look after ye. I'd've looked after wee Cecilia too, if ye'd only let me.'

She shook her head.

'I know, I know. I just can't stay here any longer.'

His face darkened, became closed to her.

'Is it someone else that ye have in mind?'

She didn't know what he meant for a moment.

'Jesus, no. There's nobody. I just want out o' here. I need to go . . . somewhere else. There's nothin' for me to stay for.'

She hadn't meant it like that, never meant to hurt him. But there was no easy way to do this. At the same time as she spoke and watched his eyes fill, a small, panicked voice inside her was asking *Are you sure? You're burnin' yer boats, you know. What else is out there for the likes o' you?*

Myles stood up. He spoke softly.

'That's grief talk. I'll not let ye go that easy. But I'll not trouble ye any longer the night.'

He began to walk towards the door. His quiet step had a heartbreaking dignity to it, and Mary had to stop herself from running after him, from throwing her arms around his neck, and begging him to forgive her. The words were there already, formed in her mind, waiting for her signal. They would come if she bade them, falling gratefully from her tongue. Myles would do his best to keep her safe, her life predictable, surrounded by all that was familiar. And who could know? Wasn't there a chance he might even succeed?

She kept her feet firmly rooted to the floor, standing her ground. Her hands were clenched by her sides, her mouth closed tight, all her senses controlled. She feared that some look, some gesture would succeed in betraying her while she wasn't watching. Then the door clicked to and he was gone.

Mary made herself tea in the kitchen and brought her mug up to bed. She sipped at it until the trembling stopped. Then she quenched the candle and lay down in the darkness.

Her head was whirling, buzzing with what she had just done. She felt cold and bereft. She stretched her hand out to where Cecilia's warm shape should be. The cold roughness of the sheet brought the tears then, and she cried until she was empty.

Part Two: 1896–1900

Eleanor's Journal

I WAS MUCH older before I found out what had transpired behind closed doors between Mama, Papa and Hannah on the day they brought her home from school. And by then, of course, everything was very different. Nevertheless, with a fourteen-year-old's heightened fear of change, I knew that nothing was ever going to be the same for our household again. I have always known that grown-ups pay very little attention to the children around them in times of crisis. The common perception seems to be that children do not understand what is happening – that they are somehow impervious to grief, or suffering, or calamity. Nothing could be further from the truth. I know that I got through those days feeling as though I were living with the inside of my skin turned out: I felt the impact of the conflict and the turmoil around me with an acute sensitivity that was akin to physical pain.

And it was not the first time I had lived like that. A full five years earlier, at the too tender age of nine, I had met similar upheaval and suffering in our house in Belfast, and I soaked up the residue like a sponge. I had learned then that shame and betrayal are no respecters of social position or comfort or contentment: they strike where they will. It was a lesson I was becoming practised in learning, one I was never to forget.

When Hannah would not look at me that day, the day they brought her home from school, I feared that, once again, catastrophe had chosen our unfortunate household. I remember I sat on the staircase outside the drawing room, trying desperately to catch anything of the animated conversation going on inside. I tried to squeeze my head between the wooden spindles, and then became frightened that I might become stuck there. I think I would have been prepared to pay the price if I could have provided a welcome distraction for my sister – and for myself. All I could do was feel the anguish of the situation: I didn't even have May by my side for some sharing of comfort. I could hear Hannah's voice, but I could not make out the words. I was too terrified to move from my step, to go any closer to the drawing room – I knew that if I put my ear to the door, it would suddenly be wrenched open and I should be discovered. Mama always had an uncanny instinct for misbehaviours such as that.

When Hannah emerged, tall and angry, I was relieved. There were no tears; to my childish eyes, that meant that nothing could be really badly wrong. As she passed me on the staircase she put one hand gently on the top of my head. I remember that I understood what that gesture was saying: not now, Ellie, not now. Of course, our conversations since then may well have influenced that particular memory, but I know distinctly that I felt reassured, included again.

It was the last time for some weeks that I was to feel anything loving from Hannah. She locked herself away, and would see no one, not even me or May. I thought she would never come out of her room, never eat, never cease weeping. I was terrified that she would starve, waste away to nothing. With my passion for ghost stories at that time, I imagined that we would break down her door one day and discover her wasted body on the bed. Her restless, unhappy spirit would return to haunt us, torturing us for ever for our lack of kindness to her. I don't remember when I was told, or discovered for myself, the cause of her grief. I seem to have absorbed the information somehow, perhaps by instinctively putting two and two together, or, more likely, by listening at doors – a bad habit which took me many years of self-discipline to cure.

Mary: Spring 1896

MARY COULDN'T STAND it any longer. The house without Cecilia was too sad, too empty, yet still full of her. Everywhere she looked, she could see her sister: brewing tea in the kitchen, seeing her way by her fingertips to the tea caddy, the spoon, the mugs; standing by the fire ironing handkerchiefs, her strong hands smoothing the fine linen; sitting in the small parlour, across the table from Mary, checking cloths for stray threads and imperfections. Even the bed felt too big to Mary.

Myles had come back again and again, as she'd been afraid he might. Sometimes, he waited for her in the mornings, accompanied her to her tram. In the evenings, he would find some excuse to come and visit. Each time, it got harder to send him away. Each time, Mary was conscious of what it looked like to the neighbours: she was keeping company with Myles as far as they were concerned, accepting his attentions, behaving in every way as a bride-to-be.

'We can look for a wee house somewheres else, Mary – we don't have to stay around Carrick Hill.'

He was sitting by the fire, his long frame almost

folded into the small armchair. Mary was ironing table-cloths. Not for the first time, the comfortable domes-ticity of this scene threatened to weaken her resolve. Myles was being his usual solid, reasonable self – picking off her arguments one by one.

'Your mother'd never move, Myles – an' it wouldn't be fair to ask her.'

He shrugged.

'We wouldn't be able to go at once, but the day would come, soon enough.'

Mary was suddenly horrified. He was a good son, Myles was, a good man – and here he was, as good as wishing his mother dead on her account. This was wrong: she didn't even want to be having these conver-sations. She'd already made up her mind, but he didn't seem to be listening. Every word she said he filled with hope, heard what he wanted to hear. She was going to have to bolt her door against him. They could not be friends, not now.

She had to put a stop to it, and soon.

Father MacVeigh listened to her, as she knew he would. He made no comment until she was finished.

'You must be sure about this, Mary. There'd be no going back.'

She nodded.

'Aye, that's what I want, Father – a clean break. I wanted to do it while Cecilia was alive, but – we never got the chance.'

He waited until her tears had subsided.

'It's very early days, Mary,' he said gently. 'You haven't even begun to get over Cecilia yet. Being among strangers, especially in service, would be very difficult for you – you can't leave your grief behind, you know. You must take it with you.'

'I know that. I just can't stay here, knowing I'll never get out, not for the rest of my life.'

'And Myles McNiff?'

'He's a good man, so he is, but he's trapped here, just like the rest of us. Father, I have to go while I still can.'

The priest sighed.

'Very well, Mary. Of course I'll help you. I'll get in touch with Father Maguire, he'll have plenty of contacts. I'll come by and see you on Friday.'

'Thank you, Father.' And Mary fled.

It was done. Five more days and she'd know. She'd take all the work York Street would give her in the meantime. Work all day, stay close to home all night, out of Myles's way. She could do it, she knew she could.

Hannah: Spring 1898

NOT ONE WORD was spoken in the brougham.

Hannah forced herself to be quiet, while the air between her parents seemed to fizz and crackle. She was not going to break this explosive silence: there was too much at stake to rush into pleas, demands, explanations. They would all have to wait until home.

She kept her eyes lowered. Her parents radiated that peculiar warm stillness of suppressed anger, a stillness long familiar to their eldest daughter. Hannah had learned to feel its presence between them, could measure its intensity by the shape of an eyebrow, the curve of a lip.

Every line of her mother's profile spoke of agitation. In the seat opposite, her father kept his gaze directed out the window, but Hannah could tell he was looking at nothing in particular. His thumbs were anchored firmly to his waistcoat pockets – a sure sign that he was keeping his hands under control, resisting the urge to finger his moustaches.

Hannah was pleased that whatever rage they were suppressing no longer had the power to distress her. She had discovered a new and secure sense of herself, a quietness inside that was unusual. She felt that she was invulnerable. Whatever it was they had to say to her, she was ready for them. She felt calm, determined, ready for a fight.

All sorts of new possibilities had been expanding before her in the last few weeks. The joy of her musical talent seemed to have opened out her life before her, like the bright promise of water. Opportunities to be other than she was, to live a different kind of life, to be fulfilled and independent of her parents – all this seemed to be there for the taking now, unfolding before her astonished eyes. Miss de Vere's praise and Hannah's own growing confidence made her life feel like *hers*, in a way she had never imagined. She would do anything to hold on to that new vision of herself, now that she was, at last, certain of the kind of life she wanted. She needed to tread carefully. Hannah felt strongly that whatever was about to happen this afternoon must not affect the shape of her future; she had to make sure of that.

Sister Claire had come fussing into the classroom during French. There was some urgent whispering between her and Mademoiselle. The girls had looked up eagerly then; any distraction was worthwhile, anything to relieve the monotony of irregular verbs in the *passé composé*. Mademoiselle looked directly at Hannah and nodded. For a moment, Hannah felt a faint flutter of excitement. Was it something to do with the scholarship? Was Miss de Vere waiting for her, nursing the news that would help her change her life?

The other girls were all looking at her. There was some nudging and whispering as she gathered up her books. She didn't care. There had been a slight frostiness in the air towards her once it became known that Miss de Vere and Sister Claire had singled her out for special attention, that she was the school's great hope for the Royal Irish Academy of Music. Now some of the faces around her were smug. They seemed to know something she didn't. Their eyes wished disappointment on her. That's what you get, they seemed to say, for thinking you're better than everyone else.

Hannah followed Sister Claire down the corridor. The elderly nun said nothing, just glided along the polished floors, the skirts of her black habit sweeping along smoothly. She looks as though she's on wheels, Hannah thought, wanting to giggle.

The principal opened the door to her office, bustled over to her desk, and nodded at Hannah to close the door behind her. She seemed nervous, more edgy and fussy even than usual.

'Your parents are coming this afternoon to collect you, Hannah,' she said briskly, seeming to recover her composure once they were safely inside her territory. She immediately began rearranging the papers on her desk. Hannah felt stung by her curtness, as though she had already been rudely dismissed. 'You will need to gather up your things.' The nun's long fingers seemed to become even busier; she had eyes only for her task.

Hannah looked at her stupidly, not understanding.

'Why, Sister Claire?' she said.

It was a genuine question, not a challenge to author-ity. Hannah felt everything around her sag somehow, slow down, while her heart speeded up. Why were

Mama and Papa coming for her like this? How long would she have to be away? She began to experience real fear, a new and profound sense of her own powerlessness. She didn't want to be taken home. She didn't want to be *taken* anywhere. She waited for an answer, still looking at Sister Claire. The nun grew cross under the girl's scrutiny. With an obvious effort, she raised her eyes.

'I understand that you have made . . . certain arrangements . . . with Miss de Vere. Arrangements of which your parents do not necessarily approve.'

'Do you mean the scholarship, Sister Claire?'

Hannah was immediately relieved – if *that* was the problem, then she was ready, eager to solve it. Miss de Vere was so much on her side that, together, they could persuade anyone of the rightness of what they proposed. *A God-given talent*, Miss de Vere had said. Who would want to thwart a gift from God?

'I am not privy to all the details, Hannah,' Sister Claire said stiffly, and Hannah knew she was lying. She had given her approval to Miss de Vere, Hannah was sure of that. No teacher in the school moved without permission from Sister Claire. She would have given it willingly, Hannah suspected, would have wanted to see the school covered in glory, basking in the success of one of its pupils. We did that, she'd be able to say; that's the sort of girl the Loreto produces. Now she was taking a step back, abdicating all responsibility once the possibility of conflict with parents arose. Hannah wanted to say all of this, but knew that she couldn't.

Perhaps if she remained calm, kept her composure, she could still get what she wanted.

Sister Claire dismissed her brusquely, and sent her off to the dormitory to pack. As Hannah made her way down the corridor she deliberately tried to slow down her frantic thoughts. She made herself think back to less than two months ago, to the day when she had played one of Chopin's nocturnes for Miss de Vere. Nothing could have changed that much, surely not within two short months? She wanted to feel the exhilaration of that day again, that sense of expanding possibilities, of a future there for the taking. She closed her eyes, remembering the stillness that had enveloped her once she'd sat down to play. Miss de Vere sat silent, as usual, to her right, one hand poised to turn the pages of Hannah's well-thumbed manuscript. Her pencilled notes were everywhere, guiding her pupil, focusing her technique. Once Hannah had begun to play for her, she felt time slip away somewhere; it was no longer a measurable quantity. She felt far from her surroundings, worlds away from everything that was familiar. Her spirit began to respond to the music in a way that was new and aching in its tenderness.

As the last notes died away, Miss de Vere had stood up from her chair and clapped loudly, enthusiastically. Her normally pale, rather anxious face was pink with delight, and now she clasped her hands together for emphasis. Her small figure was suddenly animated, as though lit from within.

'Hannah, that was wonderful, truly wonderful! Your playing was simply flawless.'

Hannah found the courage to look directly into her teacher's eyes. She felt proud of what she had achieved, full of warmth towards the woman who had made it possible.

'Thank you, Miss de Vere. I couldn't have done it without you. I'm very grateful.'

Hannah blushed as she spoke, feeling the colour creep up her cheeks. She had practised her words of gratitude silently, over and over, for days now. She admired Miss de Vere as she admired no other person in her life. She wanted, passionately, to be like her. Her selfless dedication to her music, to her pupils, to her life as a teacher inspired Hannah, made her long for the same sort of life for herself.

She'd had a recurring daydream over the last few weeks as they had worked closely together on piece after piece, preparing for the school's end-of-year recital. She had even become a little embarrassed by the vividness of her fantasy, often looking around her guiltily in class in case one of the nuns or one of the other girls was looking at her, knowing what she was thinking. She was terrified they would think her foolish. She had imagined both of them, an unchanged Miss de Vere and her older self, working together, teaching music, perhaps even running their own school. She had never thought about her future properly before, never really looked further than the end of her last term. But since last September, she hadn't been able to stop wondering what would happen to her once the security and predictability of boarding school were finally behind her. She had found herself longing to talk to Mama and Papa about what was to become of her. Over the past months, she had had the growing feeling that she was, at last, discovering the purpose of her own life.

She began to feel calmer. She welcomed the slow return of confidence in her own abilities: that glowing sense that had become stronger, more familiar over the weeks of constant, exhausting playing. Once Mama and Papa really knew, really understood that she was good, truly good, they would give her their blessing, surely. After all, they were both musical – Mama had a fine soprano voice, Papa loved opera. Perhaps it was some-thing to do with money; perhaps they were worried about fees, didn't understand that there would be a *scholarship*. Without that, of course, she would never dream . . .

Hannah wondered what exactly Miss de Vere had written to her parents. Perhaps her letter had been such an unexpected thing that they were disturbed by the novelty of what it proposed, anxious on their daughter's behalf. Perhaps all they needed was reassurance. With-holding their approval for now did not mean that they would never give it, surely?

All traces of calm suddenly evaporated and Hannah's head began to ache with the unexpected complications of what last week had seemed so desirable, so simple. She would make them proud of her, then they would see the justness of what she wanted. They would see her at the end-of-year recital, would appreciate that she wasn't just a competent musician, but that she had real talent. She would remind them of the parable that was one of Grandfather's favourites: talents were to be *used*, not buried.

There would be no help from Sister Claire anyway, that much was clear. By the time she got to the dormitory, her trunk had already been retrieved for her from the trunk room. It stood beside the bed, shiny and still new-looking. Hannah found its presence some-how menacing. It was only a *trunk*, she told herself impatiently, but she couldn't shake the feeling that its presence right here, now, conveyed an unhappy truth. It was too large, too solid – it spoke of long journeys, long absences from what she now regarded as her home.

Quickly, she put some of her clothes and books in, leaving the rest in her cupboard. She'd be back in a day or so. Her pieces for the recital still weren't perfect, particularly Satie's strange and exciting 'Trois Saraban-des'. She knew they needed more work, but she'd have time enough for that. She stacked the sheet music neatly on the top shelf, ready for her return. Miss de Vere would wait for her, as demanding and exacting as ever. She must talk to her now, before Mama and Papa arrived. She needed urgently to find out what the letter had told them, even what Sister Claire had said before she had so cravenly changed her mind. She needed to reassure herself that she had a strong chance of one of the scholarships, at least. Once she knew that for sure, she was prepared to do whatever fighting it took.

Hannah desperately did not want to let this chance go, did not want to be an ornament in her parents' drawing room, waiting until the time came to show off her accomplishments to some suitable man. She did not want to be condemned to a life of drawing pretty pictures, playing party songs on the piano and leaving visiting cards at all the most suitable homes in Dublin. That was not going to be her life. She had glimpsed another way, a way which promised dedication, usefulness, a life of significance. Even if she never became a performer, even if she weren't nearly good enough for that, she could still be like Miss de Vere, and teach. She tried to respect her mother and father, always: knew that it was her duty as their daughter to do so. But she also knew, from unhappy past experience, that parents were not always right.

She left the dormitory quickly, taking the back stairs to the music room, in case she was stopped on the main staircase. She listened outside the door for a moment; no lesson was going on. Miss de Vere must be in there on her own. Gently, Hannah knocked on the door. No answer. She tried again, knocking harder this time. Still nothing. She tried the handle, turning it slowly, noiselessly. It wouldn't give. She was surprised. Never, in almost five years, had the music-room door been locked. Pupils were always free to enter at any time, to practise whenever they had a spare moment. Miss de Vere had never believed in constant supervision: she believed her pupils had a duty to develop the skills of independent learning.

There was the distinctive sound of wheels on gravel. Keeping carefully to one side, Hannah looked out the window opposite the music room, knowing already what she would see. The door opened and Papa descended from the brougham, holding his hand out to Mama, who followed. It couldn't be helped, she'd have to go.

Hannah ran along the corridor again, down the back stairs, around the corner and into the dormitory once more. She sat on her bed, as though she'd been waiting there all the time. Sister Louisa, a sweet old nun who no longer taught due to her failing sight, appeared at the doorway a couple of minutes later.

'Hannah O'Connor? Sister Claire is waiting for you.'

'Thank you, Sister Louisa.'

The elderly nun gestured towards Hannah's trunk.

'Don't worry, dear. We'll get Mr Peters to bring it to the carriage for you.' She hesitated for a moment, then placed her hand gently on Hannah's arm. She peered up at her, her weak blue eyes magnified hugely by the thick lenses of her glasses. 'Such a shame, my dear,' she whispered. 'You have always been a delightful pupil, a real asset to the school.'

Hannah smiled at her.

'I'm not leaving, Sister Louisa, at least, not for good. I'm just going home for a day or so. My parents – I, that is we – have some things to discuss. But I'll be back again. Can you tell Miss de Vere for me in case I don't see her before I go?'

The old nun looked confused. She patted Hannah's hand distractedly, said, 'Yes, yes, my dear, of course,' and then led the way to the front parlour, where all guests were received.

Hannah knocked on the door. She entered immediately. There was no sign of Sister Claire. Mama was seated by the old fireplace, Papa was standing, his back to her, looking out the large window into the gardens.

She kissed both of them.

'Mama, Papa, I'd like it very much if we could try to see Miss de Vere . . .'

Before she'd even finished speaking, her mother stood up.

'That won't be possible, Hannah. There are some matters your father and I need to discuss with you, at home. We are leaving at once.'

Hannah looked from one to the other. Tension was etched deeply into the lines at the sides of her mother's mouth. Her face was closed, empty of all expression. Her eyes were looking down at her hands as she pulled on her gloves. Her father's face looked deeply shadowed; he wouldn't leave his moustaches alone.

Hannah decided to stay silent. The convent parlour was not the place, this was obviously not the time. She followed her mother out the door. When she got outside, her trunk had already been safely stowed in the brougham.

They made their way quickly around St Stephen's Green. The rapid blurring of the railings as they passed made Hannah feel slightly dizzy. Her stomach began to feel restless, edging towards nausea. But she would not look away. She had decided to gaze intently out the window to keep her eyes directed away from her parents. Any glance, any movement might break the deepening silence, and Hannah was determined not to speak now until she was home. She turned slightly away from them, seeming to find much to interest her in the carriages lined up outside Harcourt Street Station, and the purposeful air of passengers on their way to and from the trains. It started to rain as they made their way down the Rathmines Road, one of those always unexpected April cloudbursts. Hannah watched as the Town Hall receded into the distance, its facade darkening as the rain soaked everything on the street within minutes. Some young men dashed for shelter under the trees, women struggled with their umbrellas. It was all so ordinary. Other people's lives just carried on as normal. Hannah held on to the window frame as the brougham turned sharply up the Rathgar Road. Just one more turn into Highfield Road, and then they would be home.

Hannah was conscious of her heartbeat beginning to quicken. She glanced anxiously in her parents' direction, but nothing had changed. She took a deep breath, trying to calm herself for the last few moments of the journey. She decided to close her eyes then and play to herself the final notes of Chopin's Nocturne, Opus 15, No. 1. Hannah could see the sheet music before her, her fingers resting on the gleaming keys of the piano; could hear the dying notes, as clear and resonant as the day she had performed for Miss de Vere. She remembered the sudden elation she had felt, the strong sense that something wonderful had just happened. Her fingertips thrilled with the memory of their own success. She had done well that afternoon, and she knew it.

Everything that day had struck her as beautiful.

Waiting by the window for Miss de Vere, she had looked out on to the convent grounds below suffused with the russet glow of an autumn afternoon; the silence of the music room had been intensified by the light flooding on to the polished floorboards; even Sister Louisa's star-gazer lilies, arranged in the glass vase on the piano, seemed more highly perfumed than usual, filling the air all around her. All of her senses had felt heightened, receptive. It was as though she were living the day with the volume turned up. *Forte*; the thought had pleased her.

And now this.

Whatever her parents had in mind, whatever the source of their anger, Hannah knew that, in some way not yet defined, their plans did not include their eldest daughter becoming a teacher. Chopin's melodies faded into nothingness as the wheels of the brougham came to an abrupt, gravelly stop outside the door to her home.

Hannah could feel Eleanor's eyes on her as she ascended the steps to the front door. She had spotted her at once, the small anxious face peeping out from behind the drapes in the drawing room. Hannah had no time to speak to her, they simply exchanged a glance, sharing the intimate sisterly knowledge that something was wrong. Her mother sent Eleanor away at once.

'What is it?' said Hannah, once the door had closed behind her sister.

'We've had a letter from a Miss de Vere, about your going on to study music in the autumn.'

Hannah wondered why she said '*a* Miss de Vere' like that, as though she'd never met her. Mama well knew who *the* Miss de Vere was; why was she making it sound as though she were some anonymous person, one of thousands of Misses de Vere?

'Yes,' said Hannah, 'but only if I get the scholarship. She thinks I have a very good chance. I'm well prepared and . . .'

At this, Hannah's father raised his hand. She stopped.

'It's not possible,' he said, simply.

'But Papa, I really want this. I know I could be good enough, and the scholarship would pay all my fees. I can teach . . .'

'This is not just about money, Hannah.'

Her mother's voice was sharp. Hannah realized she had touched, too soon, on the most painful topic of all.

'Nor is life just about doing what you want. It is about doing your duty.'

Hannah stayed silent. She thought that this was probably the first time that she had really hated her mother and all that she stood for. She could feel unaccustomed anger begin to burn somewhere deep in her stomach.

'Papa?'

'We have made other arrangements for you, Hannah. You are a young woman now, ready for adult responsibility.'

He stopped.

'May I know what my responsibility is to be?'

Hannah spoke quietly. She had begun to shake

inside. She knew what was coming. She was proud of herself that she gave nothing away, no hint of dismay, no quiver of anger: her voice was cold, steady. She had the satisfaction of seeing her mother fidget with the gloves in her lap, her father's chin grow weak and uncertain. She waited.

'We feel it best that you marry, early next year. We feel it is in everybody's interest that you do so.'

Her father was not looking at her.

'May I ask how so?'

'No, you may not.' Her mother was clearly losing patience. 'You will be married as we think best. It is our duty to secure your future for you. Marriage will do that, and we are happy that we have chosen well.'

Hannah looked levelly at her mother. She would not lower her gaze. She would never have been able to utter the words, but her eyes were clear and challenging. A secure future through marriage? they asked silently. Just like yours?

Sophia flushed angrily and turned away.

'May I know to whom?'

Hannah wanted only to remain composed now. She would not let them break her.

'Charles MacBride,' her father replied. 'You already know Mrs MacBride, Constance, . . . from . . . before. They are an old, respectable Belfast family.'

Hannah wondered if he was finished yet. She said nothing.

'He's a good man, a very good man,' he added, almost appealingly.

He wanted her to absolve him, she realized. He

wanted her to make him feel better for selling off his eldest daughter. For money was at the bottom of it; of that she had no doubt. 'Respectable' families, 'good' families, 'well-regarded' families – she had become used to the words her parents used, down through the years, had learned to read the secret vocabulary they shared, the real significance that lay concealed just below the surface of their speech. All these words meant the same thing: rich families, moneyed people. Old money, new money, fortunes made in trade – her parents had a complex system of gradation for everyone they knew. Everything depended on the extent of one's wealth; once that was established, only then did the manner of its acquisition become important. Old fortunes, inherited from generation to generation, were better than new, unexpected wealth from the stock exchange; stocks and bonds were, in turn, significantly better than money amassed through trade, however old and respectable the business. Finally, old money from trade was unquestion-ably better than new. 'Nouveau riche' was the supreme insult, implying, as it did, the resources to live like a gentleman without the pedigree and the savoir faire to do so. Life well lived was a right, a *duty*, conferred by long years of privilege. Hannah felt keenly the supreme irony of her parents' snobbery. They had nothing, it seemed to her. Even this *house* belonged to Grandfather Delaney – they lived on his charity, leaving Leinster Road quickly, discreetly, on Papa's return from prison. Once the epitome of solid, unflashy respectability, her father, the government man, was now nothing more than the career civil servant turned thief.

All the old contempt for him that she had tried to suppress for five long years welled to the surface now. She didn't care any longer. They could punish her in any way they chose. Nothing could be worse than this.

'Well,' she said. 'You want me to be married. To a respectable man.'

The emphasis on 'respectable' was just enough to make her father flinch. He looked at her, without replying.

She kept her voice steady, smoothed the front of her dress. She needed to do something to stop the shaking of her hands.

'I hope,' she said softly, 'that you got a good price.'

She turned on her heel and made her way, steadily, towards the drawing-room door.

'How dare you!'

Sophia's voice exploded into the stunned silence.

'Let her go, woman!'

Her father's anger followed Hannah out of the drawing room. She stepped outside into the hallway, and closed the door very gently behind her, waiting until she heard the click.

Eleanor was sitting on the stairs, waiting for her. Hannah made her way past, holding her breath. She could not stop, not now. She placed her hand on top of her sister's smooth hair, and continued to make her way up to her room.

She closed and locked the door. She felt as though her body had become suddenly brittle, about to shatter. It seemed to be made up of millions of tiny pieces, like the cracked glaze she had seen on vases in the museum.

She climbed on to the bed, lay on her back, and covered her face with her arms. She hadn't even the will to cry. She stayed there, all night, ignoring the calls at her door.

Eventually, they left her alone. She listened as the last set of footsteps made its way downstairs. She could stay here for ever, she thought. She wrapped herself in the counterpane, still in her day-dress, and slept.

The night had been a restless one. A long thin thread of oblivion, it had been disturbed every so often by dreams which struggled to the surface, breaking into the air like shrill, discordant notes. She had been back in the music room at school again, but a room which had lost all the warmth of its recent familiarity. Everything was arranged differently, with its own peculiar dream logic. The metronome swayed silently, and Miss de Vere looked on disapprovingly as Hannah's fingers refused to touch the black keys, no matter how hard she tried.

She could feel her underarms grow damp. She tried to tell her teacher that everything had been so right, earlier. She had practised her Chopin endlessly, joyfully, for days. Her hands had skimmed delicately over the notes, loving the dip and dive of tone and rhythm, the quick swoops of bright melody and dark brooding that had flowed effortlessly from her, hour after hour.

And now it was all slipping away from her. It was as though all her skill, all her inspiration had deserted her. Her fingers felt thickened by stupidity. Even her eyes were paralysed, powerless to stop the slow confusion, the blur of notes across her vision. For a sudden moment of brittle revelation, the minims and quavers, crotchets and semi-quavers seemed to be nothing more than meaningless black marks, like tiny footprints scattered across the sheet in front of her, marching away from her. It was as though she had never seen them before, as though she had suddenly lost the power to understand their language, once as familiar to her as speech.

She crashed both hands on to the piano, sending a wave of silence washing around the emptiness of her bedroom.

Her eyes jerked open. Her palms were sweaty, her hair in disarray. Hannah covered her face with her hands, remembering yesterday, remembering what had happened. She lay very still, re-imagining the music room which up until yesterday had been filled with optimism and purpose. Now, it felt flat and stale, all its tranquillity shattered. She could still recapture the smell of wax, the sterile cleanliness of the gleaming wood, the watery midday light filtering through the crowding oak trees just beyond the windows.

Hannah wanted to hold on to those earlier feelings, when possibility and optimism had fuelled her every moment, but Papa's voice kept intruding. *You must make no plans. First and foremost, you have duties to others*. Hannah wished the words away into meaninglessness, but they would not leave her.

She would stay in her room for the rest of her life – she hated everyone, hated what they were forcing her to be. She would run away, and then they would be sorry. She would find Miss de Vere—

There was a knock on her door.

'Hannah? Your father and I would like to see you. Downstairs in the drawing room, please, at once.'

Mama's voice was brisk, matter of fact. There was no trace of appeal, no note of contrition.

Hannah did not reply.

She would not go to them. She would die rather than marry Charles MacBride.

They would never force her. Never, never.

Eleanor's Journal

I DON'T REMEMBER consciously setting out to draw
Hannah from her room, but I must have had an
instinctual understanding that the piano played a large
role in her refusal to be part of the family. I had never
known our house so silent before, so bereft of music. I
remember feeling cheated that, at a time when I could
have had Hannah all to myself, she refused to let me
come to her. And so I set about drawing her to me –
not a conscious choice, perhaps, but none the less
deliberate for that.

It was a Thursday afternoon and Mama and Papa
had gone out on their weekly visit to Grandfather
Delaney. He would rarely come to our home, certainly
not since Papa's sad and humble return from Belfast
some two years earlier. And now he was ill, unable to
leave his house. Whatever was happening, my father
was no longer left behind when my mother made
these weekly, dutiful visits. I understood later that his
presence was tolerated by my grandfather, but not
sought after. Katie and Lily were on their afternoon
off. Hannah and I were alone in the house, each of us
deemed to be responsible enough to look after ourselves

for a few hours, and after each other, should the need arise.

We had been learning some of Moore's melodies in school at that time – 'The Meeting of the Waters' was a particular favourite of my teacher's – and I decided to see if I could accompany myself on the piano. I have never been an accomplished musician – not even nearly as good as May, who in turn, was not nearly as proficient as Hannah. I left the drawing-room door open on this occasion and began to strike the notes as loudly as I could. I sang carelessly, as though I had no thought for anything but my own entertainment.

It seemed to me that I played for some time without achieving the desired response. There was no sign of Hannah, no footstep that I could hear, no doors opening or closing. I was almost ready to stop – my sister was obviously not about to dignify my poor performance with her presence – when I sensed, rather than saw, a flash of blue to my left: Hannah, come to see me at last. I went to turn around and felt my long hair being pulled suddenly and furiously. I landed heavily on my back, my arms and legs waving in the air like a frantic spider. I don't think I knew what had happened, even when I saw Hannah standing there, her eyes black with fury. The piano stool had fallen over with a crash, and sheet music poured out of its seat, lying whitely on the floor like spilt milk. I was too shocked to speak. I had never before seen Hannah in such a temper – cross, yes, even sharp and angry after the occasional exchange between herself and Mama, but never this black, unforgiving rage.

I remember I cried, hugging myself, clasping my long arms close to my body for comfort. At one point, Hannah looked as though she was ready to soften towards me, but I wouldn't let her. I howled, deliberately averting my eyes from hers. I shut her out, just as she had shut me out. I was not going to give her the joy of comforting me. I even shook off her arm as I ran out of the drawing room and upstairs to my bedroom, sobbing as I went. I cannot say that my tears weren't real, but I do know that I pursued my advantage. I had made Hannah notice me, and simultaneously feel bad about her neglect of her youngest sister. As I slammed my door, I was conscious of a small feeling of triumph. I am almost ashamed to tell you this: I fear it makes me appear shallow and callous, but I have promised myself, and you, absolute truthfulness.

It was Hannah's turn now to want my company: and I should wait as long as it took for her to come and get me.

Hannah: Summer 1898

HANNAH LEANED HER head back against the warm glass of the window. She was tired of watching the hazy countryside hurry past, framed by the streaked grime of some other day's rain. She knew that her mother willed her not to, so she closed her eyes, shutting her out, obliterating that grey gaze, those long fingers plucking at the pearls around her throat. It gave Hannah satisfaction to withdraw like this, to savour the silent power of her last defiance. She felt the sun against her face, the bright midday light making pinkly crazed patterns on the insides of her eyelids. The train jolted occasionally, but mostly its rocking motion was soothing, childlike. Hannah thought how nice it would be to sleep now, to shut everything out, once and for all.

Eleanor shifted slightly on the upholstered seat, edging closer to her sister.

'I think we're nearly there,' she whispered, her breath warm against Hannah's neck. The older girl nodded and reached for the small hand. She could feel it lying uncertainly on the seat beside her, vulnerable, slightly sticky. She squeezed gently, filled with a rush of guilty love. She would never want Eleanor to feel closed off, abandoned. This silence was not for her. The young girl relaxed at once, comforted by the strength of her sister's warm grasp. May sat beside her mother, her gaze following the restless countryside, her face impassive.

No one spoke again until the train signalled its noisy arrival at Great Victoria Street. It snaked its way along platform one, finally shrieking to a long, juddering halt. Its cry echoed harshly, bouncing off the high metal roof, sending pigeons flapping whitely above the great billows of grey steam. Porters swarmed all over the platform, pulling at the peaks of their caps, sharp eyes on the lookout for the sweetest bit of business, the unwary traveller. Her father stood up at once, sliding back the door of their first-class carriage. He adjusted his hat with the air of a man accustomed to getting things done. Before he reached the bottom step, his left hand was already raised, half in summons, half in greeting. He moved rapidly along the platform, his gold-topped cane swinging in elegant rhythm with his footsteps.

'Come along, girls,' their mother urged.

Her voice was tight, the edges of her words jagged. May was already standing, fixing her bonnet without a word. Their mother tugged at her gloves, glancing irritably in the direction of her other two daughters. Neither moved. Hannah decided to count to ten before she even opened her eyes. Eleanor sat still, paralysed in equal measure by terror and delight at her sister's bravado, drawing strength from her tightly held hand.

'Eleanor, do as I say – at once.'

Hannah gave her sister's hand an extra little squeeze

of encouragement and opened her eyes. She looked innocently at her mother.

'Are we there yet, Mama?'

Eleanor stifled a giggle.

Her mother blinked rapidly. She pulled sharply on the drawstrings of her reticule, refusing to meet her eldest daughter's eye.

'Please don't be childish, Hannah. Gather your things. Your father's gone to get a porter.'

She swept angrily out of the carriage, ushering May down the steps in front of her. Hannah watched as the feathers of her mother's hat brushed against the top frame of the narrow doorway. They bobbed wildly for an instant, their careful arrangement distorted into sudden parody. A blue peacock's eye drooped sadly, then swayed drunkenly back to its proper position again. That moment, out of nowhere, Hannah was assaulted by a feeling of sudden, raw pity for the departing back. She could see, with a fleeting, startling clarity, all the secret years of disappointments, measured by her mother's small step, by the unyielding set of her shoulders.

Eleanor's cheeks were pink with suppressed laughter, her eyes shining. But when she turned back to Hannah, her sister seemed to have gone away from her. She was suddenly somewhere else. Her gaze was fixed on something in the distance, her expression had become blank again. Eleanor had seen so much of this in recent months that she now knew not to ask. She was too young, she'd understand when she was older, she wasn't to worry. She'd grown tired of her sister's responses, all of them the same, all of them filled with nothing, empty of reassurance. Quietly, she gathered up her book, her gloves, her ridiculous straw bonnet, and waited while Hannah smoothed her dress and pinned the crown of her travelling hat to the thick coil of hair they had plaited together that morning.

Finally, Hannah turned away from the mirror and gestured towards her mother, now waving at them furiously from the platform.

'Let's go, Ellie, and get this over with.'

She led the younger girl towards the door, where a porter's outstretched hand helped them both safely down the steps. Hannah kept her eyes lowered as they made their way up the platform towards the exit. She felt the familiar lurch in her chest as she thought about this life which others had decided for her. Once level with their mother, both girls stopped and waited obediently for her to take the lead.

'Hannah, do look up.'

Hannah did as she was told, startled by the unexpected change in her mother's tone. It was no longer sharp; there was no sense of that edgy, unspoken anxiety that her eldest daughter was about to let the family down. Instead, the words had come almost as an appeal, with an undertow of resignation, a new sense of enduring the inevitable. Hannah was surprised: she had thought that those feelings were hers and hers alone. She searched her mother's face, but could find no clue there, no change in the familiar expression. Her chin was resolute, her grey eyes directed down the platform as she searched for her husband.

He was by now well in front, having made his way

through the knotty crowds, a porter respectfully by his side. He had stopped just before he reached the barrier, waiting for his wife and daughters to catch him up. Hannah could see nervousness locked into every line of his body, in the way he pulled at his moustaches: first the left, then the right. She felt a hot surge of indignation as she looked at him. She was glad that he was suffering. She wanted him never to forget the last time his family had stood on this platform; she felt cruel enough to hope that he could still feel the shame of it all.

Beyond her father's slightly stooped shoulders, Hannah could make out the familiar outline of Constance MacBride – broad, squat, vastly hatted, apparently unchanged after five years. *She* was the one who had changed, Hannah realized, with a sudden, surprised stab of revelation. From thirteen to eighteen is a long time: enough to change from child to woman, enough to know the world a little more. From sixty-five to seventy is nothing, surely, just a very small proportion of a very old and unsurprising life. Beside Constance stood a tall, solid-looking figure, a man dressed in a black frock coat, already tipping his stovepipe hat to Hannah, his eyes, even at this distance, searching out hers.

This was it, then. This was what she had fought about, dreaded, railed against for all these months. And now she was here. She walked towards him mechanically, no longer aware of Eleanor, of May, of her mother, or her father in the crowding distance. She was aware only that this would now be her future, that the rest of her years would be spent shadowed by the northern grimness she could once more feel all around her, as though she had never left. It was a city that she remembered without affection, a whole sea of memories upwashed by the harshness of the Belfast voices that now joked and jostled with each other in the air above her.

For better or worse, she was home.

Mary: Spring 1896

FATHER MACVEIGH HAD written Mary a wonderful reference. He praised her honesty, her capacity for hard work, her resourcefulness. He read it to her slowly before folding the creamy notepaper in half and sealing it in a matching envelope.

His eyes twinkled at her.

'That good enough for you?'

Mary smiled.

'I hardly recognize meself, Father,' she confessed.

'Father Maguire has already spoken to the lady of the house, a Mrs Long, and she's expecting you tomorrow. She wants her housekeeper to interview you. Just a formality, I'm sure, but put on your best bib and tucker, just in case.'

'Is it a family, Father?'

He nodded.

'Aye, three children; I think the oldest's nine. They're one of Father Maguire's wealthiest families, made their fortune in aerated waters, I believe.'

Mary felt suddenly nervous. Now that she was effectively cutting her ties with Carrick Hill, she felt adrift, full of self-doubt. Since she and Myles had last spoken, he barely glanced in her direction any more. It might be her imagination, but it felt as if some of the warmth of the neighbours towards her had begun to cool, too. And Mrs McNiff was never at her downstairs window any more, where she used to perch for hours on end, her sharp eyes missing nothing of the comings and goings of the street.

What if this didn't work out? What if nobody wanted her? She knew that there was no going back, and going forward felt much more frightening now that it was real.

'I have other possibilities up my sleeve,' said Father MacVeigh. 'You aren't to become despondent if this one doesn't work out.'

He stood up, and opened the presbytery door for Mary.

'The others are in Sydenham and in Malone Park. These new fancy houses seem to need an unending stream of servants. I think it's a case of aping one's neighbours.'

His tone was dry, resigned. Mary didn't really know what he meant, was too shy to ask. But she caught the undercurrent of disapproval, and it puzzled her. Why would anyone not want a nice house, nice things, far away from the bustle and grime of Belfast's city centre?

The following morning, Mary caught the tram just outside the railway station in Great Victoria Street, and positioned herself at the window. The tram was only half full, the early rush to work long over. Mary didn't mind the journey. At least it was something different, and the fare was only tuppence from the city centre, no matter what the distance.

She was nervous when she stepped out at Fort-william Park and tried to remember Father MacVeigh's directions. Her hands were shaking a little, but at least their ugliness was concealed by Cecilia's gloves. She had worn them for luck.

She would try this household first, then Sydenham, then, finally, Malone Park. She would keep going until one of them took her on. All her other options were now closed off, some by the random hand of circum-stance, some by her own choosing. She was dressed up in her Sunday best, and had trimmed her old hat with new flowers. The streets were wide and tree-lined and Mary breathed deeply, glad of the sensation that here there was more space and air, equal amounts for everyone.

'I see you haven't worked as a maid before.' Mrs Long was looking doubtful, turning Father MacVeigh's letter over in her hands. 'I am glad to see that you have an excellent character reference. Do you think you would be able to manage the household duties?'

'Oh, yes, ma'am,' said Mary eagerly.

She hadn't been able to take her eyes off the woman seated in front of her. She must have been about thirty, Mary reckoned. According to Father MacVeigh, she already had three children, the oldest nine years of age. Her hands were white and slender, her dress perfection.

There was only the hint of fine lines around her eyes; no swathes of grey streaked her soft hair. Women in Carrick Hill who had three children were already stooped and faded, with straggling hair and several gaps where their teeth should be. Their constantly harassed expressions bore no resemblance to this woman's serene face. And there wasn't a child to be seen, or heard, anywhere.

The room was like nothing Mary had ever seen before. It oustripped even Cecilia's wildest imaginings. It looked out on to a glimpse of green garden, the window high and wide and draped with soft muslin. There was a writing-desk in the room, strewn now with sheets of paper covered in writing that was large and looping: an educated, confident hand. Above the desk itself, there were cubbyholes filled with different coloured papers, envelopes and what looked like the spines of notebooks. A pretty inkwell stood to one side, and a pen rested in the little dish beside it. To the left, there was a small brass bell which Mrs Long now took up and rang vigorously.

'I think we'll get Miss Mulqueen, my housekeeper, to have a chat with you. She runs the household very efficiently.'

She paused for a moment, and almost smiled at Mary.

'You would be her responsibility, should you be suitable.'

Mary was immediately nervous all over again. Another hurdle. Should she just go now, and avoid being told, 'No – you're not what we're looking for'?

Maybe she should just try one of the other houses, maybe it wouldn't be quite so big and overpowering. But she had no chance to make her escape. Miss Mulqueen arrived almost at once. So quickly, in fact, that Mary wondered if she had been listening outside the door.

'Are you sure you understand your duties? Tell me how your day would start.'

Mary had followed Miss Mulqueen down to the basement, where they now sat at a vast, scrubbed, wooden table.

She was dressed in the prim manner Mary soon learned to expect from all housekeepers: black dress, white collar, hair pinned back severely. There was one small, silver brooch clasped discreetly just under the point of her collar. Her eyes were pale and clear and she smelt of apples.

'I'm to be up at six o'clock, miss, and open all the shutters downstairs. Then I'm to clean the range and light it, along with all the other fires in the house. Then I bring hot water to the washstands in all the bedrooms. While the master and mistress are dressing, I dust the dining room and lay the table for breakfast.'

Mary stopped to draw breath. The list was endless, but she was undaunted. She could sense a seam of kindness in the other woman, and wanted, desperately, to have somewhere she could call home. Miss Mulqueen raised one hand. This time, she smiled.

'That's enough, Mary. I can see that you are bright,

and quick. It won't take us long to get you trained in. Your lack of experience is no hindrance, my dear, in fact it is a bonus. It means I won't have to break you of any bad habits.'

Mary could hardly hear her own voice over the beating of her heart.

'Then the position is mine?'

Miss Mulqueen looked at her, her expression grave.

'You will have a trial period of one month. Then the position will be yours, for a further six months while you are being trained. Then, we will make our final decision. You will live in and, until you are trained, your salary will be eighteen pounds a year. Your half-day will be a Tuesday, for now, and, of course, some hours' liberty on a Sunday. We shall look at all these issues again once you have gained sufficient experience.'

Mary felt a great surge of happiness as she left Fortwilliam. Her room in the attic was small and cosy; her duties were nothing more nor less than she had done for Cecilia over the past two years, and she no longer had to worry where her next dinner was coming from.

God had indeed smiled on her.

Hannah: Summer 1898

A YOUNG GIRL wearing an immaculately starched apron and a stiff, punishing white cap opened the front door as soon as they pulled up outside the MacBrides' home at the top of Malone Park. Hannah managed to avoid Charles's eye as he handed her out of the carriage. She wished that Constance MacBride would stop talking. Her voice was relentless. She had named every one of the city streets – from Great Victoria Street to Bradbury Place to University Road to Malone Road – as they'd passed through, offering details of their length and breadth and characteristics as some sort of sacred gift to her guests. She seemed astonished that the sisters remembered so little. *Ellie was just a baby*, Hannah wanted to fume at her, *and May and I spent our time in boarding school. And have you forgotten that we all left in rather a hurry?*

Hannah spent most of the carriage journey imagining the impact of the words she knew she would never dare to speak aloud. She was grateful when their imprisonment ended, glad to be released from the stifling confines of the carriage's hot interior. It was much easier to be busy once they reached the hallway. Hats had to be removed, coats hung on the hallstand, gifts and parcels despatched to God knows where around the vast house. Hannah thought she remembered its rooms vaguely, recalling some nameless afternoon in winter, years ago, when the heat had been tremendous. She had a blurry image of her mother and Constance MacBride on a sofa, teacups in hand, while she, May and Eleanor had been brought away to the kitchen for scones and milk.

Margaret, a serving-girl little older than Eleanor, showed them all into the drawing room, and when they were seated – Constance MacBride and Hannah on the sofa, the others in armchairs scattered about the room – she curtsied her way out again, sent in search of tea. Constance MacBride pointed Eleanor to a small, stiff, high-backed chair, its tapestry somewhat faded, its whole purpose to keep its occupant bolt upright.

'Sofas are bad for young people,' she said to her, not unkindly. 'Bad for the back; they encourage lazy posture.'

Eleanor nodded.

'Thank you,' she said, as though she'd just been given a great honour.

Hannah felt sorry for her. Her soft eyes were already misted over with boredom; now she had to endure at least two or three hours of what passed in this house as adult conversation. May had almost disappeared into the background, sitting in a chair whose velvet covering was an almost exact match for the colour of her dress. Hannah admired her ability to withdraw herself from situations that promised to be uncomfortable. She simply seemed to fade away from company, to become separate, somehow, and discourage all attention. Poor Eleanor had no such opportunity: Hannah watched her as she tried to wriggle discreetly, defeated by the hard seat and the once again spectacular heat of the Mac-Brides' drawing room. She was such a good little soul, so patient. Hannah was sorry she had no way of comforting her.

'Did you find the journey pleasant, my dear?'

Constance MacBride addressed herself directly to Hannah and the younger woman blushed. It was an acknowledgement of her new status, that of a woman about to be married. She sensed, rather than saw, her mother's anxious look. Conscious, too, of Charles's eyes on her, she kept her gaze resolutely away from both of them. She turned instead to Constance MacBride. And smiled.

'Yes, thank you. Very pleasant indeed.'

She felt the air in the room relax. Out of the corner of her eye, she saw her mother cease to finger her pearls; her father finally left his moustaches alone. She hadn't intended to make it easy for either of them, but now that she was here, Hannah felt the full weight of the century's politeness settle around her shoulders like a yoke.

Expectation filled the drawing room; it was almost as tangible as the heavy oak furniture around her, as delicately oppressive as the ornaments crowding every surface in the large room. She knew that something significant would be broken beyond repair if she publicly, humiliatingly, opposed her parents' wishes. From the moment she had stepped off the train, she knew that she had given up the fight. There was no longer any point in pretending otherwise, to herself or to anyone else. The past few months seemed now to belong to another life, another person. She felt a sharp flush of bitterness, the acid taste of shameful self-knowledge. Was she really to be bought and sold so easily?

She wondered about Charles. Was this as much of a trap for him as it was for her? Was he so much under the thumb of his imperious mother that he exercised no choice, made no decisions of his own? Or was she, Hannah, his last desperate attempt at escape? He was forty, only ten years younger than Papa. She knew he'd been at sea for almost twenty years. He must have seen the world, must have had other chances to marry, unless there was something wrong with him, some terrible defect in his nature. She knew nothing of his character, other than his seeming kindness. When he'd taken her hand at the railway station, and held her gaze with his, she had noticed, briefly, that his grip was warm, firm. Despite herself, that had pleased her. Mama had once said not to trust men with unemphatic handshakes.

She would have welcomed the chance to observe him discreetly, but he stayed quietly in the background, his winged chair slightly to the left of the sofa which Hannah occupied with his mother. His gaze was making the back of her neck tingle. She'd have to look over at him soon, speak to him. But not yet. She intended to make him wait. At the same time, a small part of her was grateful for his unobtrusiveness.

Tea finally arrived. All conversation ceased as one

maid laid out the cups and saucers, plates and napkins, while the other put salvers of crustless cucumber sandwiches and scones on to the low table. Mrs MacBride waved the young girls away almost immediately.

'All right, Margaret, Jane, you can both go. I'll ring if I need more hot water.'

The tea ceremony barely interrupted Mrs MacBride's spirited tale of her late husband's business interests. This monologue was directed solely towards Hannah's father, who was sitting forward eagerly, thin forearms resting on his knees. Hannah felt her familiar contempt for his avidity, knew that he was once more absorbing this household's wealth and status, silently congratulating himself again and again on, finally, a stroke of good fortune.

Hannah was grateful for Constance MacBride's volubility. She neither wanted, nor was expected, to reply. She wanted to block out her father's greed, wanted not to hear the hidden text of negotiation and expectation that underlined every word her future mother-in-law uttered.

She let her eyes take in the immensely cluttered details of the fashionably ugly drawing room. The wooden floors were dark and highly polished, only their borders visible beyond the soft depths of Chinese silk rugs. Whatnots, lacquered screens, luxuriant parlour palms – it seemed to Hannah that all movement was deliberately restricted here, that the only activity permitted was the art of conversation.

'Sugar, my dear?'

Hannah started. In one hand, Mrs MacBride held

out the delicate bone-china cup and saucer like an accusation. In the other, she held the sugar bowl, with its silver tongs carved and ugly like turkeys' claws. Hannah felt her stomach lurch with sudden nausea. The older woman kept looking at her. Her sharp eyes had registered Hannah's distraction. They were eyes that missed nothing.

'Thank you.' Hannah reached towards the sugar bowl, nervous again. Her silence had caused offence. Now she would be made to pay for it. She tried to be attentive.

She watched, fascinated, as Mrs MacBride poured hot water into the next cup, waited until the cup was thoroughly heated and then discarded the water into a china bowl provided expressly for that purpose. She then poured a little milk into the warm cup and filled it up with tea.

'Pass that to your mama, my dear, please.'

Hannah knew what was coming. First Mama, then Papa; then she would have to hand Charles his tea. Eye-to-eye contact could not be postponed any longer.

'Thank you,' he said simply, not engaging her with more than a brief smile.

May and Eleanor drank their milk obediently, ate their sandwiches and scones quietly, politely, as they had been taught. *Don't speak with your mouth full.* Hannah remembered from home all the exhausting evenings of good table etiquette. Mama had been such a stickler – she still was. *Keep your mouth closed. Chew every mouthful twelve times.* She remembered the agonies of her childhood self trying to manipulate knives and forks, glasses and spoons, plates and serving dishes, without once lifting the elbows or altering the stiff, upright posture of her back. *Sit up straight; no elbows on the table. Keep your arms close to your sides.* She remembered the particular difficulties she had had in the days when her feet didn't even reach the floor. She would never complain: none of them would. There was the sense that once you had endured your polite agony, you would be released. You waited for that moment, your whole self straining towards the time when you would be dismissed. As a child, you were left in no doubt about your place at the table, in the family, in the whole scheme of things. *Children should be seen and not heard.*

And now, tea was over. Charles got up to retrieve everyone's cups and saucers. Hannah noticed that his hands were large, but he was not as solid-looking as he had seemed at the station, swathed in his black frock coat. She had thought he would be ungainly, awkward indoors, but he moved around his mother's treasures with a quiet grace which Hannah found she liked. Mrs MacBride suddenly paused and drew breath.

'Now then.'

Even Eleanor and May looked up expectantly at such a brisk change of tone. Hannah saw how desperately uncomfortable her younger sisters were. She felt sorry for the flushed, bored faces, sorry for the distance imposed between them. She longed to give them a hug, to tell them they would soon be able to go home. The poor things had had to be silent the whole time.

'I think perhaps Hannah might like to see the gardens, Charles.'

There was the chinking of spoon against china as Charles entrusted the last cup and saucer to his mother's outstretched hand. Hannah had a sudden, wild desire to run away. What would she say to him? Should May and Eleanor come too, as a sort of safe distraction?

'Delighted,' he replied, and offered Hannah his arm.

It was all done in an instant. She was outside in the conservatory before she had even had time to think about her arm on his, the gentle pressure of his hand under her elbow. He steered her from the conservatory out into the formal gardens outside.

'May I smoke?'

'Yes, of course,' said Hannah, confused. They were outside, in his garden. What had her permission to do with it? She felt awkward again. Had a different reply been expected of her?

They remained silent during the peculiarly calming ritual of his filling the pipe with tobacco, tamping it and finally lighting it. Charles inclined his head towards hers as he struck the match, cradling its flame with one hand.

When he looked up, she suddenly lost all fear of him. There was air and freedom out here in the garden; she felt as though she had thrown off a great burden by escaping from the house. She could breathe, at last. He seemed different, too. He was simply *himself* out here, separate, no longer standing in his mother's large shadow. He was smiling at her again, his eyes creased against the sunlight. He threw the spent match into one of the flowerbeds and held his arm out to her again.

'Don't tell Mama,' he said. 'She thinks smoking is a wicked vice.'

She wasn't sure whether to take him seriously.

'Do you?'

'Do I what?' asked Hannah.

'Think smoking is a wicked vice?'

'I've hardly thought about it at all. I'm sure there are worse sins.'

'Such as?'

She hesitated. How much did he know about her family, her father, about their ignominious retreat from Belfast five years ago? He'd been at sea, surely, during all their time here. Was that knowledge something his formidable mother would have imparted to him, or concealed from him, about his future bride?

'Well, stealing, for one. Cruelty. And Mama says strong drink is another.'

He nodded.

'Aye. I've never practised any of those, y' know, and I don't intend to in the future.'

He was looking at her sideways, his expression a comical mixture of amusement and sincerity.

Hannah felt her face redden.

'Oh – I didn't mean . . .'

He stopped and took his pipe out of his mouth and put it carefully on the white cast-iron table behind him. He took both her hands in his, forcing her to look at him directly.

'I know you didn't. But we both know why you're here. Let me be very honest with you, Hannah.'

Hannah felt suddenly panicked. Of course she knew why she was here, why they were both there, had known for months that this would happen. But now that the time was here too, everything felt suddenly rushed, hurtling her dizzily towards some fixed point in the future. It was as though her life had only now become predictable, changed and unexpected, all at the same time.

She let her hands lie between his. He was no longer teasing; his expression was serious.

'I'll be good to you, Hannah, if you'll consent to be my wife. I'm a ways older than you are, and I do like one or two wee whiskies from time to time. But I have the reputation of a gentleman.'

He stopped for a moment. His eyes still held hers. She had the impression he was going to say more, but stopped himself.

'Will you have me?'

He was smiling at her. She liked his tone, was grateful to him for his generosity in pretending that she had a choice, that either of them still had a choice. Her eyes filled. How easy it was, she thought, and how reckless, to seal your life with just one word, one instant which could prove to be your making or your undoing. All the final whispers of dissent had to be silenced. It was now time. She knew that no matter what happened, this moment would be etched into her memory for ever: the sunlit garden, the warmth of his hands, her own curious mixture of dread and elation.

'Yes,' she said.

He stooped to kiss her. His moustache was softer than she'd expected, his breath tasted strongly of tobacco. But it was not unpleasant, Hannah thought, returning, hesitantly, the pressure of his lips.

She took his arm again as they continued to stroll the length of the gardens. Now that the words had been spoken, and something apparently momentous agreed between them, Hannah felt relieved, almost faint. There was something breathless in the power of the words they had spoken, and she felt suddenly much older, much more womanly. The day now seemed at the same time to be of enormous importance and extraordinary ordinariness. They sat together on a bench in the shade of two old plum trees, and Charles pointed out the diamond-shaped flowerbed in the centre of the lawn which his mother had enjoyed digging and planting herself. He linked Hannah's arm comfortably and puffed on his pipe in silence. Hannah at once knew that this was a sound she would get used to: the faint suck and whistle of his mouth on the stem of his meerschaum pipe. When he spoke again, his tone was faintly mocking.

'She's a demon gardener, so she is, my sainted mother. Can't keep up with her, y'know.'

Hannah liked the sound of his voice. His accent was softer than those she remembered from her earlier years here, the memory of their harshness not diminished with the passage of time. His was a deeper voice than she had imagined, quieter, lilting. She wondered if he sang.

He was pointing to the plants in front of them, naming them for her. The extensive flowerbed was full of headily perfumed rose trees, pansies, cerastium, bellis. They thrived on the order imposed on them, their arrangement a formal pattern of alternating colours. The scented border behind where they were sitting was dominated by a row of sweet pea. Hannah liked the scent of the flowers, the feeling of tranquillity around her; she enjoyed the occasional dipping flight of passing butterflies, and the restful swathe of green lawn. She had a brief, unexpected desire for a garden of her own.

'You're musical, I understand.'

It was more statement than question. Hannah nodded.

'I love to play the piano. I took lessons, all through school . . .'

She stopped, embarrassed. Mama had told her to make no assumptions, to ask for nothing. They would discuss everything, arrange everything on her behalf.

'I like to sing accompanied, myself. I'm told I have a good tenor voice.'

That was all that was said; it was all that was necessary. She knew she would have her piano. Once she could have her music and the company of her sisters from time to time, she cared for very little else. They sat a while longer in the afternoon sunshine, blue tobacco-smoke spiralling upwards in the still air.

Constance MacBride: Summer 1898

'WELL?' ASKED CONSTANCE MacBride.

Her son was sitting opposite her, nursing a whiskey, their guests just departed on the evening train to Dublin. She was impatient to find out what had happened between him and Hannah. God knows, he wasn't the best candidate for marriage. Twenty years at sea and not one bit of growing up done in all that time. All that had happened was that he had grown older. Still as naive as the day he was born. She suppressed the familiar sense of disappointment, the ever-present undertow of irritation. Thinking about her two sons always depressed her. Here was the younger one, with not a shred of business sense between him and eternity. And as for his brother: better not even think about Robert, about his dissoluteness, his drinking. God alone knew what shame he was even now bringing to the family name. Their sisters would buy them and sell them twice over before breakfast. She waited, impatiently, for him to answer.

'Aye, she's a grand wee girl.'

'Did you speak to her? Did you reach an understanding between the two of you?'

'We did, surely. She'll do rightly.'

He would say no more on the subject, refused obstinately to be drawn further. His mother hoped he was right, that Hannah would do. She was certainly a good-looking girl, but there was a resistance to her, an independent streak which she didn't know if Charles was ready, or able, to handle. It worried her: she had a strong feeling that this was her last opportunity to have him settled.

But Hannah wouldn't have too many chances, either, despite her looks and her accomplishments. She had her father's reputation to contend with, although memories of his wrongdoing were probably fading now, with the years. From that point of view, it was a sensible match. Nothing like the lack of options to help people make their minds up quickly. She hoped it would work out, for all of them. She was getting too old for this, too tired to get Charles up and running at this stage of their lives. And so was he. Another few years and it would be too late. He needed a wife now, a home, children, a solid domestic anchor to distract him from the dangerous political waters he had been sailing recently. He was old enough to have more sense, but the fact was, he hadn't. She wanted to make sure he was occupied. The situation was tense enough, without having one of your own involved.

She sighed. Home Rule or no Home Rule, nothing was worth the risk of Charles getting involved in politics. Violence was simmering once more. It was only a matter of time. It was merely a question of how and when, not if, it would erupt again.

Hannah: Summer 1898

HANNAH COULD FEEL the sharp edge of her mother's anxiety as soon as Charles had left them at the station. She deliberately stood with Eleanor and May on the platform once Charles had shaken hands formally with everyone and taken his leave. He had simply pressed both her hands in his and said, 'Goodbye, then, Hannah.' She was grateful to him for not making a fuss, for not kissing her hand, for not behaving more like a lover. Let Mama wait. She would give her no detail until she had to.

Eleanor and May were both giddy. The escape from Constance MacBride's drawing room was like a sudden, physical release for them, and they wanted to whisper and giggle with Hannah about this stout, imperious woman, about her stuffy house and her vast beaded bosom. Hannah encouraged their laughter, conscious of her mother's eyes on her as she boarded the train after them.

Mama would never ask her in the compartment, Hannah was sure of that. She could sense her mother's disappointment, knew that she would have liked a quiet moment beforehand, but Mama would never discuss such matters in front of her two younger daughters.

Hannah had a sense of deep satisfaction that her mother now had to wait until the three-hour journey was over before her curiosity could begin to be assuaged. She decided to spend the journey home as she had spent the outward one: she rested her head on the overstuffed cushion behind her, and closed her eyes. She allowed her face to incline gently towards the window, keeping herself turned away, just enough, from her mother's gaze, but not so much as to elicit a rebuke for rudeness. That way, she could sleep or simply look out the window without anyone being any the wiser. She welcomed the opportunity to be silent, to mull over what she had seen and thought during the day.

Charles was not what she had been expecting. He was considerably more boyish, less stiff and formal than she had imagined. His sense of humour was a pleasant surprise too – he certainly didn't inherit that from his mother. And he had plans to become registered as an architect: an easy transition for a ship's engineer, he assured her. She liked his easy, friendly way with her, she decided. Somehow it made him seem less old, less like Papa – a similarity she had been dreading.

She would have her piano and her music, too, of that she was sure. Perhaps it wouldn't be so bad. At least she wouldn't be poor: he had already promised her a honeymoon in Holland, and a new home in Holywood, County Down. A grand wee town by the sea, he had told her. Famous for its mild climate, its spectacular views across Belfast Lough, its gentility.

She would never forgive her parents for spoiling her dream, not ever. But today had made her feel that perhaps she could live with what they had chosen for her. She had a brief moment of bitterness as she realized she had no choice, no power of her own. She brushed the feeling away – she had had too much anguish in the last few months. Live with reality she must – and, as Grandfather was fond of saying, learn to like it.

Eleanor's Journal

I THOUGHT CHARLES kind. I saw him look right into Hannah's eyes on that first day in Belfast, and smile. I remember how that smile surprised me: it was the smile of a boy. It lit up his rather large, sombre face, and creased his eyes in a most agreeable manner. I think he must have held my sister's hand for a fraction longer than was necessary, for she looked away and busied herself uselessly about the luggage. I liked the way he shook hands gravely with me, taking his time to greet me amid the bustle of the crowded train station. It made me feel grown up.

Constance MacBride was much more substantial than my shadowy recollection of her. The intervening years had not been kind: she seemed to have swollen, her flesh bulging against the severe lines of her clothing. My youthful imagination savoured the image of seams straining to splitting point, stitches exploding, white flesh spilling everywhere in a most unbecoming fashion. Even her hat was enormous – a most impressive creation of plumage and flowers, vastly superior to Mama's; but her gown was suited to mourning. I wondered who had died. Months later, I found out from her daughter

Emily that it was her husband, who had passed away some twenty-five years earlier. Constance MacBride claimed that she properly respected his memory by never abandoning her widow's weeds. Emily said that that was arrant nonsense; it was just her mother's way of frightening away men, of terrifying any potential suitor into silence. I couldn't imagine anyone fighting for Mrs MacBride's hand, not even in her younger days. Wealthy she may have been, but, apart from her lack of physical charms, she had an air about her that discouraged intimacy, that proclaimed her a woman sternly convinced of her own superiority. I felt instinctively that she was quite repellent enough: she didn't need the mourning clothes.

She bustled about that day of our arrival, shooing us away off the platform as though we were ill-behaved hens. She had a carriage waiting under the porte cochère, right at the station entrance. Jaunting cars were lined up all along Great Victoria Street, waiting patiently for business. Their drivers were wreathed in clouds of tobacco-smoke, jesting with each other in accents that were about to become familiar to me again. The air of activity everywhere was intense, as was the heat. Busy, purposeful men hurried hither and thither, the enormous clock above us seeming to measure out the minutes of their important days. I wondered where they were all rushing to.

Charles helped us all to ascend the carriage. First his mother, then Mama, then Hannah and May, then me, and finally Papa. Nobody spoke to me, and Hannah would not meet my eye. The others conversed in a polite, desultory fashion about the journey, the weather, the crowded Belfast streets. I can remember thinking how everyone knew the reason we had come, and yet deemed it improper to speak of it. With a child's logic, I wondered why a wedding was an indecent topic for a carriage – surely it was as acceptable there as anywhere else? After all, wasn't that the very reason we had all travelled to Belfast together? I had plenty of time to ponder this, and many other matters, during the lengthy afternoon I was about to spend inside the MacBrides' unbearably hot and overstuffed drawing room.

Mary: Summer 1898

MARY HAD LITTLE difficulty in getting used to her duties at 12 Fortwilliam Park. She welcomed the nightly exhaustion, the mind-numbing torpor induced by ceaseless physical work. She fell into her bed each night with no thought for anything but sleep. Her hands gradually grew tougher and dirtier, ingrained with coal-dust and black lead from cleaning the range. Her mind learned to fill itself with thoughts of the next job: washing-up after breakfast, cleaning the floor, tidying up in expectation of Madam's daily visit to the kitchen to give her orders. Then came cleaning the bedrooms and emptying the chamber pots, washing the varnished paintwork with tea-water, brushing damp tea leaves into the carpets, stoking the range and the fires. Mary was grateful for the rigour of this new existence. She was fed, watered and housed. If she didn't receive kindness, at least she learned to be content with indifference: it meant that as long as she did her work, she didn't have to spend her life looking over her shoulder.

*

Two years after her arrival in Fortwilliam Park, Mary came home one Sunday evening to great excitement in the kitchen. Cook and Miss Mulqueen were talking animatedly, their eyes bright, faces rosy. Two sherry schooners stood empty on the table between them.

Miss Mulqueen beamed at Mary as she propped her dripping umbrella beside the range.

'What is it?' asked Mary.

'Madam is in the family way again – the wee one is due to be born sometime in October.'

They both nodded at her, looking as self-important and pleased with themselves as if they had just announced the arrival of the Messiah. For a brief moment, Mary thought how sad it was, that these two women regarded the event as though they were family. As it was, those who lived below stairs rarely saw the children. They were Nanny's preserve, and she guarded them jealously. Mary thought privately that Mrs Long was a little afraid of her. Stout, plain and devoted, Nanny ruled the roost. In the mornings Madam would hand the children over to the schoolroom and the strangely timid governess; in the afternoons they were all Nanny's, for long walks in the local park, or doing a carefully planned variety of activities with a view to improving their little minds.

The first time Mary had seen the governess, Miss Taylor, she knew her to be a bitterly disappointed woman. Her chin was sharp, the corners of her mouth turned down, creased like parentheses. Her hands were large and impatient. Perhaps she was always worrying about something, or perhaps life simply hadn't fulfilled its promise. Mary sometimes thought about her, or Nanny, or Cook on the winter mornings when she got up as early as five-thirty to clean the grates, open the flues and set the fires going again. Sorry for yer troubles, Mary would think grimly, scraping the tarry residue from the inside of the flue, her hands numb with cold and effort: life left an awful lot of us behind when it handed out its parcels of good fortune.

Mary often felt sorry for the children: their lives seemed to be a constant round of duties. She had never seen them play ball in the garden, chase the dog or hug a brother or sister . . . She stopped herself.

Miss Mulqueen and Cook were still looking at her. Maybe they were right to be joyful: good or bad, this was as close as they'd ever come to their own hearth and home – as close as she'd ever come, too. Hadn't she passed up all opportunity of family, of children – hadn't that been her choice? She tried to appear enthusiastic. Luckily, they weren't all that interested in her reaction.

'Didn't you use to sew?'

Cook asked the question, looking over at Mary with curiosity. Miss Mulqueen was impatient now, her eyes eager.

'Aye,' Mary said slowly.

She wasn't sure what she was letting herself in for. Miss Mulqueen clasped her hands delightedly.

'I shall tell Madam at once. She asked me to find someone to prepare a new layette for the baby. Would you be able to do that?'

'I would, surely.'

Mary began to like the idea: perhaps if she were to

have such new duties, old ones such as emptying the chamber pots or stoking the range or carrying coal could be done by a step-boy.

'I'll tell Madam.'

Miss Mulqueen was gone like a shot. Cook looked put-out. Perhaps she was cross that the housekeeper had stolen her thunder; perhaps she was feeling left out; or perhaps she simply wanted more sherry. Mary had often seen the gleam that was in her eye now, the high spot of colour on each cheek. She would never have put two and two together until today.

The older woman stood up from the table now, her vast skirts in full sail like a Spanish galleon. She limped her way over to one of the cupboards which was always kept locked. She produced the bottle of sherry and a new glass. She poured for Mary, with a slightly unsteady hand.

'You're a good wee girl,' she said, not lifting her eyes from the bottle.

Mary was dumbfounded. She felt foolish as her eyes began to fill. It was the first expression of affection that she had had from anyone since she had refused Myles and left Carrick Hill. Cecilia appeared insistently in front of her, young, childlike, as she was before the mill unleashed its terrors. Tears began to roll slowly down Mary's cheeks. Cook was startled. Then her puffy face seemed to soften.

'Sit down now, and get that into ye.'

Mary sat and sipped, feeling the warmth grow in her stomach. She was disturbed by this return of feeling. For two years now, she had experienced existence in its simplest animal forms of work, food and shelter. The young Cecilia had hardly crossed her mind. She was there, always, in the background, almost hidden among the deepest bits of Mary's life. But the *live* Cecilia had always been absent; only her damaged and dying self ever nudged its way into Mary's consciousness. It had been easy enough to scrub it away on the front step, or beat it out of the dusty carpets. This was different. It was as though Cecilia had come back to demand her rightful place in her sister's memory.

Mary didn't know whether to be glad or frightened.

Sophia: Spring 1899

SOPHIA THOUGHT ABOUT it for a long time before she went knocking on Hannah's door. She was never quite sure these days what to expect from her eldest daughter. She had become fiercely private over the last several months, withdrawing from all family occasions as soon as it was polite to do so, giving others the minimum of herself. A calculated amount, Sophia had often reflected, never enough to please, but never so little that offence could reasonably be taken. Even when she was there, she had developed the capacity to detach herself from everybody, with an air just this side of aloofness. Her eyes would look dimmer, somehow, their usual blue light suffused with grey. She seemed to have little time even for her sisters. Sophia was aware, particularly, of how much Eleanor missed her. May was much more separate, always had been. But the youngest girl had taken to wandering around the house like a pale, lost soul, afraid, it seemed, even to touch the piano.

Sophia had taken care not to cross Hannah; she knew that the girl needed time to grow into the life that had been shaped for her. After his initial anger and impatience, Edward seemed to regard the matter as closed. He was simply not prepared to discuss it. This had more to do, Sophia was sure, with his own never-acknowledged sense of shame than with his daughter's defiance. His only response was that Hannah would do as she was told. He would grant her a little time only to learn acceptance, to submit to the will of her parents. The decision was made, finished with.

The dark burn of Hannah's anger and contempt had eased somewhat since their visit to the MacBrides in Belfast, Sophia was sure of that. Her daughter no longer avoided her eye, or left the room at once, shrouded in resentment, whenever her mother entered. In some strange way, Sophia realized, Hannah regarded what she saw as her mother's betrayal of her as a worse and more heinous sin than anything her father had ever done. Sophia had reflected long and bitterly on the irony of her daughter's outrage. She, Sophia, had done only what was expedient: none of this would have been necessary but for Edward. She sighed impatiently, stopping herself from going down that well-travelled road again: Hannah's words still kept her awake at night, cutting into her heart with the accuracy and precision of the surgeon's knife.

I hope you got a good price.

Once the house had settled into its night-time quiet, the secret creakings and sighings finally stilled, Sophia put her needlework to one side and climbed the stairs to the first-floor landing and her daughter's bedroom. She knocked on the door, more smartly than she had intended, and waited. She felt the first faint stirrings of panic. Now that she was here, what was she going to say? What words could she possibly use to bridge the gap between the two of them? Even if Hannah no longer hated her, she had certainly kept herself aloof from any of Sophia's recent attempts to console her, to mother her. She felt her heartbeat quicken. She tried to breathe more deeply. No matter what, her daughter needed her now, even if she refused to know it. She steadied herself, comforted by her sense of duty. Who else could explain to her daughter what would be expected of her, demanded of her as a married woman? She knew that some, including Edward, regarded this as a husband's, rather than a mother's duty. But she wasn't convinced. Her own experience had taught her otherwise. Nevertheless, she was filled with sudden misgiving, and decided to turn away, to think about it again more carefully, to come back when she was more prepared, perhaps even more sure of a welcome. She needed to wait until courage came to her once more.

But Hannah opened her door.

'Mother!'

She was surprised to see Sophia standing there, looking uncertain, her hands clasped in the way that Hannah had come to associate with anxiety. She looked altogether different from her usual daily self.

'May I come in?'

She was here now, and would do her best.

Hannah opened her door wider. She felt a sudden sympathy for her mother, something she had not felt for some time for either of her parents. For months, her anger had burned brightly; there had been reminders everywhere of her thwarted ambition, her stunted talent.

She hadn't been able to bear even the sight of the piano, or the sound of anyone else playing it. She had torn down the stairs one Sunday afternoon in a fury and dragged Eleanor by the hair off the piano stool, enraged by the child's playing. It was only when she saw the young girl sprawled on the floor, her small body made almost comical by the ungainly tangle of legs and waving arms, that Hannah's anger had deflated. She had been shocked by the violence of her emotions, appalled at her treatment of gentle Eleanor. Her youngest sister had said nothing, nothing at all. She had sobbed into her sleeve, resisting Hannah's remorseful embrace, refusing to meet her eyes. But all that had been long before Belfast.

'May I sit?'

'Of course.'

Hannah was puzzled by her mother's diffidence. She waited for the older woman to speak, content to sit in silence. She knew that this had something to do with Charles.

'I wanted to speak to you about your wedding.'

Hannah nodded. She was to be married in less than two months. Her mother and Constance MacBride had agreed that it was no longer fashionable to believe in long engagements.

'The next few weeks are going to be busy; very busy indeed.'

Hannah wondered what was going to keep everyone in Dublin so occupied, but still she said nothing. She knew that she would live in Holywood, a seaside town some four miles outside Belfast; that Charles and his mother would find a suitable house to rent; that there would be a small, elegant wedding from home: family only. Why was her mother so convinced of her own busyness?

'I wanted to have this time to speak to you before we ... all of us ... got ... distracted.'

Hannah felt her face begin to colour. She didn't want to believe it, but it seemed that her mother was going to speak to her about married life, about the things which passed between men and women: the physical act of which she already had some confused knowledge, knowledge she had long ago dismissed in all its enormity and improbability. Girls in school had whispered to each other about such things in the darkness of the dormitory. Giggling and snorting into pillows, the older ones had talked about men and women 'cleaving unto one another', becoming 'one flesh', about a man 'knowing' a woman: their talk had shocked Hannah. She hadn't wanted to know then, hadn't wanted to listen. She felt the same now. She wanted to put her hands over her ears, or disappear under the blankets like a child. She was afraid that her mother was going to spoil the first stirrings of romance which she had felt as she'd sat beside Charles in his mother's garden. Her first tentative thrillings of love were a world apart from the crude, knowing talk of schoolgirls. She was just becoming used to the feeling that her life might be bearable after all, that she could do as her father and mother had bid her. If that feeling went away, if her mother did anything to spoil the tiny shoots of tenderness she was nurturing for Charles, then she, Hannah, would no longer be able to endure it.

'Please don't, Mother.'

Strangely, her embarrassment seemed to make Sophia all the more determined to continue.

'I cannot leave you ignorant, Hannah. I may have many failings as your mother, but I feel that this must be spoken of between us.'

Sophia's voice was soft. For a moment, Hannah remembered how close they had once been, how her mother had trusted and confided in her, perhaps even needed her. She had a brief, blinding memory of that train journey from Belfast to Dublin five years ago, feeling grown up, a true confidante, while May slept and Eleanor sucked her thumb for comfort. All that closeness was gone now, destroyed by her father and mother's usurping of her life. She wondered if it would ever be possible to forgive her, if the ties between them could ever be the same again.

'I'm listening.'

Hannah sat across from her mother on the small padded chair beside her dressing table. She would obey, would give her outward compliance as she had learned to do over the last, painful few months. Her voice and expression were deliberately cool, controlled. She waited. A word from her would take the chalky strain out of her mother's face, would let the blood rush back to the high, prominent cheekbones. But she would say nothing, for now. She felt almost elated by the sense of power she had over this woman. It was good – a kind of revenge. Sophia's hands were a waxy white, knuckles sharp and shiny, fingers now interlaced. Hannah noted, with increasing detachment, that they were trembling.

'You will soon be a married woman.'

Here she smiled across at Hannah. She got no response.

'What you need to understand, my dear, is that what happens between a man and a woman on their wedding night is part of God's plan, but not knowing can make it frightening.'

Hannah still didn't speak. She kept her gaze steady, holding her mother's reluctant grey eyes. It was Sophia who finally looked down at her hands.

'When a man joins his body to a woman's, it is warm and natural, and, for many people, it eventually becomes rather wonderful.'

Sophia looked straight at her daughter, and now Hannah wanted to look away. Her mother's expression startled her into pity, and she did not want to feel that. She could see the chasm between what her mother's marriage had become and the hopes with which she must have started out as a young woman. Or had Sophia, too, been given no option? Had she also had her choices constrained, her life shaped by the circumstances of social and family needs? Hannah felt suddenly terrified for herself – would she be speaking like this to her own daughter one day, with more than twenty years' accumulated disappointments and bitterness behind her? She had the sense that married love had never become 'rather wonderful' for her mother. Hannah wanted to stop her, before this intimacy became any more painful.

As it was, the air in the room was charged with emotion, her mother's eyes were much too bright. Hannah did not want her to cry; she couldn't bear to comfort her.

'Mama, I think I understand what happens, and I hope I will be prepared. Thank you for talking to me.'

Sophia heard 'Mama' and wanted to weep. Ever since she and Edward had brought her home from school on that dreadful day, Hannah had refused to call them 'Papa' or 'Mama'. Instead, she had carefully articulated 'Mother' and 'Father' with all the calculation and precision of an insult.

Sophia stood up slowly. She stretched out her hand and touched her daughter's face briefly.

'Just remember this, my dear – I've always tried to do my best.'

She left the room at once, closing the door gently behind her. Hannah didn't even have time to say 'goodnight'. The room seemed very empty after she had gone, and Hannah felt an unaccountable sadness. She was edgy and restless for the rest of the evening. Everything around her irritated her. She felt hemmed in, claustrophobic. The gas lamp was burning smokily; it threw strange shadows on her wall as she moved about the room. She pulled books off her shelves, leafing through them impatiently, but the light was too dim for reading. She found herself wanting answers to questions she didn't even know how to ask. Nothing gave her peace.

She wanted her sisters. But May wouldn't be back from school until the weekend. Perhaps Eleanor would still be awake. The child had come to her so often in the past, snuggling down beside her, in search of comfort. Now the tables had turned. Hannah opened her door as quietly as she could, and tiptoed up the three steps to the second landing. She tapped softly on her sister's door.

Now it was time for Eleanor to look after her.

Eleanor's Journal

THE ENTIRE HOUSEHOLD was in an uproar for weeks. May and I might never have existed, for all the attention anyone paid us. Mama had said that the wedding would be a small one, an intimate affair, for the immediate family only. I remember wondering how life could possibly be any more frantic had the proposed party been a larger one.

I think Hannah was happy on her wedding day. She certainly appeared to be. I felt close to her again and, selfishly, that was all I cared about. She'd had time for me and interest in all my doings over the past few months, even though every moment of hers was spoken for. It felt good to have her back. She and I never spoke of the day at the piano to anyone else – now that is a secret shared among three of us: you, me and Hannah. After I had cried myself out, and feigning reluctance, had opened my bedroom door to her, I allowed her to embrace me. She had cried then, too, and hugged me close, calling me 'Mouse', and promising that she would never hurt me again, that she was so ashamed of her bad temper, that I was the best sister in the world. Such a reconciliation more than made up for the distance that had opened up between us since she had been taken out of school.

The afternoon of the piano stool seemed to break something in her. The following evening, she allowed Papa's insistence to bring her out of her room once again, to join him and Mama in the drawing room. I felt very sad for her that day. She still looked pale and unhappy, her eyes red-rimmed and sore-looking. She smiled a watery little smile at me as she made her way downstairs, and I had the strangest sensation that something in her spirit had been dulled, some vital inner light had been quenched beyond repair.

I did not know then what had passed among the three of them, closeted once more together in the drawing room. Whatever it was, Hannah ceased to rebel openly, although she still appeared to me to be restless, touchy, quick to anger. However she felt about Mama and Papa, she was quietly affectionate to me, which was all I wanted. I did wonder, though, why she never touched the piano, never sang, never tried to make herself happy again. She was no longer locked in her room, and she was, on the surface at least, obedient to Mama and Papa. I think that was all that was expected of her.

But once we had been to Belfast to meet Charles, she seemed to be more contented, more animated. I know that I was surprised, and, in my own childish way, filled with contradictory emotions. I suppose, in my black and white view of the world, I was secretly disappointed. That she seemed happy again should have made me glad: but I was sorry that she hadn't fought them all for longer. Ever since that day in the Mac-Brides' house when she and Charles had spoken together privately in the garden, she had become much more sober and sensible. I missed our silly songs, and the plays the three of us used to perform together, starring as The Bright Brilliant Sisters of Belfast. We still called ourselves that, although of course we had had to alter the title some six years previously in order to suit our return to Dublin. Ever afterwards, it ceased to have the same magic to it.

I remember promising myself that what had happened to Hannah would never happen to me. Her predicament had given me fair warning. I still had some years in which to prepare my escape. I would not be married off to anyone. I intended to choose my own life.

In her own quiet way, May was equally determined. She wanted to travel, I'd always known that. Ever since we were children, she had wanted to go to Africa, to India, to the Americas. As we got older, she longed to do the Grand Tour of Europe, as some of the girls from school had done. Italy, Germany, Switzerland all fascinated her. But she knew there was no point in hoping, no point in wishing for anything so impossible. 'If wishes were horses, beggars would ride.' Mama reminded us of this on many occasions. There was no longer the prospect of money for even the most modest 'grand tour' – indeed, if there had ever been. But May was determined – she would see Europe, or die in the attempt. Above all else, she longed to see France. She had always been enchanted by picture books of castles, I remember, fascinated by a country which had kings and queens, style, history, romance. Dublin and Belfast made her feel suffocated. She said they were too small, too stifling. They ate away at the spirit, like rust on the soul. She needed somewhere where living was on a larger scale, where there was room to breathe.

Hannah: Spring 1899

'STAND STILL, HANNAH, for goodness' sake! I'm almost finished.'

Hannah held on tightly to the bedpost. Her mother stood behind her, pulling ever more firmly on the laces of her corset. Lily was standing by, holding a freshly ironed petticoat draped across her outstretched arms. She held it the way one would carry a sleeping child, and something in her pose struck Hannah as almost unbearably sad. She had no idea how old Lily was – perhaps early thirties, perhaps early forties; it was too hard to tell. Her face had been lined and ruddy ever since Hannah could remember, her hands coarse and callused. Even her hair seemed to have been grey for ever. The way she waited, patiently, smiling encouragement at Hannah made the younger woman feel suddenly embarrassed. She saw how she must look to Lily – a beautiful young girl, with an affluent husband-to-be, the prospect of ease and children, all the things which, by rights, Lily should have had, too. Instead, she, Lily, was standing in someone else's house, serving in someone else's bedroom, holding on to the empty promise of someone else's frilled and sagging petticoat.

'That's enough, Mama – I can hardly breathe!'

Sophia clucked and fussed around her eldest daughter. Lily slid the satin petticoat over Hannah's head, smoothing its lacy edging.

'Boots?'

Hannah nodded, and quickly realized that the question was not meant for her. Sophia replied, her whole body intent on what she was doing.

'Yes – and fetch me the button-hook, Lily, please. We should be ready for the gown shortly.'

Hannah said nothing. This was how she had felt more and more over the past weeks – as if she were standing at the sidelines of her own life. Her mother had grown busier and busier, her father more and more remote. Hannah had felt as though she were a nuisance, an impediment to the advancing march of her mother's preparations. She would leave little to Lily and Katie: she wanted to do it all herself. She was rarely absent from Hannah's side, instructing her on how to stand, how to look, how to be. Hannah's frustration grew until, one day, she could stand it no longer, and openly lost patience with her mother.

'Mama! Please! Leave me alone!'

On that occasion, Hannah had stormed up the stairs and slammed her bedroom door in temper, something she hadn't done since she was a child. She had apologized, of course, hating and resenting every moment of her mother's martyred air. She still didn't know which was worse – Mama's over-eagerness to get everything just right, or Papa's air of complete detachment.

Papa had barely spoken to Hannah once the

engagement had been announced. It was as though he washed his hands of her; she was no longer his responsibility. Now he had other things to occupy him. But Mama had thrown herself into the wedding preparations with all the energy she could muster. It was as though someone had thrown her a lifeline: now she could be useful again, could arrange the perfect wedding, could see people's admiring glances and feel perhaps a small return of the old glory.

Hannah sat at her dressing table now while her mother pinned up her hair. She was vain enough to like what she saw. Her eyes were bright, her cheeks naturally coloured. Her wedding-gown would be much more modest, of course, but for now, the smooth petticoat over the boned corset exaggerated the curve of her breasts above her pinched waist. And Mama had always said she had lovely shoulders – smooth and white. She had been right to lace her so tightly, too – the restrictions of her corset made Hannah sit tall, made her appear much more elegant and self-assured than she felt. The older woman looked over her daughter's shoulder now, and both faces were reflected together, warmed by the bright morning light. Her mother's eyes were shining.

'You look beautiful, my dear.'

Hannah was surprised at the sudden wistfulness of her tone. She said nothing. Perhaps they would speak of it later. Lily brought the wedding-gown to them then, carefully draped in soft, white muslin. Sophia hooked all the buttons closed while Lily ran a critical eye over the set of the sleeves, the fall of the skirt, the perfect line of the intricately embroidered cuffs. At one stage she knelt, fixing some invisible imperfection at the hemline. Her employer had just left the room.

Lily looked up. She looked shy, awkward. She held something in her hand, raising her palm towards Hannah. It was a tiny silver brooch.

'It belonged to my mother, Miss Hannah. You know, somethin' old, somethin' new, somethin' borrowed, somethin' blue – well, have this here as your somethin' borrowed. I'll pin it here, just on the hemline – no one'll see it.'

She averted her face quickly, but Hannah could see the burn of embarrassment flush its way up her neck to the hairline. Lily turned up the end of the heavy gown and pinned the little brooch neatly on the folded fabric of the hem. Hannah felt the tears spring to her eyes.

'Thank you, Lily. I'll be very careful of it.'

'Sure I know you will, miss. And I wish you every happiness.'

That was all she had time for. Sophia returned with some small bottles and jars.

'A little powder,' she said, 'and a tiny smudge of rouge on your lips. Now. You're ready.'

I'm dressed, Hannah thought, but I don't know if I can call myself ready. She felt suddenly assailed by the doubts and fears which had been crowding around her for the last several weeks. She was afraid that her first romantic, tender feelings towards Charles were beginning to wither. She had tried desperately to nurture them, but it was weeks now since she and he had met properly, and his letters recently had seemed dry, dutiful rather than affectionate. Hannah began to feel real fear. If he didn't even try to care for her, then she had no chance. The only hope of survival she had was if they could learn to love one another. She hadn't wanted to marry at all; but if she must, then at least let her marriage be something other than the harsh, arid place inhabited by her mother and father.

Hannah gathered up her heavy skirts and followed her mother's careful footsteps down the stairs. She moved with difficulty: her heart had begun to thump and it was impossible to draw long, clean breaths. May and Eleanor were waiting for her – everyone was waiting. She had wild, sudden notions of fleeing from her parents' house, or hurling herself over the banisters to make good her escape.

But she would do none of those things. She knew that. She would carry on as expected throughout the day; she would be charming and grateful, modest and gracious. And she would be married: there was no escaping that.

Charles had left her alone in the hotel room. He had begged her permission to smoke a cigar before retiring, and had left quietly, almost discreetly. Hannah supposed she should be grateful for his delicacy, but the truth was, she felt too nervous to be left alone. The Shelbourne suite was luxurious, certainly, but none the more inviting for that. Now that the day was over, Hannah felt curiously stale and flat. She longed for another glass of champagne: she wanted to feel the fizz and bubble she had enjoyed after the church ceremony, once everybody was together again at the hotel. It was a delightful feeling, drinking champagne and being the centre of attention. She knew she had looked lovely: everyone told her so. Charles's admiring glances throughout the afternoon had made her face colour more than once. She regretted that it had all passed her by so quickly.

She unpinned her hair and let it fall heavily around her shoulders. Her head felt sore and tired: it had become an effort to stand so upright for so long. Sitting had been no relief either: she had eaten little, the pressure on her ribcage growing more intense as the wedding reception drew towards evening. At one stage she had felt faint, and Mama had had to rub her wrists together surreptitiously. A discreet whiff of sal volatile made her feel alert again, capable of seeing through the final few hours.

Now she needed to escape from her clothing but she didn't know where to start. There were hundreds of buttons, it seemed, all down the back of her dress. She began to feel sorry for having sent Lily away – what had she been thinking of? She couldn't even begin to undress herself. Nor could she sit in any comfort: she felt as though her whole upper body was caught in a vice. She was powerless, stupid and powerless. She thought of May and Eleanor, of their still uncomplicated lives in the safe familiarity of their own bedrooms. She started to cry; she couldn't help herself, couldn't stem the tears which welled and fell without her wanting them.

'Let me help you, my dear.'

Hannah hadn't even heard Charles re-enter the

room. She started, whirled around to face him, her cheeks streaked with tears.

'Oh, no – you can't – you mustn't!'

Hannah was horrified. Mama had told her urgently, more than once, how her husband would expect, would want, a shy and modest bride: she must be led by him, must not be forward in word or deed. If she were anything other than demure, then all could be lost.

'Nonsense, my dear – I'm your husband.'

She could smell the cigar-smoke on his moustache, and something else, something more pungent. Whiskey. She searched his face. She wanted to ask him, but struggled against her instinct, mindful of her mother's advice. But then, Mama need never know, no one need ever know anything that passed between them now. If she didn't ask, if she played her role as the shy and modest bride, then perhaps she would never really know him. She struggled to find the words. The silence between them had become almost painful.

'Have you – you're older – I mean . . .'

He smiled at her.

'Yes, my dear, I've done this before.'

He stood back a little from her, not touching her. His expression was grave, but the ever-present humour seemed to hover just beneath the surface.

'Do I shock you?'

Hannah shook her head. Perhaps shock was part of the overwhelming feeling she was trying to grapple with, but much more potent was the sense of relief that flooded her, drowning out fear, apprehension and all the exhaustions of the day. She hadn't wanted both of them to struggle on in silent, mutual incomprehension. Despite Mama's earlier promise that married love could become 'rather wonderful', she had hinted darkly over the last few weeks about the unnamed physical difficulties, fears and embarrassments that beset many a wedding night. Hannah hadn't wanted to listen, felt keenly her mother's intrusion into part of her life which she now wanted to keep private. She was no longer a child: her parents had seen to that. She wanted to claim her adulthood, to move away from Mama's incessant murmurings of what was right and proper, acceptable or shameful. And now here was Charles, expecting her to be shocked. She had the feeling that a great deal depended on her answer.

'No!' she blurted. 'I'm not shocked – just glad one of us knows what to do!'

The air in the room seemed to clear, and she had the sense of a bright, open space between them.

He smiled then and pulled her to him gently.

'Hannah, Hannah, Hannah – I care about you a good deal. Do you think you will learn to care for me?'

He was still holding her, and it was easier that way, easier not to have to look at him. His voice was tender, a little mocking, but she knew he was serious.

She nodded, her eyes filling with unaccountable tears.

'Yes,' she whispered. 'I should like to.'

He released her then, holding on to both her hands. His eyes were kindly.

'Good. Then all the rest is easy. Let me help you with your dress, at least – then I'll leave you if you wish.

275

God's truth, I don't know how you can breathe in that contraption.'

He was grinning at her now, his face reflected in the mirror in front of them. His expression was boyish again, just as it had been on that momentous, fiercely ordinary day in his mother's garden.

He began to unbutton her dress, swearing softly every now and again, making her laugh, letting her cover her embarrassment at being undressed by a man – even a man who, astonishingly, seemed to be her husband.

'Bloody end to them – who dreams up buttons like these?'

Finally, she was free. He loosened the last stay of her corset and turned her around to face him.

'Now, my dear, you may continue in my absence, or wait for my return if you wish. It's up to you.'

Hannah was immediately alarmed.

'Why? Where are you going?'

His voice dropped to a whisper, mock conspiratorial.

'To acquire us a bottle of champagne. I believe we've both just had a fairly trying day. You must promise never, never, to tell anyone – my reputation as a gentleman would be ruined.'

He gazed at her sternly.

'Go on, then. Promise.'

His expression made her giggle.

'I promise. But where will you go?'

'A lady must never ask.'

He leaned towards her and his lips brushed the top of her shoulder. And then he was gone. Whether it was the relief of being able to breathe again, or the sensation of a sudden and affectionate ease between them, Hannah couldn't tell. All she knew was that she felt absurdly light and free. Perhaps the beginnings of the tenderness she had felt towards him were not such delicate plants, after all. She would not scurry into her nightgown, waiting for him passively under cover of darkness. Her shoulder tingled where he had kissed her. She would wait, she would be daring and allow her husband to finish undressing her. His kindness, his humour had made her feel warm and expansive – she wanted to be light-hearted, to laugh with him, to wash away the strain of Mama, of Papa, of the last few weeks. She would trust him.

May: Summer 1899

IT DIDN'T TAKE the children long to get used to her. They had been shy that first morning, not looking at her directly, keeping their eyes on their books. She'd liked the way they said her name: 'Mamzelle May' sounded much more exotic than she felt.

The previous night had been almost sleepless: she'd been too tired and strained after the long journey, her head full of restless dreams. When May had first learned of the country home where she would spend her first four months in France, her imagination had supplied a house something like the one to which Grandfather Delaney had taken them all, years ago – near Rosses Point in Sligo. She remembered an early Victorian two-storey house, with four bedrooms, draughty windows and a vast range in the kitchen, beside which all the neighbourhood cats made themselves welcome. Although it was summer, they'd kept the range lit all through the grey, rain-filled fortnight: the tiles on the kitchen floor were the only warm place in the whole, chilly house.

Nothing could have prepared May for the sight of the carved, vaulted front door which brought the carriage to a sudden halt. She kept waiting for the journey to continue – surely they'd just stopped for a moment outside a church, or a castle; this couldn't possibly be someone's *home*. Then the carriage door was opened for her, and unseen hands flipped down the two small steps and helped her on to the shining gravel. In the moonlight, the building before her looked austere, somewhat forbidding. She adopted her mother's no-nonsense tone inside her head as she chided herself for her silly notions, exhorting herself to be her age.

A tall, dark-haired woman was standing just inside the portico. Her stance reminded May of Mama, the way she used to clasp her hands before singing one of her favourite arias. The gold jewellery, the arrangement of her hair, the fall of her elegant silk gown, all proclaimed her identity. This had to be Madame Ondart. She seemed to shimmer in the light and shade cast by the gas lamp. May felt very plain and gauche by comparison and stumbled in her nervousness as she made her way up the steps to the main door. The woman did not move towards her, nor did she extend a hand in greeting. She simply waited until May reached her.

'*Bonsoir, Madame,*' May managed. '*Je suis May O'Connor.*'

'*Bonsoir, Mademoiselle. Vous êtes bienvenue.*'

The woman's tentative smile seemed to fade as May came fully into view under the pale, single light. May was conscious that she was being scrutinized, measured up. She began to feel very uncomfortable. Wasn't this woman behaving very rudely?

'I'm sure you are tired after your long journey.

Isabelle will show you to your room. I shall see you at breakfast. Goodnight, Mademoiselle.'

'Goodnight, Madame.'

And that was it. Madame swept off down the corridor, perhaps hurrying back to more interesting company. May could hear voices and laughter in the distance, a sudden burst of conversation as a door was opened; then silence. Isabelle, middle-aged and smart, led May to a room at the top of a long flight of stairs, and then left her at once, inclining her head finally as a silent acknowledgement of May's existence.

Numbly, May undressed and lay down on the bed, too exhausted even to take in her surroundings. She blew out the candle that had been left on a small, solid-looking table, and closed her eyes gratefully. But sleep eluded her; she felt uneasy, alert to all the unfamiliar creaks and groans of the house settling around her. Finally, she fell into an exhausted doze just as dawn was breaking, the sky streaked with pink and grey brushstrokes, just visible outside her window. The knock on her door at seven startled her: it took her a moment to remember where she was. A maid entered, bringing hot water. She curtsied hurriedly and left. The silence of her departure filled May with sudden misgiving. A great wave of homesickness left her breathless in its wake. It was all beginning to feel like too much. She already missed the warmth of Hannah's embrace, the quiet seriousness of Ellie's blue gaze. And she certainly did not feel that anyone had made any particular effort to make her feel welcome last night.

*

Madame Ondart was already seated at the breakfast table. She looked up and inclined her head politely as May was ushered into the room.

'*Bonjour, Mademoiselle O'Connor.* I hope you slept well?'

Her face seemed to May to be arranged in the contours of a smile, but no warmth reached her eyes. She was all *surface*, May thought, with that vague, feathery politeness which meant she didn't really care about you at all. Her very formality seemed to be intensified by the heavy, ornate oak furniture and the morning light filtering dimly through half-closed shutters. May wished that her French was better: her reply sounded awkward and foolish even to her own ears. Madame barely acknowledged it.

'Genevieve will bring breakfast to your room for this morning. I wish to speak to the children in the schoolroom before I introduce you. Is there anything you need?'

She spoke slowly – perhaps making an effort to be kind? May shook her head.

'No, Madame. There is nothing I need. Thank you.'

'Very well. We shall discuss the children's activities together when we meet in half an hour.'

The young girl who had brought the hot water to May's room now entered the room silently. May realized that she was being dismissed.

'Merci,' was all she could think of to say before making her mortified exit. Was this how she was going to feel for the whole year? This was not how she had imagined travel, new surroundings, exciting experiences.

Nothing Constance MacBride told her had prepared her for this. She had expected warmth, the sharing of family news, the polite interest one would automatically display for even the most distant, the most remote of family friends. Instead, this was painfully awkward, reminiscent of not knowing your lessons as a child in primary school.

A bowl of milky coffee was set on a small table in May's bedroom. Genevieve put some croissants wrapped in a napkin in the centre, and a bowl containing sugar to one side. Then she curtsied hurriedly and left the room as silently as she had entered earlier that morning. May felt her face begin to crumple as she looked at the table. She swallowed hard, determined to contain her tears. She had never eaten breakfast on her own in her life. Hannah had always been there, and so had Ellie. She perched on the edge of the hard chair and tried to work out how to drink from such a large vessel with no handles. Nor could she eat. Even the bits of the pastry she first crumbled on to her plate lodged somewhere in her throat, refusing to soften. She wanted desperately not to be here.

She was glad to make her escape, to follow yet again the swift, slight figure of Genevieve who led her to the schoolroom, where Nathalie and Jean-Louis sat waiting for her. She felt an immediate wash of affection for the two slight, serious figures, dressed alike in their dark blue smocks.

'*Bonjour,* Mamzelle *May,*' they each said in turn, shaking hands formally before resuming their seats, faces shiny, full of shy curiosity. May wanted them to like her. She only half listened as Madame listed off the children's daily activities: English grammar, dictation, conversation, gentle walks while the morning was still cool, music practice . . . Instead, despite herself, her eyes were drawn to the shelves of books which filled the walls. The room was too sombre, too monochrome for children: she began to wish for more cheer. These two small lives seemed to be in need of being made brighter.

May was glad when Madame left the schoolroom. It seemed to her that the children, too, relaxed at once, exhaling with relief once the door closed behind her. They both turned to May, looking at her expectantly. They were waiting for her to produce some sort of magic, she supposed. She asked to see their school books, which they handed over at once. As she flicked through their pages, unseeing, she tried to quell the feeling of hopelessness which had begun to overwhelm her. The truth was, she had no idea what she was going to say to them, how she was going to teach them. She had never expected to be thrown in so completely at the deep end.

It was Jean-Louis who first broke the silence, speaking slowly, pronouncing the words as though he had been speaking French.

'Mamzelle May, have you brothers and sisters?'

'Yes,' she smiled, feeling suddenly easier. 'I have two sisters, one is called Hannah, the other Eleanor.'

It seemed to be so much easier after that. They named everything in the schoolroom for her, and copied from the small blackboard without being told. They were conscientious children, May thought, obedient to the point of apathy. She felt a little guilty, almost as though she were some sort of impostor. But she felt she could grow close to these two little souls, over time. Maybe then it wouldn't be so strained between them: maybe they could visit the rest of the house together, a different room each day, and she could teach them all the words the textbooks demanded, and more besides. They could learn about the outdoors as they went walking together. She could even teach them about Ireland, she thought, suddenly remembering her much younger self and her fascination with the shape and detail of maps. Perhaps it would be possible, after all, to be, if not happy here, then at least busy and productive.

Lessons were for three hours each day and for the next week the children pored, uncomplaining, over their prescribed texts. These were dusty, worthy tomes that made May itch with impatience. They reminded her of the lowest shelves of Grandfather Delaney's study, and she smiled at the affectionate memory. She had a sudden, sharp realization of just how much she missed him. She couldn't have wished him to have lived longer. He had hated his inability to pursue his routine; his lack of independence; his *stasis*, as he called it. He had told May quietly one evening as she read to him that he intended to see Hannah married, but that he could not promise to be there for her. He had stretched out his old fingers to catch her tears, and whispered that she was his favourite. All his books, he'd said, all of them, were to be hers. All she had to do was make sure she found a husband who would make room for them in his heart as well as his house. She'd laughed, tearfully, as he'd made her promise to do that, to recreate his shelves in some other home where her children would bring her as much joy as she had brought him.

In this room, however, unlike her childhood afternoons in Grandfather's study, there was nothing to help her break through the children's solemnity. Day after day, she tried to find something to make them truly curious, to make their eyes bright with interest.

Then, about two weeks or so after her arrival, they told her about Philippe. They had begun to be more open with her by then, edging their chairs closer to her desk, becoming mischievous and childlike once Madame Ondart had left the schoolroom after her usual stiff morning visit.

She'd prepared a lesson for them in English for the more relaxed hour after Madame's departure: 'My family'. She taught them clearly, patiently, and they rewarded her at once, scraps of English and torrents of French all tumbling out together as each of them vied to tell her about their Philippe, their big brother. At first she'd thought they must be mistaken: the age gap was so great. Twenty-five years old; Papa's first son; carrying on Papa's important business in Paris. Nathalie was standing by May's chair at this stage, her eyes big, voice breathless with excitement. They'd seen a painting of Philippe's mother in Papa's study, Philippe had shown it to them. He'd said it was a secret, made them promise not to tell anyone he had let them in. Mamzelle May would say nothing to Maman, would she not?

May suddenly understood: half-brother; although

she did not correct them. She couldn't put her finger on why, but it seemed to explain something of the relationship she had sensed between Monsieur and the present Madame Ondart. Although their first meeting had been brief, formal, May had been struck by an impression of distance between husband and wife, a distance that had more to it than mere disparity of years.

At eight and six, Jean-Louis and Nathalie adored the very idea of their older brother. May looked at their delicate, fine-boned faces. They looked so pale, so earnest, despite the brief illumination which talk of Philippe had brought to their features. Fresh air, she decided. These children spent far too much of their lives cooped up indoors. What harm could sunshine do them? She was not supposed to keep the children out of doors after half past eleven in the morning: the intensity of the midday sun would make them ill, Madame insisted. They must stay inside each day from late morning until four o'clock, when the heat would no longer upset their stomachs, or make them tired and listless. May looked longingly at the grounds. June sunlight streamed through the vast window. From where she sat, she could see the lawns and part of the formal gardens which were dotted with inviting pools of deep shadow.

She turned to the two bright heads, bent carefully again over the new words she had written for them to copy.

'We shall take our last lesson for today in the gardens,' she wrote in her careful French on the small blackboard, with the translation underneath. Nathalie's face lit up at once.

'I have a flowerbed of my own that Philippe helped me plant. I look after it on my own . . .'

May smiled at her. It was the longest speech the little girl had made in almost four weeks of classes. Jean-Louis looked less certain until his sister simply stood up and took Mamzelle May's hand. They both turned towards him.

'Coming, Jean-Louis?' asked May.

She hoped he wouldn't refuse, wouldn't become all grave and closed as he was in his father's presence. He didn't take her hand, but he did decide to lead the way. May was interested that he brought them down the servants' stairway at the back of the house, all the way through the kitchen gardens, around the side of the coach houses, and finally to the long green spread of the lawns. They could not be seen, she was sure, from any of the main rooms of the house. The subterfuge saddened her, for what it said about their lives. She decided to take full advantage of their seclusion.

'Do you know the best game we can play? The one we call in English "hide and seek"?'

They nodded, eyes full of mischief.

'I will count to fifty with my eyes closed. You must find somewhere to hide in that time. Then I'll come looking for you. But you must stay outside, in the open air. Gardens only, no hiding in the coach houses or outhouses. Agreed?'

They nodded again.

'Together or separately?' she asked them.

'Together,' said Nathalie.

'Separately,' said Jean-Louis.

May laughed.

'For this first time, hide together. Next time, you can each hide on your own.'

Jean-Louis wasn't impressed, she could tell, but she had spotted something akin to fear in Nathalie's expression. This was probably a big adventure – the first chink in the daily routine which they had to wear like armour. May wondered what their parents were protecting them from, out here in the peaceful countryside, miles from anywhere.

She couldn't find them.

How could two children simply disappear off the face of the earth? May could feel panic begin to rise from the pit of her stomach. All she could see was Madame Ondart's stern face in front of her eyes. What could she say, how could she explain? *I'm sorry, Madame, I've just lost your children.* Perhaps there were terrors lurking in these grounds of which she, May, knew nothing, could know nothing. Perhaps the children were kept hidden away among dusty books for good reason. May had no idea how long she'd been searching, but the sun had moved significantly since she had uncovered her eyes once she'd counted to fifty. It was lunchtime, at least: perhaps hunger would drive them out. There weren't all that many places to hide, if the children had indeed stayed outdoors. The kitchen gardens were full of low shrubs, herbs, vegetables – nothing even a small child could hide behind. She'd paced the formal gardens twice now, senses keen, alert for any sound: but there'd been nothing. She passed through the little wrought-iron gate again, back out to the lawns. Some small movement made her look up. What she saw made her laugh out loud with relief.

A great shout of blue announced Nathalie's hiding-place in the fork of a giant oak tree. She sat absolutely still; May was sure that the child was holding her breath. How on earth had she got up there? More to the point, how was she going to get her down?

She spread her arms wide, a gesture of defeat, a token of surrender.

'Nathalie – you've won! It's taken me far too long to find you – well done! Is Jean-Louis with you?'

Nathalie shook her head.

'No, Mamzelle May. He says you must find him too!'

May smiled at her earnestness.

'Aren't you hungry? I can't give you lunch up there!'

'No – you must find Jean-Louis first!'

The change in the little girl's face was extraordinary. She was pink with delight, animated, her fair curls escaping from their restraints all around her small head.

'All right – I'll find him!'

He can't be far, May reasoned, but she wanted to find him quickly. She hesitated for a moment, standing under the welcome shade of the leafy oak. The unaccustomed sun was strong; the light was almost white, blinding. It hurt her eyes, the heat burned the top of her head. She should have brought her hat, and hats for the two children. May did not relish the thought of explaining herself to Madame Ondart, or to Monsieur, for that matter, if any of them became ill due to her stupidity.

'I believe this is what you are looking for, Mademoiselle?'

The voice behind her startled her, and May turned quickly, almost stumbling in the process. Nathalie was laughing down at her. The little girl pointed to the bewildering sight of a grown man crouching in the second fork of the tree, just away to Nathalie's right, and a good three feet above her. His coat and trousers were suited to the city streets, not to the precarious business of perching in an oak tree several feet above the ground. His white shirt looked rather streaked and bedraggled, his leather boots a strange growth among the leaves. His whole appearance made May feel a complex mixture of anxiety and relief. He didn't look dangerous, his clothes were the clothes of a gentleman . . . and the children were safe. But should he have hidden them like that? And who was he anyway? She wasn't sure yet whether she should be angry. Even as she was making up her mind, she realized who he had to be. He had his arm around Jean-Louis's shoulders, his dark head a stark contrast to the boy's white-blonde hair. Despite the difference in their colouring, their similarity across the eyes was startling. All three were looking at her with delight, enjoying her speechless gaze, watching her try to work out what she was seeing.

In what seemed like one fluid movement, the young man dropped to the grass beneath, reached up for Nathalie and swung her down beside him, grinning broadly at her squeals of delight.

'Come on, Louis, climb over to Nathalie's place and jump like I showed you.'

May was filled with alarm. If he should hurt himself . . . Some instinct stopped her from moving forward, from intervening between the two of them. In front of all of them, Jean-Louis now had to jump; she could see that it was a matter of honour.

He climbed carefully down to the fork where Nathalie had been sitting. Please, please, May prayed silently. Nothing broken, please.

His high, childish voice rang out: '*Un, deux, trois . . .*'

A bright flash of blue smock, a yell of approbation from the other two, and there he was: flushed, grinning, rolling on the grass under the spreading oak tree.

'Excellent! Well done! You bent your knees at exactly the right time, just like I showed you!'

He ruffled Jean-Louis's hair and turned at once to May.

'Please forgive my manners: I'm Philippe Ondart, big brother to these two rascals. And you must be Mademoiselle O'Connor, all the way from Ireland.'

His tone was so light, so natural, that May felt no embarrassment at the unconventional nature of their meeting. He extended his hand and shook hers firmly. She liked his mobile, rather ugly face, his friendly manner. He made her think suddenly, achingly, of home.

'Yes – pleased to meet you.'

He nodded.

'As am I.'

He turned to the children.

'Now remember, the tree-climbing was my idea. Let's get washed and all have lunch together. Mademoiselle May, will you join us?'

He didn't wait for a reply. Instead, he began walking towards the kitchen gardens, his coat thrown over one shoulder, his free hand holding Nathalie's. May was taken aback. Lunch for the children, and for her, was in the schoolroom. Occasionally, on the day when Madame was not at home, the three of them ate in the kitchen with Jeanette and Genevieve. Isabelle, in keeping with her elevated status as housekeeper, preferred to take her meals alone. Somehow, May felt that young Monsieur Ondart had no intention of lunching in the schoolroom, or the kitchen either, for that matter. But the children were her responsibility, and after the fright they had just given her, she wanted to stay close to them. Besides, she was worried that she might have to defend herself when it became known that the children had been outdoors at an unapproved time.

She would soon know by Madame Ondart's face what was expected of her now, and how her recent transgression was viewed. Behaviour appropriate to the situation would be indicated by the arch of an eyebrow, the coolness of a glance. May felt suddenly depressed, a headache beginning from too much sun.

Reluctantly, she followed the three figures in front of her towards the back of the main house.

Madame said nothing to her, nothing at all. She spoke, rapid-fire, to Genevieve, who whisked the two children away, silencing their protests as she shooed them from the kitchen.

Philippe was the soul of courtesy: he kissed his stepmother's hand, answered her polite questions regarding his arrival, enquired after his father. May took her opportunity, murmured about getting ready for lunch, although nobody was listening, and made her glad escape up the back stairway to her room.

She wondered how much longer she could bear this.

The gong for lunch sounded a good half-hour later than usual. May made her way to the smaller of the two dining rooms. Madame was already seated.

When the children arrived, they looked scrubbed, their clothes had been changed, Nathalie's hair severely braided.

May felt their shiny appearance as keenly as a rebuke.

Eleanor's Journal

ON THE DAY of Hannah's wedding, May was, if anything, even more beautiful than the bride. She was not quite as tall, but her looks were dark, almost exotic. She had the most perfect skin, clear and creamy. I remember feeling awkward, ungainly, all hands and feet, in her company. She seemed never to make an ungraceful movement. When I look back on the photograph of that day, I am still surprised at how lovely the three of us look. The photographer even succeeded in creating an illusion of poise for me – he gave me some flowers to hold on my knee, so that my over-large hands were concealed very prettily.

Hannah, everybody agreed, made a radiant bride. She had chosen an elegant ivory silk gown and coat dress for the occasion. The shade was a perfect complement for her fair hair and smooth skin. Mama's dressmaker also hand-embroidered exquisitely, and the bodice of Hannah's wedding-gown, the edges of her coat dress, and the long cuffs of her gauntlet gloves were crowded with all manner of fine stitching. Her hat, too, was of the latest style – wide and deep-crowned, its feathers and trimmings an exact match for the shade of her gown.

But I digress. I don't think I really understood until afterwards what Hannah's marriage signified for me in practical terms – it took some time for the realization to dawn that my sister would, in all probability, never live in the same house with me again. On the day, however, my fifteen-year-old self was concerned only with the beautiful pale pink silk dress that Mama had had made for me, and the fact that I was permitted to wear my hair up for the first time. May, at seventeen, was going through a period of being completely disdainful of me – she would now be the elder sister of our household, and she took care to prove it by ordering me to do this and that during the weeks coming up to the wedding.

Mama and Papa were, I remember, well pleased with the day. Everything was perfect, the cake, the wine, the flowers. It was many years later that I learned of Grandfather Delaney's role in all of this. As with so many things in the previous six years, he had paid for everything to do with the wedding, and presided over the day like a grumpy old aristocrat, despite his rapidly failing health. I think the anticipation of the wedding had kept him alive – he was, in his own way, proud of his three Dublin granddaughters. He died two weeks after Hannah's wedding and May was inconsolable.

I remember him, even on the wedding day, being gruff, almost rude to everyone. I wondered at the time why Mama and Papa allowed it. Mama hushed me every time I made mention of his bad temper. I understand now, of course, that she had had to endure his off-putting manner, like it or not – circumstances gave her no choice. I have learned to feel more sympathy for

Mama as the years have passed. I know that she had to endure many things.

I had liked Charles the first time I met him in Belfast, and I liked him again now. His humour was always kindly, and he took the trouble to converse with me as though I were a real adult. He often behaved as if he and I shared some private joke, and he would frequently direct the most comical looks at me over his mother's head, whenever she launched into another one of her interminable 'what-a-wonderful-husband-I-had' stories. I remember feeling so relieved that the Mac-Brides had all stayed in the Shelbourne for the week leading up to the wedding. I don't think I could have contained myself had they – had she – been with us. Charles, however, made me laugh, often despite myself. I received a good number of Mama's glances across the table, the ones with a half-raised eyebrow, warning me to be careful of myself, to mind my manners.

Constance MacBride was patently delighted with herself that day, too. I have to confess I warmed to her, and to both her daughters, Emily and Marianne. They had a wonderful sense of humour and had no shame in interrupting their mother's lengthy and frequent stories. Emily, in particular, had a wicked glint in her eye whenever her mother's tales took flight, and her cry of 'Now, Mother!', sometimes clear across the room, brought instant obedience, and silence, in its wake. She was as unlike her mother as it is possible for anyone to be. Where Constance MacBride was large and fleshy, Emily was trim, tidy, her body giving a great sense of compacted energy. Her eyes had a manner of darting from one person to another, impressing all who met her with her quick and lively intelligence. I enjoyed watching her, enjoyed her mastery over her ever-imposing mama. Of course, I realize now that Emily had just as much mastery as her delighted mother permitted her. I see them now as a sophisticated vaudeville act, each part sparkling all the more because of the willing complicity of the other. It did not surprise me to learn a little later that Emily was, in all ways, the living image of her father.

It was she who took May under her wing, she who suggested that her mother's old friend, Monsieur Ondart, would be the perfect person for May to stay with, if she were really serious about going to France.

I remember feeling somewhat put-out – not only was Hannah getting married and leaving home, but now May seemed all set, too, to begin her adventures. Soon, I should be the only one of us left at home, and I really wasn't quite sure how I felt about that.

May: Summer 1899

FOR WEEKS, PHILIPPE'S arrival at Rouen train station was a regular event. Friday evening to Sunday afternoon his presence seemed to fill the house and gardens, whether he sat on the shady veranda with his father in the evenings, their cigar-smoke drifting lazily in and out of the heavy jasmine overhead, or played rough and tumble with Jean-Louis when Madame wasn't looking. He appeared to be deeply attached to his young brother and sister, and May particularly liked watching him with Nathalie. He would kneel with her beside her flowerbed, occasionally helping her plant something new that Old Pierre willingly gave them from the greenhouse. He would watch as she pulled out any stray weeds and watered everything with care. May could see he was careful to let Nathalie do everything herself – his role was that of advisor.

'Like this, Nathalie – see? You must soak the *soil* so that the water gets to the roots. It will just dry off the leaves in an instant, and then the plant hasn't really had a drink at all. Do you see?'

The little girl's adoration of him was sometimes painful to see; her glowing, open face was the palest, most angelic picture of innocent devotion. May found herself hoping that he would never let either of the children down. She hoped they would be old enough to cope when the inevitable happened, and someone else usurped the greater part of his affections.

As it was, the two children underwent a complete transformation in Philippe's company. They no longer behaved like miniature adults, grave and silent about their studies, small creatures of unvarying routine. Instead, they played hide and seek and hunt the thimble, even climbed trees when Madame was not in evidence. May admired Philippe's unselfconscious ease with them, his willingness to be open and childlike. She also got the sense that Madame was a little afraid of him: the children spent a great deal of time out of doors when he was around, and he simply seemed to ignore the distinction between the times which were permitted and those that were forbidden. May had seen a look pass between Madame and her husband on Philippe's last visit. Whatever she saw in her husband's face made her turn away, tight-lipped. She never intervened between Philippe and the children again.

After his return to Paris every weekend, May was the happy recipient of the children's fund of high spirits: whatever magic Philippe had wrought with them spilled over into the schoolroom during the following days. They would be full of fun, ready to laugh at even her lamest joke, eager to cooperate. By mid-week, they would be naturally subdued again, and she had learned to coax them along with promises of their brother's return. It never failed.

On this particularly hot, still Friday evening, they awaited his arrival from the station as usual. The whole week had been oppressive, the air humid and stifling. May found the intensity of the heat uncomfortable, and for once, Madame's strictures regarding the outdoors sat easily with her. There was no pleasure in being outside. Within the house, at least the dim, shuttered rooms offered some cool escape. Outside it, the air was so warm and cloying that even the shade offered no real respite. May disliked the old feelings of suffocation which seemed to nudge to the surface when the heat was this intense.

Now, at nine o'clock in the evening, sitting with the children in the shade of the veranda, May was grateful for this, the pleasantest part of the day. Nathalie was getting tired of waiting. She jumped up and down impatiently every time she heard the slightest sound. The children weren't even prepared for bed yet: Monsieur and Madame were away at a weekend house-party in Deauville, and May was determined to relax the regime just a little. In fact, the whole household was running more slowly: meals were unhurried, less formal affairs. The redoubtable Isabelle seemed to have thawed a little in the heat, agreeing to eat with the others in the kitchen rather than in her own quarters. Even the old house seemed more relaxed: it had been creaking and sighing all evening, like an old man easing his aching bones into rest. Genevieve had commented on it, too, but her no-nonsense prediction was for a massive thunderstorm.

Tonight, May had dressed with particular care.

There had been no urgency in her preparations for dinner. Instead, she was filled with a sense of pleasant anticipation which puzzled her. She had grown used to the Ondarts' stiff manner; it no longer had the power to upset her. But this evening, their absence had apparently made a huge difference to her – more than she would have thought. Why else would she feel such extremes of relief, of indolent well-being? She decided to wear her blue silk for the first time. Mama had had it made for her before she came away, but she had never worn it; her intuition had told her that Madame would frown upon it. It was not sombre enough, not unobtrusive enough, not – *grey* enough, somehow, for the governess of her children.

When May finally heard the scrunch of the carriage wheels on gravel, she was startled. She felt her face flush suddenly at the thought of Philippe. She was horrified at herself: what on earth was wrong with her? She stood up, partly concealed by the shade of the veranda, and looked wildly around the garden. She needed somewhere to hide: somewhere she could go until this extraordinary attack of confusion could be controlled. She couldn't believe it: where had these feelings leapt from? They were impossible, absolutely impossible: she warned herself not to be foolish. She couldn't possibly be in love with this man – she hardly knew him. The gap between them was much too great, their different nationalities, their backgrounds – and besides, Madame and Monsieur would never approve.

Nevertheless, she had her whole life mapped out in seconds, her thoughts wheeling, her brain whirling with all the impossibilities suddenly made possible. By the time the carriage drew to a halt in a shower of gravel, she had already married him.

The children threw themselves at Philippe as he alighted from the carriage. Amid their yells and laughter, May had time to compose herself. Her face felt cooler; she had managed to stop her hands from trembling. She had also had the time to laugh at herself. What an absurd imagination she had. She deliberately did not go towards the carriage, despite her custom. She must be careful. She would never let him know, never give him any indication of the madness she had just experienced. It must have something to do with the weather.

Later, when she was alone, she would look at her feelings calmly. They were childish, unfounded. She would never give him any indication.

As it happened, he came to her first.

She had returned to say goodnight, once the children were in bed. Exhausted from the unaccustomed lateness of the hour, they had both suddenly become quarrelsome, picking at each other, until finally Nathalie started to cry.

'Enough!' Philippe had said sternly. 'Off you go, both of you. It's late. No more fighting or we'll have no games tomorrow.'

Meekly, they had both followed May up the stairs to the room they shared. They washed unwillingly, complaining constantly as they changed into their nightwear. She had had to speak to them a little sharply more than once. Perhaps Madame's routine had a point, after all. By the time May left them, both children were sulking. Neither wanted a story. It was the first time she had ever left them in such bad temper. She stayed in her own room for ten minutes, waiting. Then she crept silently along the corridor to check. They were both asleep. Quietly, she made her way back downstairs to the veranda.

'Will you join me?'

Philippe gestured to the chair she had vacated almost an hour ago. She hesitated. Genevieve appeared then with a bottle of wine and two glasses.

'A good chablis – and it has been cooling in the cellar. Let me tempt you.'

He waited until Genevieve curtsied and left to go back inside. He poured a glass and handed it to May. She had thought her resolve strong, had promised herself simply to say goodnight and retire to her room quickly before she could change her mind. But she was tempted despite herself, her determination suddenly dissolving. Besides any feelings she might have, which she was sure she could conceal, it had been a long time since she had had any real conversation. Her French was improving, but still limited. She found the language an uphill struggle. Philippe's English, on the other hand, was excellent. It would be good to talk without strain, without her mind having to leap three sentences ahead of her thoughts to make sure that her grammatical structure was correct. She was constantly terrified of making mistakes in front of Madame. It was as though the woman waited for them, pouncing on every new indication of the inferiority of her governess. May was suddenly tired of being second best. A great wave of homesickness washed over her and she longed for home. Even Mama and Papa's troubled company seemed better than what she had here, in a foreign country. She missed her sisters overwhelmingly; particularly Hannah. She didn't want to be alone tonight.

She nodded, accepting the cool glass, beads of moisture already springing up on the delicate, lacy engraving around the rim.

'Thank you. That would be very nice.'

He took her cue and immediately answered her in English. The relief was enormous. And the wine was good. All her heady emotions of that day seemed to quieten suddenly, to settle into place, and she began to feel comfortable in his presence. She was able to chide herself for her earlier foolishness. He was a nice man, a sensitive soul. They had the care of the two children in common. They were polite and courteous in each other's company. That was all.

'You must miss your own home from time to time – you have sisters, am I correct?'

He was looking at her kindly, his expression open, interested in her.

To her horror, May felt her eyes well up. How had he known? How could he have seen inside her thoughts? It felt as though he had seen through her, to her most vulnerable centre, and decided to ambush her with understanding. It had been almost three months since anybody had spoken to her with such gentleness. She was unable to answer. Her throat felt as though it had closed over. She bent her head, not wanting him to see. A moment later, tears splashed on to her gown, and they continued to fall, uncontrollably. She could hardly breathe. It was impossible to stem the tide – holding back was beginning to suffocate her. The feeling was the same as on the day Sister Raphael had locked her into the map cupboard. But now she also felt shame, anger at having exposed herself, and a deep longing to have someone's arms around her. She stood up, mortified, poised for flight. She couldn't look Philippe in the eye. Dear God, what must he think of her?

She could sense that he had stood up, too, could hear the concern in his voice as he took the wine glass from her hand. His kindness only made everything worse.

'I'm sorry – please forgive me – I should never have touched upon such a sensitive subject . . .'

She stretched out one hand towards him – a gesture to say please, leave me, don't come any closer. Instead, he took it, and she felt the warm shock of his lips on her palm. She looked up at him, amazement and hope fighting in equal measure, already threatening to overcome her disbelief.

'May . . .'

She thrilled at the way he said her name. She forgot about her embarrassment, her tear-stained face, all the reasons why this was impossible. She felt all the strength ebb from her body. She wanted to lean against him, to use his solid presence to keep her feet on the ground.

He drew her closer to him. He kissed her eyes, her wet cheeks, her mouth. His voice was urgent, full of emotion.

'I love you, May. Don't you know that? I've loved you since that first day in the garden. I haven't been able to think of anything else.'

He held her so tight she could hardly breathe.

'Do you remember?'

She nodded. Her first glimpse of him – a strange growth among the leaves – as he hid with the children in the oak tree, was etched for ever in her memory. Each time she thought of him, that was the Philippe she saw. No other meeting since had erased the powerful impact of that first time. The city clothes, the crumpled shirt, the delicious shock of his incongruity in a country garden. And his face: mobile, pleasantly ugly, full of humour. She had not forgotten.

She pulled away and looked at him, still unable to speak. He was sincere, she was sure he was, but this was almost too much, too soon.

'Didn't you know? Couldn't you feel how I care for you?'

He whispered to her, pulling her close again, burying his lips in the softness of her neck.

She shook her head. Tentatively, she wound her arms around his back. They stood like that for what seemed to be a whole lifetime. May had the strangest sensation that she had come home, that all her previous life had been directing her towards this astonishing moment. She wanted it to last for ever. The sound of his voice, telling her he loved her. The scent of jasmine, released in a heady rush by the huge, fat drops of rain that had suddenly started to fall. The feel of his warm shoulders under her trembling hands. He loved her. That was all that mattered.

Hannah: Summer 1899

CHARLES'S PRIDE IN Holywood was palpable. A few days after the return from their honeymoon, he and Hannah escaped, like guilty children, from under Constance MacBride's maternal gaze, and made their way, alone, to their new home in Stewarts Place.

'Let's make a run for it, before Mama comes down to breakfast,' Charles had urged, his face assuming the contours of a naughty child. Hannah was ready, willing above all to find room to breathe far away from the oppressively benign presence of her new mother-in-law.

Charles insisted they drive from Belfast on this, their first occasion to visit Holywood. He wanted to show the many beauties of the scenery to his new wife: the convenience of the Belfast and County Down railway could wait for another, more prosaic occasion.

Hannah was excited at the prospect of visiting her new home. She only half listened to Charles as the carriage took them through Ballymacarrett and Strandtown. 'Bunker's Hill,' he was saying, 'this is the place that gave its name to the famous Bunker's Hill in America. Did you know that, my dear?'

Of course, Hannah hadn't known it, and he was

pleased and gratified at her apparent surprise. He was warming to his theme.

'See those hills there? They have the function of stopping the south-east and southerly winds that sweep across the bay, making the climate of Holywood ideal for those of a delicate constitution.'

He affected the sonorous tone of a solemn, stuffy newspaper report.

'Delicate like me?' she asked, archly.

He nodded vigorously.

'Just like you, my dear, and my dear susceptible Mama.'

Hannah laughed. The idea of Constance MacBride as a delicate flower in need of shelter from the prevailing winds was a truly ludicrous one.

'Does this mean that she'll be coming to live with us?' she teased.

Charles looked genuinely horrified.

'Not for a moment. Mama is very firmly entrenched among the comfortable groves of south Belfast. She does very well there.'

His tone was firm, as though reassuring himself.

Hannah smiled at him.

'Pray, Mr MacBride, do continue.'

He stopped, mid-sentence.

'You, young woman, are making fun of me.'

She lowered her eyes demurely.

'Not at all; I find your monologue most instructive.'

She raised her eyes to find him laughing at her. She knew that this couldn't continue, that it wasn't possible to be this happy for ever. When Charles returned to work, when she had a home to look after, when all the messy, intricate domestic details began to take over – then, perhaps, she would really know what her life was going to be. But for now, she was so elated she was almost afraid to breathe, lest everything around her shatter.

The memory of their honeymoon was still vivid. She could see the tulip fields stretching away from her. She would never forget the shock of their deep, flat masses of colour, rippling away towards the horizon. She had lazed in the shade while Charles painted: she was surprised at how good his eye was. Then Amsterdam with its canals and barges; a thriving, picturesque city, she had loved its busyness, its exotic streets, its *difference* from anything she had ever seen. She thought how May would have loved it.

Good food, good wine – Hannah was dazzled at the way Charles knew his way around all the things which made her feel shy and uncertain. On their last night, she was filled with regret: she really didn't want to go home.

He had teased her out of her low mood, making her laugh over nothing. She wanted the feeling of intimacy to last; she didn't want to give up feeling carefree so soon.

Finally, he raised his glass to her.

'There's just one thing, my dear.'

His face was so grave that she felt suddenly frightened. What had she done? In what ways had she disappointed?

'When we go home, it would be advisable for you to change your appearance somewhat.'

She stared at him blankly, not comprehending.

'Do you understand?'

She shook her head, feeling tears prickle. She knew it couldn't have lasted. She felt all her happiness drain away, as though something inside her had slowly begun to deflate.

He twirled the remains of wine in his glass. When he spoke his voice was very soft, with no trace of mockery.

'You'll need to temper your happiness a little. It wouldn't do for all to believe that you're a wanton woman. Mama would be scandalized.'

At first, she blushed furiously, mortified, not knowing where to look. Then she caught his eye, her words choking somewhere between sobs and laughter. She would never get used to his teasing; she never saw it coming, never knew if its sometimes too-keen edge contained a criticism of her. Now he had taken her hand, kissed it, his eyes full of remorse.

'Ah, I'm sorry, Hannah – that wasn't fair of me. I've gone too far. Forgive me.'

She was going to have to learn to give as good as she got. Now she looked across the table at him challengingly.

'Then your sainted Mama will have to get used to it. That, or you can learn to sleep in the coal-house.'

It was something she had never expected. Ever since their first night in the Shelbourne when she had lost all fear of him, their physical intimacy had grown quickly.

She was glad that he had been able to teach her, that they had not fumbled and agonized in the way that so many of Mama's hints had prepared her for. She enjoyed his lovemaking, enjoyed his frank delight in her response.

'We've been very fortunate, you and I,' he said quietly.

She nodded.

'I know.'

And now they were on their way to Stewarts Place. A modest home, Charles had told her, just for now until the property in High Street became vacant. He had had his eye on it for some time. A much grander house, he had assured her, with several good bedrooms.

'And I expect all of them to be filled. In due course, naturally.' He was smoking, looking away from her as he said this. She waited until he turned to face her again, his expression serious. Now it was her turn.

'Well, I expect that's up to you. I can't do it on my own.'

Delighted, he beamed at her.

'That's my girl.'

She didn't tell him what she already suspected. Something felt different inside her. It was far too soon to tell for certain, she knew that, but she was learning to trust her intuition. It felt good. The prospect of a baby made the excitement of having her own home even greater. She didn't care how modest it was. It would be hers, to make beautiful, show to her sisters, to enjoy as a statement of her new status as wife and mother.

She wondered at how fickle she was. For now, she missed nothing of her previous life – not her music, not her sisters, not her old home, nothing. She wondered how long it could last.

Mary: Autumn 1899

MARY WAS DREAMING. It was a dream filled with liquid noises, muffled echoes that seemed familiar but never quite came into focus. At one point, she seemed to be in the middle of the rippling, undulating noise herself, conscious that she was asleep, aware that this was a dream from which she wasn't quite ready to waken. Suddenly, the noises seemed to solidify, to be identifiable as running feet: more than that, as feet running up a stairway. She jerked awake, seconds before the frantic knocking on her doorway and Miss Mulqueen's high-pitched voice.

'Mary! Mary! Get up quickly, please! We need you to go for the midwife!'

The footsteps retreated rapidly, before Mary had time to respond. She stumbled around in the dark, pulling on her woollen dress, feeling around on the floor for her boots. She could finish dressing later – this was enough for running down the street and around the corner. She pulled her shawl from the back of the small chair and threw it over her shoulders. She didn't stop to wonder about the panic in Miss Mulqueen's voice: she was an excitable creature at the best of times. Surely there was no need for such urgency in a house as well appointed and as experienced as this one? Even in Carrick Hill, birth was, more often than not, routine. She clattered down the back stairway and ran straight into the housekeeper. The gas lamps had been turned up in the kitchen, and Miss Mulqueen was vainly attempting to light the range, which looked as though it had recently gone out. The October chill was everywhere, the damp insinuating itself into every corner of the kitchen. Mary shivered, suddenly wishing she had taken the time to put on her stockings.

'Be very quick, Mary,' said Miss Mulqueen. Her face was grey with anxiety. 'The master is worried – Madam has lost a lot of blood.'

Mary nodded. She'd better hurry.

'I'll be as quick as I can. There's some kerosene in the scullery cupboard – throw a wee drop in the back of the range, and stand well back before you light it.'

Miss Mulqueen looked horrified. Mary shook her head at her impatiently, pulling her shawl around her more tightly.

'It's safe, as long as you do it right. Leave it – I'll do it when I get back. Twenty minutes'll make no difference, one way or th'other.'

Gathering up her dress, she ran down the garden path and turned right into Dunlambert Drive. Mrs Croft lived just a few minutes away – but it was the return journey that worried Mary. The midwife was elderly now, and not sure of her footing. Mary wondered how long it would take them to get back. There was probably nothing to worry about – a fourth child should be straightforward enough; Miss Mulqueen always did like to dramatize.

Mary turned off Dunlambert into Seaview Drive. Here the houses were smaller, more crowded, some with a tiny patch of front garden – but still, a whole universe away from Carrick Hill. She hammered on the door of number seven, suddenly realizing she didn't know what time it was.

The top window opened. Mary saw the grey head, the short-sighted eyes peering down at her.

'It's Mary, Mrs Croft; Mr Long has sent me to get you. Madam needs your help.'

The window closed as abruptly as it had opened. Mary waited, stamping her boots on the damp ground, blowing on her hands with frosty breath in a vain attempt to warm them. The front door opened.

'What's up, child?'

Mrs Croft was pulling on a warm coat. Mary was surprised at its quality, until she remembered that a midwife would need such a coat, being called out at all hours in all seasons. She was frowning now at Mary, impatient, cranky at having been woken.

'Miss Mulqueen says Madam has lost a lot of blood and . . .'

Mrs Croft grabbed Mary's arm.

'Quick, child! Not another word! Go for Dr Abernethy, quickly now – mind you say I sent you . . . not Mr Long.'

And she was gone, making her way up the street with surprising agility.

Mary did as she was told.

It all took no longer than twenty minutes, but they were too late. By the time they returned to Fortwilliam Park, the house was filled with a strange silence. Time seemed to hang suspended. There was no flurry of activity on their arrival, no running footsteps up and down the stairs telling them there was still time, there were still things to be done. Mary understood that quietness, knew it all too well: that deep emptiness that filled a house when someone had gone, called by a sometimes merciless God.

Then a cry shattered the silence in waves, an unearthly howl that rushed to fill all the spaces left behind by the departing sea of silence.

'Dear God,' said Cook, suddenly appearing at Mary's elbow. Her face crumpled, tears made their way down the cracks and crevices of her old cheeks.

'Poor wee scrap,' was all she said, over and over again.

The following days were long and busy. Women came and went quietly, whispering to each other. Dr Abernethy arrived, bringing a nurse with him. A large, competent woman, she was a generous mix of warmth and briskness. Mary liked her.

'A wee boy,' she confided to Mary, outside the bedroom door, once the fire had been built up for the night and Madam was settled. 'Lived only a few minutes, poor wee dote.'

Mr Long went about his business like a quiet, grey ghost. There was an air of tension about the house which grew steadily with each passing day. Everyone felt it. There wasn't even the semblance of a return to normality. Even Nanny was worried, confiding her fears to Cook over the now nightly glasses of sherry in the kitchen.

Eventually, the master called them all together. It was just as Nanny had feared. The house was to be shut up, the trunks packed, the children organized. Madam was being taken to Switzerland, where the air was pure. A full recovery was hoped for – perhaps in six months, perhaps in a year. Whatever it took. Mr Long's voice was abrupt, clipped. No one dared question him as to their futures. Mary felt all the old fears again. Back to her needle. But where would she live this time? Her old home was closed to her, barred and bolted by now, gone for good.

At a signal from the master, Miss Mulqueen stepped forward.

'Mr and Mrs Long have been good enough to secure alternative positions for all of us. I have the details. Let us reconvene downstairs.'

A reprieve, perhaps. Mary felt her eyes fill. Too much death, too much of it. She had already seen more of its callous hand than she cared to. She wondered what was coming next.

May: Autumn 1899

MAY KISSED THE two children goodnight, feeling almost ill with anticipation and fear. It was a heady mix – a rush of emotion that kept her senses almost unbearably sharpened, her nights restless.

Philippe would be waiting for her, impatiently, out in the dusky gardens, hidden from view. It was getting more and more difficult to get away – Nathalie demanded another story, just one more. Ever since they had found the volume of fairy tales in English, hiding away in the old bookshop in Rouen, the child's appetite for bedtime stories had become insatiable. Jean-Louis pretended indifference, but May noticed that he lay very still and silent in his bed, listening as she read. Sometimes his thumb crept towards his mouth, giving May almost painful reminders of Ellie. She read aloud as though reading to her younger sister; it helped her keep the tone light and affectionate. She simplified the language for them, too, but they didn't know that.

'You've had two long stories already, Nathalie! We'll have none left for tomorrow!'

Laughing, May gave her one more hug. Privately,

she thought the children were sent to bed much too early, particularly now that the weather had grown so much more bearable. This was the time of day made for running around the garden, chasing, playing hide and seek in the cool of evening. The late-September evenings were beautiful in a way totally unfamiliar to May. Autumn had never looked like this at home. She had found too much of the summer oppressive, and had learned to respect and fear the heat of the sun. Philippe had teased her about turning into a Frenchwoman. August had proved almost too much for her; September was a welcome change. The autumnal air was still and fragrant in the late evenings, the light golden, making everything in the gardens assume an astonishing clarity, as though each tree, each flowering shrub had become a picture of itself, painted carefully against a shimmering, haze-green background.

But Madame feared what she called its 'treacherous chills': she would have none of it where her children were concerned. Running around raised the temperature, which was bad. It made Nathalie's face red, which was unladylike. It dirtied the clothing, which was unseemly. Having known her now for four long months, May had learned to give up. She and Madame had developed an uneasy distance, each circling the other warily. May had been surprised, and disappointed, that Madame so obviously disliked her. Her initial attitude of cool hostility had never wavered, and May had wondered more than once why she had wanted to employ a governess at all. She guarded her household jealously, and seemed resentful that she had

had to make space for someone else. And yet it was she who had accepted Constance MacBride's suggestion with alacrity, she who assured her that she had already been seeking a recommendation – a young woman of good character, quiet disposition, willing to teach and care for an eight-year-old and a six-year-old. The correspondence between both women had been purposeful, enthusiastic and May had arrived, if not with the expectation of happiness, then certainly with the anticipation of welcome. But that had not happened. Madame was permanently chilly, always waiting, it seemed to May, for her to do something inappropriate. And now, it would appear, all of the woman's suspicions had been well founded, though in a way she could hardly have foreseen. May felt herself begin to shiver, her stomach turning equally with dread and delight, when she thought about what she and Philippe were about to reveal.

He would have to tell Madame *soon*, and his father. May couldn't keep their secret any longer. October was almost here, and with it, the move back to Paris, the children's return to school. Preparations for that journey were well under way: Isabelle had already gone back to Paris to prepare the apartment for the family's return. She had grumbled a little before she left about the amount of cleaning and organizing she would have to do on her own.

May was fearful of this removal to the city. She knew that once Madame was aware of May's new standing, she would no longer want her, that it would not be appropriate for her husband's future daughter-in-law to work in her home as little more than a maid. Nor would May wish that for herself, although she had lain awake most of the night recently, distressed at the thought of her connection with Nathalie and Jean-Louis being cut in anger.

She had almost driven herself distracted in the last four weeks, ever since Philippe had asked her to marry him. He had warned her it would not be easy, that they would encounter a lot of opposition. She had felt ready for anything then, thrilled and amazed that her feelings no longer had to be kept in check – that he loved her as she loved him. But now, she and Philippe needed to make plans. She wanted to know what was going to happen to her once the summer was over. Was she to seek another position, or would they simply marry at once, having overcome all obstacles? What was she to go to Paris *as*? Governess, wife, disgraced foreigner? May did not like this feeling of her life being out of control. She wanted everything *settled*, so that she would know how to behave, could understand what was expected of her. She wished Hannah was here: she needed to tell her in person how wonderful Philippe was, how much she loved him, how he in turn adored her.

She made her way quietly down the servants' stairs and out into the darkening courtyard. The air was filled with the hectic cries of crickets, the evening heavy with the scent of jasmine. May felt herself expand with pleasure: this was the sort of place one should live, be happy in. It was open, free, the air warm and glorious.

Paris would be different, of course, but at least she would always have the summers to look forward to. Her life stretched before her, a wonderful vista of city and country, Philippe, children of their own.

He was standing under the oak tree, his white shirt almost translucent in the fading light. He moved towards her quickly, burying his face in her hair.

'May,' he whispered, kissing her, pulling her to him. She loved the way he said her name. 'I thought you were not coming.'

She smiled up at him.

'You can blame your little sister. She can't get enough stories.'

'I have very little time.'

He pulled away from her, his face serious. May could feel her smile collapse, her happiness crumble. Something was wrong. She had that sense of dread, familiar to her ever since she was a child, that her whole world was just about to implode.

'Philippe – what is it?'

He kept both hands on her shoulders, steadying her.

'My father needs me to go back to Paris tonight, on the late train. He got a telegram today – one of the companies is in serious trouble. The manager he trusted most has, apparently, had his hand in the till for some time.'

May began to feel weak; all the blood seemed to drain from the top of her head, making her feel dizzy. She felt all her energy and optimism sink to her feet, which suddenly became leaden. At the same time, she knew. Something more than business was wrong. Philippe was preoccupied, distracted, already miles away from her.

'I must go – he has no one else he can trust. Just hold tight, I'll be back in a few days, a week at the most.'

'Have you told him – about us?'

Philippe shook his head.

'It's not the right time – we must wait for a better moment.'

May nodded. She allowed him to hold her close again, briefly.

'You must go back now, before anyone sees you. The carriage will be waiting to take me to the station.'

'Yes.'

He looked straight at her.

'You must trust me, May. Give me time to resolve this crisis for him – then he will be ready to accept you, to accept *us*.'

She tried to smile at him, but she knew. Somehow, this was the beginning of the end. She sensed Madame's hand in this.

'Go now,' he said, kissing her. 'I love you.'

She made her way back through the gardens, keeping to the now deepening shadows. It was impossible to believe that this was the same evening, that she was the same person as moments before. What had seemed to her then a life filled with joy and light now stretched before her as some sort of frozen wasteland. She would not cry, not yet, not until she was safely inside her own room.

It was impossible to crush the intuition that someone was watching her from some window, some hidden vantage point. The silences, the hostility, the disapproval of recent days and weeks all came into focus. They knew, and she would be punished.

Mary and Hannah: Autumn 1899

MARY STEPPED OFF the train in Holywood and followed the stream of people making their way out of the station. She tried to remember Miss Mulqueen's directions. She didn't want to ask anybody, didn't want to show her hand before she had to. She followed the most likely looking group of women up Station Hill towards what appeared to be the main street. She bent her head and battled against the strong wind. At one point, she had to hold on to her hat with both hands. She turned her back for a moment, just to draw breath. The sea was a dark, pewter-toned mass, frilled with vigorous white horses. Mary decided she liked the salty tang; this was the sort of air that would have done Cecilia good, the sort of air that had the trains to Holywood and Bangor crowded every weekend in summer. She just wished it had been a little less hearty today.

Once she reached the junction at the top of the hill, she pulled the piece of paper Miss Mulqueen had given her out of the pocket of her coat. She turned left and walked briskly down High Street, through the town and past the maypole, its tattered flag snapping uselessly at the gusting wind. She could already see the squat tower of the Priory ahead of her. She began to feel nervous again. Stewarts Place, Miss Mulqueen had said, just before the old Priory, on the left-hand side of the street.

Mary consulted her scrap of paper again. She counted the letters, trying to match them quickly to the street sign before anyone could see what she was doing. The sense of relief was enormous; she was here. She hadn't had to ask anyone for help. She never forgot her way: one visit and the streets were engraved for ever on her memory. All she needed was to get there safely, just the once. It seemed to her that one of the sharper, more observant bits of her mind made up for the part that had never been properly taught how to read. Next time, she thought, she would walk here with confidence, keeping her head held high: if there was to be a next time.

She pushed open the wrought-iron gate and began to make her way down the garden path towards the front door. She had a sudden moment of blank panic: what was this woman's name? Miss Mulqueen had told her, of that she was sure, but she had no memory of it, no sound to remember, nothing. She'd just have to keep her head, she decided firmly, and try and get by without it. She consulted the scrap of paper again, uselessly. Even if Miss Mulqueen had written it for her, she had nothing to match it up to, no visible outward sign to tell her she was right or wrong. She sighed, spoke silently to herself. *Ye'd better help me here, Cecilia – I haven't your head for the readin'.*

The number twelve was in tarnished brass, just to the left of the door. It had to be a good omen, she decided. Number twelve Fortwilliam Park had been where she had learned to breathe again, to gather her forces and eventually, to survive. Number twelve Stewarts Place was going to be good to her, she was sure of it. It had to be more than a coincidence that the numbers of both houses were the same. Quickly, she took in all the telling details before her. She wanted to see affluence with just the right amount of neglect. The front door was wood-grained and in good condition, but the fanlight and the stained-glass panels hadn't seen soap and water for some time. The black and red diamond-patterned tiles of the porch could do with a good scrubbing, too. This looked hopeful: a young Dublin bride with no notion of how to keep house. Mary's spirits began to rise. She might indeed be wanted here; this could be her chance to get right out of Belfast altogether and into a town like this: bright, prosperous, with all the healthy benefits of sea air. She blessed herself furtively before pressing the front doorbell.

The sound of the doorbell was sudden and somehow shocking in the empty house. Hannah was becoming used to the map of each of her days now: the smooth terrain of the mornings, followed by the bumpier ground of afternoon visits, and finally the calm plateaux of evening.

Constance MacBride had taken to arriving most afternoons now, with several other imperious elderly ladies in tow. Hannah was convinced that the novelty of undertaking a journey some four miles north of

Belfast and the excellence of the sea air were more of a draw than the mildly intriguing presence of a Dublin daughter-in-law. Nevertheless, Constance MacBride kept arriving with grim predictability, her presence an annoyance to Betty, who liked to spend her afternoons snoozing by the fire in the kitchen with an enormous tabby cat curled on her lap. Hannah realized quite quickly that her mother-in-law enjoyed fussing around her, unable to conceal her joy at the prospect of her first grandchild.

Hannah was more than relieved when the elderly ladies eventually departed, full of tea and good humour, and she could subside gratefully into the tranquillity of evening, with her piano, her sunlit garden and her new husband, surrounded by the ever-present aroma of pipe-tobacco. She was becoming accustomed now to having her hours measured out, to knowing what each day was likely to bring her. At first, she had been surprised that she never felt bored. She had expected to miss the constant companionship of her two sisters; she feared the emptiness of her own company. Instead, she welcomed the uncluttered times of each day, times which she could fill with music and the delightful anticipation of the arrival of her first baby.

And so the early call to her door this morning startled her. She was not expecting any visitor – in fact, she was on her way out to the post office as a diversion, an escape from the constant complaints issuing from the kitchen.

She turned away from the mirror and made her way to the top of the stairs, hat still in hand. Betty was quite deaf, and may not have heard the single peal. She was just about to descend the last flight when she saw the elderly woman open the front door. She had a moment's pity for the grey, stooped figure whose feet seemed daily more reluctant to carry her around.

There was a young, slightly windswept woman standing in the porch. Hannah hurried down the last few steps when she heard the brusque, challenging tone.

'Betty?'

'Yes, ma'am.'

Betty simply turned and made her way back down the hallway. She didn't even glare in Hannah's direction this time. Hannah sighed to herself. Charles had promised her that much, and he had been right – Betty's main virtue was her unquestioning obedience.

This woman was very young, Mary thought, good-looking, with abundant fair hair piled softly on top of her head. She held a wide-brimmed hat in one hand, a long silver pin in the other. What *was* her name? Mary felt the back of her neck prickle with embarrassment: not only could she not greet the woman properly, she had also interrupted her preparations for going out. She decided to curtsy, briefly.

'Mary McCurry, ma'am. Miss Mulqueen sent me.'

'Oh – yes, please – come in.'

Mary was intrigued by the woman's accent. It was one she had not heard before, and so she accepted its strangeness. It was the faint, smoky echo of Belfast that puzzled her.

The lady of the house was about to lead the way back into the hallway when a sudden gust of wind blew the front door almost closed. She lurched forward to stop it with both hands before it clicked to, and let go of her hat and hatpin at the same time. Mary wasn't quick enough. The pin tinkled on to the tiles below and the large hat cartwheeled down the garden path, staggered drunkenly to the right, and took off down High Street. Occasionally, it paused in the middle of the road before becoming filled with air and taking flight again. Mary followed, flooded with a strong, superstitious conviction. If she managed to retrieve this hat, then the position had to be hers. If she lost it, or gave up halfway, the young woman she had just met would take that as a sign of her character: lacking in determination, unreliable.

She held her skirts well above her ankles as she ran, but she didn't care. Nobody around her would be interested in her ankles, and anyway she wore stout, unromantic boots, worth their salt for running up and down endless staircases, not for catching the eye of a passing man. She could never be accused of immodesty. One final burst of speed and she managed to put the toe of her right boot on the outer brim of the lady's rather fine hat. It looked a little sad now, though, its feathers badly ruffled, its ribbons dampened by the misting, freezing rain which had started to fall, its drops transformed into fine needles in the strong wind.

Triumphantly, she picked it up, brushed the grainy bits of dirt from its surface, and held it firmly, like an offering, in both hands. When she got back to Stewarts Place, the young woman was still standing in the doorway, her eyes and cheeks bright with laughter. Mary smiled, too. She could see that the woman's laughter was kind – one that enjoyed the fun with you, rather than against you. Something in the way she now stood made Mary look more closely, discreetly, just for an instant. There was a definite swell under the front of her dress, a gentle undulation that Mary might never have seen if the young woman had not, for that split second, turned sideways. Mary felt suddenly elated. This woman needed her: it was obvious. If she couldn't keep her tiles clean, then how on earth would she ever be able to look after a baby on her own?

The violent gust of wind which suddenly wrenched the open door from her grasp took Hannah completely by surprise. She lunged forward, trying to catch it before it slammed shut. She had no choice: she let go of her hat and hatpin, expecting both of them to land safely at her feet in the porch. Instead, her hat seemed to become possessed of a mind of its own. With some initial difficulty in finding its balance, it took sudden, gleeful flight and lurched rapidly all the way down the garden path, taking to the air as soon as it reached the main road outside. All Hannah could manage was a surprised 'Oh!' She was disappointed – she had really liked that hat. She was just about to say something when, without a word, the young woman in the workday boots literally took off after it, chasing the flimsy mix of straw and ribbons for all she was worth, driving rain and strong winds notwithstanding.

Hannah wanted to call out after her, to get her to stop. She cut a most comical figure – holding on to her skirts, sticking out first one foot, then the other, as though dancing to some mad tune inside her head. She tried again and again to trap the unruly hat, only to be defeated as it took flight again, feathers fluttering everywhere like small, demented birds – and off she went once more in apparently useless pursuit.

Hannah couldn't help laughing. Then, to her surprise, she saw the girl stop suddenly, her foot planted solidly beneath her. She bent down, and there was something triumphant about her as she stood upright, the hat held firmly now between her two hands. Hannah thought she could see her grinning to herself. At that moment, she liked her immensely. She didn't care what secrets Miss Mulqueen's character reference might reveal, she would have this girl in her house. Anybody that determined deserved a chance. It took only a few moments for the young woman to arrive, breathless, at Hannah's side, holding out the hat like some sort of tattered peace-offering.

'Come in, please, and tell me your name again. Thank you so much for bringing me back my hat.'

Mary followed her into the drawing room. She sat on the most uncomfortable chair she could find, while the young woman took the sofa, facing her unexpected visitor.

'Would you like a glass of water?'

'No, thank you, ma'am,' said Mary, quickly. She

didn't want to endure Betty's baleful glare for a second time. She would put up with being thirsty, as long as she could get this over with.

'My name's Mary, ma'am, Mary McCurry. I understand you might be lookin' for someone, to help about the house, like.'

Nervously, she pulled Miss Mulqueen's letter from the pocket of her coat. Abruptly, she stretched out her hand to the young woman who accepted the envelope, but didn't open it. Instead, she smiled across at Mary.

'Yes, I am.'

Mary continued, words tumbling over each other in their rush to get said. She described her duties at the Long household, her expertise in washing, cleaning, scrubbing, mending. She told of her diligence as a willing worker, her ability to turn her hand to anything. Slyly, she mentioned the layette she had created for Baby Long, and was immediately terrified that she had made a dreadful mistake. Was it bad luck to mention the dead baby in the presence of the living? As it was, the young woman never seemed to notice; she was much more intent on listening to all the things which Mary was promising to do for her.

Now that she was here, now that Mary had caught the briefest glimpse of sea and sky and fresh air, she wanted a future in this household, with this young woman and her child, her future children. It was one of those moments that could have no sensible explanation in the world of real things, tangible objects. It was an instinct, a feeling that she had arrived somewhere which might become home, that memories of Cecilia would be welcome here. And soon, there would be a baby to love. Someone else's, to be sure, but a baby, nevertheless.

'. . . I'm strong an' I'm willin', an' I don't know of no work in the house that's beyant me.'

Mary paused here in her long speech and looked steadily across at this elegant, beautiful young woman, who was probably not much older than she was. She kept her trembling hands as still as she could, almost holding her breath.

Hannah listened carefully as Mary outlined all the household tasks she insisted she would undertake. She couldn't even remember the duties, let alone the moral qualities required for this position – Charles's mother would no doubt have a long and daunting list. But she didn't care: this was a choice she wanted to make for herself. Betty had more or less come with the house, passed down by previous tenants like some well-used piece of furniture, still comfortable, but with sharp edges and fraying fabric becoming more noticeable with every passing year. Her character had been above reproach, of course, since she had once kept house for the parish priest. And the elderly woman had certainly done her best, although she complained constantly about being tired. Hannah had got used to her bossy ways, but now she wanted somebody different, younger, someone just like the girl sitting in front of her.

Hannah felt more and more alarmed as the number and the details of Mary's litany of essential household duties continued to grow. Was this really what this girl's life was about – emptying chamber pots, lugging coal, black-leading the range, pummelling dirty laundry by hand, as well as cooking, mending, helping with a baby? She would have to speak to Charles – surely that was far too much work for one woman? She wanted to tell Mary to stop: her eagerness to be the perfect maid-of-all-work was beginning to make Hannah distressed. She was about to interrupt when she got the strong sense that the list was coming to an end. She heard Mary's tone of voice change to one of pride, of satisfaction in her own expertise.

'. . . I'm strong an' I'm willin',' she concluded, 'an' I don't know of no work in the house that's beyant me.'

Hannah caught the small gesture with which she tried to calm the nervous shaking of her hands. She didn't need to hear any more.

'Thank you for that, Mary. I think you'll be very suitable. We don't intend to stay in this house for too long – my husband has acquired a property on High Street, and we'll be moving shortly. It would be good to have you to help with that.'

Hannah put the letter aside, on a table to her right. Her mother-in-law could look at what it contained, if she wished. She, Hannah, had no desire to. She sat back, folded her hands and waited for Mary to say something.

Mary heard the words, but not their meaning. She stared stupidly around her, disbelieving. Was it, could it possibly be, as easy as that? She couldn't speak. She opened her mouth, but no sound came out. Mary could feel the words form, somewhere towards the back of her throat, but she couldn't breathe life into them. She felt her face grow warm and glowing under the other woman's scrutiny. Finally, the words she wanted to say exploded into sound. Her voice sounded shrill, higher than normal, she could hear it echo loudly, too loudly, inside her own head. She hoped she wasn't shouting.

'Thank you, ma'am. You'll not regret it. Thank you.'

'I'll write to Miss Mulqueen this evening. Come back tomorrow, and we'll go through your duties. I'd like you to start as soon as possible.'

'Miss Mulqueen has already spoken very highly of you to my mother-in-law, and I understand you have received excellent training. You will be paid twenty-four pounds a year, plus your board and lodging.'

'Thank you, ma'am. I'll come back at the same time tomorrow.'

'That would be very suitable.'

The woman smiled at her again, a slow, warm smile that Mary had to believe was sincere. Her whole face smiled, not just her mouth. She, too, seemed to be relieved that this was over.

Mary couldn't believe her luck. Had she finally landed on her feet? She thought suddenly of Ma, of her stubborn lack of belief in good luck, in anything being put down to mere good fortune. If things go well, she'd always say, then God's hand has touched you.

The young woman, whom Mary suddenly remembered was called Mrs MacBride, opened the front door herself, and waited until Mary had reached the gate.

She called out 'Goodbye, Mary.' And then, 'Mind your hat!'

Mary laughed out loud.

'Goodbye, Mrs MacBride – thank you!'

She set off down High Street towards the station, her heart lighter than she could ever remember. She almost wished her hat would blow away – it would give her some excuse to use up the exuberant bubble of energy which seemed to rise from her feet to the top of her head, making her feel dizzy, tingly, as though her blood had just been aerated. She could imagine herself skipping down the street, just as she had done when she and Cecilia were only wains, even throwing her hat into the air with sheer delight. She cried, just a little, that her sister hadn't lived to be part of this. That woman, young Mrs MacBride, was a kind person, Mary was sure of it. If God was good, this would be her home; she would never ask Him for another thing, not for as long as she lived.

Hannah watched as Mary made her way down the garden path. She felt suddenly grateful for the comfortable life which was now hers. This young woman couldn't be any more than twenty-four or twenty-five, and yet there was almost an *oldness* to her, some indefinable sense of lived experience that had nothing to do with her years. She felt suddenly, overwhelmingly, fortunate. She was glad that she had been able to do something small for Mary – even though she was really doing something for herself, her own ease. She sighed.

It seemed that everyone's existence was not as carefully mapped for comfort as hers.

She was still astonished at the speed with which her own life had suddenly taken off – a little like the hat's manic flight down High Street. Some things had been so *easy* – getting used to a new home, a new town, making domestic decisions herself, however small, even living apart from her sisters. In many ways, it had been a momentous year, but Hannah still didn't have the feeling that all these things were really happening to *her*. Being a wife, almost a mother, was like gradually being transformed into a whole new person. It was as though she had successfully acquired all the trappings of a grown up, without actually having to be one. She knew she had blushed slightly when she said 'my husband': it still sounded strange to her ears.

And now it seemed that yet another hurdle had been overcome: she had just employed her first servant. Try as she would, she couldn't help feeling other than ridiculously pleased with herself about that.

May: Spring 1900

MAY HATED PARIS. Once Nathalie and Jean-Louis had returned to school, she found the days on her own long and dreary. Her room was a tiny one, tucked into a far corner of the vast apartment, beside the cupboards where trunks and suitcases were stored. All the openness of the countryside was gone; she felt hemmed in, overwhelmed by brick and concrete. She had spent a lot of time there, in the first couple of weeks, growing accustomed to the sounds and smells of apartment life around her. The small slatted window above her bed gave out on to a courtyard, a busy place, full of washing lines; only the backs of buildings were visible here, their grimy, paint-flaking ugliness trapped in almost permanent shadow.

And there was no word from Philippe; nothing. May's only terrified consolation was that she had bled as normal, the month after their return from the countryside. In Philippe's absence, May's abhorrence of what they had done was almost absolute. What had seemed so natural, so right for betrothed lovers at the time, now took on another mantle entirely. What if she had conceived? All of Philippe's declarations of love now seemed hollow, meaningless. May grew both angry and ashamed of herself as she tried to pry information out of the two children. She collected them from school each afternoon, and walked them home the long way, stopping off in a small local park where she felt she could breathe among the greenery. But the children knew nothing. Philippe seemed to be part of their summer lives only. May gathered that once Paris and school came around, it was natural to them that he went away again, appearing only at the occasional weekend, arriving on birthdays, Christmas, special times like that. She tried to find some hope, some comfort in their childish acceptance of Philippe's absence; but try as she might, one small inner voice kept insisting that Philippe could have come to *her*, his wife in all but name, if he'd really tried.

By December, May was missing everything and everyone that had once been familiar to her with an intensity that was close to physical pain. Hannah, Eleanor, Philippe, Rouen, Ireland – everything got mixed up into a constant ache that was there even during sleep. She had made brave efforts to get to know Paris. She felt she owed it to Grandfather Delaney. But nothing worked: not the galleries, not the arrogant beauty of the imperial buildings, not even the wide grandeur of the Champs-Elysées with its lively pavement cafes. If this was travel, then she wanted no more of it. May reflected bitterly that, if her grandparents could see her now, they would have very little to be proud of.

And then, as suddenly as he had disappeared, Philippe came back. She heard his voice in the hallway of the apartment just as she was finishing Nathalie's bed-time story. The wave of relief that accompanied the sound of his return washed away all the unhappiness of the previous three months. He was here – he had kept his promise. How could he have come sooner? Marseilles was so far away, and his father's business so demanding.

'Well, Nathalie, are you being a good girl?'

He seemed to burst into the little girl's room, full of energy and purpose. May watched as he sat on the edge of Nathalie's bed and she leapt up, wrapping her small arms around his neck.

'Philippe! Philippe! You're back!'

He laughed at her, teasing her in French which was too rapid, too colloquial for May to catch. She didn't know what to do with herself. Should she wait, settle Nathalie after his departure? Or should she make her escape now, while she was still able? She was conscious of a slow burn of anger, felt his high good humour as keenly as another rejection.

'And Mademoiselle O'Connor? Are you well?'

His voice was jovial, as impersonal as any employer.

'Yes, very well, thank you,' she said, meeting his eyes.

'Good, good! A moment, please!'

Before May knew what to do, how to respond, he had ushered her out of Nathalie's room into the narrow corridor. He closed the child's door softly.

'May,' he said, and pulled her to him. She knew they were well hidden from the main room: the only danger was from the kitchen. May understood this in an instant and her anger suddenly took flight. What did he think she was? How long did he expect her to live her life waiting for him, skulking in servants' quarters?

With a strength she never knew she possessed, she pushed him away from her. She could feel her face colour, her whole body tingle with an energy she hadn't felt since he'd left her.

'I couldn't,' he whispered, his hands extended beseechingly. 'I had no way of getting in touch. This is the first time I've been able to get away. Meet me at this address, tomorrow afternoon – please, give me the chance to explain.'

He pushed what felt like an envelope into her clenched hand. May stood unmoving. She couldn't reply, didn't trust herself to speak. There was laughter from the dining room, a voice calling: 'Where's he gone? Where's Philippe?'

She left before he did. She turned on her heel and walked quickly down the long corridor to Jean-Louis's bedroom. She knocked once, then let herself in and closed the door behind her.

Paris had never looked less appealing. Grey early morning rain spread great swathes of darkness across the roofs and sheeted down the dull facades of shuttered buildings. It felt as if the whole city had closed its eyes on her, turned its back resolutely against her. Madame Ondart had bid her a cold, formal farewell in the dining room last night before the silent dinner had been served and endured.

May still didn't know how they had found out. At

first, she'd thought that it shouldn't matter, that Philippe would simply make his announcement about their engagement immediately, rather than delaying until his father's health was better. Frankly, May had seen nothing wrong with Monsieur's health: he seemed as robust and as objectionable as ever. In the eight weeks since Christmas, Philippe had returned from Marseilles only three times. Each time, he had sworn to May that he loved her, pleaded with her to understand that the time was not right. They must wait until he was back in Paris permanently before announcing their intention to marry.

On his last visit, they had quarrelled.

'I will wait for you, Philippe. I will even come to Marseilles. But I will not live a lie. You must tell your father, or I will have to believe that you have changed your mind. Please, just tell me the truth.'

He had raged at her then, even wept a little. Of course he loved her, but she did not, could not understand. He could not assault his father with an announcement such as that – not while his whole business empire was crumbling right before his eyes. They had parted, tearfully, Philippe swearing his devotion.

Soon after his departure, something changed in the atmosphere of the Ondart household. Nothing was said to May at any stage about Philippe, about the impossibility of such a match in Monsieur and Madame's eyes, about their disappointment in her. Instead, everything was cloaked in obliquity.

Suddenly, there was a great flurry of activity. Preparations for travel were undertaken with astonishing speed. Isabelle grumbled as she shook out the dust covers she had so recently folded and put away.

Madame spoke to May with the greatest formality possible. It was unfortunate that Monsieur's business now demanded their immediate departure for Marseilles. Unfortunate, too, that the children had not made more progress in their language studies. But many thanks to Mademoiselle O'Connor for her best efforts. The children would now be sent as boarders to the Ecole Internationale, where no doubt all Mademoiselle's hard work on their behalf would ease the transition into their new environment. Of course, her salary for the remaining four months would be paid to her on her departure, *naturellement*. She and Monsieur Ondart would most assuredly keep their side of the bargain. Mademoiselle would of course understand that the children must not on any account be upset. As yet, they were not aware of the changes planned for them, and Mademoiselle would make very sure that she let nothing slip.

May had sat unspeaking through the long speech as Madame Ondart regarded her across the polished table, already set for an early dinner.

Her throat felt constricted, her chest made of stone. She could feel Genevieve trying to be kind, nudging her gently as she served the soup until a sharp reproof from Madame sent her swiftly back to the kitchen. May had not understood all that was said; the French was too sharply dismissive for her to catch, although the sense was clear. Monsieur said nothing, as usual, except complain loudly to the air, in great staccato bursts, about the quality of his burgundy. Large, sudden hand movements accompanied his complaints, filling the air around him like smoke after gunfire.

The children had been brought to say goodbye to her, one by one before bedtime. They shook hands with her, their faces filled with the sudden shyness she remembered from her first days with them. She wanted to stoop and kiss Nathalie, to ruffle Jean-Louis's hair and tease him about his latest passion for stick insects, to watch his slow serious smile once he realized she was having fun with him; but Madame had already warned her.

'The children have been told you are going on a journey. They understand you will be back. In time, they will forget. Their father and I do not wish them to be upset. Bid farewell to them simply and quickly. We'll have no displays of emotion.'

No displays of emotion. May repeated it to herself now, over and over, wanting to feel the keen bite of its bitterness, wanting it to hurt. Anger was the only thing which would help her keep control until all of this was over and she was home. She wanted to *be* home, now, without having to *get* home. The thought of the journey wearied her. Train to Calais, boat to Dover, train again to London, then Liverpool, ferry to Belfast. At least Eileen's birth had made May's journey to Holywood seem natural, understandable: of course she would want to be with her sister during such a momentous time. And she wouldn't have to face Mama on her own, to feel the keen edge of her sharp eye just yet. If only for a few days, she would have peace with Hannah, who would understand everything. Her sister, at least, wouldn't make her feel that she had, somehow, let everyone down. The baby's fortunate timing took away the need for explanations, evasions, half-truths. May knew that she could not have kept her secret from her mother.

And Philippe had never appeared. Her prophecy from last summer had been uncannily accurate. One very small part of her had held out hope that he would be waiting for her, miraculously, at the Gare du Nord, or perhaps at the station in Calais. She wouldn't give up hope, not yet, not until she had to.

Part Three: 1900–1906

Eleanor's Journal

1900 WAS A truly momentous year for us Bright Brilliant Sisters.

Hannah had just given birth to her first baby, Eileen. May had experienced the joy of travel, at last; and I was spending all my time planning my escape.

For the second time, I lived the summer apart from both my sisters, and I missed them terribly. Our house was deathly quiet; even Mama didn't sing any more. There were ladies in our drawing room on fewer and fewer occasions now, and Papa became more and more engrossed in 'business' which kept him out and about town a good deal. From what I observed, it seemed that most of his transactions took place over long lunches at his club on Stephen's Green, from whence he would return smelling of cigar-smoke and good brandy. I have often wondered how his gentlemen companions must have regarded him. He cannot have been able to conceal his past completely; his acceptance there must have been yet another result of Grandfather Delaney's magnanimity and influence. Papa made great show, too, of 'managing' Grandfather's properties all over Dublin, would murmur about his 'responsibilities' as a landlord and generally took himself very seriously indeed. Mama would turn her head away from him when he arrived home after his club days, and I could not help noticing her barely concealed expressions of contempt.

I learned later that Grandfather Delaney had been very careful to leave my father no real role in the management of his properties. After his death, all the significant business was transacted by the old and highly respectable firm of Morgan, Lancaster and Company in Dawson Street, about which not one syllable of scandal had ever been breathed. Mama received a monthly income through the hands of these gentlemen: the large, buff-coloured envelope would arrive with mathematical precision on the last Friday of every month. How much she gave my father remains a mystery – she always went with him to his tailor, for instance, and his bootmaker, and I know she paid his club bills, too. I should not, of course, know these things, not any of them, but I had the disgraceful habit of rummaging in Mama's desk on the occasions when I was alone in the house. I feel ashamed of myself even now, confessing this to you. But I couldn't help being curious; and the fact that I was also on my own with both of them meant that my parents' presence in my life that summer became, for the first time ever, a disproportionate one. I had no May to escape to, no Hannah to make me laugh. Instead, I sensed Mama's every mood, was present for any sharp exchange that might take place between her and Papa, and was in a position to observe all the unspoken bitterness that filled the air between them. I longed for summer to be over. I wanted the company of other girls, needed the stimulation of study, the safe predictability of school routine.

At sixteen, I no longer wanted to be burdened by the emptiness of failed lives. I loved my parents, naturally, but I loved the possibilities of my own life more. I knew that Hannah was happy, but her new world seemed to me to be very small. May's sojourn in France, as I subsequently discovered, seemed not to have brought her any happiness at all: I heard no more talk about Africa, the Americas or Europe. Just nine months as a governess with a wealthy French family, then back home at once to the safety of the familiar. That was how I felt at the time, how I saw things from my corner of the universe, with all the indignation and arrogance of youth.

All that spring, the newspapers had been filled with excited accounts of the preparations for, and the arrival of, Queen Victoria at Kingstown. Although thousands of Dubliners lined the streets, ostensibly to welcome her, I certainly remember no great outpourings of affection. Mama had been sadly disappointed at the elderly Queen's appearance: she had seemed sullen, almost sleepy, with no great elegance of person or dress. By summer, the newspapers were filled with accounts of a very different nature. The Boer War was suddenly everywhere: the relief of Mafeking, the fall of Pretoria, the occupation of Johannesburg. At that time, I had little interest in the politics of conflict, but I was overwhelmed by the stories of common bravery: the heroic exploits of doctors and nurses in their tending of the wounded, their extraordinary courage in bringing comfort and relief to the fallen, despite the danger to their own lives. I still have the cuttings that affected me most, now brittle and yellowing, their print blurred all along the seams where they have lain folded for many years. I began, secretly, to gather all the information I could about becoming a nurse. The nobility of the profession appealed to me, but more than that, I could make a good case for attending St Bartholomew's teaching hospital in London. Thus I should escape Dublin, my parents' house, and the fate of my sisters. Little by little, I would make my way towards another kind of life, one that awaited me elsewhere, always elsewhere. I knew that I should have nothing at all if I did not seize the first opportunity that presented itself. I had a bright vision of myself approaching an open door; all I needed now was to gather the courage to walk through it and leave my sisters behind.

Hannah: Spring 1900

HANNAH AWAITED CHARLES'S return impatiently. She had already been to the window several times, and there was still no sign of him. It was most unusual: he took the same train every evening, arriving home punctually at half past six from his office in Sussex Place. A knock on the drawing-room door made her jump.

'Come in.'

Mary stood at the threshold, wiping her hands on her apron.

'Is Mister Charles going to be very late, miss?'

'I don't know, Mary – there was no note in this afternoon's post. I don't know what could be keeping him.'

'Not to worry – I'll keep yer tea hot, so I will.'

It was really most unlike him to miss his tea. And the Burkes were coming tonight at eight – everything was set up for their musical evening together. Hannah pulled the curtain aside once again. People were streaming up from the station now. She recognized Mr Reeve, who always got the same train as Charles. His little boy was pedalling furiously beside him as they made their way up the hill together. He cycled down every night to meet his father; Charles had often remarked on the young fellow's devotion. Hannah had wondered aloud if Charles's pocketful of sweets might have anything to do with the boy's regular visits to Holywood station, and was rewarded with a look of genuine amazement. How had she known that? She refused to satisfy his curiosity, thinking that he really had led a very sheltered life in many respects – he simply did not understand how women talked to one another.

She resisted the urge now to run outside and ask whether anyone had seen Charles. She was being foolish: anything might have delayed him. He was fond of saying that his business was not an exact science. By ten to eight she was frantic. Mary came in and lit extra lamps around the drawing room, trying to soothe her.

'Don't be worryin' yer head too much, Miss Hannah. Sure mebbe he stopped off for a wee drink after work.'

Maybe he had – but he usually found some way of telling her. Suddenly, she heard footsteps on the porch. His voice, loud and welcoming, and other voices that she couldn't distinguish. Of course! The Burkes. She had almost forgotten about them in her anxiety. Charles opened the drawing-room door wide, ushering his guests in before him. There was nothing else for it – her questions must wait. She had guests to see to.

'Hannah, you look wonderful!'

Bella hugged her, laughing as Hannah's large stomach got in the way, no matter which way they turned.

James kissed her hand.

'Blooming, my dear, blooming,' was all he said. Hannah couldn't help smiling to herself. The Burkes were only about ten years older than she was, and ten years younger than Charles – yet their speech and manners seemed to have been absorbed from a much older, somehow jollier generation.

'You're both welcome: please, sit down.'

Hannah thought she might steal a moment with Charles while their guests were getting settled, but the only communication from him was a warning glance as he poured glasses of wine for Bella and for her. The evening crawled. She tried her best to be gay, to accompany Charles and James as they sang together, two full, rounded tenor voices. Then Bella and James together, then Charles and Bella. She thought she was going to scream.

When Mary brought the tea and cakes at ten o'clock, Bella leaned over to her, confidentially.

'You look very tired, Hannah. You should rest. We'll go soon.'

Hannah looked at her gratefully.

'Yes, I am tired. I really cannot get past this hour of the evening, no matter how hard I try.'

'Then don't try. Be sensible. How long is it to your confinement now?'

'Just eight weeks.'

Hannah couldn't help the surge of excitement she felt each time she admitted how close she was to holding her baby. The great rush of love she felt made her prepared to forgive Charles's late return, no matter what the reason. It would all be something very simple, she was sure of that. In a way, it was probably good that they had had to entertain people – she didn't want to quarrel with him, not now.

She was glad when tea was finally taken and Bella stood up immediately.

'We must be going, James. It's late.'

Her husband looked at her in astonishment. He was just about to reply when something in his wife's expression must have stopped him.

'Aye, of course, of course. Lovely evening, Hannah, Charles – thanks so much. Looking forward to the next one already!'

A few moments in the hall, a friendly wave, a pause until they turned the corner out of sight. Charles shut the door. He followed Hannah back into the drawing room.

'I was worried, Charles,' she said quietly. 'Is anything wrong?'

He patted the sofa beside him, his expression almost normal, but she had the sense he was making an effort.

'Nothing for you to worry about, my dear. I'm sorry I couldn't get word to you.'

She waited. He said nothing, just went through the ritual of filling and lighting his pipe. She could wait for as long as it took.

'We lost a building contract today,' he said, puffing, keeping his eyes intently on the bowl of his pipe, cupping his hands around it. 'It was a big one, so we were a wee bit disappointed.'

Hannah knew he was keeping his voice deliberately low, his attitude calm. But she was his wife, she had the right to know, to share it with him, no matter how bad it was.

'Why did you lose it? Do you know?'

'Aye. To be sure, I know. There's no mystery about that.'

'Can you tell me?'

She had never seen him like this before. He was dangerously quiet. No teasing, no mockery. It was as though he had retreated somewhere, far away from everything. Suddenly, he seemed to make up his mind.

'Och, it's just business, Hannah. Nothing for you to worry your wee head about. Haven't you enough on your plate?'

He patted her stomach, smiling at her. She felt relieved: something of his old manner had returned. She wouldn't push him any further. She had learned of late that the more she pushed, the more he dug his heels in. He would tell her in his own good time, and she would have to be content with that.

Hannah and Mary: Spring 1900

'MARY, MARY, COME quickly, please!'

Startled, Mary dropped the bundle of clothes on her way to the laundry sink and looked around her. Miss Hannah's voice seemed to have come from somewhere very near.

'Mary, where are you!'

The voice was higher-pitched now, frantic. Upstairs; she was calling from upstairs.

'Coming now!'

Dear God, Mary thought, don't let anything be wrong. Memories of the Long household started to crowd in on her. Impatiently, she pushed them away.

'Don't fret, now, I'm on me way!'

She ran up the stairs, cursing silently as she stumbled in her eagerness. Miss Hannah's voice had sounded terrified. At least it wasn't the middle of the night, and Nurse Walker was on standby only two streets away.

Mary reached the landing to see Hannah standing in front of her, her long white nightgown soaking wet to below her knees, streaked unmistakably with blood. She was shaking, her eyes two startling pools of blue in a pale, terrified face. Mary instantly became calm.

'It's all right, Miss Hannah. Yer waters have broke. It means the baby's ready.'

She smiled encouragingly, leading the frightened young woman back into her bedroom. She had a sudden rush of pity for her: she was only a girl, herself.

She settled her on the bed, wrapping a shawl around her shoulders, rubbing her arms to stop the shivering.

'This'll be a considerate wee wain, arrivin' at midday instead o' the wee small hours o' the mornin'!'

She was rewarded with a weak smile. Hannah's eyes were tearful now, her face not so frozen.

'Are you sure everything's all right?'

'As right as rain,' Mary promised her. 'Now you sit tight for five minutes, an' I'll be back with Nurse Walker.'

'No – don't leave me! Don't go, Mary, please!'

Her hands clutched at the sleeves of Mary's dress.

Mary knelt on the floor and took Hannah's two hands in hers.

'Deliverin' babies is the midwife's work: lookin' after them is mine! I promise I'll be back before ye know it.'

Finally, Hannah nodded. Mary fled before she had time to change her mind. She felt wildly excited. She had shared this child with Miss Hannah, shared all the joyful anticipation of its arrival as much as a doting aunt. And Miss Hannah had promised, if it was a wee girl, to give her the second name of Cecilia.

The whole room was filled with pain. It didn't matter if she stood, or tried to walk, or even knelt on the ground on all fours with Mary rubbing her back. No matter what way she lay or turned, there was no escaping it. Hannah couldn't bear any more of this. Tomorrow, she'd come back again tomorrow.

'Please, Nurse Walker,' she begged. 'Just let me rest for a little while, just a little.'

Mary sat behind her on the bed, her strong arms linked in Hannah's, her warm body a comfort, something solid and grounded to lean against.

'We're nearly there, Mrs MacBride, nearly there!' Nurse Walker's voice was loud, encouraging. 'We can see the wee one's head. Just a few more pushes and we'll be there, so we will!'

Mary's face was pressed to hers, her cheek warm and firm.

'Ye're doin' so well, Hannah; don't give up now. Pretend ye're usin' my strength – push, now!'

With one huge, last effort, Hannah drew breath, kept her chin down as Nurse Walker had shown her, and pushed, hearing herself groan as though from a great distance.

'Well done! That's the head now – what a dotey wee face!'

The midwife's voice was triumphant. Mary embraced Hannah warmly from behind, finding she could no longer speak. She thought she had never seen anything so magical, so simply wonderful, in her whole life. Hannah began to laugh as the baby seemed to turn around of its own accord, its small red face suddenly visible, all its tiny features squeezed together with indignation.

'One more push, now – the shoulders'll slide out easy enough!'

Hannah was rewarded with a high-pitched wail.

'It's a wee girl, with a fine pair o' lungs!'

'Look at the length o' them legs!'

'Let me see her!'

Nurse Walker was bending low over the infant, her hands moving so swiftly that Hannah couldn't make out what she was doing. Then, grinning from ear to ear, the elderly woman handed her a tiny bundle, swaddled tight in a white cotton blanket.

'Now, just once more, and we're done.'

Hannah looked up in alarm.

'Twins?' she gasped.

'No, you wee goose – the afterbirth!'

All three women laughed. Mary couldn't contain herself any longer.

'Congratulations, Hannah, well done to you! What a wee beauty she is!'

Then she blushed. In her delight, she had forgotten all formality, forgotten completely that Hannah was her employer, neither her friend nor her sister. Hannah's eyes never left her daughter's face. Her hand sought Mary's, fumbling among the sheets and towels behind her.

'She's beautiful, isn't she? Baby Eileen, say hello to Mary. Mary, I'd like you to meet Eileen Cecilia MacBride.'

Hannah squeezed Mary's hand.

'Thank you,' she said. 'For everything.'

May: Spring 1900

MAY'S EYES WERE gritty with sleeplessness. The trip from Paris had exhausted her. She had hardly slept the night before, every mile of the rattling train journey putting more and more distance between her and her hopes. Even at Calais, her eyes kept looking for a miracle, her neck straining as she searched the crowds for the sight of a tall, rangy figure making his way rapidly through the throngs to claim her. It had not happened, and she was angry at herself for the heights of her ridiculous, romantic hopes.

Alone in her compartment, she had cried for the first time since Madame had told her she was sending her home. Some instinct had made her steely, refusing that woman the pleasure of seeing her defeated. She had cried for most of the journey, and now she felt simply empty: as though some vital part of her had leached away during the night.

She had kept her eyes down for most of the ferry crossing to Belfast. A woman with a small child, then a well-dressed couple – May would respond to neither advance, watching with relief as they drifted away from her, the one looking upset, the others puzzled. She didn't care how she appeared to the other passengers: she would never see them again. She wanted no talk, no kindness, no contact with anyone. They had all left her alone with her book. She had to remember to turn the pages from time to time to complete the impression of concentration, of a woman absorbed. The grey, freezing morning in Liverpool had seemed to her exactly right: somehow she wouldn't have been able to bear it if the sun had shone.

She had gone out on deck as soon as she had heard the first booming warnings from the Reed Horn on East Twin Island. Fog, as usual. A thick, grey mass of it hung above the city; May could already smell the greasy fumes of factory chimneys, could feel the heavy air insinuate itself into her mouth, her nose, her lungs: she imagined it coating her insides with soot, layer after layer of it until she would become sick again, coughing and wheezing her way back to childhood.

She counted the buoys which now guided the ferry into port. All of them were lit, their misty beams rising and falling gently on the rolling swell. Eight black cans on the County Down side, nine red ones on the Antrim side. At some points along the Victoria Channel, all the buoys looked the same dark colour, with nothing to distinguish them in the murky water. They looked crusty, May thought, like dried blood.

The ferry announced its impending arrival, and it was as though all the sounds from the quayside were suddenly unleashed. As they drew closer, the shrill sound of sirens, the groans of distant machinery and the creaking of timber shattered the watery silence. It was as if all the looming shadows of cranes and gantries in Belfast's shipyards had suddenly come to life, stretched themselves and roared into wakefulness. May was startled by the noise and the jostling and hurrying that now surrounded her on the deck. People were crowding against the railings, pointing and shouting at the vessels that lay side by side at the quay. Towering above them all, pushing against the grey skyline, was the huge hull of a ship under construction. May thought she had never seen anything so vast and terrifying in her life.

'It's the *Celtic*, it's the *Celtic*!'

Excited voices were shouting to each other, forefingers jabbing the air in the direction of the monster. It seemed to her to be lying in wait – like some enormous beached whale hoping for the next tide. It made her feel dwarfed and vulnerable; looking up at the stocks made her dizzy and slightly sick. She wanted to be away from here, wanted to be safe within Hannah's walls.

Quickly, she began to gather her things. Most of the other passengers were still facing the hull of the *Celtic*, unable to draw their eyes away from it. Belfast's pride: a symbol of its growing industrial might. 'The biggest ship in the world,' she heard the men saying. 'Aye, bigger even than the *Oceania*.' Their voices congratulated each other on its vastness, as though their citizenship made them somehow personally responsible for this marvel. They kept repeating to each other over and over again what they must already know. She would take advantage of their distraction and make her way to the gangway. With any luck, she would not be delayed disembarking. She had her money and the piece of paper with Hannah's address folded together inside her glove. She knew that Charles would come for her if he could, but she was not to wait if he were not there before her. In a way, she hoped he wouldn't be. She wanted to look neither right nor left, but straight ahead to where Hannah's last letter had promised a line of carriages would be waiting. She wasn't ready for conversation and questions, not yet, no matter how kind. She just wanted to be with Hannah; that was home for now.

May welcomed the time alone on the last part of the journey to 107 High Street, Holywood. The small space inside the carriage was comforting, allowing her to disappear. It was as though the carriage became her carapace, protecting and sheltering her until she was able to compose her face and her thoughts for meeting her sister. She would tell her everything in time, of course, but this was Hannah's moment, Hannah's joy which must not be tainted.

Her sister was waiting for her. May smiled to herself when she saw her, imagined her standing in just that position since early morning. A swift movement of muslin at the porch window and the front door was suddenly flung open. And there she was, arms open wide. May hugged her sister wordlessly, realizing how fiercely she had missed both Hannah and Ellie, suddenly wanting never to be that long apart again.

'May – welcome home!'

'Oh, it's so good to be back! Let me take a look at you!'

She held Hannah at arm's length from her, the older girl looking suddenly shy. Her face was rounder, softer than before, her figure fuller. May thought the change suited her.

'You look wonderful,' she said softly. 'And I can't wait to see baby Eileen.'

'Aren't you tired?' asked Hannah anxiously. She looked at her sister's pale, strained face and May caught the sudden fear in her eyes. Hannah knew that there was something wrong – something more than the fatigue brought on by a long journey. This was not the moment. May shook her head vigorously.

'That can wait. I can't.'

She was already taking off her bonnet, shrugging her way out of her travelling coat. From behind, a pair of strong hands lifted the awkward garment and May found her arms slipped away easily from the imprisonment of the heavy sleeves.

She turned around to see who had helped her.

Hannah indicated a strong, capable-looking girl, whose expression instantly reminded May of Lily.

'This is Mary. Mary, this is my sister, May.'

May saw that the girl's face was at once young and somehow older than its years, her hair already lightly brushed with grey.

'Thank you, Mary.'

The young woman smiled and nodded, and May liked the honesty and kindness she could read in her open features.

Hannah took her sister by the hand.

'Will you ask Nurse to bring the baby to us in the drawing room, Mary?'

May only half heard Mary's response, half caught the echo of the strong Belfast accent which was suddenly familiar to her again. Instead, she was looking around her in delight. In front of her was a dark mahogany double door, its solid panels lightened by the presence of large panes of stained glass. The vivid, glassy blues and reds and yellows brightened the wide hallway into which Hannah now led her. An imposing staircase lay to their right, and pieces of classical sculpture nestled in the curved niches to either side. Hannah's last home in Stewarts Place had been nothing like this.

'Hannah, what a beautiful house!'

Hannah opened the door into the drawing room and turned back to smile at her sister.

'It is, isn't it? I'll show you the rest later.'

The fire was lit and the room mellow in weak, February sunshine.

'I don't need to ask if you're happy,' May smiled at her sister, feeling as though she were suddenly the older one. Hannah seemed to have recovered all her old freshness and contentment; May felt shadowy and embittered by comparison. She had a moment's extreme envy – what she saw was a happy marriage, a baby, a beautiful home. All of the things which she had been so close to having for herself. And now she had nothing; it had all slipped away.

There was a soft tap at the door and an elderly woman entered, carrying what appeared to be a fat bundle of blankets. She handed the bundle to Hannah and murmured something about tea.

'Of course! How stupid of me. And ask Mary for some scones, too, will you? Thank you, Nurse.'

May had stood up at once and was gazing at the doll-like face surrounded by a lacy, frilly cap.

'Take her,' said Hannah.

May held the baby close, feeling some of the ache of recent months drain away as she watched the barely perceptible sucking movements of the small mouth, the tiny flailings of the perfect hands.

She couldn't speak. She smiled at Hannah, her eyes full. Neither needed to say anything, and May was grateful for the silence.

May welcomed all the fuss and activity that surrounded the birth of her tiny niece. She was glad that such a small being had made everybody forget about her recent return from France. She was able to pass it off easily, expressing her delight at being home, at her new role as godmother to baby Eileen. She was half relieved to learn that her activities were of very little interest to anyone except her sisters, and marginally to Constance Mac-Bride. No whisper of her fall from grace seemed to have crossed the sea with her. When this became apparent, she finally allowed herself to believe that she need not be so anxious about being found out. She could not bear the thought of anyone probing what was still an open wound.

'Treated you well, the Ondarts, did they, my dear?'

Constance MacBride had fixed May with her stern eyes a few days after her arrival at Hannah's home. May froze. The old lady's sharp eye, her face full of intelligent curiosity, made May wonder if she suspected.

'Yes, thank you, very well indeed,' she had replied meekly, determined at first to give nothing away, filled with a sudden rush of feeling that she wanted done with the whole thing, that she never wanted to think about it again. If she ceased to remember, she would cease to feel pain. Mrs MacBride, then her mother – these were the only interrogations she need fear. She would not be drawn; she would show no sign of weakness.

'Were you homesick, then? Is that what's brought you back to us sooner than you'd planned?'

May made up her mind quickly. She looked around her, as though checking she could not be overheard. Constance MacBride's eyes were instantly alight, and May knew that she had made the right choice. The woman loved a good gossip, she was sure of it. She leaned closer.

'I'm not to say – I'm sure you understand – some little trouble over business.'

The older woman gasped.

'But I understood Ondart to be – *rock* solid!'

May hoped she hadn't gone too far.

'And I assure you, he still is. That's why they had to go to Marseilles at once: Monsieur wanted to handle everything *personally*.'

The older woman nodded, grimly.

'The only way. Time out of number, I said to my husband . . .'

May breathed a small, silent sigh of relief. It would appear she had hit the right note; now, perhaps, she would be left alone. Constance MacBride was in full verbal flight, happily rehearsing all her certainties about life and business. She didn't need an audience: the sound of her own voice delivering her favourite, familiar phrases was comfort enough for her. May sat with her politely, nodding from time to time, reminded of the day of Hannah's engagement. On that afternoon, they had all had to endure the heat and the boredom of the MacBrides' drawing room: but now she, May, was in her sister's home. Perhaps she didn't need to be so passively polite. She half listened to the torrent of recollections, waiting for the appropriate moment to make her escape. She hoped the older woman was sufficiently indignant not to ask the obvious question: why had May not gone to Marseilles with them? And then she heard the words '. . . an older son, I believe – did you ever meet him?'

May gave her full attention.

'Monsieur Philippe, yes, I did meet him.'

Then she shook her head gravely.

'Not at all like his father, I'm afraid.'

Constance MacBride nodded, satisfied.

'That's what I always thought. Don't worry, my dear, I'll say no more about it.'

Suddenly, May didn't care. Time and distance would distort the truth anyway, if it were ever discovered, and now she wanted only to be with her family.

*

Richard arrived the night before the christening. He and Charles were distant cousins, close boyhood friends, and they had kept in touch throughout all of Charles's years at sea. Richard was five or six years younger than his cousin, May thought, and perhaps a degree or two poorer. Her first impression was of a big man, with thoughtful and deliberate movements. His clothes looked ill at ease, as though they were not used to being worn; they hung, baggily, on his large frame. He had a shock of fair hair that kept falling across his forehead, and that he pushed back from time to time, with a hand rough-veined and callused by hard work. He was a farmer, he told May that night over dinner. Not a gentleman farmer, he said with a smile at Charles, but a real one, one who got his hands dirty and his boots muddy on a regular basis.

'Aye – and never was there more truth to the phrase, "Happy as a pig in muck"!' Charles teased him.

It was getting close to midnight, and May had watched as Charles became more and more expansive. Some of his hand gestures reminded her unwillingly of Monsieur Ondart, yet there was none of that man's ill humour here. She noted with amusement that Hannah had moved the decanter of wine just out of her husband's reach. It had been done discreetly, but she had caught May catching her and suppressed a smile with difficulty.

'This man,' Charles was saying, indicating Richard with a nod, 'knows every blade of grass, every stone, and the peculiarities of every single animal at Abbotsford.'

He raised his glass.

'Here's to his father, who had the good sense to leave his land in such honest and capable hands.'

They raised their glasses.

'If I may propose a toast now,' said Richard, looking around the table. 'To friends old and new, girl babies, and the honour of being . . . godparents.'

He said this last with a smile, turning to ask May's permission with his eyes. She nodded, feeling strangely pleased to be included. She felt a welcome surge of freedom and ease as she sat around this table. Nobody knew. Her secret was invisible, she could keep it for as long as she liked. Charles's and Richard's animated conversation all evening had amused and entertained her: for the first time since she had met Philippe, she had a respite from extremes of emotion. She felt neither elated nor anguished. She was glad that Richard was such a calm and easy-going man. She had been afraid that she would have to make huge efforts for Hannah's sake, had dreaded meeting this distant relative from County Meath. It was a relief to find he was such undemanding company. When all four rose to leave the table, it was well after one o'clock. May was surprised she didn't feel more tired. In some strange way, Richard's presence had made the thought of her parents' arrival the next morning easier to bear. The beginnings of the sense of peace she had felt earlier were still with her as she went to bed. It was the first release from the torment of rejection which had made her fear, at times, for her sanity. She felt sleep creep up on her. She was suddenly deeply grateful to be home. France had never felt quite so far away.

She knew she would never get over Philippe, not ever. But it was good to have the edge taken off everything, just for a little while.

Richard had to return to the farm immediately the christening was over.

'I can't leave my animals any longer,' May heard him say to Charles, 'the Duggans have their own place to look after as well. It wouldn't be fair.'

May had been gathering empty dishes and bowls from the dining room, bringing them across the hallway to the kitchen where Mary was keeping a watchful eye on two young girls up to their elbows in hot water. They could have been no more than thirteen, May thought with a pang, remembering the local girls brought in by Madame Ondart to help out at their weekend parties. May could still feel that sense of exclusion, when it was simply understood that she would keep to the kitchens or to her room – anywhere she chose, as long as she stayed out of sight.

A few moments before, Charles and Richard had left the dining room together. Charles had opened the French windows and both men had stepped outside to light their pipes. They were standing at the top of the little flight of stone steps that led down into the terraced garden. May had stood there earlier that afternoon, glad to be away from the crowded drawing room for a moment, enjoying the blue glisten of the sea in the distance. Now she gathered up some more plates from the table and moved away from the open window in case it would appear that she had been eavesdropping. She didn't hear Charles's muffled reply, but sensed that both men had descended further into the garden. She could no longer smell their tobacco-smoke.

She felt a vague sense of disappointment. She loved being here in Holywood, an instant part of Hannah's household, helping her welcome Mama, Papa and Ellie; she loved being godmother to baby Eileen, but the day of the christening had brought with it a deepening restlessness. She felt cast off, cut adrift from her own life, the one which she hadn't fitted into yet. It was the same feeling she had had in France, waiting for Philippe to decide what they, what *she*, was going to do next. She felt now that she had no talents: her French had improved during her nine months away, but she was by no means fluent, not nearly good enough to teach. And she really did not want to go home to live with Mama and Papa again. Her longing to travel had brought her nothing but unhappiness – she wished Grandfather Delaney were still alive, so that he could give her courage, tell her again that she could do anything if she put her mind to it. At eighteen, her life had begun to feel very small and narrow, unlike those days when hopeful continents had opened up to her so many years ago in Grandfather's study. The daring and piracy of Grace O'Malley, the rejection of constraints by such intrepid travellers as Lady Craven and Annie Boyle Hore, the gentle, ladylike travels of her grandmother – all seemed very far away from her now. Even her two sisters seemed far ahead of her. It seemed that Hannah's earlier suffering was over – she looked happy, fulfilled.

Papa and Mama had been right, after all. It was also clear that Ellie was taking charge of her own life – she had whispered about wanting to train as a nurse, striking out on her own, swearing both her sisters to secrecy for the moment, until the time was right.

She would do it, too. She had always had a determined, independent streak, ever since she was a small child. And May could see that she had grown and matured an amazing amount in the nine months since they had last seen each other. Of all three sisters, it seemed that only the youngest was destined to be a New Woman, deciding her life for herself, supported by work and purpose. Everyone was moving towards something new, something different, while she, May, was imprisoned, her will paralysed by the events of the last several months.

She had a suddenly terrifying vision of herself spending the rest of her unwilling life under her parents' roof, perhaps nursing them long into infirmity and old age. Her life stretched before her as something that would belong to her by default only – no choice of hers, right or wrong, would bring its circumstances about, but simply the cruel randomness of chance. The spinster daughter, the one who was left behind. The one forced into blind and dutiful obedience long into the resentfulness of a childless middle age.

Panic-stricken, she fled the dining room, and ran silently up the stairs to her bedroom. She poured water from the ewer into the basin on her washstand, immersing her hands in the cool depths. Trembling, she bent down and splashed her aching forehead. She felt trapped, as though all hope for another kind of life must be abandoned.

Single, alone, unwanted. She could not, would not, allow that to happen.

Eleanor's Journal

I WAS VERY glad to hear the news that Hannah's confinement had gone smoothly, and that she had been safely delivered of a baby girl. I am sure it is no compliment to myself to say that I welcomed the distraction which the recent arrival of my parents' first grandchild afforded me. I was no longer the focus of their attention. Mama now had somewhere else to direct the overspill of her emotions. Papa could remain quite happily in the background, secure in the knowledge that no one was about to interrupt his daily lethargy, now that a beautiful, healthy baby had arrived to fill the gaps in everyone's life.

And Eileen was a delightful baby. I had been so looking forward to seeing her, and was only a little disappointed that May was chosen as the godmother, and not I. I was very surprised when she wrote of her early return from Paris – something about her family's need to relocate to Marseilles. I did not believe a word of it. The tone of her letter was so subdued, so bleak almost, that I knew something terrible must have happened. As usual, Mama either feigned ignorance, or genuinely did not understand this; Papa continued to be oblivious to all but himself.

Of the many journeys to Belfast my parents and I had shared, this one was without doubt the happiest. We were going towards something wonderful for once in our lives, rather than retreating from something unspeakable. We conversed freely, at least Mama and I did, and she reminisced about all our babyhoods, occasionally calling upon my father to validate her memories. It struck me for the first time that our very earliest years must have been the happiest time of Mama's life. Thereafter, there seemed to be some sad, complicated relationship between our growing up and the increase in her discontent.

Charles was waiting for us at the train station. He had the air of a man who was very pleased with himself. He was his usual polite and friendly self, and treated me with exaggerated courtesy. He answered Mama's endless questions about her new granddaughter, answered them with generosity and humour, and the journey to Holywood passed pleasantly enough. He was lavish in his praise of his first daughter – the brightest, the prettiest, the best-behaved little infant who ever drew breath. I thought him quite endearing.

Amid much embracing and kissing on our arrival at Hannah's new home, I caught my first sight of May. Something within me felt squeezed, as though a painful pressure had been slowly exerted around my heart. I went straight to her and put my arms around her. I hugged her as hard as I could.

'Oh, Ellie,' was all she said.

It was enough. I could hear the sound of her heart breaking in the way she said my name. I didn't press her, didn't beg for explanations. I knew my sisters well enough to know that I would be told, again, that I was too young, I wouldn't understand, she'd tell me when I was older. I didn't mind. I knew that May had Hannah, and that she would tell her eventually what was troubling her. I also knew that she hadn't done so yet – the weight of her unshared burden was all too visible around her.

She did her best to conceal her unhappiness. I don't think that anyone else noticed. I tried not to watch her too closely during the days before and after the christening, but I was glad when Richard made her smile.

I have always found this to be a strange irony between me and my sisters. They used to think, perhaps still do think, that youth somehow precludes emotional understanding – intuition, if you will. Never mind that there are precious few years separating all of us anyway – years that seem to become less and less significant as we all grow older. And yet, they still see me as Ellie, their baby sister. Perhaps they need to do this in order to comfort themselves that they grow no older as long as I remain a child.

Child or no, I have intuition to burn. They have never understood that I possess more of it on my own account than they do between them. Does this sound less than modest to you? I do not wish to be arrogant or self-serving, merely faithful to how I felt at that time, and still feel, if truth be told.

I have always known my sisters' hearts better than they do themselves.

May: Spring 1900

THE DAYS THAT followed the christening were quiet.
May was grateful for the sudden calm that descended
on the house. All the other guests were long departed;
even Constance MacBride did not outstay her welcome,
but Mama and Papa did. She tried to conceal her
impatience at their presence – Mama was in no hurry to
leave, whereas Papa was agitated, impatient to be gone.
The friction between them was like an additional,
uneasy presence in the room, and May escaped their
company as often as she could. She took refuge in
Mary's kitchen, leaving her mother to cluck and fuss
with Nurse. May knew that Hannah was getting restless,
too – she had spent the last week being told, in all sorts
of silences and gestures, how she couldn't possibly be
capable of looking after her own daughter.

And now they were on their way, back to Dublin.
Charles had organized their carriage to the railway
station, cheerfully carried their bags downstairs, and
before they knew it, they were on their journey home.
May had smiled to herself at how he had brought it
about. There had been no discussion, no time for the
enemy to prepare its pre-emptive strike: the carriage

would be there at eleven; Matt was a good man, very reliable; he would not leave until they and their belongings were safely stowed in the first-class compartment he, Charles, had reserved for them. No, no, not at all, no trouble – this when Sophia was about to protest. May knew she wanted to protest about leaving so soon; Charles expertly turned it into a polite protest at his generosity, which, of course, he was far too much a gentleman to heed. May had to turn away. She had caught the beginnings of a smile from Hannah, and did not trust herself not to laugh. She was surprised: this was the first time she had felt like laughing for several months.

Gradually, the sisters settled into a routine. In the mornings, they rested while Nurse took care of Eileen. Hannah was determined to care for her baby herself as much as she could – Nurse's days were numbered. In the early afternoon, if the day was fine, the two sisters wheeled Eileen out in her baby carriage, ignoring Mrs MacBride's sharp observation that only lower-class women wheeled their own children about. Hannah chose to do as she pleased. The afternoon walk was a double blessing, she declared: the baby got some fresh air, and she, Hannah, managed to be absent for several of her mother-in-law's increasingly frequent visits.

It was almost a month after her arrival at Hannah's home that May felt able to tell her about Philippe. They were drinking tea in the drawing room, Eileen fast asleep by the fire in the kitchen, under Mary's watchful eye. It was much too wet and dreary to go out; March winds blew with increasing ferocity across Belfast Lough. The sisters had been sitting in companionable silence for some time.

Hannah spoke first.

'It's wonderful having you here, May. It's like being children again – I don't even *feel* like a grown-up!'

'It's been wonderful for me, too. I can't begin to tell you how much.'

'You were very unhappy when you came back from France, May – what happened there?'

May smiled across at her sister. She had always had the ability to see right to the heart of the matter, to ask questions whose directness was matched only by their gentleness.

May struggled to find the words to begin to tell her about Philippe. Instead, she started to cry, helpless to stop herself. Hannah came and knelt on the floor beside her, wrapping her arms around her sister's waist. In turn, May rested her head on Hannah's shoulder. It was a familiar pose for both of them.

Once May began to speak, she couldn't stop. All the misery of the Ondarts' coldness towards her, her struggles to teach the children, her sense of isolation – all came pouring out in the safety of her sister's drawing room. Her growing love for Philippe, and his for her; the day he asked her to marry him. Visions of him standing in the twilight, waiting for her, brought fresh torrents of weeping. It was such a relief to let it all go, not to be judged, not to feel so tainted and guilty over everything that had passed.

'But the hardest thing is, he could have found me at any stage if he had cared enough to. In Paris, at Calais – even here. His family knows Charles's family, for heaven's sake. And it's cruel to keep hoping, but I can't help it.'

Hannah stroked her hair, looking gravely at her sister's tear-stained face.

'And perhaps he will.'

May shook her head.

'No – I knew that night that he would not. I can't explain, but I know them – I know how they will arrange things so that he can't, and then he won't want to. No. I have no reason to hope. I must do something else, something useful – I cannot spend my life waiting.'

'You're welcome here – to make your home here, if you wish. You know that.'

'Yes,' said May, 'I know that. And I'm very grateful, to you and Charles. I need some more time to think, to recover my wits. I'll stay a little longer, but then I really must think of making plans.'

May could not tell her sister of the furtive night she and Philippe had spent together. What other man would marry her if he knew? If Hannah guessed, then so be it: they would never speak of it. May's regret at what she had done was matched only by her fear of being the sister who was left behind. *Spinster; old maid; odd woman.* Nor could she ever have thought of herself before this as being capable of such black ingratitude towards her parents, such wickedness. But watching them together, seeing the disappointment of their lives, their need to look beyond themselves and each other for solace, for interest, for entertainment – anything to make life worth living – May had felt herself grow cold. She needed to preserve herself, her own corner of the world. She could not be sucked back into the family home, surrounded by bitterness and failure. She would not settle into the emptiness of a solitary life, the pitiful state of an odd woman.

She would stay with Hannah a little longer, but then she would have to take charge.

Mary: Summer 1901

MR MACBRIDE was very kind to her, very kind indeed. He thanked Mary more than once in the mornings before he left for his day's work and always greeted her with something witty on his arrival home at night. He was truly a creature of habit, Mary thought. For well over a year now, he had walked briskly out of the house at the same time every day, and come home on the minute-past-six train every evening. His routine had never varied.

Never varied, that is, until the news of Queen Victoria's death sent the whole city into mourning. Mary went about her work quietly, kept her mouth shut in the marketplace, nodded politely to all around her, just as usual. But she could feel the tension in the air. All over Belfast's streets, Union Jacks hung from lamp-posts, shop windows, trams – the whole city seemed to be an undulating mass of red, white and blue. She could imagine the silence that must prevail all around Carrick Hill, the agitation behind closed doors. She couldn't help herself: in her imagination she relived all the awfulness of the riots of eight years earlier, feeling her heart clench with fear as she recalled how the days and terrifying nights had been spent waiting and watching. Even after the uproar had receded, she and Cecilia always seemed to go back to *waiting*, keeping quiet behind their own door, senses honed for even one unaccustomed sound.

Unwelcome flashes of memory now disturbed Mary's daily chores: she saw Cecilia, her face bruised and bloody, everywhere she turned. Her sleep was uneasy, filled with dreams that had her struggle into consciousness, dry-mouthed and fearful, in the early hours of the morning. Those were the times she cried, silently, missing her sister with an intensity she had believed dulled and eased by the last two contented years. And Myles. His face appeared before her more often than she cared to acknowledge, even to herself. His eyes bright with hurt, his step full of quiet dignity on the night she sent him away, had returned to haunt her here, where she had thought herself finally safe.

And while Holywood was a whole world away from Peter's Hill, with its genteel houses and discreet inhabitants, she was nevertheless taking no chances. You never knew who was listening, what damage could be done by a careless word. There were still houses in this town that let it be known, however quietly, where their loyalties lay, that wore their colours on their tailored sleeve; and then there were those that were silent.

Mary became watchful during the days following the old Queen's death. She was glad that Miss Hannah was so occupied with Eileen. And with the arrival of her sister May, she had developed an extraordinary ability to live within her own four walls, undisturbed by, and perhaps even unaware of, what surrounded her on the outside. Mary suspected that she was pregnant again, and hoped for her sake that she was. To be completely self-absorbed was the only way she could continue in ignorance about the night-time activities of her husband.

He did not arrive home on his accustomed train, and Hannah grew frantic. Mary was surprised at the depth of the other woman's distress. Privately, she thought her reaction a little bit extreme. Mary did her best to soothe her.

'The trains are all late, Miss Hannah. There's a torchlight procession tonight for the Queen's funeral. Ye're not to worry, now.'

Hannah looked at her with relief, wanting to be reassured.

'You're sure?'

'Aye. There was talk of nothin' else in the market this mornin'. They said the whole o' Belfast would be grindin' to a halt.'

Mary prayed to God to forgive her. She would burn that day's newspaper as soon as she got the chance, in case there was anything there to contradict the lie she had just told. It was only a white lie, but still. And maybe there was something going on in the city centre, anyway: there had been some demonstration of loyalty to the dead Queen, in one form or another, every night this week.

'Why don't ye rest up this evenin'? You look tired, so ye do.'

She felt easier in herself when Hannah nodded.

'I am tired,' she admitted. 'Maybe I'll do that – just go to bed.'

Mary knew she was missing her sister, too. Miss May had gone back to Dublin, just for a week, to see their Mama, who was unwell. But Mary knew that Miss Hannah feared she would not return: although the two women had not said as much, Mary had had the sense that their Mama was trying to claim Miss May's attentions for herself. There had been tears and regrets between them, and many promises on Miss May's part to return; nevertheless, Miss Hannah had wandered around the house like a lost child ever since.

'Aye. You do that. You settle yerself in bed. I'll wait up – I've a pile o' mendin' to finish, any road. I'll bring ye tea when ye're ready, so I will.'

'All right, then. Thank you, Mary. I don't know what I'd do without you.'

Mary felt herself glow. Miss Hannah exasperated her at times, with her childishness, her inability to master even the simplest household task, and her complete uselessness at managing money. But there was a core of warmth to the young woman to which Mary found it impossible not to respond. Her gratitude to Mary was heartfelt, simple – just like her view of life, Mary thought. Everything was either good or bad, black or white; people were either worth knowing, or they weren't. And the same Miss Hannah had just a little too much respect for people with money. Mary thought that Miss May was a much more down-to-earth young woman, despite whatever unhappiness was troubling her.

Mary often thought that it was as well that Miss Hannah had never tried to live her life among all the shades of grey that settled around the Belfast she and Cecilia had known. Mr Charles was a whole other kettle of fish, though. At home, he was easy-going to a fault, but he was nevertheless alert to all that was going on around him. He left the running of the household to the three women, but the running of the world was a different matter. Mary served his breakfast in the dining room every morning, and had by now become used to his outbursts over his morning coffee. At first, she had wondered why he bought so many newspapers – the *Belfast Telegraph*, the *News Letter* and the *Irish News* – as the contents of at least one of them seemed to enrage him so much on a daily basis. He had shattered a teacup one morning recently in his fury over that morning's headlines. Jabbing a finger at the masthead, he roared, not at her, but to her: 'What d'ye think of this outrageous bit of rubbish, Mary? The Irish "an inferior race, genetically incapable of ever being their own masters"?'

Mary froze. She managed so well with everyone – post office, tradesmen, church collections – that she knew he had no idea she couldn't read. He had often complimented her on her quickness with figures. But that morning, he understood her expression instantly, and his anger deflated at once. He reminded Mary of the way boiling milk seethed and then settled, once it was taken off the range. He folded the paper abruptly.

'Aye, well. That's the sort of nonsense I must accept if I insist on buying the *Telegraph*, eh?'

She nodded, grateful.

'Aye, sir.'

She understood his views, and they surprised her. He was one of the Catholics that used tò make Father MacVeigh angry on occasion, wasn't he? One of those who had escaped the fate of so many others, one who got educated and then seemed to forget about everyone else who had been given no such chance? And yet, here he was, morning after morning recently, raging over what he read, expressing views about the British Government that would not have been out of place anywhere on Carrick Hill. Maybe his years at sea had opened his eyes to the possibility of other existences less blessed than his own. His view of the world was certainly more complex than that of his wife, and yet he doted on her.

His occasional sharpness to Miss Hannah recently about overspending had surprised Mary. She had thought there was no shortage of money. By observing Mr Charles closely, however, by listening carefully to the suggestions he made to his wife, Mary believed she had a much clearer picture than Miss Hannah about the financial difficulties that seemed to be troubling him of late. He gave her the impression of a man with a lot on his mind. Gradually, gently, Mary had taken over the management of the household money. Miss May had been a great help – she seemed to be a naturally more frugal being than her elder sister. Together, although they never discussed it, they tried to teach Miss Hannah more careful ways, and bit by bit, Mary took over all the shopping and dealing with tradesmen herself. They'd not try to pull the wool over her eyes, so they wouldn't.

All in all, she knew she was lucky. She had good employers, people who were kind to her. She would not see them taken advantage of. If only she could be sure that Belfast was not going to erupt again: Mr Charles's bad temper over his morning paper was a bad sign. Her dreams of Cecilia were another: trouble was brewing again, she was sure of it.

Suddenly, Mary thought she heard the front door open. She stood up, letting the pile of mending on her knee slide to the floor. She walked out on to the landing and stood, alert and listening. No sound from the bedroom; Miss Hannah hadn't woken, at least. Nor had the child.

Mary tiptoed downstairs, her heart beating a little faster than usual. What could there be to be frightened of? It had to be Mr Charles – he had let himself in with his key, after all. But that was unusual, too, for he rarely brought his key. He had his own signal, his own little tattoo which he would beat out gently with the door knocker, and wee Eileen would recognize it at once. He would wait for Mary to let him in, scooping up his small daughter, making her squeal with delight as he carried her on his shoulders into the drawing room, back to her Mama.

Mary made her way now down the long corridor towards the kitchen. As she got closer, there was a faint but peculiar smell. She grew alarmed; it was like tar – was there something on fire? She quickened her step and pulled open the kitchen door. In the almost complete darkness, she collided smartly with another body in the process of lighting his pipe.

'Mr Charles!'

She couldn't help it. Relief had made her tone accusing. How *dare* he frighten the life out of her.

'Hush, Mary. Not a word now. I need some old clothes from you.'

She stood, staring at him stupidly, trying to make out his features.

'Now, Mary; as a matter of urgency.'

There was no trace of mockery in his voice, none of his usual teasing humour. Instead, his tone was anxious, a little impatient. She turned at once and made her way towards the scullery. Bending down, she pulled the basket of laundry out from under the sink. She would do as he asked, without question, almost hoping he would not explain. She did not want to have to keep anyone's secrets. She rummaged until she found a pair of trousers and a shirt, the same ones he had discarded just that morning. Wordlessly, she handed them to him. As he took them, she could see him more clearly now, her eyes grown accustomed to the dim light.

His hands were almost covered with some dark, sticky-looking substance, his clothes spattered with what looked to be the same. Suddenly, she recognized the smell that had been puzzling her. Bitumen. How could she have forgotten?

But Mr Charles was a grown man, a wealthy one – or, at least, a professional one. Surely he couldn't be up to the same thing as all those youths from Carrick Hill?

Daubing slogans was hardly the occupation for a gentle-man. And this week above all? Police would be all over the city like flies, keeping sharp lookout for anything that might disturb the dignity of the old Queen's send-off. Mary was shocked. She remembered the painted signs, scrawled on walls around where she and Cecilia had lived. 'Home Rule Now!' and 'Self-Government for Ireland!' 'Irish Parliament for an Irish people!' Cecilia used to read them all to her, while Myles told them of the ones on the shipyard walls. Obscene ones about the Pope and the horrors of 'Rome Rule'. Was it really starting all over again? And had it now spread its tentacles to catch her out, just when she thought she was long enough and far enough away to have escaped?

'Leave me while I change, Mary. Then I want to talk to you.'

She nodded and left the kitchen at once. Her stomach turned with sudden nausea. She tried to reassure herself. God knows, Holywood was a good distance from Belfast, and divisions weren't quite so easily spotted here. Money and ease tended to cushion any differences which might exist, and the churches seemed to live together peaceably enough. But here was Mr Charles, ready to draw ruination on all their heads if he continued to lose the run of himself. She was still trembling when he leaned out of the kitchen into the corridor and called her name softly.

She went at once.

'Not a word of what you've seen tonight, Mary. Not to anyone, mind, particularly not to Miss Hannah.'

She nodded, finding it hard to swallow.

'Aye, sir.'

He was rolling down his shirtsleeves, his hands and forearms red raw from where he had scrubbed them. Her stiff brush and the washing soda were still on the laundry sink.

'If you can't clean the clothes, tell me. I'll dispose of them myself.'

He looked more closely at her.

'Don't be frightened, my dear. I promise you you're safe here. I'll not bring trouble to my own door.'

She nodded.

'Aye, sir.'

'Do we understand one another?'

'Aye, sir,' she said again. It was all she could think of.

'Good. Off you go, now.'

She fled. She knew she'd be able to clean the clothes, to remove all traces. Paraffin, brown paper and a well-heated iron. That wasn't the problem. The problem was the next time, and the time after that. Mary was sure that the RIC didn't come to homes like this with anything like the frequency they visited Carrick Hill. But still.

The whole thing made her uneasy. And she didn't like keeping things from Miss Hannah. It looked as though a good night's rest was going to elude her for some time to come.

Eleanor's Journal

How COULD I ever have known what awaited me on that autumn morning when Mama and I set out for London? I still remember the day as clearly as if it were yesterday. Dun Laoghaire harbour was bustling – there was an extraordinary sense of suppressed excitement, of delighted anticipation, on all the faces I saw around me. My own experience of travel extended no further than the train journey between Dublin and Belfast. A sea voyage seemed much more daring to me, far more adventurous. No doubt my own frame of mind influenced what I saw reflected in the expressions of others – but no matter.

The sea was flat calm, with that intense blue that comes only with the autumnal clarity of early September. I could feel my heartbeat quicken as the time came to board our ship. I know I felt terrified that Mama would have forgotten something, that our tickets would not be valid, that our papers would, somehow, not be in order and I should be turned away. It was not an idle fear: Mama had been most reluctant to permit my removal to London. She and Papa had had a rare moment of unanimity on the evening, some two months previously, when I had told them of my plans to study nursing – and to do so at St Bartholomew's, far away from home.

Mama's face had gone quite white, and Papa had looked surprised, but, above all, irritated. It was as though I had disturbed his quiet existence, his comfortable assumptions that he had finished with domestic upheaval in all its forms.

'Nonsense, Eleanor,' Mama said. 'I shall never allow it. Nursing is no life for a young woman like you.'

My arguments in favour of what I had already decided were logical, reasoned: times were changing; the new century brought greater opportunities for all young women; I had a deep need to make myself useful to others. I spoke quietly all the time, while my heart beat wildly in my chest. I knew that I was fighting for my life.

Papa had blustered at first, and then seemed to lose interest. But Mama had been more tenacious. During the following days and weeks, she moved from outright opposition to appeasement. There were perfectly good nursing schools at home, she had claimed, in a tone which tried to be firm, but lurched instead towards desperation. I had to fight my instinct to feel sorry for her, to want to make up to her for the sad emptiness of her life. She wanted me safely by her side in Dublin, to keep me close, now that my sisters had, as I believe she perceived it, abandoned her. Mama had developed a slightly aggrieved air, an unconscious aura of martyrdom, which she wore like a veil. Through this gauzy filament she regarded her world, now blurred and distorted by maternal disappointment: it was as though her children had treated her with nothing but unkindness.

I could not allow myself to be persuaded.

The fact that my escape had been organized methodically, deliberately, secretly, was an even greater blow to her. She could not claim that her youngest daughter had been seized by a sudden, irresponsible flight of fancy; instead, she had to endure the painful process of accepting that I, the baby, had consciously chosen to leave her, to make my life elsewhere. In the weeks preceding my departure, Mama suffered greatly. I know that. It is to her credit that, after her initial outburst, she never again threatened to withhold her official permission.

My sisters had both wished me well. Hannah pressed some money into my hands when Mama was absent from the room, and silenced my protests by putting her finger to my lips. May, on one occasion when we were all together, had drawn me aside from the others, and warned me not to weaken.

I must do as my heart dictated; I must not let this opportunity pass. In truth, it was her words which gave me courage in the final days before departure.

I was a little disappointed that my first sea voyage was not more eventful. I remember thinking that it resembled a smooth, silent train journey: with a little more motion, certainly, but what movement there was, was both gentle and soothing.

I insisted that Mama did not accompany me from our hotel to St Bartholomew's on my first day. Perhaps I was cruel, but I could not bear for one moment longer to see her quivering lip, her averted eye, her hand clutching at her throat. Every sigh of hers made me more determined to free myself from the shackles of family, or, more accurately, from those of my parents. I ascended the carriage which was to take me to St Bartholomew's, my trunk safely stowed, my travelling coat wrapped warmly around me. London was even colder than Dublin.

Mama stood at the open window, issuing last-minute instructions to me, dabbing at her eyes with her lace handkerchief. Impulsively, I leaned out and kissed her. It was the surprised gratitude of her expression that finally made the tears spring to my eyes.

'Thank you, Mama,' I said softly, 'for being with me. I shall write soon, I promise.'

I felt wretched as we drove away. Every time I think of Mama now, that is how I see her – an elegant figure, but one with the lines of frailty already etched about her person, waving her handkerchief at the departing carriage, her left hand clutching restlessly at the pearls around her throat.

But I was already intent on looking forward, not back. I was filled with the excitement that comes from intense, youthful conviction: the sense of mission that makes one believe that one's life can make a difference to others. I knew that I was no Elizabeth Blackwell – I did not have courage enough to be a pioneer. I had not the vision then to aspire to a career in medicine: I believed only that I was good enough to be a nurse. I had read everything I could about St Bartholomew's. I knew of the hospital's work among the poor, of the excellence of its patient care and the high standards of its training. I saw my future unfold itself before my delighted, terrified eyes: a life of caring for others, of womanly independence, of fulfilment. I could hardly bear to wait.

Those first months at St Bartholomew's hospital were more terrifying than anything I have ever endured, before or since. But for you, I believe I should have gone truly mad.

The homesickness from which I suffered had an intensity that was akin to physical distress, a wound inflicted which took many months to heal. While it mended, silent and invisible to others, its residual ache lasted for months. I hope that I have used the memory of my then unhappiness to good effect in the training of my nurses over the years. You cannot heal others unless you have first learned to heal yourself.

I remember well my extraordinary confusion in those days: I had made good my escape from home, planned and executed it with admirable efficiency in my own eyes. And now, suddenly, the only thing I wanted was to be back. All I could think about was Papa calling me 'Mouse' with that wonderful tenderness that had lit up my childhood; and Mama – tending chilblains, braiding hair, making tears go away. Ironically, the routine of hospital life probably helped to save me. Gradually, the tearful occasions became fewer. After fourteen-hour days, all I wanted was to fall into bed and oblivion before the whole demanding cycle began again. All forty of us were on the wards by seven o'clock, emptying bedpans, making beds, feeding and washing patients, disinfecting every surface: there were many times when I angrily compared our lives to that of a step-boy. Where was the healing hand in our work? Where was the bravery, the occasion for compassion, the bringing of comfort and relief to the sick?

For that first year of our training, the lessons we learned most frequently were humility, discipline and the ability to hold your tongue when provoked beyond endurance by the unreasonable demands of Sister. Even the patients were obedient, cowed into silence by each unvarying day on the ward, by the need for immaculate beds, dust-free surfaces, and no visitor to disturb the relentless march of routine. I am sure that patients often felt themselves to be an inconvenience. Sister Sheridan could run the ward a lot better in their absence – their presence did nothing to assist in the smooth preparation of her domain for the visit of Almighty Doctor. This was not how I had imagined Florence Nightingale to behave in the Crimea, nor did it seem to reflect the newspaper accounts of the glory of ministering to the sick and wounded in the Transvaal. I was experiencing the terrible disillusionment of the young idealist. However, in the circumstances of our rigorous training at St Bartholomew's, there was little time and less energy for fomenting rebellion.

Along with the natural disillusionment of those days came the valuable realization that I was tougher than I had thought. The sharp rebukes, the lack of physical comforts, the daily humiliations inflicted for some small transgression all served to make me more determined to finish what I had come to London to do. I grew an outer shell, a carapace that allowed me to survive underneath while pretending stoicism, patience and even humility whenever I was in the presence of Sister.

Wedged into our narrow beds at night, with freezing sheets and ice forming frequently inside the windows, we girls would whisper to each other about Sister's peculiarities – her dry cough whenever she was displeased; her irritating manner of intertwining the fingers of both hands, one thumb rotating around the other as she waited for the answer that her victim almost certainly did not possess; the silent eyebrow-arch of disapproval which could stop a young trainee in her tracks at forty paces. We would replay the day's events, borrowing and inventing freely, with the express purpose of making the others laugh. Sometimes the laughter became hysteria, and we would have to stuff our fists in our mouths so as not to be heard beyond our dormitory. Despite our tiredness, we would often lie awake in the darkness, giggling again and again at some remembered foible, sending each other off once more into paroxysms of helpless laughter.

And so I passed the first, and the hardest year of training.

May: Autumn 1901

IT HAD ALL taken very little on May's part, really.

She had written to Richard at Hannah's request – one godparent to the other – and sent him the photograph taken on the morning of Eileen's christening. The baby sat, in tiny solemnity, on her mother's knee. She wore Hannah's own christening robe. The guipure lace reached almost to the floor, giving the child a strange, elongated appearance. Charles had sat to Hannah's left, while May and Richard stood, one to each side of the baby, in the traditional pose of guardianship. All the adults had remained breathlessly still, each hoping that Eileen would not choose *that* moment to move, to sneeze, or cry out with boredom or hunger.

Richard had written back at once, professing himself delighted with the photograph. His new god-daughter, he said, now adorned his mantelpiece, and very fine she looked, too. Other letters followed, and Hannah responded regularly, charmed by Richard's apparently insatiable appetite for news of his small god-daughter.

Finally, there was the invitation for everyone – Charles, Constance MacBride, Hannah, May, Eleanor, indeed, all the O'Connor family should they so wish –

to visit him at Abbotsford, where he would attempt to return the generous hospitality he had received at everyone's hands in Holywood. He should be delighted, he said, to host his god-daughter's first birthday in his home. May encouraged her sister to make the visit – Hannah had been ill and lethargic at the beginning of her new pregnancy, and May was concerned about her, felt that she was ready for a change of air.

Somehow, May's plans to move out of Holywood never came to fruition. First there was the joy and novelty of helping to look after baby Eileen; then Charles asked her to stay on, confiding that current difficulties in his practice kept him from home more than he would wish; then Hannah became pregnant again, and was too unwell to look after the now highly active Eileen. Somehow, a year and a half had passed. May was conscious that it was now high time for her to go, to find some way of making her own life. Even Mama had started making discreet enquiries about when they could expect her back in Dublin.

In the event, Hannah, Charles and May were persuaded to make the visit to County Meath, bringing baby Eileen with them. Within a day of their arrival, Richard had spoken to Charles, who spoke to Hannah, who spoke to May, and somehow it was all swiftly resolved.

Richard held May's small hand in his, and amid much stumbling and faltering, told her he had loved her since he first saw her. He could promise her devotion, fidelity, respect – all the things by which a man defined his integrity. Money, ease or elegance were a different matter. Farm life was tough, but he had never wanted for anything that was truly essential. If she would have him, he would be deeply honoured, would share everything he had with her.

Yes, she'd said, I will marry you.

Philippe still blurred at the outline of her vision, and she tried hard to keep her eyes focused straight ahead. At least the way in front of her was brighter than it had been in some time: its edges were no longer crowded with the bitter weeds of grief and disillusionment. The prospect of spinsterhood, solitude and the unremitting yoke of filial duty finally began to recede a little into the yellow fields and gentle hummocks of a substantial County Meath farm.

Hannah: Autumn 1901

CHARLES CARRIED THE sleeping Eileen on to the train, her head lolling across his shoulder like one of Hannah's childhood dolls. May hurried behind him, blankets at the ready. Hannah smiled to herself. May would make an excellent mother: she had a gravity which calmed Eileen and soothed her tears into chuckles. Richard walked behind them, carrying their cases with ease. It was just as well there was one strong farmer among them, he'd said with a wide grin: the station was far too small to boast a porter at this hour of the evening.

Hannah was glad for her sister. Richard was a good, kind man, generous to a fault, fond of children. Rather like Charles, in fact. May had chosen well. Hannah had no doubt that her sister had been first to choose here: Richard had followed, of course, more than willingly, hardly able to believe his good fortune. Money, though, would always be a problem. They would never have enough, and Abbotsford was a draughty, sparsely furnished place. Hannah shivered at the memory – no matter how early the young girl from the village lit the fires in the bedrooms, no matter how high Richard had piled on the logs in the drawing-room grate, Hannah's memory of the entire five-day visit was of having felt the cold.

Charles turned back now to help her on to the train.

'All right, my dear?'

He had been particularly kind to her since she'd been ill with this next baby. He always thought ahead, planned for her ease and comfort, and yet she knew something was troubling him. Some weeks back, she had asked him, tentatively, was he angry that there was another baby on the way. He had looked so genuinely astonished that she had felt relieved at once, reassured that she was not, somehow, the cause of his worry.

'You must never think that, my dear, never.'

He had grasped both her hands in his, his voice urgent.

'I am delighted to be the father of a growing family. The prospect fills me with nothing but happiness. I am concerned only that your health should not suffer.'

She had felt lighter after that, less weighed down with guilt. She suspected that people were not paying him as promptly as they should, and the thought depressed her. The last thing she wanted was to repeat her own mother's history: fighting and complaining over money. But once Charles had reassured her that he longed for this baby as much as she did, everything seemed to change. As if by magic, she began to feel better in the mornings, no longer racked by nausea. Charles seemed to slot back into his old routine, too, coming home on the minute-past-six train each evening. And now the glad news of May's wedding: Hannah knew she was selfish to want to hold on to her sister until then, but she couldn't help it.

May had written home the very evening she had accepted Richard's proposal. Hannah had gone into her room just before dinner to hug her all over again, to make plans, to tell her what a wonderful man Richard was – quite the best, in Charles's estimation, quite the soundest man he had ever known.

'I don't want to go home just yet, Hannah. I couldn't bear Mama's fussing.' She paused. 'May I stay with you until a few weeks before the wedding?'

What May did not confess to her sister was that she couldn't bear the thought of Mama prying into Richard's affairs – how much land he had, what his income was, how May's life with him would be. She knew, no matter what Richard's virtues, that his worth would be subtly, perhaps even wordlessly, but nonetheless unfavourably, compared with Charles's.

According to Mama and Papa, they were delighted and proclaimed Richard 'a gentleman'. May was only a little resentful that they appeared almost uncaring about the details of her forthcoming marriage. She thought they were glad to have her off their hands at so little trouble to themselves.

Once the others were settled in the compartment, May went back on to the platform to say goodbye to Richard.

'Come back soon,' he said softly, pressing her hands between his. 'Now that I have someone to work for, you won't recognize Abbotsford the next time you visit. I'll make it right for you.'

'Don't, Richard – please don't change too much on my behalf. I love it just as it is, truly.'

May returned the pressure of his large hands, feeling an overwhelming affection for this gentle man. And she meant what she said. She loved the old charm of Abbotsford, had found the slightly worn rooms to be warm and comfortable. She already thought of it as her home.

Impulsively, she reached up and kissed him. She didn't care who was watching; she would soon be his wife. Then she turned and fled, back to Charles and Hannah.

Hannah had watched her discreetly, the whole time. That kiss, she felt, more than anything else, meant that the ghost of Philippe had finally been laid to rest. And Richard would never reject her, should he ever discover her secret. His need for her was every bit as great as hers for him. They really were a perfect match, she thought.

Hannah: Spring 1902

WHEN HANNAH WOKE, the room was full of light. Mama was still in the rocking chair beside the bed, asleep, her head resting on one hand. Maeve was in the Moses basket beside her. Hannah didn't know how long she'd slept, but she felt better, much better. Suddenly, the silence seemed strange – the baby had to be hungry – why wasn't she crying? As though her new daughter had heard her, a thin wail arose from the depths of the basket. Her mother started, setting the rocker in sudden motion. She reached towards the basket and lifted out her tiny granddaughter. Then she turned to smile at annah, her whole face lined with sleep.

'Here you go, young mother,' she said softly. 'Breakfast is required.'

Once the baby had started to feed, Hannah turned to her.

'Thank you, Mama, for being here. You've been wonderful.'

'I'm so glad I was here for this little one's birth. You've no idea what it means to me.'

'Was Charles here?'

Her mother laughed.

'We had to forcibly eject him, three times. He's the proudest father I've ever seen. He didn't want to wake you.'

Hannah nodded. She hoped it was true, that he was proud and happy with another baby girl.

'He made me promise to waken him, so I'll do just that and leave the two of you alone.'

Hannah watched as her mother stood up stiffly from the chair. With a pang, she realized that she was no longer young. As though she'd heard her, Sophia said:

'I'm afraid I'm past the age of sleeping in chairs all night!'

'Get some proper rest, Mama. I'll be fine now.'

'I'll see you later, my dear. Sleep all you can.'

Charles seemed delighted enough. Hannah watched his face for any sign that this child was less welcome than Eileen, any indication that she had disappointed his secret hopes. Whatever he may have felt, his outward self was smiling hugely, eyes bright with love.

Hannah was grateful for the hours he spent with her that morning. She had discovered, although Charles had never told her, that he was losing contract after contract to the Protestant firms all over the city. He, and firms like his, were being sidelined by the politics which seemed to dog this part of the world everywhere she turned. Hannah didn't even pretend to understand the bitterness and prejudice which seemed to have the whole of Belfast constantly on edge these days. As yet, there were none of the overt terrors of the carriage ride to the station all those years ago; instead there was a subterranean sea of silences and secrecies and bigotries which threatened to erupt and carry everyone with it in a tidal wave of unprecedented fury.

She knew that her furtive reading of Charles's post had been wrong, but she could never get him to share the truth of his other life with her: the one which happened between eight and six, and late in the evenings when he was delayed or, simply, chose some activity other than coming home. Perhaps all men existed under the same pressures, forced to divide their very selves into acceptable domestic and public faces, no matter how the two collided. She was disappointed; she had hoped that they would do better: that by sharing, they could somehow halve the trouble. But Charles resolutely kept his concerns to himself, and she had learned that she could not change him.

There were times when Hannah feared for her children, all the others she knew she would have. While they were small, living in the protection of a tolerant, civilized town, all could still be well. But when they were grown, what would happen to them then? Would they have to endure being regarded as second-class citizens, watching people's faces change when the names of their schools marked them out as taigs and fenians? Would they have to live among hostile others who asked 'What are ye?' rather than 'How are ye?' as a greeting? She did not want her children to absorb the mindlessness of tribal hatreds, to feel that their place was always the lesser one because someone else's tradition had deemed it so.

Hannah had grown to love her adopted town. She had even learned to appreciate the poetry of the surrounding countryside, with its liquid, magical names. Wolf Hill, Ardglass, Kilkeel, Annalong . . .

But Belfast, and all it stood for, would never claim her heart.

Eleanor's Journal

I LOVED ABBOTSFORD from the moment I first saw it. I loved its rambling oddness, the solidity of its comforts, its innocent lack of modern elegance. May brought me to see her future home just a few days before her wedding. Mama did not want us to undertake the journey, given that the wedding preparations were so far advanced, so demanding of everyone's time, but May was insistent that I see her home before my return to St Bartholomew's.

'I want you to take this memory back with you,' she said. 'I can't describe it well enough in letters – you must see it for yourself.'

Richard came in the trap to collect us from the station. I thought both my sisters fortunate, in their different ways, in their choice of husband. Richard was a plain man, direct in his ways, open in his devotion to his future wife. I was glad. I could see the tenderness she felt towards him, and I hoped she would be happy, as well as secure. It was to be many years before Hannah told me about Philippe, about her conviction that he and May had been intimate; many years, therefore, before I understood how May must have needed this marriage.

The farm was a good distance from everywhere. There was no village close by, and we passed but a few farmhouses on our journey, each scattered from its neighbours by long tracts of ploughed land. I wondered would May be contented to be so much alone. Then I thought that the openness of the countryside would most probably suit her: she had always found Dublin and Belfast difficult. She needed room to breathe.

A long driveway led up to the house, green lawns sloped away on all sides, and as we turned the corner into the yard, the glittering waters of a stream were just visible in the distance. I turned to my sister, surprised to catch the mute appeal in her eyes.

'It's beautiful, May – the house, the view – everything about it! I shall very easily imagine you here!'

Richard looked gratified.

'My father's house,' he said, nodding. 'And his father before that. Our roots run deep here.'

The pony came to a halt in the middle of the cobbled yard and Richard helped May and me to descend from the trap. A large grey and white dog lay sleeping beside the water pump, his pink tongue lolling. He opened one rheumy eye as we stepped into the yard, and his bushy tail gave a single, feeble wag.

'All right, Boy, it's all right.'

Richard's voice was kind as he leaned down to stroke the old dog's head.

'Just about had it, poor old Boy,' he said. 'He should go in his sleep any day now.'

I felt a stab of sympathy for the animal. If my memory is accurate, Boy died the morning Richard and

May were married. When they returned to Abbotsford, the Duggans had already buried him.

Inside, the farmhouse was cool. Having been in Hannah's home so recently, I was struck by how shabby everything was here. It was all clean and neat as a new pin, but it had not had a woman's hand for some time. Richard cooked and cleaned for himself, I learned, and had done so for the previous ten years, with occasional help from a girl in the nearest village, some five miles distant. It was clear that he had survived well, but the finer points of cleaning incandescent mantles and removing dust from picture rails were obviously way beyond his capabilities. Or perhaps Sister Sheridan had just made me oversensitive to such matters.

I was charmed by all of it. We walked the land at Richard's invitation and he provided us with excellent afternoon tea. I felt rather sad leaving – I should have liked to spend a longer time there. My cold dormitory began to seem even more unattractive after my brief visit to this homely, welcoming place. I felt quite depressed on our return to Dublin.

The wedding passed as all weddings seem to do – with a great deal of fuss beforehand, large quantities of cake and wine on the day, and so many sad and wilting flowers afterwards. May had not wanted the Shelbourne; she preferred the intimacy of home.

Papa behaved himself on that day; by early afternoon, Mama's anxious looks were diminishing in frequency. Hannah had both her babies at the wedding:

the now highly active two-year-old Eileen, and her placid, two-month-old sister, Maeve. Charles was even more the doting father this time around – he really was a most unusual man. I was loath to leave all of them. All I could think of was the year ahead. I should be engaged once more in scrubbing toilets and enduring the sharp tongue and beady eye of Sister Sheridan.

For some time after May's wedding, I think I even envied my sisters a little. Now, I find that ironic. I had not even begun to comprehend the range and depth of your love, already in the process of transforming the rest of my life.

May: Spring 1902

RICHARD LOOKED NOT so much uncomfortable as incongruous in his good suit. He was a man who cared little for clothes in his everyday life, but it was clear that he had made an effort for the day of his wedding. And yet, although his suit fitted him well, May couldn't help feeling that it had been made for another man altogether. It seemed to hold itself apart from Richard, or he from it, so that they appeared to be two separate entities. There was Richard; and there was his suit.

When May walked down the aisle towards him on her father's arm, he turned to greet her, his big face transformed by the warmest smile she had ever seen. He looked almost handsome, she thought, his face coloured, but not yet weather-beaten, by his outdoor chores. He had chosen to invite only the Duggans, his friends and neighbours from a nearby farm. May had insisted, in the interest of fairness, that her number of guests be small, too.

'My dear, you're a picture.' Bridie Duggan beamed at her, hugging her close as soon as she could get May on her own. They had bumped into each other on the stairs at home, after May had removed her hat and

Eleanor had laced flowers into her dark hair. The guests waited downstairs, and May was glad to receive Bridie's kiss, to return her hug.

'He's the best of men, you know that. And a lucky one. Now don't forget – there's no formality in our part of the world. You call on me whenever you need anything, d'ye hear me?'

'I do indeed, Bridie. I shall look forward to it.'

May felt warm towards everybody that day. Mama had done a beautiful job in arranging the wedding breakfast. She had placed posies of spring flowers everywhere, and May appreciated all her efforts to make the day special, despite her disappointment at her middle daughter's choice not to have a more public display at the Shelbourne.

Hannah had brought Mary with her to help. Katie had long since retired from service and Lily had surprised everyone by getting married a year ago, to a small farmer from her home town in Tipperary.

May was so glad at making her own escape that she felt able to be generous, affectionate and deeply grateful towards her mother. In the early afternoon, the Duggans left, anxious to tend to all the animals. Richard had told May they could stay as late as she wished – they had no need to be at Abbotsford until tomorrow. The Duggans had promised to look after everything until their return.

She watched him as the Duggans were leaving. He looked suddenly forlorn, as though a connection with something essential had just been broken, or stretched beyond endurance. She slipped out to the hallway, catching a last glimpse of Mick and Bridie as they ascended the carriage.

She slipped her warm hand into his.

'Let's go very soon,' she said.

His face lit up, his eyes darting towards the departing carriage as though very soon could mean right now, this minute.

Then he recovered himself.

'Don't you want to stay longer?'

She shook her head. She was done here.

'No,' she said. 'I'd like to go home.'

He squeezed her hand, his open face full of joy. She knew it would take them some time to get away, but she wanted to make this gesture, to reassure him that she would never keep him from what he cared for. His land would always come first, and she knew that, had grown to accept it. It was a fair exchange, she thought.

She no longer actively thought about Philippe. He was there always, colouring everything she did, acting as the standard against which everything was measured. But she could push him away more easily, now. More and more, he resided somewhere below the top layer of the life she was living. She could manage quite well without him. It was only when something disturbed the carefully arranged surface of her life that he struggled upwards, eager to fill all the empty spaces.

Eleanor's Journal

ROUTINE HAS THE most extraordinary effect of dulling the senses, does it not? I believed I should never become accustomed to the sight of blood, the stench of gangrene, the helpless moans of those afflicted by the diseases of poverty, and yet by virtue of mere familiarity, all these things somehow insinuated themselves into the interior of my everyday life. I grew used to the ebb and flow of each long day, learned to rejoice in the comfort and security offered me by Sister Sheridan's immutable daily structure. I remember the early winter mornings most of all, with so many of us Irish girls running through the already bustling meat market as we made our way to Ely Place for six o'clock Mass; I remember our breathless arrival on the wards afterwards, frantically settling our caps into place, smoothing our blue and white striped dresses. Our faces were raw from the wind or from a hasty dousing in cold water. I remember, too, the sharp smell of bleach which heralded the start of the all-consuming cleaning duties. I even grew to enjoy the physical demands of mopping and scrubbing – I liked the feeling of alertness which followed such exertions, the sense of being truly awake, the blood singing in my hands and feet. I even grew to understand the need for the terror which Sister Sheridan inspired, to regard it as instrumental in the refinement of my skills, and the development of my natural abilities as a nurse.

Do you remember our first days on the wards? The fear of being caught out, of being found wanting in some vague and ill-defined way, filled my dreams at night – that is, once I finally succeeded in sleeping. You, on the contrary, seemed to me to be so calm, so knowing. I began each day safe in the knowledge that, with you as my daily partner, I could survive all the difficult hours ahead, learn something new and gather my strength to respond to the faces, the pleading eyes, the mute appeals for comfort that greeted even the most inexperienced of us. It was deeply humbling to see the powerful effect of a kind word, a soothing hand. You, more than anyone, taught me by example. Where I saw merely the symptoms, or the injury, or the difficult patient, you saw the individual pain, the need for reassurance, the terrible vulnerability of the old or ailing.

Imagine my distress, then, on the day that Sister Sheridan separated us. She was right to do so, of course. I can see how much I relied on you, trusting your judgement above my own on all occasions. She was quite justified in forcing me to confront my problems on my own. Sister Sheridan simply took you away with her, leaving me with three other girls I barely knew, and Staff Nurse Smyth. I was bereft. How was I to get through this ordeal without you? I watched as you joined your new group and marched away from me, ascending the staircase to the second floor, your shoes eerily silent on the green linoleum.

That was the day I first encountered the wonders of anaesthesia. My fascination with this new process was complete: I forgot to feel nauseous at the sight of so much blood. As the surgeon drew his scalpel along the patient's distended abdomen, I held my breath, waiting for the young woman to sit up, to howl in sudden agony. The bright red line extended from navel to pubis, scarlet beads quickly forming in the wake of the knife, and still she never moved. Even when the surgeon pulled back the strangely white flap of skin, her face remained impassive. She continued to sleep peacefully, her breathing deep and regular. We watched as the surgeon plunged his hands into her abdomen, retrieving the small and miraculous body of a healthy baby girl. Her high-pitched cries soon filled the theatre and I cannot describe the joy of that triumphant moment.

That was a turning point for me. It was at that instant I lost all fear – fear of the human body, fear of failure, fear of not being good enough for the work I had chosen, or which had, in truth, chosen me. I was filled with the most extraordinary sense of elation. There had been no mistake: this was how I would spend the rest of my life. This was modern medicine on the march; these doctors and nurses were now my family; this was true healing, true caring for those whose lives were blighted by poverty and loss. It was all that I had wanted, longed for desperately, ever since the dawning of my adult consciousness.

From that time onwards, my sense of dedication was

no longer that of a wide-eyed and innocent young girl. I had acquired a focus, a clarity of vision which has never left me. I feel fortunate in the path I have been able to follow: blessed in that, as in so many other things in my life. All subsequent decisions flowed from that day, including my wish to work among the poor, to help above all those women whose entire lives were an endless cycle of pregnancy and struggle. I knew that once my training was finished, I should return to Ireland.

I decided to go back to Belfast. The thought of Dublin made me uneasy: I did not want to slide into Mama's clutches again.

I had had to harden my heart to her letters: Papa was simply disintegrating. I have often felt guilty over that decision. I could have nursed my father before the street urchins of Belfast, but I chose not to. My rationale was that he was responsible for his own condition, whereas they emphatically were not. He simply drank too much. They starved to death.

I did not want to become acquainted with the private disappointments that may have driven my father to his current state. I was far too afraid of returning to an unhappy household from which I might never escape. Besides, I had the excuse of Hannah and her children. I hadn't seen them in so long.

My first visit to Hannah's home in Holywood after my return from London in 1903 was another turning point in my life. In many ways, it was as momentous and shocking as the week of my father's arrest in Belfast, which had taken place exactly, to the week, ten years earlier. I have spent many years trying to untangle the threads of why the warp and weft of my sister's life had such a profound effect on me at that time. On the surface, all was well with her – more than well. A loving husband, two beautiful daughters, affluence, respectability – Hannah wanted for nothing.

I think that many things contributed to my sense of shock at that time. First of all, I was no longer Ellie, the baby sister. I was then nineteen – as old as Hannah had been when she became a married woman. I had skills that she did not, experience of the complexities and injustices of the world that had passed her by. I was amazed to find myself suddenly her equal – more than that: in many ways I felt older, wiser by far than she. Then there were all the ways in which she reminded me of Mama. She no longer played the piano, no longer dedicated herself in any serious way to a discipline which demanded her focus and attention. Now she merely tinkled – accompanied others for the rather staid and superficial musical evenings which reminded me so much of my parents' drawing room. Do you think I judged her too harshly? I remember being struck by how Mary seemed to perform all the household, and family, tasks which I firmly believed should have been my sister's duty.

Perhaps most importantly of all, I could not help but be personally hurt by the contrast between my sister's life and the lives of those I served. In all the ways that mattered, Hannah's home might have been a million miles away from the streets of Carrick Hill.

All of these thoughts and observations bore fruit in a strange way. You, my love, were not with me that week to listen to my confidences with sympathy and affection. I had none of the calming presence of May to help give equilibrium to my perspective. Nor did I even have Charles's company to provide humour and distraction. He seemed to spend all his life at business in those days.

And so I was consumed by the desire to begin a journal, to chronicle the events which had fashioned my family and given shape to all our different lives. I knew even when I began that whatever I wrote was not to be handed down to any children of mine: destiny had other things in store for me.

By then, I knew that I had already met the companion of my heart; knew the love that was to sustain and comfort me for the rest of my life. It was for you that I began, and for you that I continue.

It is, in the true meaning of the phrase, a labour of love.

Constance MacBride: Spring 1903

AFTER A SMALL hesitation, Constance MacBride accepted the carriage-driver's assistance, and stepped, stiffly, on to the pavement below.

'Come back for me in two hours, like a good man,' she said, pressing a handsome tip into the leathery palm.

'Aye, ma'am,' he replied, tugging briefly at the peak of his cap.

Mary already had the front door open for her. A good wee girl, Constance thought, practical and frugal, by all accounts. And not too pretty, either, which was just as well. Men could be such fools.

'Good afternoon, ma'am.'

'Afternoon, Mary. Is your mistress at home?'

Without waiting for an answer, the elderly lady swept past her and knocked smartly on the drawing-room door. She entered at once.

'Hannah, my dear, you're looking well.'

She stretched out her arms to her daughter-in-law, accepting Hannah's kiss.

'And how are my wee beauties this afternoon, then?'

She sat heavily on the sofa, and Hannah set Eileen and Maeve beside her, so that she could kiss them.

'Never better, Grandmama, isn't that right, girls?'

Constance turned to look at her sharply, catching something in Hannah's tone. A weariness, a resignation, bitterness perhaps?

'Are you well, my dear?'

'Very well, thank you. A little tired, that's all.'

There were blue-tinged shadows under the girl's eyes, Constance noted, a strain about her whole person. She had seen this before, knew already what it heralded. Now she spoke softly.

'Is there anything you'd like to tell me, my dear?'

Hannah smiled, her eyes suddenly filling at the sympathy in her mother-in-law's voice.

'I'm in the family way again; Nurse Walker believes it's twins.'

Constance patted the sofa beside her. Hannah lifted her daughters back to their toys on the floor.

'How may I help, my dear?'

Privately, the older woman was pleased. With twins, perhaps Charles would have the son he longed for. Perhaps then he would be content to stay closer to the domestic hearth. She knew what her son was up to. Not the detail, of course, just the broad brushstrokes of what she firmly regarded as his stupidity. 'Wee' Joe Devlin and his Ancient Order of Hibernians were at it again, rabble-rousing all over the city. And Charles, despite his years, still had not a titter of wit. Did he not know by now that any association with this strident, defiant form of nationalism meant trouble for him, for his family?

They had quarrelled bitterly the last time he had come to see her. He had insisted that Devlin's voice was a legitimate one, that Catholics had to look after their own. She, in turn, had insisted angrily that they were no better than those they professed to oppose: Orange Order, Hibernian Order – whatever Order you liked, man dear – what in the name of God did he think they were at, parading up and down with their bands, rousing passions that were much better left dormant?

She regretted their quarrel, now. She knew Charles of old: he would simply stop visiting. Or, if he did come to her, he would stubbornly refuse to be drawn. She sighed. She was getting on in years, too old to cope with this any more. Before she died, she wanted to be sure that his life was safe, settled. Besides, his wife and family needed him, now, far more than any cause.

Hannah sat down beside her, trying to smile.

'I will be pleased, really I will, as soon as this awful fatigue lifts. I have hardly energy for anything any more.'

Constance took both her hands in hers.

'Let us have some tea, dear, and then you must rest. Mary and I will gladly take these two for a walk. You mustn't worry about a thing.'

The girl looked at her gratefully. Constance suddenly felt very sorry for her. She had forgotten how all-consuming the physical demands of small children were. Now was not the time to tell Hannah that, no matter what age one's children, the only thing to change was the nature of those demands, not their intensity.

'Thank you,' said Hannah. 'You're very kind to me.'

And she stood and rang for tea.

Mary: Spring 1903

IT WAS SOME time since Mary had let Constance MacBride in, and still Hannah had not rung for her. Perhaps she should knock discreetly to enquire if madam would like tea, or else just bring it anyway. Mary was unwilling to do anything untoward – she feared that any slip on her part would reflect unfavourably on Hannah. Just then, the bell tinkled, filling her with relief.

Hannah opened the drawing-room door herself, Maeve in her arms.

'Will you bring tea, Mary – and can you take the children for something?'

Her face was very pale, Mary thought, and her eyes looked suspiciously bright.

'Of course, ma'am,' she said quickly, lifting Maeve, holding out her free hand to Eileen, who had come to the door at once on hearing Mary's voice.

She took the two babies with her to the kitchen, settling them both on the rug across from the range. She loved them, both of them, but her heart warmed more to Eileen Cecilia. She always thought of the older girl as Eileen Cecilia, and she had never stopped being grateful to Hannah for the generosity of this one, heartfelt gesture. Seven years had passed now, almost to the week. It was difficult to comprehend that Cecilia had been gone that long. Missing her got easier, mostly, but at times her sister appeared to her in sleep, bringing with her a ferocity of grieving that still took Mary by surprise. But she was happy here. Her only worry now was that Mr Charles would go too far with his politicking, and that she would be left without a home for the third time in her life.

She prayed to St Jude every night that it would not be so. She didn't think she could bear it.

She handed each of the two little girls a piece of bread and butter dipped in sugar as she waited for the kettle to boil.

No matter what happened, she had no control over any of it. She'd do her work, keep her counsel and trust that her favourite saint would hear her yet.

May: Spring 1903

BRIDIE DUGGAN WASHED her hands vigorously, the drops of water chinking against the sides of the blue-rimmed enamel basin. Steam rose from her hands as she turned the soap over and over, working up a good lather. Her hands looked even redder and coarser than usual against the delicate white froth. May was conscious of her warm presence, content in the peacefulness of her bedroom, soothed by the crackling of the flames in the fireplace. Occasionally, a log spat and fizzled out into the air, its flame lost in the early morning sunlight streaming through the window.

Richard had finally given in to exhaustion and gone into the small bedroom next door to sleep.

'You gave us quite a scare, my girl,' said Bridie, drying her hands now on the towel that hung by the washstand. 'Thank God and his holy Mother ye're both safe. This little fellow was in a right hurry to make his appearance.'

May smiled up at her dreamily. Her eyes kept closing, but she didn't want them to. She wanted to keep awake for ever, to keep on looking and looking at the small, perfect form in the cradle beside her. A little boy. Richard had wept with relief and gratitude as the tiny wail had pierced the silence at five o'clock this morning, four short hours ago. They had been awake all night, May disbelieving that it was time: she had another three weeks to go, at least: it was only a pain in her back, it would go away if she walked, if she had a hot-water bottle, if she had another cup of tea.

But it didn't go away, and at one o'clock there was no longer any doubt. There was a great, warm, slippery gush under May's skirts and she touched herself quickly to make sure it was water, not blood. Richard cursed himself for not having gone for help earlier. He finally threw his overcoat over his shoulders, torn between wanting to stay with his wife and wanting to get Bridie to help her through the birth. He was afraid of what she was about to endure, afraid she wouldn't have the strength for it. But she surprised him.

'Go, Richard,' she'd said, calmly. 'It will be some time yet.'

When he returned with a breathless Bridie in tow, she had already built up the fire in their bedroom, and spread layers of old hemp sheets and flat, cotton towels over their bed. She was in her nightgown, barefoot, and paced the bedroom with one hand pressed into the small of her back, the other rubbing her distended stomach. Richard had charged up the stairs, taking them two at a time. He could have sworn he heard her talking as he reached the bedroom door. He couldn't make out the words, only the tone: comforting, reassuring – for herself or for the child, who could be sure. She'd turned and smiled at both of them as Richard opened the door.

'Thank you, Bridie – I'm sorry for getting you up at such an unearthly hour.'

'Now, child, you don't need to be sorry about anything. Will ye lie down on the bed for a bit and let's see what this child's intentions are?'

Richard sat on the bed beside her, and took her hand. He knew what was ahead of her, and he was terrified for her safety. Cows calving, horses in foal, ewes lambing – he had seen it all, been up to his own elbows in amniotic fluid, blood, faecal matter when the animal was in distress. But this was his *wife*: he couldn't plunge into her body if things were too slow, harvesting her child as if it were just another one of his flock. This was women's business: she wouldn't want him there, and Bridie was the next best thing he knew.

Bridie's cloak was already off, her sleeves rolled up, her wide, honest face full of good humour. Five sons of her own grown and gone, and 'nary a one o' them a farmer' she'd say cheerfully, with no trace of bitterness. She'd acted as unofficial midwife for years in this corner of Meath, helping out most when the babies made their appearance unexpectedly or tardily. Nothing made her flap, May thought. Her very presence brought comfort and confidence.

'Hot water, Richard, if you please, and some soap, there's a good man.'

Richard took his dismissal humbly. He waited in the kitchen until the water boiled on the range, filled the enamel basin and carried it carefully upstairs, the new bar of soap nestling in his waistcoat pocket.

'I'll be right outside if you need me,' he said, kissing

May on the forehead, tasting the saltiness of the sweat that was already beginning to build up there.

'Go and smoke yer pipe, man dear. 'Twill be a while yet.'

Bridie nodded encouragingly at him, her eyes telling him to go now, her arm around May as they walked slowly up and down the room. May seemed to have forgotten his presence, her face filled with frightened concentration.

Richard smoked and prayed. He boiled water, in case more was needed, made tea for all of them and occasionally made his way upstairs to the landing, just to listen at the bedroom door. Once, he almost went in, when May's cries pierced him to the heart. Then he heard Bridie's voice above it all, hearty, urging her on, and knew all was well.

He could do nothing except wait.

He thought he heard his name being called, but it became confused with a small, high-pitched wailing somewhere in the back of his dream. He jerked awake, suddenly realizing where he was, suddenly remembering.

'Richard!'

Bridie's voice was loud and clear, and unmistakably cheerful. Thank God, oh thank God and his Holy Mother it was over, she must be safe, both of them must be safe.

He bounded up the stairs, stumbling on the last step in his eagerness. There was the most tremendous sense of calm in the bedroom. May lay in their bed with a tiny swaddled form close to her. He noticed with a shock how clean she looked: her nightgown was different, her hair brushed, her face warm and shiny. Bridie was busy with a pile of sheets in the corner.

'It's a little boy,' May said softly.

He searched her face. Her eyes were bloodshot, veins broken with the effort of giving birth. He had seen that in ewes, too. He felt a lump gather in his throat. He kissed her hand.

The baby was smaller than he could ever have believed possible, its body fitting almost completely into his own large grip.

'Thank you, thank you,' was all he could say, a sob strangling him.

'Do you still want to call him John?' she asked, pulling the blankets back gently so that he could see his son's face more clearly.

He nodded. She smiled up at him.

'Then John it is.'

She closed her eyes.

He sat beside her, unmoving. All he could do was gaze on the red, wrinkled cheeks of his baby son. Bridie went about the room quietly, building up the fire, touching May's forehead from time to time. But there was no anxiety in her movements.

'Is she well?' Richard whispered after a time.

She smiled at him.

'Fine. She's stronger than ye think. An' the little fellow's perfect. A bit thin, but that's what ye'd expect: he'll catch up, right enough. Fed an' all with nary a complaint.'

She continued to fold the bloodied sheets and towels and her simple busyness filled Richard with gratitude.

'I can't thank you enough,' he said.

'Aye,' she said, 'ye'd take none yerself the time ye saved half our flock when the lower field flooded.'

'That's different,' he protested. 'That's friends and neighbours, one as much as the other.'

'So's this.'

'Thank you anyway.'

'You're welcome.' She bobbed politely in a mock curtsy. 'An' now I'm goin' to soak these sheets in cold water 'til tomorrow. Will you stay?'

He nodded.

'Of course.'

'I'll be just a while. If ye're worried, call me. I'll not be far.'

When she came back, he insisted she rest. She refused to leave the bedroom, nodding off instead in the old armchair beside the fire. She woke suddenly, seconds before the baby wailed into wakefulness, and helped May adjust his tiny mouth on her breast so that he suckled contentedly.

'You get some sleep, Richard,' said May, after they had watched Bridie change and clean the whimpering baby. 'You'll have the animals to tend to in a few hours.'

Eventually he gave in, feeling no exhaustion, only a sense of pure elation. He had been given what he'd accepted as impossible for so many years before May. A son to take over the land, a boy to work for, to build the farm for, a child to make it all worthwhile.

He slept, his dreams filled with future.

May: Summer 1906

THE LAKE-BOAT WAS tied up where it always was. Richard liked to see to things like that himself. He'd checked that the bow line was secure; didn't want the boat drifting off downstream. John had loved sitting in it, trailing his gleeful hands in the water while Richard kept a firm grip on the straps of his small son's trousers. He was glad the child showed no fear, neither of the farm animals nor the water. This land would be his; he would learn to respect it as he grew older, and whatever measure of fear came with that respect was enough. May was still nervous around the cattle; they sensed it and were jittery in her presence. He was glad that his son, even at three, showed that he was made of better farming stuff.

Yesterday, Richard had taken him in the boat for the first time, despite May's initial reluctance to allow it.

'He'll be safe with me. He has to start getting used to the water sometime. The younger the better.'

May had known better than to argue. Richard was rarely insistent in matters concerning the boy; he was usually content to let her be Mother. But when it came to the things necessary to men who worked and lived the land, his quiet stubborn streak would not be gainsaid. She had held out only for a little while, more for show than anything else, then given in gracefully. She liked giving Richard the satisfaction of having his own way, liked the dark burn of desire in his eyes afterwards. She had stood watching from the river-bank as he had shown the little boy how to pull on the oars. They could both see the surprising strength and determination of the small arms as John sat safely between his father's legs and tried to pull as he had been shown. He believed that his was the strength that moved the lake-boat smoothly away from the wooden jetty and off downstream. His blue eyes were ablaze with excitement.

'Pa – Mama, look! Me row Pa's boat!'

May had kept to the river-bank, keeping pace with them, cheering John's progress.

'Who's a clever boy! Sit close to Pa, now, no jumping about!'

Richard remembered how girlish she had looked, looping her long skirts over her left arm, almost running at times to keep up with them, her face prettily flushed. It had been a perfect afternoon. He felt proud of his family, proud of his life, of what he had made – what they had made. John's small presence permeated every aspect of their lives. Since his arrival, May had been completely happy. All traces of her former brittleness had disappeared. It was like watching someone being made whole again. Richard had always known that there was a great need in her, right from the first time he'd met her. There had been someone else before him, that much was plain. He had never cared, and they had never spoken of it. He still thanked God each day that the unbelievable had happened: somehow, May loved him enough to be his wife. He knew that he and the boy, but above all the boy, had gone a long way towards making her life complete.

Richard surveyed his fields now, grateful once more to his father for the opportunity to make this his future. The old man had defied convention, leaving the farm to the one who loved the land best, passing over the elder son in favour of Richard. He felt only a little regret that Matthew, now a prosperous publican in Dublin, saw fit never to speak to him again after the reading of their father's will. He'd never cared much for him anyway, him or his self-satisfied wife. He remembered how she had darted greedily around the farmhouse, her small, sharp eyes calculating its worth, already seeing the auctioneer's gavel strike out all the financial uncertainty of her husband's latest ventures. And that before the old man's body was cold in the bed upstairs.

This was what he cared for now – this farm and this family. He liked the slow tasks of walking the land, noting the breaches in the fence which waited to be fixed, keeping a close, almost paternal eye on the animals that roved freely across his lush green pasture. The river was unusually low just now, the summer heat blue and intense, shivering just above its surface. Heavy rain was forecast, and Richard watched the sky anxiously. The land was parched, but too much rain at once brought its own problems. He wanted to be prepared. Two of the Friesians stood in the water's lazy depths, tails swishing, ignoring the clouds of midges that had suddenly descended from the trees above the river-bank.

'All right, old girl.'

Richard's voice was soothing as he waded knee-deep into the water, patting the flanks of the younger animal, making no sudden movements. She turned her head and gazed at him blankly, rolling her huge, brown eyes. He could see himself reflected in their translucent depths: a figure made suddenly tiny and insignificant. He smiled to himself. A cow's-eye view of the man's world. He stroked her head, still murmuring.

'That's the girl, good girl, Dolly.'

Swiftly, he passed the halter around her neck. It was done in an instant; immediately, the animal began to tremble. Richard could see the movements of the powerful muscles jerking beneath the silky hide. It was always the same – she slithered and stumbled her way down into the cool, glad water, but it was quite another matter clambering up again.

'Good girl, good girl.'

Richard continued to pat her, and began very gently to draw her with him towards the sloping river-bank. The mother watched, shaking her head from time to time as though despairing of her daughter's stupidity. *She* could look after herself. She'd begin to follow at once, Richard knew from past experience. She was older, more sure-footed, less likely to startle than the younger creature. Her baleful eye never left him as he began the gradual ascent back up to the pasture, stooping to pick up a switch he had cut earlier. One sharp strike across Dolly's rump would be sufficient to make her scramble up the first reluctant few feet on to the field above, and safety.

'There y'are now,' he said, slapping her encouragingly as she lumbered off to graze under the trees. The mother scrambled after her, fear illuminating her eyes as she made the last desperate effort to heave herself up the remaining foot or two of the slope. Her front knees buckled and Richard thought she wasn't going to make it. He moved towards her to help pull her forward. At the last minute she steadied herself and walked away with stately dignity to join her daughter. Richard grinned after her affectionately. Same performance every evening during hot weather; talk about not learning from your mistakes. It was always these two; the others didn't bother. Otherwise, he'd have to start thinking about a fence. Bloody expensive, though, all along that stretch of river. He'd take his chances; hadn't lost one of them yet.

May sat at her writing-desk in the dining room, glancing occasionally out the bay window. She never tired of the view. Laurel trees with their long, frond-like leaves framed either side of her garden, which in turn led gently on to the sloping front pasture. She had to remember to keep the gate closed, always, otherwise the animals trampled everywhere, devouring her plants. John had learned quickly how to duck between the gate's five bars, and recently she had seen his small, grinning triumph as he had managed, a little unsteadily, to climb right up to the top and over the other side.

She could see Richard's tall figure in the distance, stooping from time to time to tend to one of the animals. He was worried about the mysterious fungal infection which had recently swept like fire through the herd. He had never seen anything like it before. He had been silent, preoccupied, occasionally short-tempered over the past few days. The last thing May wanted to do was worry him about money. She sighed and wrote her signature with a flourish at the end of her letter, the fourth she had composed that afternoon. Perhaps it would buy them another few weeks; Richard had always been a good customer, they deserved a little credit when times were tough, just to tide them over.

John was asleep on two cushions by her feet, one plump, dimpled arm draped around the soft neck of Molly, their golden Labrador. Ever since Mick Duggan had given them the pup, one of a too-large litter, John hadn't wanted to let her out of his sight.

'Lovely nature,' Mick had promised them, taking the tiny golden bundle out of his inside pocket. John's eyes had widened in delight and disbelief.

'Her mother's the sweetest-tempered bitch I've ever owned,' Mick said, stroking the puppy's silky head. 'This one'll be good with the little fella, you wait and see.'

And she had been good, right from the start. John's shrieks of laughter had filled the kitchen as the new puppy tried desperately to gain her balance, all four paws sliding off in different directions on the polished linoleum. Richard had been pleased at the boy's response, at his gentleness in handling the warm, floppy body.

'It's good for him, getting used to animals like that. Next thing's for him to learn they're not only play-things.'

He had approved later, too, when his son smacked Molly sharply on the nose, a fitting retaliation for the sharp, snapping nips the puppy had suddenly started to inflict on his small hands.

'That's it; show her who's master. Only as much force as you need, mind. There's never any call to be cruel.'

May had drawn the line at Molly sleeping in the child's bedroom, but had softened enough to provide her with a basket in the warm corridor between kitchen and scullery. She had very quickly become the fourth member of their family.

The little boy stirred in his sleep as the puppy shifted under him, straining to get up. Like clockwork, May thought. She stood up from her desk and bent down to stroke the bright head.

'Time for dinner, Molly?'

May spoke to her gently; she lightly scratched the soft flesh under the pup's ears. Molly stretched her neck in appreciation, closing her soulful brown eyes, licking May's wrists whenever her tongue reached far enough. She was a gentle creature, one whose name suited her surprisingly well, May thought. She smiled as she remembered John's insistence on naming all the farm animals to rhyme with Molly.

'Come along, then.'

The dog now wagged its tail frantically in anticipation of dinner. May was just about to lift the sleeping child when Richard's distant voice reached her through the half-open window.

'Tom! Tom! Where the hell are you, man?'

He sounded strange, almost panicked. May stood on tiptoe, holding on to the top frame of the sash, straining to catch a glimpse of him. Her eyes scanned the lower field. Nothing.

She gathered up her dress, not for the first time frustrated at how the long, cumbersome skirts slowed her down. Molly managed to get between her feet, making her trip and stumble.

'Stay!' she commanded.

John woke, wailing. She hadn't the time to stop.

'Stay with Molly, John! Mama will be back directly!'

Something in Richard's voice told her she had to hurry. She flung open the door into the hallway.

'Annie! Annie!'

There was a scuffling sound from upstairs.

'Annie – look after John, please! I'll just be a moment! Mr O'Brien needs me!'

She ran all the way down to the river. She could just see the top of Richard's dark head, bobbing around in an odd manner. As she got closer she could see what was happening. The Friesians were in the river again. Richard was struggling with Dolly, who kept slipping back into the water, unable to find purchase for her hooves on the muddy slope. The river was higher than it had been in weeks, as a result of the previous twelve hours' torrential rain.

Richard turned towards her, head straining over one shoulder.

'She's lost confidence, and she's already gashed her front legs. I need Tom to push her while I try to pull her up the slope – where the hell is he?'

'I haven't seen him – not at all this afternoon – can I help?'

Richard's appearance alarmed May: he was sweating, breathing in great gasping breaths, his face a peculiar, mottled red.

'Hell roast him anyway! See if he's above in the yard, will you?'

'Let's see if I can help, first.'

Richard hesitated.

'All right – you stand here, at her head. Just take the halter and talk to her. Try not to startle her.'

Abruptly, Richard turned and waded into the river. He bent down, leaning his back against the terrified animal's rump.

'I'm goin' to push her on three, May – you pull on the halter at the same time. One, two . . . three.'

May had a dim memory of a child, a bright flash of blue smock, leaping from a tree in white June sunshine. Jean-Louis's grinning face now swam before her eyes as she pulled on Dolly's halter, watching as fear rolled around her wide wet eyes.

'Easy, easy, girl,' she said firmly, just as she had heard Richard do. But the animal would not budge.

Richard stumbled and crashed into the muddying water, regaining his balance again with difficulty. He cursed softly.

'It's not goin' to work, May. You'll have to find Tom. I'll stay with Dolly. For God's sake tell him to hurry up!'

May gathered up her soaking skirts and half ran, half fell up the muddy bank to the field. In the distance, she could see Tom's large figure beginning to lope towards her. She ran, as quickly as she could, waving her arms to attract his attention.

'Tom – Tom – hurry, please!'

He quickened his pace, settling his cap lower across his forehead.

'Quick – Dolly's stuck in the river. We need help to get her out!'

He nodded, his eyes already scanning the swollen water. May had a fleeting thought that there was something wrong – he seemed unwilling to speak, to look at her.

'Where's Annie?'

Still there was no answer. Perhaps he hadn't heard her. May was suddenly filled with a sense that something was wrong, or about to be wrong. She could feel a return of the old anxiety, a feeling of suffocation, of being trapped in some dark place from which there was no escape.

She pushed open the back door, ran through the passageway between kitchen and scullery, out into the broad, sun-filled hallway. She flung open the door to the dining room. Her letters sat innocently on the

448

writing-desk, the two cushions still bore the imprint of her son's small body. But there was no John.

Annie was coming down the stairs, fixing the strings of her apron. She was startled to see May, frightened by her air of urgency, her panicked breathlessness.

'What is it, mam? Is everythin' all right?'

'John! Where's John!'

'I ... don't know, mam. I've been ... cleanin'. Upstairs.'

Annie was nodding, as though agreeing with words spoken by someone else: words which had supplied her with an answer she'd been searching for. Her demeanour was strained, almost guilty. May felt her panic growing. She couldn't read her way into the young woman's expression.

'Didn't you hear me call? I told you to look after the child!'

'No, mam. I didn't hear nothin'.'

She straightened her shoulders, smoothed her apron firmly.

'Like I said, I was busy.'

Her face was now openly defiant.

'The dog – did you hear the dog barking?'

Annie shook her head.

'Come with me, quickly.'

May ran back towards the scullery, her throat now so taut with fear she could hardly breathe.

'Hurry – go tell Mr O'Brien. I'll search the house. Tell him to cover the yard – the byre – the river – anywhere he can think of. Get Tom to help him! Run!'

Stumbling on the muddied hem of her dress, May

449

went on hands and knees up the stairs and tried to call out to her son. Her voice was choked by sudden, hot tears. She prayed that she would open the door to John's room and find Molly tearing at the curtains, eating the rugs again. She tried to tell herself sternly to calm down, to stop being hysterical, but something deep inside was warning her that her moment had come. That indefinable sense of dread which she had carried with her all her life was now about to be made flesh.

His room was empty, too quiet. Muslin billowed in the wind, voices carried from the water's edge. All the rest was silence.

One last heave and Dolly finally lurched forward with a suddenness that made Richard stagger in her wake. He brought the switch down with unusual violence across her rump and she hurried up the last few feet to the pasture.

'Bloody animal!' he roared after her.

As if he hadn't enough to contend with – the whole herd infected with God knows what, and money suddenly owed to everyone, everywhere. He turned angrily to Tom.

'And where the hell have you been?'

Before Tom had time to answer, Annie arrived at the edge of the river-bank, breathless, wiping her forehead with her sleeve.

'Please, sir, quickly, sir – Mrs O'Brien says to look for the boy. He's not in the house – we're to search everywhere.'

Richard looked at her stupidly. What boy? What was she talking about? He looked blankly from her to Tom.

'It's little John, sir, he's gone missin'.'

Richard felt his anger drain away, leaving a cold and empty space where it had once been.

'Since when?'

He stood still in the grainy water, Tom just above him on the sloping bank, Annie bending towards them from the edge of the pasture. Something about the way they all stood there struck him as odd, theatrical almost. It was as though this were really happening somewhere else, the three of them on stage, displaced, representing somebody else's reality, not his. He noted the fierceness of the sun over Tom's left shoulder, and how the man's large face was thrown almost completely into shadow. Fear paralysed him.

Annie had started to cry.

'Don't know, sir. Missus came runnin' into the house a few minutes ago, screamin' that he was gone. That's all I know, sir.'

Richard caught the glance between her and Tom that made something seem clearer to him, but he didn't know what. Couldn't put his finger on it. He scrambled up the bank, pushing both of them out of his way.

'Get back to the house, Annie – help Mrs O'Brien. Tom, you come with me. Now.'

He wanted to separate them, wanted them not to be together, to whisper away the uneasy guilt he'd seen in both their eyes. He'd deal with whatever it was later: for now, all that mattered was his son. He sent Tom downriver, whistling for Molly. He made his way upstream, calling cheerfully to John, wanting the boy to know by his tone that no punishment awaited him, no matter what he had done.

Some instinct brought him towards the lake-boat. It bobbed innocently on the small waves, tap-tapping gently against the side of the wooden jetty.

'John? Son? Come on out to Pa, now. We'll go in the boat together. Would you like that?'

His words were returned to him on the breeze. Something had gripped his insides, hard. He didn't know whether it was hope or despair. He made a bargain with God – if his son lay silent, playing hide-and-seek in the bottom of the lake-boat, or sleeping under the willows on the river-bank, he would never ask for another thing. Please, God, just let him be safe.

He approached cautiously.

At first it looked to him like an unbleached flour sack, swelling gently with the movement of the water. He laughed out loud in relief, a short, sharp sound, more bark than mirth. One occasionally floated down from the flour mills a quarter of a mile upstream. On still days, the fine, white, powdery residue clung like a cloud, a sort of hazy halo above the stiff material, before they both sank slowly into the greenish eddies just beyond the bend in the river. Kneeling on the slippery wooden planks of the jetty, Richard rolled up his sleeve and plunged his hand into the restless water.

At the same moment, the flour sack stirred and turned, its lazy billow disturbed by the tug of his fingers.

Quietly, almost innocently, it revealed its secret to the kneeling man. Small, cold face. Eyes closed. Bruise like a sad poppy stretching from cheekbone to hairline, its outer edges already turning purple, pewter, indigo.

The watery silence was shattered by the sound of a man's voice howling. His own.

'Ah, Jesus, no. No, no, no, dear Jesus, please!'

He gathered his small son into his arms with difficulty, almost losing his balance on the treacherous surface of the jetty. The child felt so heavy, so unfamiliar, that for a moment Richard wondered was this really his son, or was it someone else's, someone who had strayed on to his land, or perhaps a body washed down to his farm from further upstream, a mill-child, an orphan, a son that nobody wanted, that no father would miss. It was an impression he couldn't shake for several minutes. He pushed the fair hair back from the swollen forehead, looking for signs, for something to recognize. Eventually the plump curve of the child's blue-white forearm brought weeping so harsh that he believed he would never be able to bear the pain. He buried his face in his son's neck, wondering wildly how he could hide him, bury him, keep May from seeing him like this.

He was so little, so cold. Richard had nothing to wrap him in, no coat, no jacket. He tried again to struggle to his feet.

And then May was beside him, stumbling, kneeling, tearing at her son's white smock, covering his body with hers in a futile attempt to warm him.

'No, no, dear God, no! Richard, he's cold – fetch a blanket – no, no, go – tell Dr O'Connell to come at once! John, John, my little angel, open your eyes!'

Her cries were those of a wounded animal; their fierceness shocked Richard back to the present again, back to where he was kneeling, sobbing, one large hand on the fair head of his dead son.

Looking up, he caught sight of Annie, her face buried in her apron. Tom stood awkwardly, his hands hanging loosely by his sides, suddenly too big for his body. His eyes were focused on the distance, on nothing in particular. He stood apart from Annie. He was very carefully not looking at her. It was the distance between the two of them that finally made everything clear to Richard.

He leapt up the slope and put both hands around the older man's throat. Roaring in a voice he did not recognize as his own, he pressed hard on the man's windpipe, needing, wanting to kill him.

'You! Both of you! You're to blame for this! Fornicating while my son drowned!'

All the blood had drained from Tom's face. He was gasping for breath, tearing at Richard's hands, his own useless in the face of such terrified, white-hot strength.

It seemed to be Annie's screams which eventually made Richard loosen his grip and step back, shocked into silence. Instead, it was a thought that had its own clear logic, its own beauty of resolution. Almost forgetting his grief, he strode off in the direction of the house, his mind sharp, clear, like a clean blue light.

He no longer heard May's sobs, no longer saw her bent over the lifeless body.

The shotgun was always locked away. He was a careful man about such things. He reached up and took the key from the dusty surface at the top of the cabinet. He took what he wanted and locked the cabinet after him again, replacing the box of shells on the second shelf, putting the key into his pocket this time. No loaded guns in the vicinity of the house; it was his father's one unshakeable rule. He carried the shotgun under his arm like a broken branch, and made his way towards the river again. He waited until he was close to the last line of willows before he placed both shells into the breech. He had no idea how long he'd been gone; it was puzzling – everyone was just as he had left them. In a way, he had expected something to have changed.

All three turned around at the sound of the shotgun being loaded. Richard raised it to his shoulder, drew the sight closer to his eye. The long barrel pointed like a finger, direct, unflinching. He watched, unmoved, as Annie ran towards her lover, screaming, clutching at his chest. With one arm, Tom swept her behind his back, meeting Richard's eye for the first time.

'We din't do no wrong, Mr O'Brien, sir. We din't hear the Missus call . . .'

May was crooning softly, her mouth buried in the soft, milky flesh just under John's ear, his small body arcing back over her arms, one hand just brushing the surface of the jetty gently, uselessly. Richard felt something give inside his chest. He was consumed with an unbearable tenderness towards his son. His eyes filled, and for a moment, Tom's face with its peaked cap blurred and swam before him.

'Go,' he said softly. He motioned towards the farm gates with the barrel of his shotgun. 'Get out, both of you. If I ever see either of you within a ten-mile radius of here, Christ help me, I'll shoot you.'

Sobbing distractedly, Annie reached for Tom's hand. She dragged him up the bank, away from the river. He followed, unwillingly, it seemed to Richard. He had a split-second, wild desire to shoot the man in the back. It was the only punishment that felt fitting.

May was silent now, rocking her son back and forwards, back and forwards.

'Poor little scrap,' he heard her whisper, over and over.

Richard knelt behind her, placed both hands on her shoulders. He spoke quietly into her ear, avoiding his son's face, which was becoming somehow featureless, almost formless.

'Let's get him up to the house. Let me carry him.'

She shrugged him off with surprising strength.

They stayed like that, for hours it seemed to Richard. He found her rocking motion soothing. He swayed with her, holding her close, until the breathless arrival at the water's edge of Mick Duggan and his wife Bridie.

They'd found Molly's body, trapped in the reeds by the fence at the bottom of their lower field. At first, Mick had thought it was a young fox, maybe poisoned or shot for killing chickens. But he was puzzled – no news of any foxes on the prowl had reached him, and Bridie was always on the alert, clucking like a demented hen herself at the first sign of danger to her little beauties.

He'd climbed carefully between the wires of the fence, holding the dangerous barbs as far away from his body as he could, easing his large frame safely through. He went closer to the river to have a good look. Molly's coat was matted, covered in green slime, but Mick had recognized her instantly once he knelt at the water's edge.

He pulled the swollen body out of the water, and felt a surge of compassion. He'd been really fond of that little dog, and her gentle mother. He had a sudden stab of misgiving. He knew Richard O'Brien to be a careful man: if something like this had happened, then it was likely there was some sort of trouble above at his neighbours' farm.

He manoeuvred his way with difficulty back through the barbed wire, still holding on to Molly's waterlogged body. He walked quickly back towards the house. Bridie was feeding the chickens, letting them roam freely around the yard as usual, occasionally stooping to pick up an egg that she had missed earlier. She was proud of her chickens. She still had a sense of wonder at the large, warm eggs that they produced, just for her. She loved handling their translucent shells, loved the tiny, breathy feathers that often clung to their speckled surface. She had grown to regard them as a sort of fragile daily miracle that she was fortunate enough to witness. She smiled as she saw Mick approach, then her face froze.

One look at his expression was enough.

'What? What is it?' she said fearfully.

At the same time, her eyes rested on the sodden bundle under her husband's arm.

Mick held out the puppy's body to her, wordlessly.

'Ah, dear God,' she said, her eyes filling. 'Poor little thing. How did that happen?'

Mick shrugged his shoulders.

'I don't know, but I'll tell you this – something at the O'Briens' is not right.'

Bridie stroked the puppy's cold nose.

'What a shame. Little John will be broken-hearted. Let me leave these eggs inside and we'll go down together.'

She gestured towards her husband's burden.

'I think we'd best leave Molly here. We might be able to pretend she's gone missin', or somethin'. Better that the child doesn't see her like that.'

She took off her apron and pulled the door closed behind her.

'Let's go,' she said.

They set off together down the road that led to the neighbouring farm. Almost at once, Bridie spotted two figures hurrying off into the distance, something vaguely comical about their ungainly speed.

'Isn't that Tom?' she asked her husband. 'And Annie? What on earth are they doin' runnin' off like that?'

Mick didn't reply. He quickened his pace and Bridie put her arm through his, almost trotting to keep up with him.

They reached the farm, but neither of them called out. As they crossed the front pasture, the total silence suddenly unnerved them. The air around them seemed to have stilled, as though time had stopped itself in its own tracks. All the doors of the house were wide open. Curtains bellied and sagged gently through upstairs windows. There was no one to be seen anywhere, no movement of man or animal. They made their way automatically towards the river, Bridie holding on very tight to Mick's solid arm. Still they saw no one.

Suddenly, Bridie heard a sound that made something chill inside her. She gripped Mick's arm, hard. He had heard it too, and for an instant, his big face looked wide open, helpless.

'Come on, love,' Bridie said, steering them both towards the sound, in the direction of the jetty. At first, all they could hear was the swell and hurry of water, indistinguishable now from the rush of wind through swaying, leaf-laden branches. Once they made their way around the gentle bend in the river, they saw them.

Hoping, dreading, praying for it not to be so, Bridie saw May and Richard kneeling over something white. She didn't need to look any closer. May's body was despair made flesh. Richard was kneeling behind her, clutching her to him, holding on. A few more steps and Bridie saw, all too clearly, the small, drained face, the livid bruise, the lifelessness.

'Dear God, no,' she whispered.

She made her way on to the jetty, placing first one foot, then the other, carefully planting the sole of each sturdy boot, still holding on to Mick's outstretched hand. She bent down, her face level with May's. She looked for a moment into Richard's eyes, and looked away again. She couldn't bear to hold his gaze. She put her hands on May's shoulders and squeezed them gently.

'Come on, love.'

She caressed the cold arms, waiting until the younger woman looked up at her. Then she took one of May's hands gently in hers.

'Come with me, pet. Let his dad carry him to the house. Come on now.'

It made her sad, looking into May's empty eyes.

'It's John,' she said, her voice full of wonder.

Bridie swallowed.

'Let's take care of him in the house. It's warmer there.'

May rose obediently, allowing Richard to take the full weight of the small, still body. She clung to Bridie's hand, not letting go even when they had to scramble up the bank together.

Bridie put her arm around May's shoulders, keeping her moving towards the house. She didn't want her to see as the two men struggled to climb the bank, holding on carefully to the now awkward, absent body of her dead child.

May woke, her heart pounding. For a moment, she lay in the darkness, trying to piece together the fractured details of her dream. She let out a little cry of relief.

'Oh, thank God, thank God it was a dream!'

Richard was awake beside her at once. But there was

still something dark beneath the surface of her memory which she could not place. It puzzled her.

Richard took her hand.

'May? Are you all right?'

Something in his voice broke the spell and she wailed, clutching at him.

'Oh, no, no – I don't want it to be real! Please don't let it be real!'

She sobbed harshly, holding on for comfort. When she felt the tears on his face, she knew she was lost. It had happened; it was real. He could not make this better. She could not make it better. They held each other for a long time.

With John's death, she felt part of herself slipping away. She watched it go, wondering how much of herself would be left. Wondering if she cared.

Hours somehow slipped by, becoming days. Richard still fed the animals, tended the farm, but it was all too much for him. He worked the longest hours he could, welcoming the exhaustion of his labour, sometimes working until he dropped. He toiled savagely, punishing the soil. Shovelling animal shit was better, easier than watching his wife disappear bit by bit in front of his eyes. At night, he slept badly, an uneasy, dream-filled state which brought him no rest. He was aware of May's weeping, of her wanderings around the darkened house. He felt powerless; they spoke less and less.

May spent her days aimlessly. With no Annie and no Tom, the house gradually began to sag. Bridie still came and brought food. She tried to get May to change out of her nightgown, to clean up a little. May never said a word to her. She knew that Bridie would eventually go back to her own life, leaving her in peace.

This morning, she sat listlessly, counting. She had taken to sitting in the rocking chair in John's room, sometimes looking out the window when the bright sight of water had ceased to hurt. The first Monday without John; the first rainfall; the first full week, then the second week. She wanted Ellie and Hannah to be with her, but she angrily didn't want her sister's daughters, her twin boys. Life wasn't fair. Hannah had babies all the time. May had nothing, nothing at all. Why hadn't God taken one of *her* baby boys? She'd still have plenty left.

There was a sudden movement in among the laurels. May sat forward and leaned her head closer to the window. She could see nothing. Sunlight was filtering through the trees, making a constant lazy pattern on the grass beneath. She sat back again; it hadn't been that kind of slow, leafy movement, but something altogether more familiar, more recognizable, although she couldn't put her finger on it. She would wait. Something told her it would happen again. Suddenly, the air in the bedroom became very still; in response, she stopped the soothing, rocking motion of her chair. And then she heard it.

'Mama?'

The voice was unmistakably his. She was filled with such joy that she could hardly breathe. Slowly, she stood up, and moved as close to the window as she could get.

She pressed her body against it for support. Everything was trembling; she didn't trust her legs to keep her upright. She clung to the top of the sash. John was standing there, under the trees, in his white smock. He held his right hand to his face.

'Mama, face hurt.'

Still May didn't move. His words were clear; she heard them distinctly inside her head, as much John's voice as if he'd been standing right beside her. She had known it all along; he would never leave her. She knew that the thread of connection between them was much too strong for him to break. She smiled down at him, but didn't speak. She knew she had to tread very gently, carefully, in case he took fright.

He took his hand away from his face and she saw the bruise. No longer dark, it was again poppy-coloured in places, silvery in others. It changed emphasis as she watched. She was afraid to leave the window, afraid to let him out of her sight, in case he disappeared on her again. She wouldn't be able to bear that.

'Wait,' she whispered, finally, and it seemed to her that he nodded in reply.

She lurched down the corridor, holding both arms straight out from her shoulders, needing to feel the wall solid under her fingertips. She stumbled on the top stair, and had a bright vision of herself hurtling downwards, out of control, to the hallway below. Its clarity frightened her. She gripped the banisters tightly and walked carefully, step after unsteady step, down the stairs. She prayed that he would wait for her.

The front door was already open. She stepped

outside and moved quickly to her right, where the shade of the laurel trees was deepest. She stood in the spot where she had first seen him, and closed her eyes. She was able to see him again, that way, as he really was. His face, the day he'd seen Molly for the first time. His small, plump arms pulling strongly on the oars of the lake-boat. His smell at bedtime, wrapped by her body, listening with wide eyes as she and Richard told him a bedtime story.

She stayed very still, only moving her head a little as her eyes now searched the rest of the garden for him. She could be patient.

And there he was. Just out of arm's reach.

'John?' she said.

'Mama.'

'I love you,' she said.

He nodded and smiled at her. Then he began to move back towards where the trees were thickest. May felt rooted to the ground, paralysed in that dream-like way, as though her feet had gone deep underneath the soil. She couldn't move, couldn't follow him.

'Will you come again?' she asked, watching as he moved away from her. He turned and nodded. Then, just as suddenly as she had seen him, he was gone.

The feeling began gradually to return to her legs. She stood, almost breathless, as the most profound surge of tranquillity seemed to come from the soil beneath her, filling her whole body, soothing her mind. It was the first time she had felt alive, that she wanted to live, ever since he had gone away.

The gate whined as Richard came through into the

garden. He bolted it behind him and turned, startled to see May standing there, thin and pale in her long nightgown.

'May? Are you all right?'

His voice was tentative, unhappy. She turned to him, her face calm, her eyes bright in a way he had feared never to see again.

'Yes,' she said. 'I'm all right.'

She looked down, as though suddenly noticing her nightgown for the first time.

'I think I'll have a bath. Will we have a cup of tea, first?'

Richard's eyes filled. He couldn't speak.

'I miss him, too,' he blurted, his whole frame racked by sobs. May put her arms around him, drawing his head on to her breasts. She held him close, kissing the top of his head, murmuring words of comfort. Together, they made their way towards the house, Richard's long body weak and stumbling with relief.

As May turned to close the front door, she saw him again, standing just where she had seen him first from his bedroom window. He was gone in a moment, leaving behind him the certainty of his return.

Eleanor's Journal

I CANNOT BEGIN to tell you of the heartbreak endured by May and Richard all that summer.

I went to them at once, as soon as Mama telegraphed me to say what had happened. Richard was consumed with despair – I know he blamed himself, although he never confessed as much, for having permitted John, even once, to accompany him in the lake-boat. I have seldom seen a man so desperate. For her part, May never reproached her husband, not once. Perhaps she was too distracted even to make the connection. I have never seen my sister so absent from herself.

Nothing brought her ease, or comfort, or even one hour of repose. I felt so helpless, so hopelessly inadequate in her presence, in their presence. For the first time since I had so proudly declared myself a fully-fledged nurse, my efficiency, my competence, my professional manner all counted for nothing. My cures were for the body only; none of my ministrations brought any lessening of anguish to the hearts of my sister and her husband. They had no need of me.

I was forced to recall your words to me, on the occasion when you gently suggested that I needed to learn a little humility; that my sense of mission sometimes blinded me to the subtler needs of the human spirit. As ever, you were right. I know, however, that it gave you no pleasure that I began at that time to gain some small understanding of myself and others at the expense of my sister's unspeakable suffering.

How could I begin to tell her, or indeed Hannah, that my greatest happiness had coincided with this tragic time in May's life? That I had found love where I had least dreamt to seek it? I had always known instinctively that I was destined for another kind of life, one different from my sisters' in as many ways as is possible for lives to diverge. But nothing could have prepared me for the depth of the bond that had grown, almost imperceptibly, between you and me. In our work, our home, our friendship we achieved an intimacy which I could never imagine sharing with any man. We seek neither society's acknowledgement of who we are, nor its approbation. God has made us, Stella, and the love we bear one another. It is enough.

I know that I returned home to you that summer filled with gratitude that I needed to explain nothing – that you knew and understood all the enormity of a family's grief. And I did learn some resignation, too – I know that I continue to rage against God sometimes, that I cannot discern His plan among the unfortunate people we care for and the work that we do. The difference is now that I am learning, simply, to accept that there are some things that even you and I cannot change.

EPILOGUE

Autumn 1906

HANNAH SAT QUIETLY in the sunshine, allowing the sound of the river to lull her into peacefulness. Eileen and Maeve played on the grass beside her, pressing smooth pebbles into a mound of sand which Richard had just brought in a bucket. They had been shrill earlier, quarrelling over spilt lemonade. As usual, Mary had come to the rescue. The two girls always stopped being pettish when Mary scolded them; Hannah seemed to have little effect on them herself. At six, Eileen was particularly conscious of her status as the eldest. When she and Maeve, younger by two years, played together, she became especially fractious if she did not get her way. Earlier that afternoon, their shrieks had set Hannah's teeth on edge. She could feel her temper rise, sure that Eleanor's silence indicated disapproval. Mary's swift separation of the two small bodies and her low, urgent voice had brought about reluctant reconciliation far more quickly than Hannah ever could have.

Alec and Patrick were nearly three: twin boys, tow-headed, slight in frame, gentle with each other, who did not take kindly to the bossiness of their older sisters. Hannah sighed, still not opening her eyes. The boys were so much *easier*, so much more simple in their needs and straightforward in their adoration of their father. Nevertheless, four children were a handful – both hands full. She didn't know what she would do without Mary. The last pregnancy had ended before it had hardly begun, and she been filled with nothing but gratitude for her loss, followed rapidly by an enormous guilt. She had never even told Charles: there had been no need. Mary had helped her, cleaned her, comforted her, mistaking her sobs for grief. And now, unless she was very much mistaken, she was carrying again.

May watched as Richard spread the sand on the grass below the oak tree, her heart turning over as he smiled at the high-pitched delight of Hannah's two little girls. Automatically, her head turned towards the laurel trees, although *he* tended not to come to her if there were others around. Perhaps she would just take a walk in that direction, anyway, just in case. Hannah seemed to be asleep, and Eleanor had had her head buried in some journal or other for the last hour.

She glanced in Richard's direction before she stood up. As usual, he was looking at her. She tried to smile, and made as though she had simply been changing her position on the hard, wrought-iron garden chair. Her hat shaded most of her face, she knew that, so for once he shouldn't be able to read her expression.

He had been worried about Hannah's visit, had tried to persuade May against it. Not because of Hannah, of course, but because of her four children. He was afraid that the presence of high, childish voices might upset her. May knew how deeply he feared for her, could read the concern that was now a permanent feature of his expression – as ingrained as though he had suddenly acquired a scar that wouldn't heal. Tentatively, he had asked May was she sure, was she strong enough – perhaps she should wait, perhaps next year would be better. He tended to *watch* her so much these days: she had to be constantly on her guard.

She had insisted. It was so long since they had all been together. Besides, Hannah was bringing her maid. If things got too much, then Mary would simply take the children away, take them for a walk, bathe them, do whatever needed to be done to children.

She hadn't told Richard that she wanted the exquisite pain of her sister's brood around her. She wanted to see if she could bear it, knowing that she had a secret among the laurel trees.

May and Richard have made us very welcome. In the four months since I last saw her, my sister has grown even paler and thinner. I do not believe she will ever recover from the loss of John. I despair sometimes of a God who will not send her another child to take his place – such a simple thing to do, such an easy way to give her back her old, uncomplicated happiness. I worry about her. There is something almost insubstantial about her presence among us – her gaze is frequently directed elsewhere, as though she is searching for something, someone. It struck me very forcibly today that she does not truly believe that John is gone, or at least, that he is not coming back. There is such a yearning, such wistfulness in her eyes that it breaks my heart.

Richard looks years older than the last time I saw him. He looks frayed and shabby, something like Abbotsford the first time I saw it. I am puzzled that May has no one to help her here – I seem to remember that there was once a man about the farm, and a young woman to help with the cooking and cleaning. It is not my place to ask; I fear that money may not be as plentiful as they had hoped. Is this another legacy to be passed on from generation to generation? As you and I know, poverty is no less difficult to bear simply because it is covered with a discreet cloak of gentility.

The sudden sound of metal on china woke Hannah. She sat up straight instantly. Had she really fallen asleep? And for how long? Guiltily, she looked around at her two sisters. They hadn't moved, it seemed, and the children were still playing as before. Mary was setting a large tray with tea things on the low table in front of her. Hannah coughed, and settled her hat more comfortably, shading her eyes from the gently sinking sun. She must only have nodded off for a moment. Everything seemed to be as before.

'Will you pour, ma'am?'

Mary directed her question to May, a fitting respect towards the lady of the house. Hannah was grateful to her. She always got it right, always did the correct thing, the required thing. She could have been forgiven for letting things slip a little from time to time, given the informality that now reigned in the house in Holywood. 'Ma'am' had given way almost imperceptibly to 'Miss

Hannah' when they were alone, and after last year's miscarriage to 'Hannah', once there was no one else around. Hannah had encouraged her – how could you be stiff and formal with the woman who had helped deliver your babies, who kept your husband's dangerous secrets, whose strength kept you from impatience with those small bodies whose every need now dominated your life?

May gestured towards Hannah. She gave a little laugh.

'Oh, I feel too lazy to move. Let Hannah be Mother.'

The warm air around them seemed to freeze for a moment. Eleanor looked up quickly, her intelligent eyes darting from one sister's face to the other.

Hannah stood up at once, replying lightly, 'Oh well, if I must!'

She was relieved when Mary appeared once more at her elbow, carrying a plate piled high with new scones. She had even brought the hot water to warm the cups. Despite herself, Hannah smiled.

'Now, then, my dears! You can all once again witness the intricacies of the MacBride tea ceremony!'

Everyone laughed. Conversation became animated; even Richard joined in. As she poured, Hannah was overwhelmed with memories of her first visit to Belfast, of the MacBrides' drawing room, of her first hopeful yearnings for romance. She had hoped so much for another kind of life. She bit her lip. This was not the time, nor the place.

But she couldn't shake the feeling of helplessness which engulfed her more and more often these days. Charles was losing too much business, his native city becoming more bitter and divided by the day. *Taig; fenian; antichrist.* His potential clients didn't use such words, of course – wouldn't even think them. Professional men would never lower themselves to such working-class terms of abuse. But, behind their smooth regrets and sound financial reasons for doing business elsewhere, the same ugly reality lurked. These were difficult times, they said. Best not to ruffle any more feathers, they said. She knew that Charles was being driven inexorably into the company of men who painted slogans in bitumen on city walls in the seething darkness; men who refused to lie down, as they saw it, and accept the crumbs from the rich man's table. None of this was new: Constance MacBride had let something slip to her recently, and then immediately become silent. But it had been enough: Hannah understood, with a bright flash of intuition, what the older woman's fears were. She had hoped, as his mother, that marriage would put an end to Charles's dangerous dabbling. His naivety and his recent, growing sense of injustice were an explosive mixture.

Where would it all end? Wasn't half a loaf better than no bread? What was to become of her, of all these children, if Charles put himself into foolish danger, becoming sucked up into a cause whose consequences he did not truly understand?

Hannah handed Richard his tea. Mary reappeared

with more lemonade and ices for the children. Silence descended again, broken only by the chinking of spoon against china. Hannah wanted to stay where she was for ever, in the tranquil shade of the laurel trees, with the bright promise of water beyond the sloping lawns.

She sipped, wondering what was coming next.

I am sometimes impatient with my eldest sister. I know that I am more fortunate than either Hannah or May, that while I feel my world expanding with work and with loving you, they each seem to inhabit a relentlessly shrinking universe. Hannah really has no understanding of what exists outside the four walls of her terraced garden, her comfortable, fortunate existence. I can sense her growing exasperation with her children: such lovely children, too, each of them a living arrow fired into May's poor, sore heart. I find myself becoming more and more angry with Hannah – she has no right to be discontented, no right to be ungrateful. The world has been nothing if not kind to her. But poor May – it is as though grief has shrivelled her world, making a prison of even the broad expanse of land and water which had once given her the freedom to breathe.

Last week, when I was sent to Abbey Street, that wretched place just off Peter's Hill, I had to tend to a Mrs Brent, a woman already in labour. She was giving birth to her seventh child. The filth was indescribable. She could have been no older than Hannah, yet she had already lost two children to typhus. The others stood around, barefoot, faces streaked with grime and tears. They were like steps of stairs – the oldest being no more than six. They were frightened by their mother's wailing.

Foul-smelling straw served as Mrs Brent's birthing place. I knelt beside her, my stomach revolting against the stench despite my best efforts. I tried to keep my manner cheerful, encouraging. She looked at me. Her eyes were huge, full of pleading. I listened for the baby.

'A good, strong heartbeat,' I told her, making my mouth smile. She turned her eyes away from me then and faced the wall. I have seen so many other women look like this. They are filled with an appalled hope which they cannot voice. And now, another mouth to feed. The world is a badly, cruelly divided place. In due course, her baby was born, a little boy. Small and puny, but healthy enough. I had wild notions about snatching him away from her, bringing him to May. But I could not; I cannot. I wish I could feel differently. It would not be the first time a midwife had found such a solution. Perhaps the mother, like many others before her, may well find her own way out. Suffocation is swift and painless.

And my sister suffers because her children spill lemonade.

Mary carried the tea things back into the bright kitchen at Abbotsford. Hannah had told her to take some time, have her tea in peace. She sat gratefully, suddenly tired by the heat, the quarrelling of the children, the strangeness of the atmosphere in this new place. She sighed. She wanted to be gone, well away from here; something was making her uncomfortable and she couldn't quite put her finger on it. The divil ye know, she thought, is better than the divil ye don't. And she was getting along quite happily in Holywood. She couldn't ask for more, really. She had kindness, food, shelter, something approaching love from the four children. It was what she'd chosen, after all, what she'd hoped for some ten years back. It didn't make up for the loss of Cecilia; but then, nothing could do that.

As she waited for the water to boil, Mary heard a strange ticking sound behind her. She turned, and saw the orange and brown-streaked wings of a butterfly flapping wildly against the dusty windowpane. Time and again, it dashed its frail, shell-like body against the glass, searching for air and freedom.

She stood up.

'C'mere,' she said softly, scooping its papery lightness into her cupped hands. 'Ye'll knock yerself senseless doin' that.'

She walked to the back door and opened her hands. The butterfly seemed to stagger in flight for a moment, unsure of itself and the sudden sunlight. Then it disappeared into the dense foliage of the laurel trees. Mary watched it go. Her eyes were drawn back downwards again, to the picnic scene on the lawn. Hannah was watching the children, minding them in her absence, as she had promised. Miss May was still unmoving, her body looking even more tense and delicate from this distance. She looked as though she was carved out of something brittle. Poor woman, Mary thought; her fragility had reminded her more than once of Cecilia during her last days. And there was Miss Eleanor, scribbling away as usual. A kind woman, Mary thought, but almost too efficient, too *virtuous* in her caring. One with a secret, though. Of that she was sure.

The kettle suddenly whistled in the background and

Mary turned to go back inside. Two more days of this, and then back to Holywood.

She'd be glad to be home.

Richard had had enough of everyone. He knew he'd been unwise to bow to May's insistence that her sisters come and visit, but she had given him no peace. Her normally gentle nature had changed recently: she seemed to become pettish, almost childlike, if she thought he was about to deny her anything. He knew she was conscious of him watching her. He couldn't help it. Her absences from him, from their life together, were becoming more and more frequent. Every time it happened, she seemed to move further away from him: it was as though something was drawing her away from all that was solid and earthy, and both of them were powerless to stop it.

He had thought she would come back to him, after the day he'd found her standing in her nightgown, among the laurel trees. He had been joyful then, filled with hope that he could give her another child, that he could put back together the pieces of her life which had shattered that afternoon beside the lake-boat. It had not happened. He felt suddenly old, too old.

He counted the minutes until everyone would be gone. He wanted his wife and his home back to himself, so that he could watch her, cherish her, protect her.

I must finish for now. I shall be home to you soon. I have had much time for reflection here, despite the

*activities of my nieces and nephews, and my growing
concern for May.*

*My thoughts keep going back to the first day we
met, almost five years ago now. I can still see the hard,
narrow beds in the nurses' home right next to each
other. I remember that I recognized your accent at
once, caught the fleeting shadow of something familiar.*

'Are you from Belfast?'

*I spoke very softly, already intimidated by the
authoritarian frostiness of our recent welcome. Sister had
just left us in no doubt as to the standards of cleanliness,
neatness and godliness that were expected from all of us
as a matter of course. We were surrounded by rows and
rows of grey-blanketed beds, the white walls bare and
cheerless. Some forty girls were already unpacking bags
and trunks in a silence which had quickly become
uneasy. Do you remember, Stella? Do you remember
how you looked across at me and smiled broadly?*

'Bangor,' you said. 'And you?'

'Dublin, and Belfast too.'

*We quickly shared all we had in common, words
tumbling over each other in their eagerness to get said,
to establish a connection, to claim each as the other's
friend at once before anyone else could take either of us
away. I felt that I had discovered a small piece of
home; your presence was like having a smooth stone or
shell in my pocket as a talisman – something which I
could touch and hold whenever comfort was needed.*

*And I remember how much I needed comfort. Each
night, before we slept, your warm hand would seek out
mine across the divide between our beds. Saying
nothing, you would hold my hand in yours until you
judged that my nightly storm of silent weeping was
abating.*

I do not think that I would have survived that first year without you. And I should never wish to have survived the subsequent years without you.

I feel fortunate; more fortunate than either of my sisters. Your heart is mine, mine yours.

Keep it safe, and know that I could never bear to see you suffer.

Acknowledgement

THE AUTHOR GRATEFULLY acknowledges the patience and professionalism of the staff of the Linenhall Library, Belfast, who responded to all requests for information – no matter how complex – with good humour, courtesy and perseverance.

Bibliography

The description of Cecilia McCurry's attack in the chapter entitled 'Mary and Cecilia: Spring 1893' is taken from '*Belfast Riots 1893: The Catholic Reply*', Linenhall Library, Belfast.

Holywood Chronicles: Volume I and *Volume II*, Linenhall Library, Belfast

A Record Year in My Existence as Lord Mayor of Belfast, 1898, James Henderson, Belfast, 1899

A Shorter Illustrated History of Ulster, Jonathan Bardon, The Blackstaff Press, Belfast, 1996

A History of Ulster, Jonathan Bardon, The Blackstaff Press, Belfast, 1992

Belfast: A Century, Jonathan Bardon, The Blackstaff Press, Belfast, 1996

Liquorice Allsorts, Muriel Breen, Moytura Press, Dublin, 1993

In Search of a State: Catholics in Northern Ireland, Fionnuala O'Connor, The Blackstaff Press, Belfast, 1993

The Making of Modern Ireland, 1603–1923, J. C. Beckett, Faber and Faber, London, 1966

Northern Protestants: An Unsettled People, Susan McKay, The Blackstaff Press, Belfast, 2000

The Belfast Anthology, ed. Patricia Craig, The Blackstaff Press, Belfast, 1999

The Catholics of Ulster, a History, Marianne Elliott, Allen Lane, The Penguin Press, London, 2000

Images of Ireland: South Belfast, George E. Templeton and Norman Weatherall, Gill and Macmillan, Dublin, 1998

Picking Up the Linen Threads: A Study in Industrial Folklore, Betty Messenger, The Blackstaff Press, Belfast, 1980 (First published by University of Texas Press, 1978, with the assistance of the Andrew W. Mellon Foundation)

Ripples of Dissent: Women's Stories of Marriage from the 1890s ed. Bridget Bennett, J. M. Dent, London, 1966

Sexual Anarchy: Gender and Culture at the Fin de Siecle, Elaine Showalter, Bloomsbury, London, 1991

A New Day Dawning: A Portrait of Ireland in 1900, Daniel Mulhall, The Collins Press, Cork, 1999

Ulster Since 1800, ed. T. W. Moody and J. C. Beckett, BBC, London, 1957

A Century of Northern Life: The 'Irish News' and 100 Years of Ulster History 1890s–1990s, ed. Eamon Phoenix, Ulster Historical Foundation, Belfast, 1995

The Blessings of a Good Thick Skirt: Women Travellers and Their World, Mary Russell, Collins, London, 1988

Female Activists: Irish Women and Change 1900–1960, ed. Mary Cullen and Mary Luddy, The Woodfield Press, Dublin, 2001

ANITA DIAMANT

Good Harbor

PAN BOOKS

From the bestselling author of *The Red Tent* comes a rich and moving novel about the tragedy of loss, the insidious nature of family secrets and the redemptive power of friendship.

When Kathleen meets Joyce, each has come to a turning point in her life. Kathleen, whose sister died of breast cancer fifteen years earlier, has just been diagnosed herself and finds her world abruptly thrown into terrifying turmoil. At the same time, Joyce is struggling to cope with her awkward adolescent daughter and burgeoning career as a writer, and is growing increasingly distant from her husband. Neither woman realizes that their chance meeting will result in a life-altering friendship.

With her trademark wisdom and humour, Anita Diamant explores the lives of modern women who manage the precarious balance of marriage, career, motherhood and companionship. Good Harbor is at once a poignant and refreshingly honest novel.

'Immensely moving and delicately told. Anita Diamant's second novel fulfils every iota of promise of the first ... I was entranced by every word of it'
Daily Mail

CLAIRE MESSUD

When the World was Steady

PICADOR

Emmy Simpson believes she makes her own luck. After an austere wartime childhood in London, she joyfully grasped at her first sign of good fortune and left for Australia. Her sister Virginia doesn't believe in luck at all. She made no more than a brief foray to the other side of the city. The sisters made their choices, made steady worlds for themselves. But now, middle-aged, they find those worlds disintegrating.

'In its rich detail and its humour, this is an awry, uplifting book'
Independent on Sunday

KATE GRENVILLE

The Idea of Perfection

PICADOR

Winner of the Orange Prize for fiction 2001

Well, he said, and laughed a meaningless laugh. A moment extended itself into awkwardness. Well, he said again, and she said it too at the same moment. Their voices sounded loud together under the awning. She felt as if the whole of Karakarook, behind its windows, must be watching this event that had burst into their silent afternoon: two bodies hitting together, two people standing apologizing.

The Idea of Perfection is a funny and touching romance between two people who've given up on love. Set in the eccentric little backwater of Karakarook, New South Wales, pop. 1374, it tells the story of Douglas Cheeseman, a gawky engineer with jug-handle ears, and Harley Savage, a woman altogether too big and too abrupt for comfort.

Harley is in Karakarook to foster 'Heritage', and Douglas is there to pull down the quaint old Bent Bridge. From day one, they're on a collision course. But out of this unpromising conjunction of opposites, something unexpected happens: something even better than perfection.

'From these two reticent characters, besieged by two lifetimes of regret, doubt and dismay, Grenville manufactures an extraordinary comedy of manners, made all the more powerful by her own reticence as a writer'
Guardian